REQUIEM FOR A SPY

Alberto Giovannetti, a native Roman, was a member of the Vatican diplomatic corps for many years. In 1964, he became Permanent Observer of the Holy See to the United Nations, the first to be appointed to the post. He is the author of books dealing with the Catholic Church in Communist-controlled countries and has written two widely known volumes on Pope Pius XII's policy during the last World War: *The Vatican and the War* and *Rome Open City*. Monsignor Giovannetti's latest book published in the United States, *The Italians of America*, is a concise story of the struggles and successes of Italian-Americans. He now divides his time between Rome and New York.

REQUIEM FOR A SPY

ALBERTO GIOVANNETTI

TRANSLATED BY
FRANCES FRENAYE LANZA

DOUBLEDAY & COMPANY, INC.
GARDEN CITY, NEW YORK
1983

by Alberto Giovannetti

Fiction
REQUIEM FOR A SPY
IL GONFALONIERE ALVISI

Nonfiction
THE ITALIANS OF AMERICA
WE HAVE A POPE
THE RED BOOK OF THE PERSECUTED CHURCH
THE VATICAN AND THE WAR
ROME OPEN CITY
THE GLASS HOUSE
ROME SPEAKS TO THE CHURCH OF SILENCE

The characters, situations, and events depicted in this novel are creations of the author, and any resemblance to actual persons, situations, or events is purely coincidental.

Originally published in Italian as *Requiem per una Spia* by Bietti copyright © 1978 by Alberto Giovannetti/Bietti

Library of Congress Cataloging in Publication Data
Giovannetti, Alberto.
Requiem for a spy.
Translation of: Requiem per una spia.
I. Title.
PQ4867.I6348R413   1983   853'.914
ISBN: 0-385-15612-X
Library of Congress Catalog Card Number 79–8926
English translation copyright © 1983 by Doubleday & Company, Inc.
All Rights Reserved
Printed in the United States of America
First Edition in the United States of America

Acknowledgments

The author is grateful to Frances Frenaye Lanza for keeping in constant touch while doing the translation to English. It cannot have been an easy job.

His gratitude also extends to Samuel S. Vaughan, who read the manuscript with kindness and sensitivity.

This English language edition of the novel differs in some aspects from those that preceded in Italian, French, Spanish, and German. The resulting improvement is due largely to the suggestions made by Mr. Vaughan. They were edited by Randall Elisha Greene, who added suggestions of his own showing great understanding. His is the final editing. The author would like to acknowledge here his debt. He is grateful to Betty Heller for her assistance in guiding this manuscript to publication.

Having written only books on history and essays, the author felt the need for congenial and serene surroundings so as not to become discouraged in attempting his first novel. This atmosphere he found at Sacred Hearts and St. Stephen's Rectory in Brooklyn. The book was completed while the author was a guest of Luigi and Evangelina Lisi in their beautiful California home. Signora Evangelina with her affection, patience, and espressos (no smoking allowed!) did her best to help the author safely and quickly to the finish line.

A.G.

259574

PART ONE

EVERYONE SAID IT WAS THE BEST ESPRESSO IN TOWN, BUT to him it was just bitter, murky soup. Like all other espresso, anywhere in the world. Except that here it was worse.

So typical, Panin muttered to himself. At the UN they can't even make coffee. Nonetheless, he ordered one from Ramirez, the barman in the North Lounge, then waited for it to be brought to his table. The gurgling of the espresso machine competed with the ringing of a telephone somewhere in the back section of the lounge.

As the barman came to the table, Panin complained in Spanish, "Chico, have you forgotten that Italians don't go for lemon peel?"

"Ambassador Faraglia doesn't hassle me about it." His two-handed gesture seemed to say, Understand?

"Well then, let's say Italian priests, not Italian ambassadors."

Panin felt himself thinking more and more like Monsignor Righi: "How long since you've written to your mother in Ponce, by the way? Do you remember to send her something from time to time? I'd hate to start an anti-tipping movement here. . . ."

"I'm okay, Father. My mother and my women get taken care of. Chico looks after his old lady back home and his old ladies here, too." There was a dance in his step as he gathered empty glasses at the adjoining table. "No woman will ever complain about Chico—in Brooklyn or in Puerto Rico."

Panin was enjoying Chico's impertinence, but he knew it would disturb the Monsignor. So he fell silent.

Without enjoyment, he sipped the coffee. Why, he wondered, would a Righi take it so hard? So what if this twenty-year-old claimed to be a Latin lover? Panin smiled. If Chico really had "old ladies" in Brooklyn then he would be less likely to strip every passing woman with his eyes. As the barman was doing just now while a slender blonde left the rest room and headed for the lounge door.

Ah yes, Righi, you ought to pray that Chico finds a good girlfriend in Brooklyn.

Then Colonel Panin grimaced. Idiot, he reprimanded himself. He knew all too well that thinking one's own thoughts, too much of this dual dialogue, was the beginning of failure. On previous assignments, he had always played his role to the hilt. Traveling salesman, union leader, businessman, impoverished grand duke, porter. Now, just because his cover was a clerical collar . . .

No, Panin and Righi, colonel and monsignor—they had to be virtually one and the same, as if living in symbiotic alliance. Otherwise neither would survive. It was certain they shared the same fate, they now worked for the same purpose. Together they would sink or swim. Meanwhile, only one character could rule.

The professional within Panin asserted himself once more, and he became the austere and serene Vatican Monsignor seen every day for the last month in the corridors and meeting rooms of the United Nations.

The representative of a small but opulent emirate on the Persian Gulf sat down two tables away. He did not look around, but dug into his briefcase and removed a pile of papers over which he immediately leaned, oblivious (or so it seemed) to both the barman and the Monsignor.

Righi had been introduced to Ambassador Ahmed Badr and he knew something of the Ambassador's reputation for spontaneous harangues. But the Ambassador, it appeared, was studying a prepared speech. Nothing impromptu this evening.

Righi had been at the UN long enough to realize that a written speech did not guarantee that Badr would be less than long-winded. Neither the yawns nor the yawning absences of other delegates ever seemed to affect the Ambassador's self-absorption. Righi pulled a note card from his vest pocket, scanned it, then moaned to himself. We're in for a couple of hours of Badr, at least . . . and, my God, Colombia and India and Tanzania are scheduled to follow. What did I do to deserve this punishment?

For the third consecutive evening, Righi concluded, he would have to miss supper. Others can phone their missions or embassies and have something kept waiting—hot or cold, as they wish. But where can I call? The rectory, where supper is on the table at six-thirty and Mrs. O'Rourke goes home by eight sharp?

The espresso machine's latest gurgle interrupted his thoughts. He could hear Chico's low whistle as the barman brought Badr a steaming cup, though the Ambassador continued to concentrate. Righi shook his head, realizing that if Badr had written the speech himself, it would be scholarly and unbearable—but if he hadn't written it, he had his head buried so that he could improve his chances of understanding it. The priest glanced at Badr's reflection in the mirror.

The Arab delegate's face was beaming like that of an ancient poring over holy writ.

Righi decided that he was probably right the first time. Badr had written it. His smile seemed to say that he would nail the Zionists once again. He wielded his pencil, underlining, as if each stroke exposed a new outrage in the long list of their historical misdeeds. Or possibly he was underlining—God forbid—quotations dug up by his staff, pithy pomposities from the Talmud, the Encyclopaedia Judaica, the collected works of Rabbi Shlomo Ben-Hellul: all the writing that he believed bared the foul motives behind the unspeakable Balfour Declaration.

Outside there is such temptation, Righi sighed: the arrival of Indian summer a week ago.

Righi began to daydream of a long walk down First Avenue, approaching the Brooklyn Bridge; watching the sun set over the low-lying hills of Staten Island; then a leisurely return as he ambled up Second Avenue. But he knew that this warm, bright October afternoon promised no such respite. The Security Council was to meet in an hour (if it kept to schedule) and there would be a vote on some innocuous or impossible resolution presented energetically by several minor countries.

Still, there would be a debate. Several states, not members of the Council, had asked to take part. And the Council never refused. It was one of its wiser policies, as Ambassador Faraglia had once reminded him. Debates serve as a decompression chamber, a safety valve, a forum for venting anger; as long as there is discussion, there is less likely to be shooting. Even victims reap some satisfaction from airing the injustices inflicted upon them.

Quite right, Faraglia.

Righi called for Chico to bring a second espresso—to which the barman rejoined in a voice mimicking the Monsignor's, "And this time no lemon peel, remember?" Both men laughed and Righi realized how much he appreciated this barman for his verve.

When Chico brought the cup, Righi asked, "Are you on duty this evening?"

"Until midnight. After that, I have better things to do." Chico's smirk promised everything.

Righi pretended not to notice. "Great. Would you have two tuna sandwiches made up for me? I'll pick them up about eight. And thanks, Chico."

Righi saw Martha Winthrop as soon as she walked toward the bar at the end of the lounge. He had gone to the rest room, where he had washed his face and combed his hair—having decided that he could not skip the Ambassador's speech. And there *were* Colombia, India, and Tanzania to consider. Then he saw her stride. Grenadier Winthrop—there was no mistaking that walk. It was emblematic of the drive necessary to be the kind of UN correspondent of whom the radio network UBC could be proud.

She ordered ginger ale. Then she slowly checked her makeup in the lounge mirror. Righi resisted highly uncharitable thoughts about her false eyelashes, plucked eyebrows, Hollywood teeth, and her dangling, nearly lethal earrings. But he had other reasons to dislike her.

He had not forgotten the way she had used him, as new man, two weeks before. They had been at a reception given by the delegation from Mauritius. While he peacefully sipped a scotch and soda, she and her earrings had crept up behind him with another ginger ale (their drinks, he thought, were symbolic of their two worlds). Then, with all his escape routes cut off, she shot at him, "Monsignor, what do you think of the Middle Eastern situation?" There was a smoothly ingratiating smile on her face.

"It's worrisome," he had said.

Two hours later, UBC had defined relations between Syria and Israel as critical. Proof? The Vatican's Permanent Observer did not share the optimistic views just voiced by the Danish Secretary-

General Eriksen. Within days of arriving, Righi was in trouble and he had Martha Winthrop to thank.

From then on, Monsignor Righi had avoided the press.

Particularly women.

The thought reminded him that St. Paul had something to say about women—but Righi couldn't recall the text. Well, no matter. At least men such as Chico Ramirez don't have such problems.

He realized that Ms. Winthrop had planted herself in front of him, her grasshopper legs rising from absurdly high-heeled boots. She looked like a native of an underdeveloped country given a costume by passing tourists. Her blond wig and thrift-shop beads rattled with every breath though she was simply standing still.

"Hello, Monsignor. Am I interrupting a meditation?"

He forced a grin and reflected. The only Anglo-Saxon thing about her was her name—if indeed it was hers. "Not at all. I wasn't meditating. I was just doing something even more rare—thinking. About St. Paul, if that gives you any clue. And also about our barman. An irreverent combination—don't you think? But they were humanitarian thoughts."

"Oh? I'm sorry. I'd imagined darker, hidden, secret thoughts. Mind if I take a seat?"

She plopped herself down in front of him—taking particular care to cover her thighs, as much as her dress allowed. Even Panin appreciated the slight deference.

But Righi responded, "In this *glass house*, what secrets can there be?" And, to Chico: "If the lady wishes, please bring her another—"

"He knows." Then her voice returned to its flat, nasal tones. "Such a sense of humor, Father: secrets in a glass house. So *typically* Latin and you say it with such a charming accent." Her eyelashes began a rapid flutter toward her tag remark. "May I quote you?"

"Quote what?" Once bitten, twice shy.

"You on the subject of secrecy here."

The Monsignor started to shake his head, but she pressed on. "I'm thinking of doing a piece on the Vatican presence at the UN." He immediately corrected her.

"The presence of the Holy See—"

"My apologies. Shows that I'm not a Catholic, merely a WASP."

Perhaps due to the grasshopper-like image in his mind, Righi said spontaneously and without malice, "This wasp is some sort of bug, no?"

Her laughter came in such an outburst that Chico dropped a glass. "Monsignor, you're a *riot*," she said. The barman disappeared behind the waist-high bar; Righi could hear the brushing of a broom over broken glass and Chico's rapid mumblings in Spanish.

"But now I am getting lost: you are a bug and I am a riot? Is this American slang?"

"Just colloquialisms. A riot is someone who's funny. And WASP stands for White Anglo-Saxon—"

He silenced her with a gesture, waving his left hand: "*Protestant*—I should have guessed. It is obvious that you and I have a different sense of humor. And maybe a different sense of the ridiculous."

Martha Winthrop twisted uneasily in her chair.

"But this is the era of ecumenical spirit, is it not?" he said. "And the diversity of cultures makes for a diverse world, so we must allow for differences. Correct?" The correspondent sipped on her ginger ale as if it were a dry martini; her eyes spelled mischief. "After all, won't everything be weighed in the balance, when we have come to the finishing post . . . when we are called upon for a final accounting of our lives? How do you call it: the bottom line? Isn't that what spurs us toward living life well—the certainty that our human adventure must come to an end?"

The woman seemed to have no idea what the Monsignor was talking about, but she knew when to interject, "Communication. That's what greases the wheels." Her smile showed off her expensively capped teeth.

A priest, he thought, should think of communion at this point. "You are quite right. Communication, communion, and dialogue are our stock-in-trade, our business."

She added, "Our tools."

It was then that Righi perceived, There is both coyness and contempt blended in this woman's manner. She is playing the insider, one of the *cognoscenti*. "Tools, if you like—" he made a point of looking at his watch. "But why write a piece on the Holy See through a—what?—profile of its UN Observer? Aren't there more important matters right now? I should think the burning question would be Palestine, for example."

Panin knew he needed more time. Such a profile could be dangerous, no matter how innocently handled.

So his Righi face became a wall.

"That's true, Father, but doesn't the Palestinian issue involve the Vatican?" She hesitated. "Okay, the Holy See." Apparently the term affected her. "The essence of it: the *Holy* See and the *Holy* Land, holy places of all kinds, even the Holy Sepulcher. Isn't the problem essentially a religious one?"

That's when Ambassador Badr intervened from the nearby table. They were surprised, having thought him to be intent upon his work. It became obvious that not a word of the conversation had been lost on him.

"Exactly. It *is* a religious problem—sacred." The Ambassador was leaning across two chairs to make his point. "I've been saying so for years. Zionism is essentially antireligious. I'll be stating this once more"—and he laughed, showing a kind of halfhearted humility—"in my speech this evening. Can I count on you, Ms. Winthrop, to give an accurate report of it on the air tomorrow?" He looked toward the Monsignor. "That is, if she reports it at all— because with the number of Jews here in New York, you know . . ."

Righi listened without comment. It was as he had noticed from his arrival here: whenever someone mentioned the Palestinian question, Arabs and Israelis seemed to outdo themselves in courting the Vatican.

A summons from the loudspeaker: "Monsignor Righi is wanted on the phone."

Courteously he excused himself, leaving the woman and the Arab in the thick of what was obviously an old argument.

At the indicated phone booth, Righi picked up the receiver. "Hello, this is . . ." To the apparent discomfiture of the secretary from a small African country, who remained on the alert, standing in the next cubicle, he spoke in soft monosyllables. Righi realized that the fellow was on assignment. Ambassador Faraglia had ex-

plained the practice: secretaries and low-grade staffers were strate-
gically deployed by various countries so that what they overheard
could be used in their employers' best interests. Faraglia had been
adamant: "The head of a mission must never let down his guard."

When the Ambassador said it, Panin had enjoyed a silent
chuckle. But now, as the target of an eavesdropper, he appreciated
the advice. Faraglia was a good friend.

When the priest finished his conversation, he headed toward
the North Lounge. Through the window he could see that the sun
was setting fast; he'd never make it to the Brooklyn Bridge.

Righi turned to see the barman going to the telephones.
"Chico, do you need a dime to call Brooklyn?"

The Puerto Rican looked puzzled. "Yes, Father—but how did
you know?"

"Because no one tips in dimes anymore," the Monsignor replied, "and because you live there. 'I must call home' is written
across your face like icing on a cake. *Hasta la vista.*" He handed
him a coin.

Then, as the barman slid into the phone booth, he leaned out,
balanced on one foot, and called, "I know: don't forget the sandwiches."

The session ended at midnight, after the approval of a resolution
proposed by the nonaligned nations. In Jerusalem, people were already up and dressed for a new day. Who knew whether they had
resumed shooting, too? Or would care about resolutions?

Still, nobody in the North Lounge asked such questions.

Badr's ideas took center stage. He had stolen the limelight, and
conversation over fresh drinks seemed like a replay of the session
just ended. Someone credited Ambassador Kalman with topping
Badr's remarks with the counterargument that "Jerusalem belongs
not to Israel, but to the world. Is it not like Athens or Rome?"

Righi surprised them when he extended Kalman's point: "Jerusalem belongs to the world *more* than Athens or Rome." Chico and
a waitress were busily shuttling sandwich plates from the order
window. A third voice added in a thick accent: "Gentlemen, we
cannot forget Cairo, seat of Islamic culture."

"Along these lines," Kalman said, "there are also Benares and

Lhasa, plus all the cities in which religion, art, and philosophy have made a universal contribution. These cities have advanced civilization."

Moroni, counselor to the Italian mission, mumbled into the Reuben sandwich just brought to his table: "They've forgotten Florence. They're the losers!"

"Yeah," Chico said. "And Newark and Jersey City. And Brooklyn."

Moments later, as Righi slipped out of the great building, a gust of wind blew over him. Oddly, the surface of the East River was barely ruffled. Across the river, toward Queens, the colored lights from the Pepsi-Cola sign was mirrored, wavering in the dirty current. The wind wafted a foul, oily smell. A tanker must have recently gone by. Over the opaque web of the Queensboro Bridge, a crescent moon hung.

From the sidewalk, Righi could see the delegates' limousines moving up First Avenue. On Forty-seventh Street, he turned west and passed the United Engineering Building: through the windows he could see women cleaning offices.

In Moscow at this hour, Panin thought, the women are sweeping the streets.

As he arrived at the rectory of the Church of the Nativity, he was running through the names of cities in his mind: Jerusalem, Athens, Rome, Cairo, Benares, Lhasa, Brooklyn. He was rehearsing his memory for the report he intended to send to the Vatican the next day.

Not Brooklyn. Panin checked Righi. The man was momentarily of two minds.

As he took the rectory steps two at a time, it was Panin who thought, "Vatican" is just as acceptable as the "Holy See"—and a little neater.

[II]

OVER THE YEARS, HIS SUPERIORS AT THE MOSCOW OPERATIONS Center had come to appreciate the considerable skills of Vladimir Efimovich Panin. Time and again, he had eluded traps set for him by various counterespionage services, time and again he had brought back the information or achieved the results in even the riskiest missions.

All this was in the field. Everything else about him was in the files. He was born in the Ukrainian city of Kiev in 1922 and his father had named him for the great Bolshevik leader. Of course Comrade Efim knew that Ilya Ulyanov had given the future Lenin the name Vladimir because it was that of the first Christian ruler of Russia, who was later canonized. But such a weak reason, comprehensible even if reprehensible in 1870, was positively absurd after the glorious October Revolution, which had given all power to the Soviets. From that historical moment on, Vladimirs would honor Lenin rather than the saint venerated for centuries among the masses downtrodden by czars, boyards, and priestlings. And, as in the case of the Lenin-to-be, Volodya was to be the boy's affectionate name.

In the file was his outstanding school record. When he was ten years old, his father was posted to Moscow, and the family went there, pleased that the Party had appointed Efim to a job in the Ministry of the Interior. Efim Panin was proud of his son, although not in the usual, fatuous, bourgeois manner. Volodya was not only a good student and a good athlete, he was a faithful participant in Komsomol gatherings and later in Party meetings.

When Panin was nineteen, Stalin called upon him to defend his native land. He suffered a wound in his left leg in the battle for the reconquest of Kharkov, where his captain recommended him for a medal and where, given his response, his fellow soldiers awarded him the name "Nitchevo." *Nitchevo*, it's nothing, was the only word he had uttered when, thigh shattered by a hand grenade, he was carried on a stretcher to a first-aid station. His file also recorded the fact that as soon as he was conscious, he asked to be sent back to the front.

When he was a civilian again, women were attracted by his athletic body and proud features, but were put off by the coldness of his expression. The files contained copies of many letters and an inordinate number of observation reports, each confirming that Volodya Panin knew how to control his sexual impulses, however urgent. One interview quoted him as saying he was a bachelor by choice: success in his profession and the safeguarding of his independence made it mandatory.

But no one could read Panin's thoughts and few could guess at his ambitions or tastes. The file only hinted at these. Evaluations showed that although a loyal Party member, he was no fanatic—a fact that pleased his superiors. One supervisor noted, "After all, it was Lenin who said (and forty years of Party history have confirmed it) that an excess of zeal is often a sign of emotional instability." Another ended his evaluation with: "The Revolution needed its zealots, especially at the outset, but even more it now needs well-balanced men with iron nerves—men like this Panin." Every yearly report gave him superior ratings.

"Dedicated to the cause, yes; but with a sense of perspective and of reality, and with a sense of humor." This was how General Leonid Rostov had described Colonel Panin when the KGB supervisor had assumed authority over Panin and other special agents.

The sense of humor was something which Volodya himself declared lacking in Communist circles. But no mention of this could be found in the files, because he gave vent to it only when talking to himself—ordinarily spicing it with typically Ukrainian sarcasm.

But one top secret note in Colonel Panin's record was puzzling. It was an anonymous observation recorded in the early '60s:

In spite of his broad cultural interests, Panin lives in a vacuum. His isolation is something of a state of grace—a term borrowed from the language used by Christians when they speak of their saints. I use this phrase with care, but I use it purposely, for Panin is a man of faith, a strong Marxist-Leninist faith. A faith which not only allows for no other, but a faith which also gives him an increasingly pes-

simistic view of his fellow men. My concern is that, over the years
of his training, Panin has constructed a strong circular wall around
himself from which he has made fewer and fewer efforts to emerge.

The full range of Colonel Panin's stature could be easily traced
through his assignment records. Recommendation papers accompanying his appointment to the NKVD show that he accepted the appointment at once. And mission reports indicate that from the start
he did a good job, enduring shake-ups at the top as well as at lower
levels in the organization. None threatened his career.

He began to rise through the ranks until 1954 when, after the
death of Stalin, General Ivan Serov organized the KGB. He took
Panin with him without hesitation and enrolled him in courses to
train agents for special foreign assignments.

Panin's first mission abroad was in Trieste, as a junior member
of the Allied Control Commission. There, in three years, he per-
fected his knowledge of Italian, which he had studied before. As he
practiced what he had been taught, Panin became increasingly valuable. By 1968 he held the rank of colonel.

His files contained several awards and medals, which—due to
the jealousy that they might evoke from Panin's immediate colleagues—had not yet been awarded him. A typed schedule indicated
when each would, most likely, be presented.

Colonel Panin was the unanimous choice when the KGB devel-
oped an audacious plan involving the UN. It would be a demanding
role and Nitchevo was by 1970 one of their consummate actors.

At the end of the summer of 1970 he had just returned from a
highly successful mission to Canada. He had been sent there to seek
the latest conventional weapons innovations. When he received a
summons to report to KGB headquarters for a meeting with General Leonid Rostov, rumors scurried among Panin's colleagues that
the Colonel was in line for some lavish benefits—maybe a *dacha*
or an extended vacation in one of the Black Sea compounds.

But when he arrived at Dzerzhinsky Square and was greeted by
the General, Panin was given nothing more than a tape recorder and
two long-playing tapes.

"For your amusement," Rostov had laughed, "and also for
your *education*, comrade. Listen well."

Then Panin was left alone with the recorder and tapes in a small room hardly larger than a travel compartment on a train. And less comfortable. The chairs were wooden and devoid of any upholstery. One ashtray, cracked and with a pie-shaped section missing, kept the recorder and tapes company on top of a wax-gummed table.

Three dead flies hung upside down in a dust-matted cobweb that occupied the other chair, one that Rostov chose not to use during his brief minutes in the room with the Colonel.

What else could he do? So Nitchevo lit a cigarette, then placed it in the ashtray, not touching it again. He did not smoke—but his "character" in Canada had. The assumed habit lingered, even after the role had been abandoned. The tape began to play.

It was a discussion. His KGB superiors were debating the wisdom of an operation. Within seconds, Panin realized it was to be his mission.

"What, after all, is to be gained by going through the files in the Observer's office? Who cares about papers exhorting peace, disarmament, Third World development, or—get this for the record, Pyotr—resolutions on the rights of parents to determine the number of children to have, rather than having population control forced upon them." Panin recognized the voice as that of a general whom all the agents hated. Most refused to even say his name.

The discussions went on. He could hear the crumpling of paper as some reports apparently were passed among the superiors, scanned, and then tossed. He could almost see the waste basket—torn sheets scattered around it, waiting to be shredded.

"It will give us a new window on the collusion between the Vatican Secretariat of State and the U. S. State Department, even the Pentagon now and then. The kind of stuff we have gotten so far from our people both in Washington and Rome doesn't satisfy me." The voice was high-pitched and the accent distinct, but Panin could not identify the speaker. "Since our propaganda speaks of this collusion, wouldn't it be helpful to have something to put on the table?" Several men laughed. And one mumbled what sounded to be an aside to the effect that such had never stopped propaganda —*good* propaganda—before.

"There's code data. We can always justify a probe if there's evidence that a code might be broken. Who knows how useful the Vatican codes might be in our efforts, say, in Poland or Mexico or Spain?" Somebody far from the recorder mike appeared to object. Panin could barely make out the comment, but it seemed to indicate that many of these countries had no papal representatives, so that communication was carried on not in cable code, but by means of hand-delivered letters. "Any new and hard information on the procedures these priests use with such letters—I can see real benefits for our agents in the Catholic-dominated countries. It would be great to nail the cross-kissers at their own petty game."

General Rostov interrupted. Panin listened more intently as he heard the superior among superiors make his succinct point. "This operation already has Kremlin approval. It must be carried out, even if it provides nothing more than the latest prayers."

But the General added another reason—one that pleased Panin greatly. "This project," the older man explained with some admiration, clear even in his recorded voice, "represents something quite new in any agent's experience. It would prepare Panin for a greater assignment someday. One, for instance, aimed to penetrate foreign intelligence operations."

The room grew so quiet that Panin could hear several men breathing.

"Comrades, a priest arouses less suspicion and less interest than almost any other cover an agent might assume. It is delightful to imagine how handy such a fellow might become under circumstances totally unconnected with the UN or the Vatican."

Amid the mumblings that Panin could discern thereafter, he heard several joking (and possibly a few serious) suggestions as to what such "totally unconnected circumstances" might one day be. Then Rostov's voice interjected, "Do not forget that Volodya will have diplomatic privileges and immunities. There are a hundred and thirty-six member countries at the UN and many of them have already made their missions into espionage centers, primarily aimed at their host—naturally." Some tired chuckles blurred the tape and someone's chair scraped across the floor, making the tape even less intelligible for several seconds.

When the voice became audible and clear again, the General was arguing, "Despite strict surveillance upon our mission there, we have obtained solid indications that the Permanent Observer's office plays an important role in many questions, particularly that of Palestinian concerns. Many Catholic countries line up their votes with Vatican views and instructions. Volodya can filter such communiqués to us."

An hour or so later, after Panin had listened to both discussion tapes, he pushed the buzzer on the compartment wall, and seconds after his third ring the door opened. A guard appeared and the Colonel asked to see General Rostov once again.

Panin was taken to an immense file room. It was the size of two or three hotel lobbies and, for whatever reason, not another person was in sight. The guard left him alone. He immediately felt the awkwardness of being in such a cavernous place, and of knowing that the stories of a million people (maybe more) surrounded him, but that not one file drawer or compartment cabinet would ever be open to him.

He provided information; it almost never came back to him.

A voice called out his name.

"So what did we miss in considering your upcoming role, Volodya?" Rostov was speaking with Panin, the voice was coming from speakers scattered throughout the vast room, but the man himself was nowhere in sight. Panin smiled; his mind tried to work as he imagined a priest's might work: this voice and the authority behind it, all unseen, was it not like talking to God?

"I was cut out to be a man of the cloth, Comrade General. You know that I am a character in search of an author." He could hear Rostov's laugh from many sides. It was eerie; where does one look when talking to an echo chamber? "I think you have written the script I was born to perform. A priest. It's amazing. Who knows what miracles Nitchevo can perform?"

Then, for the next half hour, Rostov instructed the Colonel concerning specific preparations. Now and then the room echoed with growls and belly laughs from Rostov as he detailed what Panin would be doing so that religious instruction and priestly manners could be added to the long list of his talents. The General seemed anxious for the time when he could observe the transformation, when Panin would bring this Catholic pope to life.

Such theatrics, Panin thought. This meeting place, these speakers, the power of his unseen presence. Maybe Leonid Konstantinovich Rostov would really have preferred directing plays instead of commanding spies in the KGB. Then Panin grinned a sly smile. He is both: the world is Rostov's stage and all of us are his actors. We special agents are particularly sensitive to his way of shouting "Cut."

KGB Colonel Vladimir Efimovich Panin's file did not reveal everything.

It did not say, for instance, that he had been baptized.

It was a fact that no one among the living knew. His maternal grandmother had stealthily taken him to a Ruthenian church, where against his parents' wishes she had had him baptized and secretly given religious instruction. Before his family had moved to Moscow, he had received communion in a private house. The administering priest had been from the Byzantine rite and Panin had never forgotten the taste of that wine and wafer.

Shortly thereafter his grandmother died. Soon the memories became very vague in his mind. In any case, he did not even nominally consider himself a Catholic.

In 1945 when Stalin took a hard line toward the Ruthenian church and the government legislated it out of existence, deporting Archbishop Slipyj, the twenty-three-year-old Volodya had no reaction, not even a thought about how great his grandmother's sorrow would have been had she been alive. Within the KGB, the Colonel considered himself no longer Ukrainian, but Russian.

But the day he left Moscow Center he could not help but remember his grandmother and first communion, even the smells of the old Ruthenian church. He knew immediately that it would be of great help as he began building his new role as priest.

[III]

NEARLY NINE MONTHS AFTER COLONEL PANIN BEGAN HIS preparations for his mission as a priest, a report arrived at Moscow headquarters. The Soviet agent in Rome confirmed that the Papal Secretariat of State was about to transfer Monsignor Faddini, Permanent Observer of the Holy See at the

United Nations. Faddini would move to a higher position and his replacement would be one Monsignor Righi.

General Rostov stirred his office staff into a frenzy. They had less than three months to prepare for a classic switch.

The obvious had to be handled first. Soviet agents followed, photographed, studied, almost vivisected the Monsignor, who was himself busy making preparations for his move to the United Nations.

As he wrote letters to friends and family announcing his new post, KGB agents were able to compare these communiqués to the biography they were uncovering. Soon they knew Righi's friendships; his strengths and weaknesses; the languages he spoke; the dialect of his native region, Romagna; even the intimate details of his close relationship with a sister who lived with the parents of her dead husband in the countryside near Rome.

The Monsignor, unwittingly, could not have been more helpful. As the surgeon specialists studied the photos, it became apparent that the choice of Righi to succeed Faddini was a piece of extraordinary luck for the KGB. He and Panin had the same hatchet face; the two were of approximately the same height. The Monsignor's slight limp, the result of a skiing accident on Mount Abetone in the Apennines, was even on the same side as the slight irregularity that Panin carried from his war injury. "Just proves once again," the surgeon had said, grimacing, "that we are all interchangeable cogs in the world's many fine machines."

The face to be sculpted, once again, had been hidden away at a villa in the Crimean, formerly the property of Prince Lermontov, though more recently an essential KGB installation. Panin was almost overwhelmed by the enormity of preparations necessary to become *any* Permanent Observer of the Holy See. In a note to the General, Panin had said his earlier training had been child's play by comparison. After all, he now had to immerse himself in Latin, theology, canon law, Vatican diplomatic history, and the organization of the Church in North America—not to mention the tedium of the minutes of the United Nations and related materials.

Languages were less of a problem, since in the course of his career he had become fluent in Italian, French, German, and Spanish. He only needed to add an Italian accent for his English. He accomplished this by early morning practice sessions using recordings, motion pictures, and a fine tutor who loved to play chess.

Then the news came that he must also prepare to become a *specific* Permanent Observer. With professional pride, he tightened his daily regime and astounded his colleagues once again by continuing his other studies at their original pace while thoroughly memorizing the Righi files.

Panin's method was not merely to absorb the details of any person whom he was to impersonate, but also to add, when possible, that man's story to his own. For example, this Giuseppe Righi had been ordained in 1941, the same year that Panin had had his baptism by fire. After some study, Panin could actually envision the ordination, seeing it almost as vividly as his own trench memories from icy days and nights on the front. When Panin awoke one morning and remembered dreams from both his own war years and the priest's days of ordination, the KGB Colonel knew he had that part of Righi within him.

And so he proceeded. Becoming Righi as a professor in the diocesan seminary and as a student at the Academia Ecclesiastica. Or in 1960, as Righi entered the Vatican diplomatic service. Still later, as Righi served abroad in Bolivia, in Chile, then Kenya before being called back to Rome. . . .

During the three months remaining at the Crimean villa, his KGB colleagues actually began to miss Colonel Panin as the austere Monsignor Righi, like a possessing demon, overpowered almost all of what had been—for so many lively months before—the energetic and accomplished Nitchevo.

What with a different haircut, new features (thanks to surgery), even a different posture and manner, and of course the accent—there was almost no trace of Panin to be found. A transformation. It was worse than when the Colonel had slipped away for an intensive practicum in Lithuania. During those weeks the villa had been dishearteningly quiet in the Colonel's absence. Upon his return, many of the villa staff members delighted in the evening, which few would forget, when Panin abandoned his Righi character and, for one last time, joined them in vodka and jokes. His stories about the Catholic Church in Lithuania surfaced ironically in conversations on the Lermontov estate. He gave them his imitations of church rituals and mimicked priests baptizing and chanting. And his poignant story—not actually told for any humorous effect—about how the mass reminded him of . . . No one objected. It was the vodka and the talk of old people's lives. The heart of Mother Russia. "It seemed right," one fellow had concluded.

Soviet agents in Rome worked with their usual efficiency—at a speed rare for that city—to convey confirmation that Monsignor Righi would be leaving for New York, via London, on an Alitalia flight on September 8. Moscow Center was delighted, as a Heathrow switch had over the years become something of a routine operation. They waited. When the bursar of the Papal Secretariat of State purchased a tourist-class ticket for the eighth and gave Righi's name, General Rostov had his staff prepare for one of the "first-class operations." They knew Alitalia.

On the eighth, as Panin, in disguise, handed his colleague the unused tourist-class ticket and went to the first-class waiting room at the Fiumicino airport, the Colonel laughed to himself. Rostov had been right again: Alitalia *had* transferred the ticket-bearer from the Vatican, giving him a seat in first class for his tourist-class fare.

And the priest would have a companion in first class: Panin in the guise of a cheerful engineer.

"Excuse me, Monsignor, my name is Morlacchi. I introduce myself because it appears that there'll only be four of us in first class." Panin used great care in avoiding any lapses of accent in his Italian, lapses that might betray the Romagna dialect. "Probably because our companies are paying—but you can't be taken for a company man. . . ."

Monsignor Righi had no idea he was in a sense talking to himself when he responded: "Quite so. At a time like this and indeed at any time, we clergy should give an example of austerity. It's no more than proper—but you know how it is." Panin's mind was working rapidly, memorizing voice tones and gestures and mannerisms—all the while being sure to appear just a friendly listener. "Alitalia may want to pay respect to clerical garb, or possibly to the position which the wearer is going to hold abroad."

Panin could not help observing: How cold yet innocent the man is.

Righi continued. "How can anyone refuse? And I must admit, the twenty extra pounds of baggage allowance is very convenient."

It will not be difficult, Panin thought, to keep this fellow talking. "You're quite right. Only our native Communist rabble-rousers could see anything out of the way about such an arrangement. Don't give it another minute's thought."

Just then Panin suffered a momentary surprise as he observed how much like Righi's were his own hands—the priest had folded his arms so that his hands rested just above his clericals' elbows. The Colonel knew that only his face had undergone plastic surgery.

Yet the hands were almost identical.

"But Father—may I call you that?—things aren't the same abroad. No one mistakes a mere creature comfort for conspicuous waste." Panin pointed toward a bartender who smiled back at the two passengers. "Meanwhile, shall we order a drink? And not because they're free. . . ."

Righi laughed comfortably, as if he had thought of the joke himself. "No, thank you. They'll be offering us one as soon as we're airborne." From the waiting room window two fellow priests reappeared and waved at the Monsignor. Apparently they had accompanied Righi to the airport, then had excused themselves momentarily. An announcement indicated that the flight to New York was now boarding. The priests, halted by the announcement, merely waved again and walked out of sight.

The two men left the waiting room and boarded the plane together. While the Monsignor walked ahead, Panin cautiously adjusted his pacing and posture in motion to mirror Righi. The Colonel was applying a fine tuning, up close, to the imitative traits he had practiced at long distance.

As they approached the first-class compartment, Panin kept close to Righi to ensure that no one else sat near him.

It was the Monsignor, to the Colonel's delight, who suggested that they sit side by side and also the Monsignor who ordered the first round of drinks. The plan was working almost too perfectly.

"So you have to do with the steel mills, do you? That should be interesting." The priest was pursuing their exchange of introductions, in which Panin had described himself as a representative of an Italian steel consortium that was sending him to open a foreign office. Righi noted the similarity between their upcoming positions.

Panin persisted in encouraging the Monsignor to be talkative.

"Not as interesting and rewarding, I suspect, as your contact with human souls must be."

"Perhaps." Righi was suddenly not quite convincing. "My contact with souls will be somewhat polluted by politics."

Panin said nothing and the priest continued, "I'm going to represent the Holy See at the United Nations."

"Fascinating." Panin was as enthusiastic as he thought an engineer should be at such news. "Must be very absorbing work."

Monsignor Righi found the flight enjoyable. This man, Morlacchi, spoke of rolled steel and structural steel in terms that—to the priest's surprise—made the subjects seem somehow human. And he had gotten Righi to talk about spiritual matters. Had almost drawn the thoughts from him.

Righi felt a quiet sense of pleasure at having told Morlacchi about the inherent—even if unconscious—riches of every human soul. It was the first time in months that he could recall the feeling that his remarks had come across as enlightening rather than unctuous. Congeniality, he decided, could work wonders.

Then the plane landed at Heathrow.

An announcement from the flight attendant explained that they would be grounded in London for an hour, so the engineer offered to show the Monsignor the way to the duty-free shop. Morlacchi added, "I know the byways of Heathrow like the inside of my pocket . . . and I can promise a special bargain that you couldn't have imagined."

The two men walked down a well-lit corridor that opened up onto the cargo arrival space. From behind—had anyone been there to notice—the pair could have passed for brothers.

The empty corridor suddenly went dark as two men grabbed Righi and forced him into a delivery truck whose motor had been running since its driver had received the radio message that the plane had landed.

They took nothing from his briefcase except the baggage claim checks attached to the ticket folder.

Fifty minutes later, when the Alitalia plane took off, there were still only four passengers in first class.

But one had come aboard at London.

[IV]

THE OPERATION HAD GONE SMOOTHLY, BUT NEITHER MOSCOW Operations Center, nor the agents in Rome, nor Panin himself gave in to self-congratulation. They could remember more difficult assignments from the past; in this line of work, Panin reminded himself, only failures made the front page.

The front page of the New York *Times*, September 8, 1971. Dozens of papers faced the men waiting at JFK Airport for the new Observer. Monsignor Maguire, pastor of the Church of the Nativity, purchased a copy of *Reader's Digest Best Inspirational Stories* and Father Belli, the Italian-American priest who worked (at an hourly rate) for the Observer's office, chose salted peanuts.

It was Belli, in charge of the office since Faddini's departure, who was at the airport in an official capacity; Maguire's appearance was an act of courtesy toward the Vatican's envoy. Until the arrival of Monsignor Righi's plane was announced, the two priests hardly spoke to one another.

But Maguire opened up considerably once the three men were in a cab headed for midtown Manhattan. He not only welcomed his new guest warmly, but—like a good Irishman—also put in an immediate bid for Righi's spare-time services.

"How's Faddini?" he asked, and for a quick moment Righi confused the names of the Ambassador to the UN from Italy, Faraglia, and Righi's predecessor, Faddini.

"Beg your pardon?" Righi gestured toward the open cab window, implying that the noise prevented his hearing.

"I said, 'How's Faddini?'" Father Maguire appeared slightly puzzled. "You did see him before you left Rome?" When he saw Righi nod yes, the parish priest continued, "What a good friend he was. Gave us a hand—when he was not at the UN. Hope that you can do the same." The cab was bouncing from pothole to pothole along the expressway. Maguire leaned closer so that Righi would be certain to hear. "We're the UN's parish church, so to speak. We

have to hear confessions in French, Spanish, Italian, German. God
knows what. Yesterday, a good woman asked for someone who
could listen in, I promise you, *Swahili*."

Righi professed himself willing and able, "Except for Swahili
and Russian—but the Russians don't come to confession."

At supper, the entire rectory "family" was present—except for Father Potocki.

"He's arriving any day from Detroit," Maguire explained for
Righi's benefit. The pastor also handled the introductions, politely
repeating "Giuseppe Righi" each time. It was both friendly and
awkward.

When he came to his assistants, Fathers Nevins and Vaccaro,
Maguire mentioned that the latter had an Italian background. Righi,
however, could see that in Vaccaro's features.

But Vaccaro immediately corrected Maguire: "Sicilian."

Righi interjected what he hoped would be a pleasant observation. "Then Father Vaccaro has history on his side, at least as far as
America is concerned. He understands that before the mass immigration, Italians were divided up, according to most Americans,
into Genoese and Sicilians. The first represented the north; Sicilians,
the south. But after the first year of the tidal wave—1885—there
came to be three categories: northerners, southerners, and Sicilians. . . ."

While Monsignor Righi continued, Maguire thought, This new
guest will give these fellows some food for thought. Faddini was a
good man, in his way—but a bit sentimental. This newcomer is
sharp—possibly argumentative, probably critical. But I must caution Potocki . . . his reputation as a busybody—no matter how
good a priest he may be—might annoy this diplomat.

Vaccaro was the first to respond to Monsignor Righi's remarks. "I'm pleased about your understanding of our place in history." His manner surprised others in the rectory family, who
knew Vaccaro to be a calm and reasonable man unless someone
mentioned Sicily, when he often lost his head. Now he seemed
unruffled.

Actually, he was quietly pleased. His eyes gleamed as he
thought, This *paesano* will side with me against these Irishmen. And

since he knows something about the history of immigration, he probably knows how they've stepped on us in the churches. Vaccaro frowned: Or rather, in the church basements.

During that first meal, it became quite apparent that the Church of the Nativity had its own problems. One, as in most parishes, was its debt and another was the usual clash between the Irish—in this case, Father Nevins—and the Italians—represented by Vaccaro.

Righi observed how diplomatic Father Maguire attempted to be, conceding that the Italians were "good people" and that they had made many contributions, including a substantial increase in the number of Catholics in America.

But Righi also noted that Maguire refrained from continuing that point with regard to the Irish. The newcomer held the distinct suspicion that Maguire was one of those churchmen who maintained—however silently—that the breakthroughs and prosperity of the Catholic Church in this hostile Protestant America were due almost entirely to the Irish.

Righi decided that this was his landlord's weakness, and diplomat that he was, he listened, hoping to take a tack that would please Maguire, even as the parish priest forged ahead with his opinions. "The Italians were discriminated against, just as the Irish were." Righi could see in Maguire's face the man's struggle not to become impassioned as he spoke. "But your grandparents, Sal, did find a better climate when they got to these shores—better than my grandparents found. We were often forced to arm ourselves so we could protect our churches, schools, and sisters' convents. And despite the need for manual labor and the fact that Irishmen were good workers, my great great-grandfather was confronted with a sign which read: 'Men wanted. No Irish need apply.'" Maguire, in a final gesture, aimed his pointing finger rigidly toward Vaccaro. "This hardly happened to your grandpa."

That's when Righi interrupted. "But you passed through the test magnificently. You were formidable fighters, obedient to the priest. You trained for political combat against the English and remained ready to retaliate whenever an Orangeman put you down. And you soon realized the importance of a vote in America—not to mention the power of the police or the unions."

While Righi was appeasing Maguire, Vaccaro looked like a man betrayed. His response was immediate. "But *they* had the enormous advantage: they spoke English. Their first generation could enter the fray immediately."

"That's true, Father." Righi had to agree.

"And our countrymen had another *great* advantage which the Irish never attained." Vaccaro's eyes widened innocently, exposing an intense and naïve look. "They were sober. They drank simple homemade wine and not whiskey." Then Vaccaro pressed his attack further, as if tossing out a challenge for a real argument. "With the result that their earnings made it home—not to the bars or to betting on horses."

Father Nevins' face turned beet-red and he was halfway into a stuttering rebuttal when Maguire stopped conversation with the dictum which Righi would hear quite often in the months ahead: "No fights in the rectory. We are one big family: Irish, Poles, Italians, Germans. *Ô, Église Catholique, que tu es belle.*" Then, over laughter at the pastor's French, he hastened to add, "Which I say in bad French because a Frenchman—I don't remember exactly who—said it first."

Thereafter, Righi had not been able to ignore how absorbed Father Nevins became, as if doing an analysis like some amateur experimental psychologist. It soon became apparent that Nevins' subject was Righi, so that Righi came to suspect, from the look in the Irishman's eyes, that Father Nevins thought him to be the victim of a "complex."

Later, alone in his room, Righi smiled and Panin, the hidden mind behind that grin, whispered a quick afterthought: "He thinks I have a superiority complex. He distrusts me."

Nevins, Panin decided, would probably never be a threat, but his suspicions had to be dealt with . . . and soon.

The next day Monsignor Righi arrived early for work in his new office.

It consisted of three rooms next door to the church; Maguire had explained that this small building belonged to the parish.

The first thing Righi did was to type a letter to Anna Maffei, the Monsignor's sister, telling her that his trip had been good and that he liked the accommodations that the rectory provided. "Don't expect too much in the way of letters, dear Anna, because I'll be busy these next months."

From the many copies of letters that Panin had studied—Righi's correspondence had been intercepted by Soviet agents in Rome—he was certain this note would satisfy Anna. As he had practiced so many times before, he penned a scrawl over the typed signature: "Peppino."

At nine o'clock, Father Belli arrived from his parish in the Bronx. He had been whistling rather loudly until he spotted his new superior immersed in papers and fell silent. He shoved his briefcase on the swivel chair, then stepped through Righi's doorway before offering a greeting, an apology, and a compliment: "You hit the ground running, I see."

Righi looked up in consternation. "An expression," Belli explained. "You are a hard worker. You don't waste any time."

Righi held up a finger and hurriedly scribbled a note. Belli stood quietly, thinking. The impatience in his expression seemed to say: Well, Faddini started out at full speed, but he soon slowed down. We'll see how things are, say, three months from now.

The new Observer understood—more than Belli allowed—that the General Assembly was due to open within a week. Righi intended to be fully prepared so that he could follow each of its sessions. So this first morning he took the bit between his teeth.

He asked Belli to fill him in on the past three months. The Monsignor's questions were so much to the point that the young Belli appeared stunned. The interrogation, casual as its tone was, nonetheless lasted over an hour.

Afterward, the Observer summed up his reactions as Belli sat, drained by all the early morning questions and answers: "The United Nations seems to be an organization where everything works efficiently, except for the member states. But we won't lose heart, will we, Belli?" He noticed that the assistant was still making some notes on an already well-used legal pad. "And we're expected to work only toward the ends that keep faith with those noble purposes which were set out in its beginning."

Belli's expression was blank.

"Just as the Holy Father said—do you remember?—when he spoke here on October 4, 1965."

Belli didn't seem to remember, but he quickly explained that he had been a seminarian at the time. "You can count on me, Monsignor," he added hastily, "I'll do the little that I can do." Righi nodded. He expected that it would be little enough.

Left alone once more, Righi scanned his notes, calculating which subjects would probably occasion the sharpest debate once the Assembly opened:

—a seat for the People's Republic of China
—the further spread of nuclear arms, colonialism, foreign military bases
—apartheid
—the Middle Eastern or Palestinian problem.

This last was what interested him most, not only because of instructions from the Papal Secretariat of State, which Righi had found that morning in the office files, but also because the subject promised to be inordinately complex and difficult. He knew that after almost thirty years, attempts toward peace between Israelis and Arabs had become a diplomatic maze. In the last twenty-three years, three wars had taken place. A fourth now threatened.

And so the first days passed. From his post, Righi heard what he had expected to hear: endless debate over usurped land, Palestinian refugees, rights and injustices. According to the Arabs, everything had been revolutionized in Palestine, everything from the surface of the earth itself to the age-old ways of people who could no longer inhabit it. As for the Israelis, they felt entitled, after two thousand years in diaspora, to claim the right of cultivating a soil which had lain fallow after the deportation of their ancestors.

Outside the Assembly, the Holy See's Observer learned more detailed and disturbing information. The important thing was what was being said in the political affairs commission and in the emergency meetings of the Security Council.

Soon Righi became recognized increasingly often, so that in the hallways and at parties he prudently and impartially could approach both Israeli and Arab delegates. The basic issue remained too serious for a smile, but he did overhear things that were comic to the point of paradox.

One American delegate, for example, said to him that it might be opportune for the Holy Father to exhort Arabs and Israelis to try reconciling their differences in a "truly Christian spirit."

And there was the observation of Faad, counselor of the Egyptian mission: "The best way to knock out Zionism is to do away with anti-Semitism."

These first weeks provided Monsignor Righi with enough material to fill his reports to the Vatican Secretariat of State.

The news was hardly of overwhelming interest, but the general point Righi was able to make confirmed categorically that the Holy See's presence at the United Nations was appreciated and that he personally was receiving courteous attentions.

One report made mention of an observation that, much later, Righi would reconsider . . . would reconsider when he once again allowed himself to think as Panin:

> It is from Ambassador Badr that one gets the most overt expressions of religious feeling. His speeches usually begin, "In the name of Allah, the merciful, the compassionate," and his most recent one ended in a kind of beseeching: "Allah, the merciful, the compassionate, send peace among us."
>
> Otherwise, there is almost never a mention of prayer at the United Nations. At the opening of the General Assembly, the delegates are asked to dedicate a minute "to silent prayer or meditation." But there is never a motion at the end of a session to thank God for allowing everyone to get through the marathon of speeches and the flood of resolutions.

Monsignor Righi concluded the report by speaking well of Monsignor Maguire and Father Belli while voicing the hope that he would soon come to enjoy the company of Fathers Nevins and Vaccaro and Potocki.

Such recommendations never hurt in church reports.

And he did not fail to attach a short special report devoted to the incident with Martha Winthrop.

A week or so later the Vatican sent a reassuring reply: It had troubles of its own with the media.

[V]

STANISLAUS POTOCKI WAS BORN IN A GALICIAN VILLAGE NEAR the border of the Ukraine. He had emigrated to the United States when he was fifteen; he and his family had been waiting, idled in a German camp for displaced persons. It had taken a year and a half to get the visa. The Potockis settled in Detroit. There young Stanislaus entered the seminary and was ordained priest. Years later he arrived in New York to begin his second pastoral assignment.

He was a homesick man. Homesick for Detroit, but, above all, for the Ukraine. It was as though he cultivated distress over the loss of his native land to Soviet Russia—cultivated that suffering, even after so many years.

"Autumn—and already I have my first cold," were the Permanent Observer's first words as he entered the rectory and was introduced to Potocki. The priest from Detroit barely caught the name: "Righi?" Whatever. At any rate, the fellow seemed no more impressed by Potocki than Potocki seemed to be by the Vatican Monsignor.

The Observer continued what to Potocki was irrepressible chatter about how much he liked New York. "It's sprawling, dynamic, explosive, unmistakably money-mad." Potocki could not help but notice how the others gathered around the speaker, each listening with deference as he concluded, "almost a nightmare vision of the future: metropolis and jungle, rich and bankrupt, cynical and generous—but I can't take it in the rain."

Righi peeled off his overshoes as the truth of his remark made everyone laugh. Except Potocki. He sat quietly, trying to decide why he had taken such an immediate dislike to this fellow.

"How was the political affairs commission?" Belli asked. Potocki had chatted with him earlier, found him down to earth. No pretenses. Just another guy.

But Monsignor Maguire interjected his own question before the Observer could answer Belli. "Do tell us the latest news from the Glass House." Potocki abhorred such treatment of subordinates and let Belli know that by sending a quick expression in the assistant's direction: I know how you feel, fellow.

The Observer responded, oblivious to Potocki or Belli. "Nothing special—though I did have the satisfaction of hearing the foreign minister of Ecuador say that the Vatican diplomacy is the best in the world."

"And you blushed with pride, I suppose?" was Maguire's reaction.

"Not at all, Monsignor. I played modest." Righi's words amused Potocki, who couldn't imagine the Observer as modest, except by device. " 'If our diplomacy is first-rate,' I answered, 'I can't imagine second.' "

This time even the Polish priest laughed.

"Apart from this," Belli said, trying once more to get his new superior's attention, "has there been any remarkable intervention in the debate?"

"Why, yes." Monsignor Righi shook the rain from his London Fog coat and showed particular interest in giving Belli the details: "The Peruvian delegate, Belaunde. He said something which will last, I think. 'At the UN, something is always disappearing. When there's a controversy between two small countries, the controversy disappears. When the dispute, however, is between a large country and a small one—the small country disappears.' " The Observer paused, as if for maximum effect, then added, " 'And when two great powers are entangled in controversy, then the UN disappears.' "

All the rectory companions laughed once again and the priest named Vaccaro slapped Righi on the back, calling him "paesano." Still Potocki could not feel relaxed. Not as relaxed as Nevins, who wore off-duty attire: a limp turtleneck pullover and dark gray slacks.

Then Righi spoke to him. Potocki felt as though the Observer had somehow sensed this other newcomer's discomfort. There was a sudden genuineness that affected Potocki. This fellow was now asking Potocki about where he had gone to seminary, what his major had been, how Stan had enjoyed his first pastorate and the city of Detroit. The Observer was so engagingly cordial that the Polish priest was surprised to find himself telling stories about his past. And he was surprised to find this diplomat listening more attentively than the others.

Potocki said, "The bishop told me I'd get the experience of ministry in a big city." His words made him sad; he could feel the smile fade from his face. "As if Detroit had been nothing." Thoughts of all he had tried to do seemed to engulf him. "And here I'm afraid I won't even have the consolation of preaching or hearing confessions in Polish."

For a moment no one spoke. Potocki could see from Nevins' expression that the Irishman, who had been only half listening, felt no sympathy. Nor did Vaccaro, who continued flipping through *The New Yorker*.

Only Righi attempted to console him. "*Habent sua fata . . . superiores.*" But Potocki—like the other priests in the rectory—had little Latin and even less acquaintance with Horace. He could only hope that the Observer was trying to be sympathetic.

Finally Maguire spoke up. "In Detroit you had the world's biggest automobile companies. That's something. But here in New York—in time—I suspect that you'll find a lot to interest you—starting with the United Nations. And ours is no ordinary parish; it's a church in the service of the UN. Financially, we may be in the red, but we do have a mission all our own."

This seemed to challenge Potocki. Maybe there could be a spiritually satisfying dimension to such a godless place as this? "Very good. I like that: to satisfy the spiritual needs of the international community. Then we must find ways to give such parishioners special treatment."

The thought of it made Potocki feel, at last, that this might be a good place for him. He opened his roundish, almost bovine eyes in a wide glance around the room, searching for whoever might affirm his feelings. But his blue eyes saw only a silent cynicism.

"Special treatment, Father, as you say. But I advise dispensing it on the installment plan. That is, as they furnish proof of their credibility." Monsignor Righi was the only person to comment and his words made the Pole feel even more lonely than before.

He lowered his head and said nothing more as the rectory family proceeded to the table for lunch, the chunky Mrs. O'Rourke's chunky beef stew. He sat across from Righi.

Midway through the meal, musing, Potocki happened to notice

the Permanent Observer's hands. There was something about them —or about the way in which Righi used them. The hands bothered Potocki. The fingers were slender and the nails, well manicured; the manner was befitting a Roman prelate, since the Monsignor was possibly of aristocratic rather than peasant origin. Still, Stan could not help but feel that the hands were somehow . . .

Father Nevins interrupted Potocki's ponderings with a loud expounding of his theory that "young people—even if they are doing their own thing—are nonetheless closer to the Gospel than all the old ladies who show up for mass in a taxi, but do no more than keep our pews warm." Stan listened as the Irishman continued, citing characters from the Village whom Nevins knew "from first-hand experience" to have real purpose in their lives. "It's narrow-minded to judge them by the patches on their blue jeans—unless you've got a complex for living in the past." The Pole was not so certain.

But Righi seemed to support Nevins. "You might add that these presumably godless prophets often have rosaries strung around their necks—like talismans." There was a dry tone to the Monsignor's voice.

"Well said, Giuseppe." Maguire actually applauded. Then he turned to Vaccaro. "And what do you say, *paesano?* Do you have anything against old lady churchgoers?"

It was a conversation that Potocki considered to be disrespectful, so he allowed his mind to be distracted once more as Righi's hands regained his attention. Stan was no chiromancer, but he did remember how a Detroit parishioner had explained that a priest's character could be read from the way he approached the consecrated bread and wine. The parishioner had observed that some priests grasped the host and chalice firmly; others held them up timidly or with something akin to dismay. Then he had added that the gestures of the faithful after they receive communion— each one of these reflected a state of mind. Potocki remembered some of those gestures: some folded their hands over their chests; others lay one hand over their heart while flailing the air with the other. . . .

Potocki had made the observation of hands a sort of private guessing game, one that from time to time yielded results. On trains and buses, he remembered having seen the hands of men whom he

could have sworn were at one time ordained priests. Once in a
while, when he had chatted with them, they admitted that it was so.
But no matter how well they had adjusted to the secular world, Potocki knew that their hands had retained their ritual qualities.
Handshakes communicated messages and an innocent wave of the
hand seemed like a blessing.

Then Monsignor Righi grasped his glass, drinking his water
though seemingly absorbed in Nevins' convictions about saints in
jeans.

"*Matka Boska*, just so," Potocki whispered to himself. This
fellow does not have the hands of a priest. That was what had been
bothering him all along.

He raised his eyes to look into the Monsignor's face, just as
Righi teased Father Nevins: "Those young men of yours will come
to a bad end—if their ambitions go no higher than their belt
buckles. I think you'd do better to be less permissive and to try and
bring them back into civilization. It will not be by defiance of the
law that these boys you so admire will . . ."

Then Potocki's eyes narrowed. I've seen this fellow before—
and not so long ago. . . .

[VI]

THE SECURITY COUNCIL WENT INTO ANOTHER FRENZIED SES-
sion. A South American whispered to Righi, "Let's see
who can stick it out longer," referring to arguments after
a raid by the Palestine Liberation Organization. Of course there
had also been an instantaneous and implacable Israeli reprisal.

But the Middle Eastern crisis did not impede the progress of
the autumn's social calendar. It was a circumstance that Righi took
some time to figure out: How could these people argue by day and
party each evening? Nonetheless, every ambassador felt it his duty
to give a reception in honor of the head of his country's delegation
—usually the foreign minister, an undersecretary, or an important
parliamentary leader.

Between mid-September and Christmas week, there were often
three cocktail parties a day, followed by a multitude of dinners.

But, one reasoned, it could hardly be otherwise, with a hundred and thirty-six member countries, plus six permanent observers.

Today, for example, Monsignor Righi received seven embossed invitations. Each for an afternoon three weeks hence. Of course the new Observer had not fallen into this social whirlwind without some prior warning from Italy's Ambassador, Faraglia.

The genial diplomat had phoned Righi as the first flurry of invitations began arriving in the mail. Faraglia's voice over the telephone sounded rich and resonant, like a stage actor's from the old troupes of Europe. "It's an obstacle course race, from one hotel or apartment to another. But diplomatic custom prescribes attendance. In fact, it would be counterproductive not to go."

So the Observer of the Holy See went, making the rounds. An ex-seminarian, now his country's UN representative, had spotted the new priest in the crowds. Ambassador Mwambutsa was his name, and he seemed to perceive Righi's hesitancy. The African ex-seminarian quickly changed the Monsignor's attitude, however, when he explained, "Agreements that have misfired at official sessions are often reached in the corner of a crowded room—a place where both parties become more relaxed and agreeable, huddled with glass in hand."

Righi soon came to see another value in such parties. It was as though, in the eyes of the other guests, one's presence at the party of a host country affirmed friendship.

On this rainy evening in late November, Monsignor Righi felt as though he was dancing from place to place. And he understood Father Belli's comment about how lucky Righi was to be living in midtown—because tonight he would venture no more than twenty blocks from home, though his destinations included a reception at the Waldorf, another at the Plaza, drinks with two delegates at the Pierre, and promises to drop by other gatherings at both the Hilton and the UN dining room, should time permit.

How thankful he was that at evening's end, he would not have to drive out to the suburbs, as many delegates would—each of them, as he would be, soaked in whiskey and stuffed with shrimp.

At the reception given by the Grand Duchy of Luxembourg, the liquors were what a British guest called "top drawer" and the canapés, what Martha Winthrop described as "widely assorted."

For that woman was there. Righi had seen her from the corner of his eye. How could he have missed her gleaming gown of purple and gold?

He decided to avoid her by sweeping across the crowd on the other side of the receiving line. Instead he wound up in front of the bar. Guests pressed behind him so that he could not retreat without ordering a drink. The best vodka he had seen since— Panin was tempted, but Righi quickly chose a dry moselle wine. At least he hoped it would be dry.

"Hello there" came an assault from behind, words accompanied by a clap across his back that sent wine splashing down Righi's right coat pocket. He turned to see the Israeli ambassador.

"Shimon?" There was more enthusiasm in the Monsignor's voice than he really felt. The jacket had just come from the cleaners. "What's up?"

"*Ein breira*, as we say: there's no alternative to being well." As if to underline his words, the Ambassador reached for a glass of champagne and emptied it with a single swallow.

This was Bar-Hillel, born Tannenbaum, whom Righi had come to appreciate as a friend during the recent spate of parties. And, when he wasn't spilling drinks, Righi found him quite entertaining. Plus, he was Jewish and—for Panin's purposes—Righi felt as though he needed to combat an inherent anti-Semitism by befriending Shimon.

For Righi had discovered Bar-Hillel to be sensitive to any sign —genuine or presumed—that hinted at anti-Semitism. After all, he had been Tannenbaum in Germany while Hitler was ascending into power. That was when Shimon had emigrated to a farm in Palestine.

In fact, Bar-Hillel had checked the Observer on several occasions, claiming to have detected such signs in Righi. But each time Shimon had openly attributed them to the Vatican—needling Righi about the fact that the Holy See had never formally recognized the State of Israel and that, historically, the Catholic Church did not have an exactly admirable record concerning its treatment of Jews.

Righi—suppressing Panin's prejudices—knew better. But like a diplomat, he demurred. It was sufficient to allow the men frequent and lengthy conversations—each of them becoming convinced that he had elicited valuable information from the other.

Their reports stood as proof.

Bar-Hillel's most recent reports to his country's Minister of Foreign Affairs had been based largely upon what the Observer had told him concerning opinions that Arabs had shared with him. As for Righi, in writing to his Secretariat of State, he had quoted Bar-Hillel extensively—making due allowance for calculated misguidance. Israel was known for such, done with an eye toward their own aspirations, intentions, and—now and then quite brazenly —some of their concrete projects.

The two men carried their drinks away from the crowd at the bar and maneuvered toward a corner with some privacy. It was Righi who launched into what had become one of their routine, friendly exchanges. The two men enjoyed tossing scriptural quotations at one another. "So, Shimon, have you found time this week to count the grains of sand on the seashore?"

Bar-Hillel grinned, remembering their lengthy argument about this godly promise to the ancient, Abraham.

The Monsignor persisted. "It seems to me that these words could apply equally to the United Nations. Have we not multiplied 'as the stars of the heaven and as the sand—' "

The Israeli burst into laughter. Champagne splattered about his cupped hand surrounding his glass.

"But those who have sprung from the loins of Father Abraham are not as numerous as the stars." Righi was alluding to their argument, a few days before, concerning the hundred and thirty-six member countries and how such a number both helped and hindered the UN. "Just think of all the permanent representative offices; the people who come for the General Assembly meetings; the employees of the Secretariat, hundreds of them all over the world where the UN has sent them; the cleaning women; the newspaper reporters (God help us)—"

"And the spies."

For a moment Righi's natural reaction was silence. Panin had risen up from within him—and spies, like diplomats, cannot afford to answer back. At least not indiscriminately.

"There must be some, of course—but I haven't run into one."

Bar-Hillel's grin grew wider and he stepped back a bit, giving his next words a slightly larger stage: "You will meet them, if

you're not on guard. And I see that you're easily caught *off* guard
—because there is a spy talking to you this minute."

Both men laughed—a fact noted by several newspaper reporters present at the Luxembourg reception.

Panin took particular note of Bar-Hillel's manner during the
minutes that followed. He knew the subtle language of men who
were spies. And he knew the quips of those who were not.

When the time came, he would know—for certain—into
which category Shimon Bar-Hillel actually fit.

[VII]

FEW PEOPLE TOOK SERIOUSLY THE AMBASSADOR OF A SMALL
Persian Gulf emirate whom Monsignor Righi had most
recently befriended. The man was Ahmed Badr, whose
last speech renewed his reputation for long-windedness, for contin-
ual self-quotation, for a total absence of humor.

Nonetheless, Righi was convinced that most of Badr's detrac-
tors were in error.

The priest had learned that Ahmed Badr's government had
kept him at the United Nations for such a long term because they
could not practically do without him. His intimacy with American
financiers and oil magnates and stock brokers had made him irreplaceable. He was considered an expert on the stock exchange, and
on Wall Street he was reputed to be in absolute charge of investing
his sovereign's share of oil royalties. And thanks to oil, he had accu-
mulated a small personal fortune, further augmented by Wall Street
windfalls.

He used his wealth in a manner well suited to a man interested
in extending the frontiers of his knowledge. History, not politics,
was his real passion.

He was—to Righi's mind—a dean among diplomats. He knew
everybody at the United Nations, having been there ever since its
first meeting in London. When his vanity was appealed to, he could
be a mine of information.

For the purposes of both the Observer of the Holy See and

Colonel Panin, such a friendship was extremely valuable. After all, reports from the Vatican's Secretariat of State had confirmed that Ahmed Badr—by virtue of his extensive connections with the commercial enterprises of American Jews—possessed ongoing sources of information concerning intrigues both inside the United Nations and outside. Most recently, background information on Palestinian commando operations had been traced through his office.

So when Badr phoned to ask Monsignor Righi to lunch at the Algonquin, the priest said yes without hesitation.

In that venerable hotel lobby, the two men were seated near the ornate grandfather clock. A silent waiter, looking more like a diplomat than either guest, had just brought their drinks; Righi could hear the ice settling as Badr continued discussing his proposed book.

"Do you think the title a bit much—*Squaring the Accounts of the History of Man When All the Chips Are Down*?"

Righi responded, "Striking, graphic," though he actually thought, A bit premature, considering that—from a historical, sociological, or anthropological perspective—we're not quite ready to "square the accounts." "And certainly legitimate for a scholar." This last comment Righi felt compelled to make because—out of deference—he did not want to underestimate the Ambassador's abilities.

Badr did own one of the richest privately held libraries in the field of Jewish studies. Bar-Hillel and others had frequently mentioned this to the priest.

Badr himself had described in some detail his ongoing regime of studies in Judaism, Zionism, the pogroms. He had alluded to many late nights of reading works that, to Righi's memory, included the ten volumes of Barn, the eight of Dubnov, eleven by Graetz, and numerous others by key historians. Specifics could be found in Righi's notes.

"I do all of this," Badr had once explained, "because in order to safeguard the rights of the sons of Ishmael, I must know everything that one man can about the sons of Isaac." Righi's notes from that day included quotations from Herzl, Gobineau, Maurice Samuel, Begin, Ben-Gurion, certain Talmudists—all in the discussion of subjects ranging from Hellenistic innovations within the Diaspora to the Aristotelianism of Maimonides, the mysticism of Ben-Eliezer, even Isaac Bashevis Singer's remarks on the rationalism of Spinoza.

A table in the adjacent room became available.

The waiter, efficient and detached, paused until the *maître d'hôtel* had led Badr and Righi toward their table before he removed their drinks from the lamp table and carried them to the dining room.

"It's a gentleman's sort of place, is it not?"

Righi could not deny this Arab that, incongruous as they both may have appeared, dining in this celebrated midtown gathering place.

There was, Righi thought, no predicting what Badr would do next. "This man of the desert," as the Swiss Permanent Observer had called him.

The Arab began with one of the most penetrating of the issues in the Palestinian question.

"Is it not true, Monsignor, that we Arabs are the seed of Abraham?" Badr's eyes were dark and gleaming. "Even if Hagar wasn't the legal wife of Abraham, he did recognize their son, Ishmael." The Arab's glance at the menu was quick and disinterested. "But what are the Zionists, those transplants into the so-called State of Israel?"

Righi had no answer.

"Well, I'll tell you. A mass of impostors who were of *European* origin—not to use that hateful word 'race.'" Badr was using the table as if it was a podium back at the UN. "Khazars: that's who most of them are—pagans from southeastern Russia, from the Caucasus."

I know it well, Panin thought, but for the Monsignor's sake he appeared puzzled, a priest ignorant of Russian geography.

"You don't know the place? Then you've missed a lot, that is, except for the Communists and atheists."

Righi hastened to answer. "Those are the ones I consider myself lucky not to know."

"Well, the Khazars are a Tatar tribe who were converted to Judaism by an unknown rabbi in the eleventh century. You'll know the period as prior to the arrival of Christian missionaries from Byzantium." The historian in Badr sometimes jolted Panin. He leaned forward and looked deeper into Badr's dark eyes. The Ambassador seemed satisfied. "It was then, Monsignor, that these Khazars were converted for motives of self-interest. They had been told that if they continue to practice idolatry terrible days lay ahead for them. And with their conversion, they soon lost their identity as Khazars."

For a strange, imperceptible reason, the word "conversion" broke straight through the Righi veneer. For a fast moment, he felt vulnerable and exposed, as if this Arab had subtly penetrated his cover.

Panin shivered. He felt as though a draft had circled into the warm, paneled dining room and whirled around his chair.

But Badr was so absorbed in his own argument that he seemed to notice none of this. "I tell you, there's not a drop of Semitic blood in their veins—yet these Tatars (and mind you, I have nothing against Tatars in general), these are the ones who now claim ownership of Palestine, a land that has always been Semitic." The Arab seemed captivated by his own words.

It had been just a whim. This fellow knew nothing of Panin— and only tidbits more of Righi. His cover was safe, though that still did not explain the feeling of exposure that the word "conversion" had evoked. Later, and alone, Panin would have to sort this out.

But now he had responsibilities to Righi. He interjected a counter to Badr's argument. "If that is true—and it must be, if a scholar of your caliber says so—then the fact still remains that for centuries they have been Jews. Whether descendants of the biblical Jews or of eleventh century converts, nonetheless, they are all alike today in their age-old sense of historical continuity."

The waiter, frustrated at having tried several times to take the men's orders, now stood quietly but insistently beside the table adjacent to theirs. His pencil and pad were raised.

Both Righi and Badr ordered sautéed calves liver. Before the starchily-clad fellow had gotten half a table away, Ahmed Badr launched back into his subject with renewed vigor. "So I ask you, Monsignor, have you ever seen a government as arrogant as that of Israel? The UN has had occasion to condemn them a hundred and twenty-seven times. That's a statistic you, as Observer, should know. And some of them know what it is doing to Judaism."

Badr paused, as if to gather Righi's deeper attentions.

"As my good friend Rabbi Shlomo Ben-Hellul says repeatedly,

'Judaism has no worse enemies.' Believe me, that hurts us. We sons of Ishmael, even as we fight for our rights, never forget that the children of Jacob are our cousins. After all, we lived together for centuries and no one had objections. . . ."

"But now you don't want them at your door."

Righi's boldness was immediately matched by Badr's challenge, "Monsignor, you can write to the Pope if you wish. You can publish it in the *Times*. I do not care who knows: it is *Zionism* we do not want at our doors . . . and none of us—whether Moslems or Christians or, yes, many Jews—intend to allow a band of Khazars to tell us what to do with the Holy Land sacred to three monotheistic religions, which otherwise might come to some accord."

The Ambassador had one last stab to inflict. "No sir—take a Moshe Dayan. Have you ever seen a more Tatar face? And the arrogant threats with which he tries to force us to accept—*de facto*—the existence of his supermaterialistic state? That theocracy has no more faith than a flea."

The one-sided argument persisted throughout the meal. And to Righi, the calves liver was tough, overcooked, moistened too little in the pan before being served. He felt nauseous and tense.

But retiring to the lounge for what Ahmed Badr promised would be a quick coffee, the Arab's manner suddenly lightened. The Ambassador became almost playful. No hint of the anti-Zionism or impassioned Semitism remained.

"Monsignor, may I confide in you?"

The two men sat around a drinks table no larger in circumference than a small tea tray. A bowl of cheese crackers took up most of the surface space. The priest held his cup as a protective prop. But what could Badr mean by *confide?* Isn't that what this dean of diplomats had been doing throughout the meal?

"That goes, or should, without saying." In a gesture he had observed at the rectory, Righi's hand clasped to the cross around his neck.

"I see something of two young women. Israelis. Turtledoves who might have come straight out of the Song of Songs . . ." Ahmed Badr had changed suddenly into a warm, almost bashful man.

Both the priest and the spy within Righi were amused.

"Two?" was a question which both a spy and a priest might—for different reasons—need to ask.

"*Two*—delectable women raised on the slopes of Mount Carmel." Badr became even more convincing. "Women, I suspect, whom you could not fail to take an interest in, since I have reason to believe that they do need spiritual guidance." The Arab was smiling, man to man. "Unfortunately, neither rabbis nor men of Islam seem capable of attracting them. However, it just may be that Catholicism—"

Righi returned the smile. "I understand."

"Good. Then you might come and have a cup of coffee with us one of these evenings? There's a little Israeli bar on Broadway. The pastry's first-rate—or so I'm told. I can't touch anything sweet. Diabetes . . ."

The priest nodded, sympathetically.

"I only suggest that you wear different clothes."

Righi, realizing that indeed he was dressed in clericals, agreed. "Of course. You may expect me in dark-green corduroy trousers and a tan turtleneck sweater—what in Italy they call *alla dolce vita*. I'll even wear a sports jacket and a camel's hair coat."

Ahmed Badr struggled to stand up in the tiny space around the drinks table. "You'll be most fashionable."

Righi pulled the table toward himself to allow Badr more room. "A priest in mufti should show some good taste, shouldn't he? After all, clothes make the man—if not the monk."

They left, agreeing to rendezvous with the Israeli women day after tomorrow, a Wednesday evening, at nine o'clock.

PART TWO

IN THE RECTORY'S GROUND-FLOOR OFFICE, FRANCIS MAGUIRE was wrestling with figures. He was angry with the archdiocesan officials—and for good reason.

They had insisted upon demolishing the old church—a quite adequate structure—and then replacing it with this one. All this, "in order to meet the spiritual needs of the personnel of the United Nations": that's how the chancery ordinance had put it.

As a result, the new pastor was still paying off the interest on mortgages while the population of the area continued to thin out. With parishioners diminishing in numbers and most new members less affluent than churchgoers from earlier eras, the budget was strained.

This was the bottom line for most urban American Catholic churches finances: dwindling income, rising costs.

So the Church of the Nativity was in hot water and Maguire had sent off a complaint—to which he received this curt response: "But you have a ready-made congregation. The UN." The archbishopric acted as though they didn't know that most of the UN personnel lived in the suburbs, as if they didn't know that these people only came into the city Monday through Friday. Where were they on Sunday, when the offering was collected?

Maguire scratched his head. According to his figures, they had no hope of repaying any of the capital this year; they would be lucky if they kept up paying as much as they were scheduled to pay month by month. "I studied theology for five years," he complained to the silence of his slightly chilled office. "So I end up in a place where my main worry is balancing the budget."

A bronze plaque of appreciation shone back at him, its dusty plate reflecting a shift in the sunlight filtering in. A gift from the UN that seemed a kind of an answer—but Maguire called out again, arguing with the silence of his empty office: "The United Nations! You can have them."

The thought reminded him that—further down the expense column—his parish was also responsible for paying costs to provide board and lodging and office space so that the Observer of the Holy See could spend his time . . .

The intercom rang.

Father Potocki was calling from two floors above, asking if he might bother the pastor for a minute. "It's a serious matter," he had added.

"Please do," Maguire responded. He needed the diversion, so he cleared the budget papers from his desk and waited for Potocki to arrive.

The fellow must be finding it hard to get used to New York, Maguire thought. Well, we're not all the same. Not everyone can be like Righi, who the day after he arrived seemed to be a native New Yorker.

Potocki's four taps on the door were nervous and light.

"Come in, Stan."

When Potocki entered and walked to the edge of Maguire's desk, the parish priest saw that the Pole's face was as glum as the ledgers that Maguire had just put away.

"Monsignor, I hope I haven't interrupted—"

This will be no diversion, Maguire realized. "You're not disturbing me. Please sit."

Potocki came straight to the point. "The matter is Monsignor Righi." The Polish priest's frown intensified.

"Righi. The perfect guest." The word and its budgetary implications did not escape Maguire's sense of irony, though he proceeded. "I wasn't aware that during these last two months he had been a bother to anyone. He is very Italian, of course . . . and he does go in for a sharp repartee that doesn't always correspond with our sense of humor." Maguire was falling victim to the lure of his own voice. "Nevins has complained about that—but then Tom often asks for that kind of rough teasing. Still—you didn't know Righi's predecessor, did you? Well, Righi doesn't cause us to miss Faddini, I can assure you—"

Potocki interrupted in an insistent tone: "Monsignor—I don't believe that this *italianissimo* Monsignor Righi is Italian."

Maguire was not amused.

"Stan, I may not be too far from the age of arteriosclerosis, but your blood vessels should be in good order. Righi is the most Italian of Italians that I've ever met—and in the years I've been here and at St. Patrick's Old Cathedral, I have met plenty. If this man isn't Italian—who is? Doesn't he continually ask Mrs. O'Rourke for spaghetti? And the espresso that he drinks at all hours—"

"It's playacting." Potocki's bluntness seemed to surprise even himself.

"Stan, you must go in for detective stories. Or are you having indigestion these days; sometimes a move to a new place will create such an upset." Maguire's true reactions were far less kind.

The new priest could surely see this—but he seemed determined to say what he had come to say. "What's more, I don't think he's a priest."

This fellow is frightening, Maguire thought.

And his first impulse was to push the button which opened a side door leading onto the street. An escape.

But staring into his assistant's eyes, Maguire saw no look of mad obsession. The pastor's hand fell away from the button. It would be better to have the matter out.

"Do you promise me that you're feeling up to par?"

Potocki appeared prepared for just such a reaction—as if the priest from Detroit had genuinely been discomforted by the feeling that Righi was somehow not who he appeared to be. He would not be stopped from speaking his mind—not now.

"I am upset. And there's a reason. It all began the first day after my arrival. . . ." Seeing Maguire lean back in his chair, ready to listen, Potocki embarked upon his story. He told of his uneasiness at that initial meeting, then launched into his theory about priests and their hands. He became so heated in his explanation that Maguire found himself examining his own hands.

When he realized what he was doing, he stopped Potocki's discourse. "Oh glory, it's all we need. Another self-made psychologist in the rectory. Haven't we enough with Nevins and his almost Freudian interpretations of original sin, his confidence in the efficacity of psychedelic lights and posters, his delight at what he calls the 'explosion of the unconscious'? Tell me how these things draw a soul one inch nearer to God?"

Potocki resumed his story.

When he finished—having ignored Maguire's reactions—he found the pastor was noticeably miffed.

"Stan, you are bringing serious accusations against a fellow priest and you are basing them upon a few superficial so-called observations. Do you not think there are reasons why our theology manuals speak so often of 'the temerity of judging our neighbors'?" Maguire reached for his pen, seeking an object to fiddle with during the conversation; then, seeing his hands, he changed his mind. Ah, this fellow. "Let me ask you again: what books and magazines have you been reading? Some printed matter depresses our spirits and some sows suspicion of everyone around us. I suggest that you read Mark Twain. You'll be grateful to me."

Potocki appeared to realize that his argument needed stronger, more specific evidence. . . . His eyes brightened, as if he felt that he had just the thing. "Monsignor, have you ever seen a Catholic make the sign of the cross from right to left?"

"Why no—"

"Well, I have, this very morning. That's why I decided to talk to you."

Maguire was not convinced. "Have you never made a mistake in saying mass? Why, I remember a gross one I made at St. Patrick's Old Cathedral, and on Easter." The parish priest pushed back his chair and stretched, causing his recounting to sound more lighthearted than the conversation thus far had been. "All during Lent, the choir had been practicing a Gloria in four voices. They were so proud of it. And you know what I did: forgot to give them a cue. I tried afterward to explain what a natural mistake it was after having gone through all of Lent omitting the Gloria—I just forgot that we had finally reached Easter. Poor *paesani*—the choir was mostly Italian—they never forgave me."

Potocki seemed unable to hold back a smile.

"Yes . . . once I forgot the Creed. And you should have seen the looks on the congregation's faces. When I realized what I had done, I said, 'How would it be, if we were to make a profession of our faith?' It was humiliating."

"So, Stan, it can happen to anyone."

"But making the sign of the cross is something you do automatically—it's second nature. A Catholic, no matter how distracted, would never make the sign in reverse." Potocki was struggling and Maguire sensed that it came out of a certain sincerity.

"Unless he were a Catholic of the Byzantine rite."

The comment was for Maguire only half serious. But Potocki seized upon it and was hardly able to mute a note of triumph in his voice.

"Suppose our Righi had come not from Italy, but the Ukraine. Just suppose. If so, when he becomes tired or distracted or lost in his devotions, might he not go back to his old way of making the sign of the cross . . . the way that in fact is second nature for him?"

The idea struck Maguire as having some validity. He sat for several moments, pondering the possibilities, then he argued, "But Giuseppe Righi from the Ukraine? How could that be . . . why would the Vatican send a Ukrainian?"

Potocki appeared to have run out of answers, so he revealed his other discovery of that morning.

"Monsignor, there's more. Today when I saw him cross himself, it came back to me. I had had a feeling—as if I had seen this man somewhere else. But until this morning, I couldn't remember when or just where. Then I saw that right to left crossing. It was the motion that had surprised me at a Ruthenian church in Winnipeg. As you know, there are a lot of Ukrainians in Manitoba, going back as far as the last century. And I was born in Galicia, which is the Polish part of Ukraine. So when I heard of their folklore festivals, I decided to travel from Detroit with friends and attend. It was 1970—"

Monsignor Maguire had been listening intently and the date alerted him. "But I distinctly remember Righi explaining that he had spent a portion of 1970 in Kenya—not Canada. The dates don't match."

Momentarily this fact seemed to shake Potocki's line of reasoning. He blushed and continued, his voice sounding less certain. "I'm simply saying that Monsignor Righi, whoever he may be, just might not be completely honest with us. We should keep our eyes open—there are reasons for that."

"All right, Stan, if the idea is reassuring to you. It is probable that there may be matters which the Holy See does not want us to know." But Maguire retained mixed emotions of his own—both about Potocki and now about the Observer.

He did not like being uninformed.

Or misinformed.

They continued the discussion a bit longer, aided by a couple of highballs.

By the time Mrs. O'Rourke came to the office to announce dinner, the two had worked themselves into a wavering and disturbed state of mind.

Luckily Monsignor Righi was absent from the meal, having phoned Mrs. O'Rourke that he had business of his own.

She made a point of telling the others how polite and apologetic the Observer had been.

And Maguire felt guilty: Righi seemed so Righi.

[IX]

ALEXANDER LEWINSON SOLD RELIGIOUS ARTICLES. IN SPITE OF the approaching Christmas season, he waited in his shop for customers who didn't seem to be coming.

Short, stoutish, a man with small, shrewd eyes and a bristly, graying beard, Lewinson appeared to be around sixty years old. His fellow merchants on Barclay Street called him "Rakoczy." To them he was gruff and likable, this fellow who claimed that his grandfather had emigrated from Hungary to the United States, changing his name upon taking up American citizenship. This teller of stories.

The balding religious articles merchant was as much a fixture on the street as the green wooden newsstand on the corner.

Today, near closing time, Lewinson turned to the counting of the day's meager receipts. He thought rather enviously of other businesses along the street. Maybe he should switch to some other line of merchandise, something more salable?

Pat Maloney, the shop assistant, mumbled to himself as he read another of his detective stories.

Lewinson added the figures, allowing one fleeting thought: Maybe I should rid myself of this red-haired, freckle-faced do-nothing?

But Maloney looked up from his book and smiled. He seemed to know what time it was, even if he couldn't determine just what his boss was thinking.

A woman entered the shop, sending its rusty bell jabbering as the door swung open, then slammed shut.

Lewinson whispered, not loud enough for the woman to hear, "Her—just because she's the housekeeper for the Church of the Nativity. She's nothing more than another complainer to me." But louder, in a honeyed voice, he greeted her: "Dear Mrs. O'Rourke, how are you and how are all your monsignors?"

Her response was a grumble that interested Pat Maloney far less than the up and down motion of the woman's breasts as she searched in her purse for a receipt. Lewinson could see the boy's eyes wander.

"The only worry I have is the worry of worries—"

"You mean how to live longer?" Lewinson knew the script to all of Mrs. O'Rourke's standard complaints.

The woman's answer was a deep, body-trembling sigh that seemed to delight Maloney even more. His boss could almost read the boy's detective-story mind.

"So, may I have the pleasure of your order?" he asked, noticing that she had one of his receipts clasped in the palm of her sweaty hand. "And I've got good news for you: the two statuettes of St. Anthony—they arrived yesterday afternoon. Pat, won't you go get them? The parcel wrapped in light-blue paper."

The assistant lingered at his book long enough to note the page number, then closed it. He was already through the door when Lewinson yelled after him. "*Schmeggege*, shut the door. Can't you feel the cold?"

Maloney spun around and closed the door.

"Could I see some rosaries?" Mrs. O'Rourke asked as she moved to a rickety display case. "Those, the ones on the right?"

Lewinson pulled out the objects she indicated plus several others he needed to get rid of. "These I only got recently from a Carmelite convent in Normandy. Real style, am I right? Beads made of the finest bone and a silver chain. And such a case—

genuine Moroccan leather. How about those French when it comes to works of art? What can I say?"

Mrs. O'Rourke's response sounded more like a grunt. "I've seen better."

"What do you mean? Lewinson imports the very best. Not that it makes much difference these days. People—who needs them? Since Vatican Two, everything has to be modern. Who invented that word? We'll pay. Just you wait. What we may live to see . . ."

"About the Council, I agree"—Mrs. O'Rourke leaned toward him—"but these beads—" Her face hovered over them, as if to examine their attributes more closely. What she softly whispered could not have been in more marked contrast to their bantering: "*Holy Synod wants to see Tolstoy.*"

"Only four dollars and, let me see, ninety-five cents." Lewinson frowned back a smile—for he did abhor these code names—then answered quietly, "*The usual place, Friday at three p.m.*"

Mrs. O'Rourke shrieked with the voice she usually reserved for reprimanding the fish market vendor when his prices were too high. "Four ninety-five, sweet Jesus. I'll be finding a bargain somewheres else. Like the shops around St. Patrick's." But her moaning and leaning over the glass counter did not prevent her from interjecting a final whisper: "*He'll be there.*"

Pat Maloney struggled with the door.

When he finally got it open and stumbled into the shop, he appeared disgruntled. A glance at the clock indicated that indeed closing time had come and gone. "Sorry it took so long," he said half-heartedly, "but the parcel wasn't shelved with the new arrivals. I had to search through—"

But Lewinson's attentions were exclusively upon Mrs. O'Rourke. "You should be happy, at least, about these. With the discount, these statuettes are—such a price—ten dollars."

She did not seem pleased. With an awkward snatching motion, she took the parcels from Maloney's arms and slapped a ten-dollar bill on Lewinson's glass counter top.

Again the bell jabbered as she wielded the shop door.

The balding Lewinson sighed, "A windbag." Slowly he put each rosary back in its box and then placed the boxes back inside the case. "She says to me, 'Get them out.' So I get them out. She says, 'How much?' I tell her how much. She paws and she complains. Then she says to me, 'Four ninety-five, sweet Jesus . . .' I ask you, why waste time on a customer like that?"

Pat Maloney's voice seemed to say, "I just want to go home," as he noted, "She bought the statuettes."

"Some Rockefeller—two miserable five-dollar pieces. Not like the old days. Then we had customers. People of means, not foundlings and housekeepers. They flocked in here, buying everything in sight." Lewinson put his hands on his hips and the stout man mimicked a kind of dancing about. "Now people are sophisticated. Who wants religious articles? They want ecumenism." His left hand gestured a dismissal to no one in particular. "I can't even say it. But you'll see: one of these days they'll have a Star of David in their churches—a star in the place of the cross."

"But you're a Jew," Maloney questioned, "why should you mind that?"

"Whoever pointed you toward business?" Lewinson shook his head, his jowls wobbling like a boxer's. "My father—God keep him —he'd have another heart attack if he could see what has happened to the business he started."

While his boss continued, Maloney moved, as inconspicuously as possible, to get his coat.

"One more thing." Lewinson nabbed the assistant just as he reached the door. "Run to the deli and get me two pastrami sandwiches before you go. And tell them to put in a carrot. Here's the money, and you can just drop the change in the bag. I'll count it later."

As soon as Maloney left, Lewinson waddled rapidly to the telephone on the wall. His short legs made him strain to see the dial.

"Harry? St. Anthony has granted the grace. Such a high-class saint, that one." He could hear Harry's chuckle. "So I'll be getting other statuettes. We should meet: how about Friday at *shul?* Yes. Same synagogue. Okay, give my best to your wife. Until we speak again . . ."

After he hung up, his small eyes seemed to sink deeper into his full, wrinkled face, though his expression was not without a hint of satisfaction. Accomplishment. It's better than the day's receipts, he thought.

Pat came back breathless. He dashed in with the bag and

grabbed at Lewinson's sleeve as he spoke. "Do you know what they're saying at the deli?"

"That the heating oil deliverymen have gone on strike? The bastards—do they care that it's cold?"

"They say a bomb exploded in the offices of that Russian airlines—"

"Cold? They wait until it's cold so they can strike—"

"It's a big scare, the radio says." Maloney's voice was earnest.

"Jew-haters, all of them."

Maloney sometimes appeared worried about his boss and the old man's anger. "Mr. Lewinson, do you know what Father Donovan said in church the other evening?" It would be worth a few minutes more, Maloney thought, just to acquaint Lewinson with some understanding of mortal sin.

"No, I don't know—but you'll tell me anyway. So tell me."

"Well, Father Donovan said that anti-Semitism is a mortal sin."

"Is that so?"

"He said also that prejudice is the reason of fools."

"Father Donovan should have preached to Germans in the thirties; I don't want anyone to die—Christian or Jew. And what would your Father Donovan say about wishing for any man's death? Isn't that a mortal sin?"

"It's a mortal sin," Maloney answered, a half-groan audible in his voice. It was getting late and this conversation wasn't communicating what he had intended; his freckle-faced expression said it all. "A lot of things are mortal sins."

"So who got killed in the explosion?"

Maloney was backing toward the door. "Nobody. The radio said it was just a big scare."

"Good news, somebody scared the Russians—a big scare is good for the health. Food for thought. Now give me the sandwiches already, then close the shop. Who could be coming today? Business is rotten. . . . People would rather buy bombs than prayer books."

[X]

PANIN WOULD HAVE LOVED IT IF TONIGHT'S PLANS HAD BEEN a true diversion for him instead of merely an evening out for the priest he was pretending to be. It made his role even more difficult. All these people at the UN were such talkers. And these priests. And espresso.

Colonel Panin was genuinely drained.

Then he came within sight of Hey, Daroma!, the small café on upper Broadway where he and Ahmed Badr were to meet the Israeli women.

The neighborhood, Badr had explained, was once a well-heeled section of Manhattan. Good families had comfortable, spacious apartments in which to raise promising children. The butcher shops had been the best and the pastry shops, a city-wide delight. That was fifty years ago.

This evening the neighborhood surrounding Hey, Daroma! seemed a well-defined slum. He had to step over drunks and walk around garbage heaps just to reach the walkable portion of the sidewalk leading to the café. Inside, however, the place was exciting to both the priest and the spy. Panin took special pleasure in each detail—the ill-lit rooms, the psychedelic posters with ragged edges, the photographs of surrealistic still-lifes blown up to distorted proportions.

It was a meeting place of Israeli students, exiles of sort because of their pro-Palestinian views. The bartender explained all this to the customer who had just walked in and introduced himself as Mr. Colella.

"But we serve anybody."

A blackboard indicated various teas and coffees, but no alcoholic beverages. The man called Mr. Colella acted genuinely disappointed.

"No drink drinks?"

The bartender answered, almost out of habit, "No liquor license."

Mr. Colella ordered an espresso and sat at the table nearest the door. Ahmed Badr would see him there and he wanted to introduce himself as Colella rather than have the Arab call out "Righi." It would save embarrassment. Panin understood delicate arrangements—all too well.

Apparently, so did Badr.

As soon as he spotted Righi, he launched into a banter of nonsense as he rushed up to his friend. He hugged Righi and used the opportunity to whisper, "In this place, I'm known as Gabriel Menachem." Badr kissed his friend on both cheeks.

During the second kiss, Righi whispered back, "And call me Colella." Both men laughed.

It soon became apparent that Gabriel Menachem was a habitué here. The Israelis knew him as a Sephardic Jew with a heart of gold and the loosest of purse strings. They tolerated his obsession of continually attempting to convert the young to Orthodox practices.

His looks and ways—in this Gabriel Menachem disguise—certainly appeared to be those one might expect from a dealer in Oriental rugs, which is what he claimed to be.

"Bring your espresso, Colella, and let's move over there." Badr proceeded toward a corner table.

Once they were settled in and Badr had nodded to the bartender for his usual, he turned to his guest and urged, "If you don't mind, just run through who you are and how you want to be introduced. Our turtledoves should be here any minute."

Righi explained that he had chosen the guise of a liberal priest not in particularly good standing with the bishop. He tapped the tarnished peace symbol that hung on the metal chain around his neck. "And the name Giovanni Colella is borrowed from an old friend. A boyhood pal."

For several minutes, their conversation and the atmosphere made both Righi and Panin feel relaxed. If only this could be tea or vodka and not espresso, the Russian thought.

He was just imagining how deliciously refreshing a glass of vodka would taste when his host motioned toward the door. "Ah, here are my doves."

The Israeli women walked arm in arm into the dark café, slowing their pace to allow their eyes to adjust to the change in light. They spotted Gabriel at his table and waved, while their heads leaned together, whispering.

They were indeed quite beautiful: chiseled features, eyes shining. Neither the priest nor the spy within Righi was fooled. These were no innocent doves.

The taller woman was introduced as Gila Ben-Ami. Her large black eyes took only momentary notice of the man named Colella, then she leaned her slender body against Badr so that her black hair fell across his chest like a scarf.

The shorter woman was Shulamith Arieh. Her emerald-green eyes and vague, gentle smile showed no hesitation in expressing how much she appreciated Giovanni Colella.

Menachem helped both women remove their furs and Colella saw that Shulamith noticed him admiring her long blond hair and the delicacy of her ears and neck.

Both the priest and the spy within Colella agreed: Shulamith seemed to have stepped from a painting by Botticelli . . . tonight *would* be pleasurable.

Gila interrupted his thoughts. "Mr. Colella, I'm an El Al stewardess . . . and Shula works in the company's New York office. When I fly into New York, I stay with her. We have a great apartment on the East Side—don't we, Shula?" They both giggled, but not girlishly.

"But terribly expensive." Shulamith coquettishly fingered her golden hair. "And you, Mr. Colella, I'll bet you're a poet. I know such things—"

He leaned back, as if to emphasize his attire—the corduroys and turtleneck sweater, the camel's hair overcoat—then he surprised them by answering, "Why, I'm a priest—can't you see?"

They laughed heartily, then Gila queried, "A *Nazarene* priest?" accompanied by a wink apparently for Menachem's benefit.

"I guarantee I'm a priest—though I may not be for much longer. A little trouble with the bishop—"

Shulamith's voice was not malicious, but quite interested as she said, "Woman trouble, is that it?"

"Not yet." He smiled toward her. "Our differences are theological. An explanation might be boring. Let me order for us."

He did, and his manner seemed to charm both the Israeli women. At one point in the conversation, Badr nodded toward him, as if to say, Monsignor, you're doing just fine.

Then, after the waiter had served them additional drinks and fresh sandwiches, Shulamith asked Mr. Colella how it happened that he became a priest.

"It's hard to say. There have always been priests in my family." The voice was directly from Righi's life story, as toyed with just now by the actor Panin. "You might attribute it to the weight of tradition."

Shulamith displayed dimples in her cheeks as she smiled. "You mean the kind of tradition handed down father to son?"

Gila sent a kick under the table, aimed at Shula. "You must forgive her, Mr. Colella—or should I call you Father?—Shula's just an *innocent;* there's much that she does not yet know."

The priest turned toward Shula and saw that in her embarrassment she seemed even more attractive than before. "There's nothing to forgive. And please call me Giovanni, if you wish. We are in America, aren't we?" Then his voice softened. "The fact is, Shulamith, we priests do not marry."

"But that's terrible. I mean unbearable." Shulamith's emerald-green eyes became intense. "Rabbis marry and I see nothing against it." Then as an almost calculated afterthought she added, "Quite the contrary."

He was obviously perplexed. And he could see that she was enjoying that fact. "Priests are, first of all, not like rabbis; the reasons why we do not marry would be a longer story than why I'm in theological disagreement with the bishop. And, I must admit, being unmarried is not always easy; we have to stop and think of the *why. . . .*" For a moment his voice trailed off. "But never mind. Let's talk about you. Do you intend to get married?"

Gila rather than Shula was the one to answer. "Not me and not now. I want to enjoy myself."

The sage Menachem overexaggerated a frown, making the women laugh once more. "My little doves, how light-headed. Just because you are young and pretty and pleasure-loving"—his voice played upon the descriptions—"can't you think of anything besides your bodies and the enjoyment which they can give you?" His eyes gleamed with the look of a tease, but his voice grew even more somber. "What about your souls? What's to become of you, once your charms have vanished? And they will. Have you considered what then?"

"Gabi, you *skirt-chaser—please*." Gila used her accent for its most comic effect.

The minutes passed, each couple easing into conversations that isolated them from the other. Casually Shulamith edged her chair closer to Colella's. Her voice was low and more knowing than it had earlier seemed.

"Giovanni, you are very much all right. Today there are so many men who tell Shula one thing but have something quite different in mind. You understand?" She patted his arm in a friendly manner. "I'm glad we have met. I feel as though I could tell you the story of my life. About my very soul, if you like."

Her words were a kind of welcome though familiar music to both the spy and the priest whom she knew as Colella. He placed his hand over hers. The touch was for the moment unmistakably the gesture of a priest. "You tell me when and where."

Thus, while Menachem and Gila held hands and laughed over her stories of a night in Tel Aviv, Shulamith gave Mr. Colella her address and telephone number. "I'll be alone this Saturday night. Gila goes back on duty."

Then he left, explaining that he had mass at half past six the next morning. Shulamith seemed disappointed, but Gabriel and Gila were far too involved in their conversation to do anything more than nod a good-bye.

Potocki was waiting.

When Righi's cab stopped at the corner and he jumped out for a brisk walk to the rectory, he could not miss the priest, leaning with his shoulder against the brick wall.

"Stan, what are you doing out here in the cold?" Potocki's face was blue. And his response was jerky, unconvincing.

"Uh, I've been for a walk, a long one. I really like the cold, you know, Monsignor."

Righi felt for the collar of his overcoat, making certain that it was buttoned to the neck so that the absence of his clerical collar would not be noticed.

"Well, since you've had your walk, shall we go in? The cold is not for me—it positively congeals me."

Potocki's almost frosted eyes stared after Righi. "Not me. When it's cold, I'm happy. It reminds me of the *Ukraine*." He said this last word as if he expected it to smack Righi across the face.

Instead the priest exaggerated his shivers. "The Ukraine? I've never been there. But you have?"

"As a boy." Potocki appeared to be trying to imbue his voice with a sense of darker meaning. "The kind of thing one doesn't forget."

Monsignor Righi stopped. The fog from his breath wafted into the younger man's face. He held the silence like a weapon. "Childhood memories, eh? Good. Then say a prayer for me—from the heart of a child—won't you?"

He left Potocki standing in the cold.

[XI]

IT WAS AN UNUSUALLY COLD NOVEMBER—THE NEW YORK City winds were sharper and bolder than Stanislaus Potocki had expected.

When he got off the bus at the United Nations stop that Friday noon, he did everything he could to shield himself from the north wind, which rode the East River as if it were a sleigh. He pulled his overcoat collar up and turned his back to the wind. He huddled among the small crowd waiting to cross Forty-seventh Street. A shiver engaged his shoulders.

Stan was just regretting his boast about not suffering from the cold when he saw Righi rush out of the UN Secretariat Building and into one of the idling taxis.

Potocki watched as the cab turned onto First Avenue and joined the traffic on the downtown ramp of the FDR Drive.

A half hour later, the Observer was the only person missing at the rectory lunch.

"Isn't my illustrious *paesano* eating with us today?" Vaccaro was quizzing Maguire, who nibbled at a salad tray that Mrs.

O'Rourke had provided. It was a Friday routine of hers; she fixed the pickle assortments just for him.

"Sal, you know how diplomats are. He'll be entertaining in a restaurant across town." The pastor grimaced as he bit into a dill pickle that he had expected to be sweet.

Mrs. O'Rourke set the soup tureen down abruptly; her voice showed that she felt insulted. "Monsignor Righi isn't entertaining. He was thoughtful enough to notify me that he would be having lunch today with the Secretary General himself. So there. And it would do the likes of you good were some of his manners to rub off on you."

"Would that lunch have been downtown?" Potocki asked, but continued when no one answered, "That's the direction I saw him headed in." His expression spelled distrust.

His fellow priests, however, were too hungry to notice.

"Like I always say," the taxi driver yelled as the cab bounced along the streets of Brooklyn, "if the Pope don't make no trouble for us non-Catholics, let the man say what he thinks. I do."

His license and photo indicated that he was Moshe Greenberg. He had argued with Righi for ten minutes or more, jabbing at the Church's position on birth control. He had succeeded in bewildering Righi.

"Believe me, I *know* what the joes of this world are thinking. Protestants and Jews—they all pass through here. Know what I mean? And they tell me . . . they say, Moshe, whatever happens in our bed is our—you'll forgive the expression—business. Priests and ministers and rabbis should—thank you—keep their noses out." He turned his head toward the back, even as the cab lunged forward. "That's what they tell me."

The taxi stopped at Clark Street and as Righi gave Moshe Greenberg his tip, the priest voiced the hope that the driver would clean up his language. Then Righi disappeared into the cavernous lobby of the St. George Hotel.

Inside, Righi crossed the lobby on his way to the subway line and when various old ladies spoke to him from their positions along a worn bench, he gave a friendly blessing.

All in all, he thought, priests in this country have a good thing of it.

At the newspaper stand within the subway station he bought the New York *Times*, folded it under his arm, then took the next train for Grand Army Plaza.

At the appropriate stop he got off and walked toward the exit he had been instructed to take for Prospect Park. Once on the street level, he realized how windy the afternoon had become. Prospect Park and the streets around it appeared deserted.

Good.

He went straight for the trash can inside the entrance to the park. Reaching in, he threw in the newspaper, which he had folded around a small parcel.

That was all.

He returned to Grand Army Plaza and took the subway directly back to Times Square, then rode the crosstown bus to the UN. By the time he reached the General Assembly, he saw that he was only ten minutes late. He smiled, having done Panin's work on Righi's time.

It was nothing. *Nitchevo*.

TOLSTOY had watched HOLY SYNOD put the newspaper in the specified trash can within Prospect Park.

After the latter had left, TOLSTOY scurried into the park, his short legs making rapid steps, as if to outrun the cold. At the trash can he found the New York *Times* and quickly made certain that it contained the small parcel he was expecting.

He shoved the parcel into his broad overcoat pocket and then scurried back out of the park. At the curb, he stumbled.

Throughout the entire scenario, Alexander Lewinson acted more like a nervous, idiosyncratic old man than the experienced agent he was. But that was his trademark, this Mikhail Sukhotin: the fumbler.

Who would suspect a spy to be so obviously graceless?

Nobody—which is why Mikhail Sukhotin was so successful.

The FALCON was the person most anxious to receive the small parcel that—he hoped—would contain photographic negatives that his superiors had been waiting for.

He sat at *shul*, quietly praying. Now and then he glanced toward the door; TOLSTOY had a disturbing habit of being late.

And, the FALCON remembered all too well, TOLSTOY had also made the mistake, once before, of not coming to this synagogue on Water Street in Lower Manhattan, but to another, twenty blocks north.

It's a good thing that fumbling has served TOLSTOY well, thought the FALCON, or I would report his foolishness immediately.

"If God wills."

The voice behind the FALCON was unmistakably TOLSTOY's.

As the FALCON turned around in his seat to face the speaker, Alexander Lewinson grinned and greeted the man who had been praying. "Your devotion is a model to my heart, Harry Goldstein. Say a prayer for me."

Ivan Bolonski merely shook his head. "You'll be the death of me, Lewinson." And the FALCON meant it.

He was convinced that one of these days the fumblings of Mikhail Sukhotin were going to trip both of them up.

"This is something for the FBI. . . ."

Maguire had taken Potocki with him, following lunch at the rectory. The pastor was on his way to visit a parishioner at New York Hospital and no one would question his taking along an assistant. Plus, the time outside the rectory would allow Maguire to talk to his priest about Monsignor Righi. Maguire had become worried.

There was still no reason to believe that Potocki's allegations might be on the mark. But he was relentless. He had been urging Maguire to take the matter to the chancery.

Maguire had suggested, "This is something for the FBI, not for the Church." He had to divert Potocki somehow. Better that the complications from all of this fall on Potocki, rather than the parish or its pastor. Going to the FBI would guarantee that the matter would be either resolved or dismissed. "A priest would only muddy the waters. The more we stay out, the better." Maguire was struggling for a more persuasive approach. "What—what if someone mixed up in this affair—if in fact the affair is anything more than supposition—what if someone were to come to you—say Righi himself were to come to you and ask to make his confession? Your lips would be sealed." The parish priest stopped so that their stroll was abruptly halted and Potocki was forced to look Maguire directly in the face. "Is it not better to involve the FBI—say some good Catholic in the FBI?"

Potocki submitted and after their visit, Maguire got the telephone number of a "good Catholic FBI agent" from one of his seminary chums now ministering in the Bronx.

The name and number were of one James McNeil.

"My seminary chum says that McNeil is a real Irishman. His great-grandfather came from County Armagh in Ulster. He's Irish two, no, three times over." Maguire indicated each of his reasons by holding up another finger. "One, because St. Patrick is buried in Armagh. Two, because its people are strangers in their own houses, since Ulster, quite wrongly, is part of the United Kingdom. And three, because the McNeils finally emigrated, leaving behind the oppression which had been shoved upon them by Cromwell's colonists and their descendants."

Potocki was just glad to get the number. He rushed back to his room and telephoned. McNeil answered and was matter of fact. Sure he would be happy to meet and talk. How about a coffee shop near Columbia University, tomorrow at half past four? "And come in civvies, Father," the agent enjoined.

Even after four-thirty, that Friday remained a busy day for the people who had met at Gabriel Menachem's corner table in Hey, Daroma!

Shulamith received a phone call from the bar on Second Avenue where she and Gila went whenever they wanted to be alone. The bartender always shielded them from the unwanted company of men. The strawberry daiquiris were the best on the East Side.

He phoned to say that "her uncle" was in town.

She quickly changed into a wool pants suit and rushed to meet Jehudah Tamir, the first secretary of the Israeli mission to the United Nations. Their encounter along the brass-trimmed bar appeared, to any onlookers, as the casual Friday afternoon greetings of people who don't see one another often.

The noise level in the bar was end-of-the-week loud.

It made it easy for Tamir to explain what he had learned. Photos taken of Giovanni Colella at Hey, Daroma! had been routed through the Israeli mission, where the poet-looking priest was identified as Monsignor Righi, Permanent Observer. . . .

Shulamith received her instructions—to wait in the apartment tomorrow, in case Colella should call. Her feelings about them were mixed. "Fall in with any proposal he may make," Tamir urged, "particularly any proposals which direct the next meeting toward your apartment."

At six o'clock Righi left the United Nations and went directly to the rectory: Panin had some work to do.

By the time the gong had rung for supper, he had already gone to his quarters and deciphered the instructions contained in the false bottoms of the statuettes that Mrs. O'Rourke had most graciously provided for the decoration of his room.

KARENINA is so smooth, Panin smiled. Statuettes of St. Anthony.

Panin hoped their influence could have some benefit for a Russian; with these new instructions, he needed some help.

For HOLY SYNOD was being asked to verify the accuracy of information received via other sources. The Pentagon was signaling its intentions concerning short-range missiles bearing atomic warheads—at least those being coordinated with the Israeli army. HOLY SYNOD was to ascertain why, for instance, an entire zone of the Negev had been declared off-limits. And there were additional instructions updating HOLY SYNOD's efforts to get hard information about NASA's space shuttle program and American spy satellites.

He was given the names of several "good Catholics" at the Princeton plasma physics laboratories and also at RCA. These were to be probed, using his priestly cover and his stature as Permanent Observer. Somebody would cooperate.

Panin had enough money available to him should his priestly manner need assistance.

Given time, something would turn up.

The second gong convinced him. Mrs. O'Rourke would be upset if Righi were late for Friday night supper.

It was a weekly event. Morale always received a boost in view of the upcoming pastoral duties of the weekend. A kind of pep rally among priests.

Vaccaro was the first to greet Righi as he came downstairs. "*Paesano*, can you tell us what the Secretary General said at lunch today? Only what wasn't confidential, of course." There was no predatory tone in the young priest's voice.

Righi responded by performing such a true to life imitation of Sven Eriksen that his audience blended laughter with a smattering of applause. Tom Nevins in particular echoed Righi's near-perfect rendition of "I am deeply concerned," the phrase that recurred in almost all of the Secretary General's press conferences.

"But the conversation did take a spiritual turn," the Observer concluded, knowing that his fellow priests would focus on this tidbit. "The Secretary General said that the United Nations needs not only politicians, but also charismatics."

Nevins seized upon this. "And what did you say?"

"I said that he was quite right. Unfortunately, charismatics often turn out to be second-rate politicians and politicians have a bad reputation for decapitating prophets."

[XII]

STAN POTOCKI WAS SEATED SOMEWHAT UNCOMFORTABLY IN a booth near the entrance of the Hickory Pit. From the juke box came the sound of Joan Baez: "The Night They Drove Old Dixie Down." A waitress was whistling along. The priest had decided that she must be from Tennessee. She had the accent he remembered hearing among factory workers in Detroit, the ones who kept talking about the hills of Tennessee.

Otherwise the coffee shop near Columbia University was empty. Hardly anyone came here at this hour; mealtimes and late evening were the Hickory Pit's peak periods. It was a student gathering place, particularly favored by those who passed up the meal plan so they could spend time with a girl or boy friend.

Potocki's discomfort stemmed from his attire: a faded red ski jacket; a green cap whose brim had not been stiff for years; and a pair of worn, colorless trousers—all garments that an observer might have thought belonged to a campus rebel.

The priest waited for an agent of the FBI.

He sipped at cold coffee and pretended to leaf through a literary journal, *Antaeus,* but he was extremely nervous. He had deep regrets about getting involved at all. He missed the calmness of hearing confessions in Polish at the Detroit parish. He missed everything he considered normal.

"Stan, how goes it, buddy?"

The warm-toned voice caused Potocki to look up from the unread magazine to see a tall, well-built, clean-shaven man hold out a hand in greeting—a hand as firm as his own was trembling.

He looks like the agents on TV, Potocki thought; he could devour a criminal like a hamburger.

James McNeil did not introduce himself; instead he sat down, then waited for the Tennessee waitress. He asked her for coffee, black, and an English muffin. "Haven't seen you for a dog's age. How's the family?"

The agent's comments left Potocki in a quandary.

"All right," he said slowly, then quickly added, "And yours?" as though he had finally caught on to the game.

"Same old story. Mildred's about to have another baby—next week, maybe. I'll let you know."

Potocki had nothing to say.

McNeil launched into another and then another of the "old buddy" stories until the Tennessee waitress served him, freshened Potocki's coffee, and then turned her attentions to the juke box, which for the moment had fallen silent.

Potocki felt as though he was playing a stupid role in a B movie.

For nearly fifteen minutes, the awkwardness continued, McNeil creating each conversation and Potocki following along clumsily. The priest was greatly relieved when the agent finally said, "Okay, let's go, pal. Have I got a lot to tell you." McNeil took the check. "Please. My treat."

As they left, the Tennessee waitress listened to an instrumental on the juke box: "Grazing in the Grass."

Outside, the two men walked a block to McNeil's car. In seconds, the agent was driving them both toward the Bronx.

"So, Father, what's the story?"

Potocki had waited so long to unburden himself of what he

had to say, he told McNeil virtually everything he had noticed since the day of his arrival at the Church of the Nativity.

McNeil made no interruptions—not even when he was tempted to question the theory about priests' hands. When Potocki finished, the agent's only comment was, "There may be something muddy in this affair, Father, but I'm not sure it's of interest to the Bureau."

Potocki slumped, his head sinking into the piling of his red ski jacket; he seemed so dejected that McNeil found himself apologizing.

He slowed the car for a stop light and turned to Potocki saying, "I'm sorry, Father. I know how you feel—but you must realize that we need a solid reason for going into action. And even then, we have to move slowly. We just don't have the men or the time to pursue every lead which comes to us from unsolicited informants."

The priest's expression showed no signs of agreeing.

"There's only one step from fantasy to fanaticism; keep your feet on the ground, Father. I'd never presume to tell another man how to run his business—particularly if that man is a priest. I hope you'll do me the same courtesy. Fair enough?"

"I guess I let myself get carried away." Potocki stared out the window at the passing cars—his voice sounded unconvinced.

"Hey—it's okay. Forget about it, Father. Just remember: if your head's in the clouds, you'll muck everything up. Excuse the expression. But, let me ask you some questions, just so we can establish any facts there may be in this story of yours. Okay?"

McNeil's questions kept Potocki talking until the car reached the Castle Hill section of the Bronx. There they parked, Potocki answered questions, and McNeil took notes.

The priest finally felt more at ease, believing that he was being taken more seriously.

At last, the questioning complete, McNeil closed his notebook and proceeded to give Potocki some instructions. "Do nothing. If there is something going on, it will take time to determine just what. Just keep your eyes open and don't put anything into writing. Talk about this only to Monsignor Maguire. I hope to meet him one day; in the meantime give him my regards. The two of you can compare impressions. I forbid you to say anything of this to anyone else in the rectory. Including that Mrs. O'Rourke."

The Polish priest struggled to hide his glee at the prospect of working with the FBI. "But how, Mr. McNeil, how will I contact you?"

"Don't."

Potocki's face fell.

"We'll contact you. I'll be JOE O'BRIEN, a friend from the good ol' days in Detroit."

"JOE O'BRIEN," the priest repeated as if to impress the name in his mind, but also to confirm his compliance.

"I have a hardware store in the Bronx. Got it?"

"Right."

"I became a drop-out in high school, but we've stayed in touch. You keep telling me to do everything I can to prevent my sons from following such a bad example. You're checking into several schools for them. Okay?"

Potocki nodded yes and resisted a salute.

"Now, I'm going to drop you at the nearest subway station. Go back to the rectory and try not to let the Italian Monsignor see you in these clothes. When the time comes, I'll be in touch."

At the rectory, the priest in the red ski jacket ran up the stairs, taking them three at a time. He was in a good mood and also in a hurry, anxious to avoid an encounter with Righi.

After he had changed into his clericals, he looked for Monsignor Maguire in the pastor's study.

"Stan, that you? I've been waiting. Sit down and have a drink. And tell me about the Bureau."

"Helpful."

"And McNeil. What did you think of him?"

"You mean Joe?"

Maguire twisted his head toward Potocki. "*Joe?*"

"Jim, I mean. A good Catholic, an Irishman, reliable, on the level. He'll be in touch, he says." Then Potocki lowered his voice. "Is *he* here?"

"At a UN party. We're free to talk. . . ."

Apparently Shulamith Arieh was not in.

This was the third time that Righi had slipped away from the party to phone her number. He no longer used the scrap of paper she had given him, having memorized the digits.

The phone rang four, five, six times.

The Observer decided that ten rings would be the limit, this call. Seven, eight.

She answered, "Ben-Ami and Arieh," in the midst of ring nine.

"Shulamith, hello. This is Giovanni Colella; I hope you remember me?"

A tinkle of laughter came at him through the receiver.

"What a wonderful surprise! I can hardly believe it. And do I remember you? I thought you had forgotten me. Giovanni—how could Shula fail to remember the Nazarene who promised to take care of her soul?"

Righi did not hide the pleasure in his response. "Daughter of Jerusalem, when may I see you?"

"Tomorrow?" Her voice was both eager and cautious; he liked the blend. "Or can't Nazarenes pay a visit on their sabbath?"

"Tomorrow. At four in the afternoon." There was no hint of indecision.

"At four. And, Giovanni?" She waited until she was certain he knew she was serious. "I'll be happy to see you. I make good, strong coffee. *Ciao*, Father."

As Righi showered in the moldy stall in the bathroom of his rectory quarters, he allowed her voice to repeat, "*Ciao*, Father." It was the memory of a sound that he couldn't yet figure out how to control.

Moments later, after the Observer had dried off and dressed in pajamas and robe, Father Vaccaro knocked at his door. "Monsignor, can we chat for a moment? I hope I'm not disturbing you."

"Not at all, Sal. Come in. That chair's best—what's the problem?"

"It's the Irishmen here, *paesano*—you don't mind if I call you *paesano?*" Vaccaro settled into the chair, but still moved with jerking motions, anxiously, while he spoke. "I just can't get beyond what they did, historically, you know? Even though today their attitude is changed, I keep remembering how for my grandfather, being Italian meant going to mass in the basement. It's a hindrance."

"Be on your guard, if you wish, *paesano*—but don't take it too far. After all, we are Catholics and Monsignor Maguire is right in emphasizing, *Ô, Église Catholique, que tu es belle*." Then Righi lowered his voice. "However, next time he says it and repeats that he doesn't remember who said it first—just tell him, De Maistre. Joseph de Maistre."

Vaccaro did not seem impressed. Instead he went immediately to the question that, apparently, he had come to ask. "Tom Nevins and I have been arguing about immigration and the making of the Church in America again. Can you help? Tom says without the Irish immigration, the Church would still be a ghetto Church. I say he doesn't take into account the German and Polish and Lithuanian —not to mention Italian—immigrations. But he says the Irish brought leadership. I tried to argue that they brought *bossism*. Is there any other counterattack I can use?"

Righi could feel his eyelids growing heavy. The shower had drained him. Not to mention the events of the day.

But he needed allies among the rectory priests and thus far Vaccaro seemed the most likely. He would have to give some answer to the fellow.

"The Catholic Church does owe much of its prosperity in the English-speaking world to the Irish, as Tom says. The Irish implanted the Catholic Church in regions which had been the preserve of the WASP or the Orangeman. And the Irish brought discipline and order. The priest was boss. As a result, Catholicism enjoyed, in the United States, a stunning, spectacular development. To America, the Irish *were* the Church—at least along the influential Atlantic coast."

Salvatore Vaccaro shook his head as if in final defeat. "So Tom is right?"

"No. Tom's wrong. The Irish held on to the Church in America even after the times had changed. Irish bossism lasted too long, to the displeasure of everybody. What, for example, did German Catholics have to learn from the Irish—other than the English language?"

"And Rome—did it have nothing to say about this?"

The subject had worn Righi down, and as for Panin, the answers had probed near the bottom of the Russian's memory from a compact year's studies. So the Observer added one or two additional details that he hoped would satisfy Vaccaro, then he pointed toward a decanter on the end table. "It's past history, Sal. Let's toast the catholicity of the Church and, *paesano*, finish the evening with a drink."

[XIII]

THE APARTMENT WAS ON THE FIFTH FLOOR OF A NEW building on East Seventieth Street, not far from the Hunter College station. Shulamith Arieh and Gila Ben-Ami had—from the perspective of the FBI—a suspiciously fine address. And they had a lot of visitors, among them a number of men also known to FBI files.

These were just a few of the reasons why the doorman in their building had been hired by the Bureau and asked to keep notes on the visitors who pushed the button next to the names Arieh and Ben-Ami.

Just minutes after a Giovanni Colella had registered with the doorman and proceeded to the elevator, which took him to the fifth floor, the doorman sent a Xerox copy of the register, a brief description, and film from the lobby camera via taxi to the Bureau office. The doorman and the cab driver were high school buddies from Flatbush. The latter delivered many packages from the building. He didn't concern himself with the "to whoms" or "from whoms." Tips erased his memory like a pint of Kentucky Bourbon.

Shulamith was wearing a broad smile and a very short green skirt accented by a black silk blouse. The clothes were tailored to show off her shoulders and breasts to their best advantage. "Good afternoon, *Don* Giovanni," she greeted him at the door.

Her visitor extended his hand. "*Et pax tecum.*"

"Which means what?" she questioned as she helped him take off his camel's hair overcoat.

"It's the equivalent of *shalom*—for our liturgy." He could tell by the way she watched him as he walked: she liked the way his *dolce vita* sweater fit his taut build. Several mirrors in the room reflected each of them for the other's observation.

"Then, *shalom uvraha!* Which, in instant translation, means 'peace and welcome.' Make yourself at home."

Colella gave the tastefully decorated room and foyer a slow, considered gaze. Shulamith seemed to watch him, proud as she saw delight in his expressions.

"So, you like Shula's place?"

"Very much."

She leaned forward in her chair, allowing her breasts to shift, quite innocently. "Shula is so pleased."

Then she saw that Colella's gaze had stopped at the leather-framed portrait of an air corps pilot.

"Good-looking fellow. Is he your boy friend?" There was restraint in the priest's voice.

"Only in Tel Aviv. I haven't seen him for fifteen months. He's far away—and we haven't promised anything to each other. You know how it is. For the moment, I'm—"

"I see." There was a hint in Colella's tone that possibly he did not want to know the rest. Shulamith became quiet.

"My conscience is clear: I'm all right and he's all right. We Israelis don't put too much stock in form. . . . How about a drink?"

"Scotch . . . on the rocks."

The room remained quiet, but not awkwardly so. The sounds of bottles tapping against glasses. Of ice cubes. Of two people trying not to appear other than casual.

When she returned with the glasses, Colella took his and smiled. "I only drink to bolster my English. Does that seem strange to you?"

"From you, yes. You speak English very well for an Italian. Gila tells me, from her trips into Fiumicino airport, that you Italians murder the language. Cheers."

Colella took two hefty swallows. "Well, I get along. I only wish that I knew Russian and Chinese. That's where history is headed: Moscow and Peking. What do you think? Is the world of the future going to be following Lenin or Mao?"

Shula's face flashed an expression both of puzzlement and flirtation toward the priest. "You're a brain, Giovanni. I saw that from

the start. And you're smart enough to know that Shula is not. Don't
waste your time asking such questions of me. Talk to Shula about
feelings—not philosophy or politics." She sat across the sofa, pulling her legs up under her skirt. The green material edged across her
thighs at an almost strategic mid-length. "For example: Tell me
how it feels to slip away from the place—whatever you call it—
where priests have to live?"

"Not like escaping from prison, if that's what you mean." The
priest's face gave every indication that he had no intention of either
seducing or being seduced.

Panin at work behind Righi disguised as Colella: the Russian
was too professional to do anything—however pleasurable—without
adequate caution. His face adopted its most neutral veneer.

"But, Giovanni, all of us are in some prison," she retorted in a
voice so mildly different from the one she had used earlier that the
priest, at first, did not notice the change. "I know very little—too
little—about the Nazarenes; excuse me, I mean Christians. I need to
know more . . . to emerge from my ignorance." The eyes staring
at him were childlike, innocent. All flirtation had suddenly disappeared.

"There is an overwhelming desire to communicate these days.
'No man is an island' may never have been more true than today.
Take our friend Gabriel Menachem: he's a devout Sephardic Jew
who, nonetheless, has a host of Christian friends. And it may
surprise you, but Menachem is presently studying the New Testament."

Shulamith laughed. "Gila will be more surprised than I am."

Then the two allowed the conversation to dwindle. For a moment they looked across at one another as if to determine just how
genuine the other's intentions really were.

She was the first to break the silence. "That stuff, Giovanni, do
you really believe in it? Is it in your heart as well as your brain?"
Her voice was both husky and pleading.

"If you mean the Gospel," the priest replied with confidence,
"I do."

Shulamith seemed determined to pursue the subject. "Then
why are you in trouble with your boss—the name you Nazarenes
use for your chief rabbi?"

"The bishop," Colella chuckled. "He didn't approve of a sermon I gave not long ago. My ideas on the meaning of sin appeared to have offended him."

There was only seriousness in Shulamith's response. "What is sin, Giovanni? Is it sleeping with someone who's not your spouse—is that sin?" There was a deliberately alluring manner to the way she added, "Or would it be a sin should a priest sleep with a woman —me? You are a man who has always been chaste—aren't you?"

The priest was taken aback by her openness. He thought for a long stretch of seconds. "All of us are sinners, Shula."

"Oh, there's no question that I'm a sinner," she sighed, abruptly moving her legs from the sofa so that her feet settled silently onto the carpet. Her uneasiness was, by appearance, sincere.

Colella stared at her, his face wearing regret with a certain detachment. "My dear, we can be sinners and still not abandon hope. That—am I not correct?—would be the most unforgivable of sins?"

Instead of agreeing, the pert young woman seemed to recover her self-possession and clapped her hands, meanwhile laughing the laugh of a girl. "Then, *Father*, what's so special about being a priest?" Her words were accompanied by a piercing, almost mind-reading look.

"Usually," he answered, "we don't lapse into the same kinds of sins. That's all."

Shulamith persisted. "What sins could anyone commit other than those common to all of mankind? Priest or no priest, Giovanni, you are just a man"—her bearing and voice, even the gleam in her emerald-green eyes asserted the most womanly brand of intensity—"though certainly a man most eloquent, with eyes and the language to move a listener's heart."

She did not wait for his response. Instead she took his glass from the table and returned to the bar, where she fixed fresh drinks. Her movements stirred the air around him. The aroma was a perfume, French, of course, that seemed to come and go, a kind of teasing. When she returned to the sofa, the priest seemed more vulnerable.

"Thanks," he said as he took the perspiring tumbler into his rather pale hands. "You are an attractive woman—I mean it."

Her free hand gestured, implying mild annoyance.

"I hear that too often, Giovanni. It's a compliment which has come to bore me. It says that men can never see past my body; no one cares if Shula has a soul. Sometimes I wonder if I really do?"

The eyes watching her were not priestly. Had she not been looking down into her drink, Shulamith Arieh would have had a momentary glimpse of Panin—not the spy, but the man.

But the actor in him recovered almost immediately. His answer was vintage servant-of-the-Lord. "You have a most obvious soul, Shulamith. An *immortal* soul."

Her voice broke as she half whispered, "I'm no child. My soul feels older than my twenty-six years."

He whispered back, "I could be your father."

There was no reaction. She stared, heavy-hearted, at her hands folded in her lap.

"Do you pray, my child?"

"I don't know how." There was no trace of deception in her voice. "Will you teach me?"

Colella remained in her apartment for another two hours, during which he gave Shulamith an elementary notion of Catholic dogma while he consumed three more scotches.

There was virtually no indication that the two were anything more to one another than priest and catechumen. Finally, when the priest stood at her apartment door and was ready to leave, he patted her on the head, "*Pax tecum*, Shula."

As he waited by the elevator doors, he could hear her repeating, "*Shalom*, Giovanni, *shalom*."

That same evening, Shulamith phoned Jehudah Tamir; she was calling from a phone booth at the Bloomingdale's subway station and the phone that the first secretary of the Israeli mission answered was his contact number with her. A mobile unit number.

Her evaluation was well considered. It contained the tone and directness that she knew Tamir would expect. But it did not contain her own personal feelings. "He's ripe for seduction and he may be the worst liar I've encountered since that Egyptian bodyguard. He misquoted the prophet Isaiah—I think?—and he spoke of his parish church as being on a block which I just rode along when taking a cab down here. There's no church. He also seems confused about the sins of Catholic rabbis." She paused, restraining herself from making this first report any stronger.

Her heart would not let her go further.

Something about this poet-priest, whoever he might really be, had affected her. Therefore she concluded with a remark that contained both overt and hidden meanings: "Tamir, if this fellow's a priest, then Shula is a longshoreman for sure."

"But you're talking about Monsignor Righi, the Holy See's Observer at the UN." Tamir's voice, even amid crackles in the mobile unit connection, sounded disbelieving. "Why would such a recognizable priest get involved with you, yet remain in disguise? And why these gaffes?"

A yowling interference interrupted the transmission of Shulamith's response, so once the line sounded clear again, she repeated, "He's coming back on Wednesday. Maybe I can get to the bottom of this then. Do you have any instructions?"

"I'll let you know the day before." The transmission line broke off completely, so that Tamir's "Here's wishing you luck, Shula. *Shalom*," never reached beyond his transmitter.

Shulamith was just glad that the report call was over.

As she walked out toward Lexington Avenue to hail a cab, she felt a sense of relief. A song came to her mind: she hummed "Stardust" as the dirty yellow taxi swerved to a halt just beyond the night shadows of the Bloomingdale's marquee.

HOLY SYNOD did not go directly to the rectory from Shulamith's apartment. Instead he phoned TOLSTOY, who had promised to wait at the Second Avenue kosher deli until an immediate report could be made. Panin just hoped that Lewinson, the renowned fumbler, had not gone to the Fourteenth Street deli instead.

TOLSTOY answered the pay phone. "Hello and don't go 'way." Then Panin could hear Lewinson barking to someone else, "It must be some drunk. He's crying into the phone. Aren't you glad you let me answer the calls at this one?" Apparently a roomful of people were Lewinson's audience and they laughed loud enough for Panin to hear.

Amid the noise, TOLSTOY whispered into the phone, "Now tell me."

HOLY SYNOD wasted no time. "She's a Zionist spy. I'd swear to it. And if she's an airline employee, then I'm a priest." He paused as if to weigh the next statement. "And she's probably a whore, though a subtle one. She's an actress—which makes it hard to get anywhere: she keeps me on the defensive. But I'll manage. I'll be seeing her again Wednesday evening."

TOLSTOY made no response. The Russians were not chatty over telephones—certainly not like the Israelis. Panin realized that TOLSTOY was giving him time to say it all. He decided to ask about the next regular communiqué. Lewinson had not included any promises in the last one.

"Any more statuettes soon?"

"One—coming to you by Tuesday." Lewinson's voice was rapid-fire, as if rushing to respond before someone approaching him could get within hearing distance. "Meanwhile, I'll pass along what you've told me."

HOLY SYNOD was left with a buzz in his ear; TOLSTOY had, without warning, hung up. It was his style: the fumbler never said good-bye.

So Panin left the phone booth near Sixty-fourth and Third. He was humming and did not recognize the tune, "Ochi Chornye," until an elderly lady passed him, then called back, "What gives you the right to be happy?"

The assault from a stranger hardly affected him because Panin was too absorbed with his own thoughts. Rather than "Ochi Chornye," "Dark Eyes," according to the song of his native land, he had eyes of emerald green on his mind.

Not from the mind of a priest or even a spy, but from the heart of a man who—for the moment—felt like being neither.

[XIV]

IT WAS THE COLDEST LATE NOVEMBER MORNING IN TWO decades. The wind had raged all night and at dawn was followed by a dense snow. By the time most New Yorkers were waking up, the grinding snowplows could be heard in most neighborhoods as the blades scraped across snow-laden pavements.

More than on most mornings, a warm bed looked appealing. This was particularly true for those who had passed through a sleepless night and were the victims of early-morning torpor. Mrs. O'Rourke felt this way, as did Ahmed Badr.

By the looks of his puffy eyelids, Monsignor Righi probably felt worse.

James McNeil nicked his chin twice while shaving.

There seemed to be more in the air than just snow.

Mrs. O'Rourke grumbled to herself as she struggled through the snow on her way to the rectory. It was a habit of hers, this talking to herself. A habit that had been her grandmother's as well.

The grandmother of Marfyona Alexandrovna Popova, that is.

For Mrs. O'Rourke was, in the KGB files, not Mrs. O'Rourke at all. Nor was she as unworldly as this housekeeper's role had required her to appear. Not this KARENINA. At least, she grumbled, I can recognize the fragrance of Guerlain's *Chant d'Arômes* when I smell it. Late last night, she had discovered that fragrance clinging to HOLY SYNOD's clothing as he passed in the rectory hallway.

She was in full conflict with herself as she turned the corner and was forced to turn her back to the howling, snow-filled wind that came at her from the East River end of the street. How can Colonel Panin allow himself to turn into a degenerate member of the bourgeoisie—the type who strolls down Piccadilly wearing a suit tailored on Savile Row? She thought of the retired members of the British Admiralty, dandies she had loathed during an earlier mission. Let the Polish priestling spray himself with eau de cologne, but not a Russian with the nickname of Nitchevo!

It was not that she wanted to preach to him.

"A man is a man," she called out to the trash cans mounded with snow. She knew that Volodya Panin was still a virile man entitled to some relaxation. And not everyone can be as sexless as that newcomer from Detroit, her mind reasoned; not everyone relies so exclusively upon sticking his nose into other people's business. . . .

KARENINA understood all too well that HOLY SYNOD had to be careful to play the part of a churchman and a distinguished churchman at that.

In this case, such a role meant that there must be no betrayals through carnal weakness. She knew the rules. She also wanted to give Panin some benefit of the doubt.

Maybe, she suggested to herself, he has been discreet and last night went to a prostitute? But the perfume remained an even stronger argument. She doubted that the woman had been merely a prostitute. *Chant d'Arômes* implied the kind of high-class woman who represented real danger to an agent under cover.

KARENINA was worried. Her first instinct had been to report her suspicions to TOLSTOY. But as always, she had definite instructions not to initiate anything on her own; her role was that of a vehicle of communication.

This had led her to consider the unconsiderable: to confront Volodya in person. Just as a check.

Nonetheless, the idea contained enormous problems, not the least of which was the rule of rules, which said that KGB agents known to one another did not make contact—except by instructions and by special means.

Thus, Mrs. O'Rourke reached the rectory door with much more than the weather weighing on her mind. She slipped her key into the lock. Once the door opened, she tapped her boots one at a time against the brick before entering.

She was barely past the threshold when her mind switched, with professional precision. There was housework to be done and a rectory of men to be waited on. Time to get busy, she grumbled to herself.

As for Panin, he had slept—according to his calculations upon looking at the alarm clock—no more than an hour all night.

He was obsessed by Shulamith and what her body stirred within him, despite all the detachment that his professional sensibilities had interposed.

The alarm rang for the third time and he slapped at it, ending the shrill bell once again. "I am certain she's a spy," he reiterated in an argument heard only by the statuettes of St. Anthony.

Panin struggled toward the bathroom and slowly washed his face.

His instructions had been to make all possible contacts with the Israelis, he reasoned: but did that mean taking risks that brought him to the brink of capture by a Zionist network?

He stared at himself in the mirror, water dripping from his

chin, eyebrows and nose like those on the face of a man just pulled from the deep. "But what does she want from me?" he whispered. "Is it love she wants? Does she want me in her bed?"

Of course this couldn't be allowed. Not as spy or as priest.

He dried his face with a fresh towel and brushed his teeth, removing the lingering taste of too many scotches.

Then the more dangerous implications came back to him. What happens if and when she discovers that Giovanni Colella is Monsignor Righi? Dare he even hope that the Israelis would let the chance pass—the chance to blackmail Righi with this priestly game of doubles?

Panin felt foolish.

Then the anger returned. Why had he allowed Badr to throw him into the arms of this woman in the first place? And what was Badr really after?

Panin could only laugh at himself. And shower. It could, at least temporarily, ease most any tension.

When Badr awoke, the first thing he did was phone the agent who had just hours before jarred him from his sleep.

"Hello? Badr here. And it's my turn—since you sound as though you were sleeping soundly." The Arab proceeded to berate the agent for having phoned in the middle of the night. He insisted that he was as angry this morning as he had been last night. But that was not all. He also insisted the agent mention his report to no one. Did he understand? The agent's response contained the sounds of freshly conjured fear.

Badr went to his bedroom door and opened it to find the breakfast tray his maid always left. Even through the thick linen napkin covering it, he could feel the chill of his juice glasses.

"But why, Giuseppe?" Badr began, launching into a discussion with the absent Monsignor. "Why did you go and visit that woman?" The Arab Ambassador clumsily fingered through the dishes and linen on the tray, his interests focused more upon this imaginary interrogation than upon the food. "It was only a game. I wanted to see how the Vatican diplomat would react to the pro-Arab Israelis at Hey, Daroma! Nothing more. But now this?"

Badr's impassioned argument did not hint at the underlying

jealousies. Righi had indeed invaded the apartment that the Arab had, until now, considered to be something of his own romantic domain.

But what about blackmail? This entire episode might lead to future troubles. Not to mention scandal.

Badr's thoughts silenced him. How could either the Monsignor's or his own Arab concerns benefit from putting the Vatican in such a bad light?

And what would all of this do to his Gabriel Menachem disguise? He had worked so hard to establish a position from which he could put these women—seductive operatives of the Israeli spy establishment—onto well-designed false trails.

All for what?

So that he, an Arab Ambassador, might lead a Roman Catholic dignitary to the bed where Israeli spies make love for their job?

The thought sickened Badr to the point that his breakfast tray lost what little appeal remained. Even the juices.

James McNeil applied small swatches of toilet paper to the shaving nicks on his chin. "Mother of God," he beseeched, "what did I do to deserve a heavy beard?" It was a question he had asked before and that had never received an answer. Still he continued asking. He knew the procedures.

"If I am nothing else," he often explained, "I am a man of procedures." Which is what this morning distracted McNeil, causing the cuts while shaving.

He was running the vague and ambiguous Potocki information through his mental procedure to discover the real concerns hidden amid the heaps of petty ones.

One: Probably Potocki was just another oversensitive, nervous fellow. McNeil encountered dozens of them each month.

Two: Any pursuit of a UN Observer could prove embarrassing and, most likely, a wild goose chase. McNeil, however, specialized in wild goose chases.

Three: There was the coincidence of another report alluding to a *priest.* . . . The doorman at that East Side apartment building had reported a Corella or something like that . . . a fellow visiting the Israeli women whom the Bureau knew to be connected with Jehudah Tamir. The doorman's description had said that this

Corella didn't dress like a priest but "talked like one." McNeil knew that the description was probably fantasy once again.

Four: Two stories about priests and the UN coming into the office in two separate reports in a handful of days was suspicious. McNeil was just enough of a Catholic to let this stuff brew a while longer.

And Five: There were a couple of so-called *facts*. Potocki had taken down a taxi license-plate number and the driver, a chatty Moshe Greenberg, had expressed some suspicions of his own about the priest whom he remembered dropping off somewhere in Brooklyn. Greenberg had promised to check his route sheet for the day McNeil had indicated, then report back.

But Six: What did any of this prove?

James McNeil thus far had gotten two shaving cuts from pondering a lot of obscure and unrelated meddlings.

Thinking FBI, he admitted, was a lousy way to start the day.

By ten o'clock that morning, TOLSTOY had done some checking on his own. FALCON had gone to El Al Israel Airlines and had made a reservation. He had also confirmed that a very attractive Miss Shulamith Arieh worked there. "HOLY SYNOD did not exaggerate about her charms," FALCON assured Alexander Lewinson.

"So, Harry, what's to keep you from enjoying your work? You'll like the looks of the woman you'll be keeping under observation." The fumbling Lewinson left an amused Harry Goldstein munching an Almond Joy.

"Mikhail Sukhotin was good at that," the FALCON murmured, "long before he became Alexander Lewinson."

Later that afternoon, after he had had a chance to run Jehudah Tamir's report through officials in Jerusalem, Shimon Bar-Hillel seemed to be the most surprised of all the people reacting to last night's incident.

When Tamir had phoned him, Shimon had laughed. "What? The scripture-quoting Monsignor Righi?" Jehudah had then explained how Righi first met Shulamith Arieh at Hey, Daroma!, then how photo comparisons had proven Righi to be the man disguised as Colella. . . .

So Bar-Hillel had asked his government for instructions. The involvement of such a highly placed churchman made this matter one that required more than routine procedures.

Jerusalem's answer had been swift. They had made inquiries of Papal Rome, only to be given immediate and unqualified assurances that Monsignor Righi was Monsignor Righi.

Jerusalem's instructions to Bar-Hillel had read as follows:

Churchman's credentials are O. K. Seduction desired, if possible. Object of contacts with Churchman: definition of his links with any Arabs, including his companion at Hey, Daroma! More directives to follow.

Just before supper that night, Potocki intercepted Maguire in the hallway. He was whispering like an amateur ventriloquist, struggling to speak without moving his lips.

"*He* came home last night and he was reeking of scotch and some expensive perfume—"

Maguire seemed puzzled at the word "reeking": "Drinking in the rectory hallways, was he?"

"Shhhh," Potocki hissed through taut lips. "I said reeking."

The parish priest sighed, then pointed to the dining room. "Not now, Stan. Just keep cool and wait for the next call from J-O-E."

"Shhhh!" trailed Maguire as he left Potocki to his brand of domestic intrigue. The Polish priest's face was several shades of red.

Monsignor Righi did not return to the rectory until late that night. Debate at the General Assembly had lasted through the supper hour once again and—despite the lingering headaches that plagued him throughout the day—the Permanent Observer had felt obligated to remain at his post until the very end.

By the time he left the UN to walk to the rectory, the New York night was cold and damp. The streets were slush and patches of ice; the sidewalks were mounded with snow. He slipped four times and once fell against a snow-covered car.

Inside the rectory, he went straight to his room.

There, awaiting him, was a letter placed conspicuously upon his desk. The return address on the envelope was Friars of the Atonement apparently located in Garrison, New York.

He opened the envelope and was genuinely surprised to find an encoded message. The ink was badly smudged, so it took him some time before he could decipher what turned out to be a message from KARENINA.

His first reaction was anger.

Both of them knew better than to make such direct contact.

But there was a hint of maternal care in what she had written; he could sense that, despite the indignation in its language and tone:

Volodya! Do you have to go to bed with a high-class whore— the kind who goes in for French perfumes? The safety of your cover is at stake. Just forget the sex. A priest is to be celibate, remember? Nothing good can come of women.

Slowly Panin tore the paper into minute fragments and flushed them down the toilet. He knew that enormous feeling must be behind such a breach of procedure; such actions could be very costly to her.

Panin decided to do nothing. He certainly did not intend to report her to TOLSTOY. Not yet.

He only hoped that she would exercise much restraint concerning him. After all, it had been a bad, bad day.

[XV]

THE NEXT MORNING WAS UNUSUALLY DEMANDING. IT WAS the kind of diplomatic day that reminded Monsignor Righi of the quotation that his colleague the Swiss Observer was fond of repeating: "Adlai Stevenson said it first; it was his way of answering the question, 'What is it that you UN people do?' Stevenson would look at them and say quite seriously, 'Protocol, alcohol, Geritol.'"

But the Swiss Observer was always quick to add a fourth dimension, one that occupied Righi today and which seemed to have burdened the Swiss Observer for a number of years before now. "It's the obligation to meet VIPs at the airport and entertain them for the duration of their stay in New York City." Stevenson, whose homeland also served as host to the United Nations, did not have to cope with the same flow of visitors that other representatives did.

Today was a day of visitors for Monsignor Righi.

Earlier he had met France's Cardinal Devreux at the airport, then had accompanied the venerable gentleman into Manhattan, where the Monsignor helped the Cardinal prepare for the peculiarities of a UN press conference.

A heavy cloud of cigarette smoke hovered, like fog in the harbor. Beneath it was a group of mostly complacent reporters. A few appeared to be taking notes. All were crowded into the press conference room on the second floor of the Secretariat building.

They were listening to the Cardinal's speech.

These radio, television, and newspaper journalists were being given a factual and concise account of the work being done by Caritas Internationalis to aid the victims of the war in Ghafra, the dissident province of the republic of Takabuland in Africa. Cardinal Devreux was Caritas Internationalis' president. He sounded earnest and unselfish.

He also coughed a lot, apparently discomforted by the smoke.

At one point, he stopped and wiped tears from his eyes—not so much from the fervor of his own words and emotions, but from the impact upon his vision created by the shafts of light projected onto his face from the area set aside for television cameras.

Righi sat quietly to one side of the floor space just beneath the speaker's platform. He appeared to be calmly absorbed in the French Cardinal's presentation. In fact, he was numb with fatigue.

"Now ladies and gentlemen, I am at your disposal, if you have any questions." The Cardinal had finished his speech rather abruptly, though the tone of his voice remained amiable. There was a sudden disruption among the reporters, first as they realized that the speech had virtually derailed instead of concluded, and then as they scurried to vie for questions.

It was immediately apparent that the Cardinal held at best a tenuous working relationship with the media. His manner implied that he did not think them trustworthy. Nor did he seem to derive much comfort from the non-media people who were present. He had told Righi that he knew that both the head of the UN Information Office and the Ambassador from France, Jean de Beaupré, were in attendance only for reasons of duty and protocol. It did not seem to matter to the Cardinal that the information official had been extremely agreeable and helpful.

Devreux only seemed interested in the attentions that the Permanent Observer of the Holy See could give.

All of this made Righi nervous—a circumstance that caused him to react with a distant air toward the Cardinal, no matter how duly deferential the Observer's gestures may have been. Even after he had seen a certain suspicion in the French Cardinal's eyes earlier, when they had spoken of the Gallic church and its troubles—even then Righi had not been able to warm toward the Frenchman.

And Panin was uneasy about his next-day meeting with Shulamith—for which he still did not have any instructions.

It was unavoidable then that Righi would show some signs of having a few problems.

It didn't help when Martha Winthrop was the first correspondent to ask Cardinal Devreux a question. "Your Eminence," she called out in her nasal voice, "it has been said that the Church is furnishing arms to the Ghafrans under the guise of food parcels. Would you give us your comment?" She stood at an angle, positioned between the television cameras and the speaker, so that the features of her sweater-clad body could be amply observed by all.

The Cardinal stared at her as if some Martian had landed in their midst; nonetheless, his answer was curt and direct. "I have no comment to make, Madam—other than, there is no substance to this hearsay. Caritas Internationalis helps people who are dying from hunger. And we cannot furnish arms for one simple reason: we have none."

At that point, while most news reporters were jotting down the Cardinal's reply, the head of information intervened, whispering to Devreux, then announcing to the audience that he, the UN official, would preside over the remainder of the questioning, "so that our guest can feel free to concern himself exclusively with his answers."

An important Indian newspaperman was then recognized.

"I have three questions." His manner was timid and yet quite serious. "First, isn't the Catholic Church trying to win back for its missionaries the area of Takabuland where its influence was lost following that country's declaration of independence from Great Britain?" The Indian's singsong voice immediately speeded its pace so that the Cardinal could not interject an answer. "And secondly, since the UN has declared that Ghafra's secession is not under the jurisdiction of the international community, isn't the Church interfering with Takabuland's domestic affairs?"

The moderator spoke up, attempting to limit the Indian so that the Cardinal might answer these first two before—but the Indian persisted: "Third, third. Isn't the Church taking a position in a political dispute while at the same time it affirms its neutrality? And one question more: Doesn't the Church risk creating enemies in a continent where its enemies are already abundant, due to past links between the Church and former colonial powers?"

The Indian sat down, but not before looking around among the reporters for approval.

The Cardinal did not give them the time. "By my count, sir, you've asked four questions, not three." The Indian leaned sideways in his chair so he could see around the person in front of him, thereby giving the Cardinal direct eye contact as the French churchman delivered his barb. "And, I might add, your four seem to have been, at least in my modest opinion, prefabricated." Several of the journalists joined the UN head of information in a quick, nervous laugh. Cardinal Devreux continued, "Our purpose is not politics, but to stand beside the poor and the afflicted. As for colonialism, the Church neither invented nor, with a few exceptions, has given sanction to it."

For nearly two minutes his answer continued, covering such topics as "neocolonialism" and the many "emotional superstructures" associated with it. Monsignor Righi remained expressionless. The Cardinal was delivering many of the lines that earlier the Permanent Observer had used when prompting the French dignitary for exactly this type of question.

"Therefore," Cardinal Devreux rasped, his throat now dry from speaking and tension, "let us stick to the facts: the Ghafrans need food; we are trying to supply it. Unfortunately, our best efforts are only what some of you call 'a drop in the bucket.'"

The questioning continued for another fifteen minutes. Following a few of the Cardinal's answers, some of the correspondents applauded and, throughout his period of giving answers, most of them took notes in a manner far more active than they had been during his speech.

At the end the head of the Information Office and the Ambassador from France courteously took leave. The exhausted Cardinal was left alone once again with Monsignor Righi. Devreux did not appear to even try to hide his anxiety. "God be praised, it's over." His hands trembled slightly and the stoop in his shoulders was far more pronounced than Righi had remembered from the airport this morning. "What do you say, Monsignor? Personally, I'd prefer hard labor to interviews with the press."

Since a few of the journalists lingered, chatting in groups of two or three, a couple not yet finished with their note-taking, Righi's response was tactfully low. "The United Nations doesn't furnish a continuous stream of news. What there is of political significance is often very difficult to popularize. It's behind-the-scenes work. These media people rely heavily upon press conferences—especially when such conferences are for persons in the public eye, such as Your Eminence." The Cardinal smiled, feeling complimented, even as he wiped the perspiration from his tense face. "But it also means that on such occasions the reporters can be ruthless, each one fighting to gain on their competitors, even if it means speeding in the wrong direction."

"Well, I don't envy them their profession."

"It helps sometimes to remember that they are not here to hear what you are saying," Righi added as the two ecclesiastics retrieved their coats from the cloakroom and proceeded out of the building. "They might have gone on to accuse you of counterrevolutionary plots, of forming a fifth column among the working masses—"

Suddenly the Cardinal grabbed at the handrail as if to steady himself against a misstep. "That's quite a Marxist vocabulary for a priest from Rome, isn't it, Monsignor?"

Righi laughed, as if the reaction were absolutely the most absurd of responses. "That's very possible, Your Eminence—because this place is swarming with reds. It's infectious. But have no fear: I've contracted nothing more than the vocabulary."

Not until Panin had finally come to the privacy of his room—not until then did he pull the envelope from his coat pocket, where earlier he had been surprised to discover it when shoving his hand into the pocket for warmth.

When he realized that it contained a message in code, he was again surprised. How and why had TOLSTOY chosen to open a new line of communication? Something must be wrong.

Quickly he deciphered the words:

> *Girl knows you're Righi. Stick to that role at any cost. No sexual contact. Girl confirmed as useful to us for Zionist intelligence connection. Justify relationship by beginning instruction aimed at conversion. Report back Friday.* KARENINA *will resume responsibility for next contact—indicating method morning before.*

[XVI]

VOLODYA PANIN WAS PUNCTUAL ON WEDNESDAY EVEning, even though he had walked around in the neighborhood where Shulamith lived and had rather aimlessly stared into the shop windows and up the side stairways. To any observer who might have cared to consider, he looked very much like a man in love.

However, once Panin entered the apartment lobby, he removed the overcoat that had shielded him from the heavy cold of these last days in November. The doorman's face registered the first surprise—Giovanni Colella now appeared in clerical dress.

"Good evening," Panin spoke with an air of dignity that he had not used in his last visit. The doorman immediately became more deferential; he stood graciously to one side while Panin signed the register: Father Giovanni Colella.

Even when the doorman phoned the apartment to announce Shulamith's guest, the man remained reserved, as if somehow everything had changed upon his seeing this priest.

While Panin waited for the elevator and during his ride up, the disguised Russian reminded himself once more of the necessity of holding this woman at arm's length. He understood why his instructions had been as they were: an agent may dream of *la dolce vita*, even cultivate such fantasies, but it is absolutely out of order to turn fantasy into reality. His assumed identity had to rule his every action; it was the price of absolute control.

And lust? Most of the time that had to be confined to the imagination, during spare moments. If ever there were spare moments.

The elevator door opened two floors beneath his destination, and Panin caught a glimpse of his priestly image from the reflection of a hallway mirror. He winked at himself just before the doors closed, but he recognized that the fleeting smile he saw in his own image was weak and unconvincing. It was almost a reminder of something that he had been pondering for several days: A spy's life is harder than that of either a priest or a monk . . . and of greater merit, too, because across a spy's path lie infinitely more temptations.

"But, Giovanni, why have you come in uniform?" Shulamith stood half leaning in her apartment doorway. She was wearing a gypsy-type blouse and a black silk skirt with silver embroidery. Her emerald-green eyes revealed both delight and puzzlement at the sight of her visitor dressed in clericals. "Didn't you have time to change?"

"I had time, Shula—but I didn't want to." Panin entered and walked past her, creating an awkward distance between them. As she closed the door and turned, he held a parcel toward her. "I have something for you."

"Oh, thank you. What is it?" She began to tear at the parcel, then appeared to realize that her guest was still holding his overcoat. "Oh, I'm sorry. Let me take that."

Panin stiffened as she rubbed quite nonchalantly against him, then took the coat from him and headed toward the closet. "Please, make yourself a drink."

While Panin fixed two scotches and tasted fresh almonds that Shula seemed to have just put out for the visit (an empty plastic bag lay beside the bowl), she sat childlike in a chrome-legged chair and quickly opened the package. It was a book, and she examined it with mild suspicion, evidenced by an expression that instantly seemed to dispel the girlish glee that just seconds before had enlivened her face.

"It's The Jerusalem Bible," he explained, then placed both of their drinks on the table between the pair of chairs.

"Oh, you shouldn't have," she protested in a voice of fashionable politeness. "Surely I could get that cheaper in Jerusalem. What with shipping costs and customs, foreign books in this country are very expensive."

It was just the kind of remark that shattered the ice in Panin, sending him into easy laughter. Once he had recovered and had explained how this particular English translation of scripture had gotten its name, Shulamith's face took on an appealing blend of disappointment and embarrassment.

"Ah, then you're still interested in my soul—right, Father?"

"Very much"—Panin choked back the remaining laughter in his voice—"and so should you be." A resoluteness seemed to come upon him; he made certain that she was looking him directly in the eye, then he continued in tones more appropriate for a challenge: "But I must tell you that 'Father' is not the right term to use with me."

There appeared to be longing in her eyes as she answered a bit peevishly, "You won't let me call you darling, I suppose? What can I say?"

Panin leaned toward her so that his answer would have maximum effect: "Monsignor."

A look of candid bewilderment flew into her eyes. She stammered, "Why 'Monsignor'?"

Panin was caught between admiration for what he had to believe was superb acting and a genuine affection. This woman was temporarily trapped in a reversal that, he suspected, she could not have foreseen. Yet her surprise was acted to perfection. Dealing with you, Shula, he thought as she sat in astonishment before him, will be the kind of challenge which stimulates me.

"Shulamith, there's more that you should know. I'm not Father Giovanni Colella. I'm Monsignor Giuseppe Righi, Permanent Observer of the Holy See at the United Nations."

It took a few moments for her to sort through this, including an explanation of what the "Holy See" meant. However, once she appeared to have gathered her emotions, she was immediately indignant.

"You, Monsignor Righi, have lied to Shula." Her emerald-green eyes glowed, alternating fresh disappointment with anger. Otherwise Panin could observe no indication that she was thinking what in fact he knew she must be: Why is he suddenly telling me the truth?

He decided to see how far an apology would get him.

"Shulamith, I'm sorry. But much of this is the fault of Gabriel Menachem. He persuaded me to go to the café, then he introduced me to you as Colella." No matter, for the moment, that this also contained a lie. "But these double games are not for me. I had to tell you the truth."

There was no softening in her manner. She seethed at him: "Very good of you, Monsignor. Now I suppose you'll tell me that Menachem is not Menachem?" There was a gauntlet in the shrillness of her voice.

Panin decided that at this juncture, nothing could be gained by matching his playacting against hers. He responded dryly. "You are right. Menachem is Ahmed Badr, ambassador of a small emirate on the Persian Gulf."

Shulamith rose from her chair, her face pale and her expression deeply troubled. Panin was most affected by the dullness that came to her eyes. Her voice broke throughout her response: "An Arab. Only more lies." She turned away, making her slender neck and arched back an indictment. "And to think that Shula welcomed you with open arms. Poor Gila. She was so proud to have you two as new friends." Her walk away from him spoke of bearing and grace under pressure. "If the two of you intended to humiliate us, you've succeeded." Her whisper was low and full of repulsion. "An Arab."

For an awkward stretch of moments she stood at the bar. Her guest could have been across the East River for all she seemed to care. Then she turned and spoke slowly, as if nothing he might say could matter any longer.

"What should I think of you, very reverend Monsignor, now that you've lent yourself to the game?"

Panin was momentarily taken aback. There were many meanings to the word "game."

But she continued: "After this, who can we trust? 'Beautiful daughter of Jerusalem' you called me." She hid her face in her hands and her shoulders heaved as she moaned through her fingers, "And all the time, I trusted you."

The professional in Panin felt extreme admiration: in her, spying took on the aura of an award-winning performance. Truly, she
seemed sexy enough to damn a saint—all the more beautiful now, as
tears deepened the green in her eyes. Yet he also felt the warmth of
genuine affection. This woman was getting to him—not just to the
priest she thought she was performing for.

The paradox from Oscar Wilde came to mind.

An actress is more than a woman; an actor, less than a man.

Compared to this Israeli spy, Panin suddenly and unexplainably
felt inferior—but he still had to play the game. "Shulamith, my
dear, please sit down. Use your reason. Shouldn't we talk this thing
out?"

She nodded, took a cocktail napkin from the bar and dabbed at
her eyes, then sat across from him once again—one leg tucked
under her, striking the pose of a teenager instead of a seductress.

"I realize that you're hurt," he continued, "but you needn't be.
Badr is my good friend, a colleague at the UN, and an esteemed
historian. Before we met you and Gila, Badr must have spoken of
you two at least a dozen times—more than once mentioning that
both of you had some interest in religion. It was only natural,
therefore, that I came to want to meet you." He could see that she
had stopped crying. "Hasn't it been all to the good for both of us?
No real harm has been done and I remain genuinely interested in
your soul." He paused, waiting until he could see some response—a
faint smile—then he continued: "And it is I who owe something to
you. You've made me remember that in addition to being a diplomat, I'm also a priest . . . a priest in the service of people, including
those who may not be, as you say, Nazarenes. Do you see? Surely
you can't be angry with me any longer, yes?"

Shulamith stiffened her left arm, pressed her closed left fist
against the slender mound of a leg under her black silk skirt; she
leaned forward. All her weight appeared to be resting on this
stiffened arm, pressing down upon the ankle tucked under her. It
was a body movement exorcising disappointment—yet also a gathering up of strength.

"No, Monsignor, I'm not angry. You're an honest man. I must
forgive you. But a man such as you should not be tangled up with
this Arab." There was knowledge and caution in her voice. "It
might be risky—who knows that he is not a spy? All I can think of

are the months of lies which he has been serving up to Gila and me. . . . Believe me: I am afraid."

Panin was suddenly alert. There was more than the designs of a spy in this woman's words. He decided to counter her approach.

"Afraid? Why should you be afraid? There's nothing to fear from either of us. Badr may be an excitable old man—an intriguer and sometimes a busybody—but he wouldn't hurt a fly. Why should he—particularly, why should he have it in for someone like you?" Panin placed his hand upon his chest as he continued, allowing his fingers to caress the cross he wore. "You're hard-working, Shula, and you've done nothing which lends itself to gossip, intimidation, or blackmail. All you need to worry about, my child, is your soul."

"You're right," she whispered and Panin could see that her eyes were now more tender and loving than he had ever seen them. Tears clung around them; even when the tears slipped and rolled down her cheeks, they were thick and slow-moving. "But I must never see that Arab again. He betrayed our trust—yours and mine—I can't help but be afraid of him."

Panin stared at her, his eyes as penetrating as he had allowed them to be in months. He was surprised at himself for what he was feeling. He wanted to make certain. It was crucial.

He was actually believing that at this particular moment, Shulamith Arieh was not acting. He had to know for certain, so his next words were carefully chosen: "Does that mean that you are also afraid of me?"

His most discerning abilities as a listener could only detect tenderness and innocence in her voice as she answered, "No, you are a good Nazarene and I cannot be afraid of you. I only warn you that you should stay away from some people. Association with Arab spies might make your chief Catholic rabbi fire you."

Panin laughed as he had not remembered doing—not in years.

"We call him 'Il Papa' or 'the Pope' and he won't let me go. As for Badr, he may think he's a spy, but—as the Americans say—he's 'only kidding himself.'"

"But what would Il Papa say if he knew you were calling on an Israeli woman in her own apartment?" Her voice was very calm.

"Nothing. Not even if he knew that the woman was as pretty

as you. Intentions, rather than actions, you see—those are what count."

Panin suspected that rapid contradictions were being batted around in her head as she asked him quite directly: "And what are your intentions? Do you want to make Shula a believer with the Nazarenes?"

"What do you want? That's the question."

"I want to learn. I want to find out as much as I can. I can't say what I'll do after that. Now, is Shula being direct enough with you?" Though she still sat in the girlish pose, there was nothing but womanly bearing about her.

Panin nodded his head. "Perfect." He did not allow himself to scrutinize her words for whatever double meanings of espionage there might be hidden among them, calculated and well disguised. "And believe me, from now on I'll be straight with you. You say you want to learn and I have brought you the book to begin that learning. Reading it is a course with the best of all teachers."

"For Gila, too?"

"Of course. If the two of you read it, maybe we can discuss your feelings and questions the next time I visit?"

"How about Sunday?" Shulamith suddenly became a child again, squirming in her chair as if invigorated by the promise of some new adventure. "She'll be coming back then. Will you have time to pay us a call? Or shouldn't I ask?"

"Why not? I'd be delighted."

For nearly an hour, their visit continued.

Panin used The Jerusalem Bible and a list of scripture passages that he had earlier typed up; these, he explained, would be excellent introductions to the relationship between what he called "*Brith haDasha*" or the "New Covenant" and the foundations of the faith, which he presumed were already in the hearts and minds of the Israelis.

Shulamith listened carefully and asked a number of questions.

Often, however, she sat quietly, as if admiring an entirely new dimension to this man who had come into her life.

He is more, her expression seemed to say, than I had imagined him to be.

Nor were her implied feelings lost upon Panin.

As their discussions ended and he was leaving her apartment, he refrained from repeating the pat on the head that he had given her on the last visit. Instead he blessed her, being careful to avoid any reference to the Trinity.

Even as he walked to the elevator, waited for it to arrive at her floor, then entered, Shulamith remained in the doorway, her head bowed.

The spy had nearly become a priest. Panin went home to the rectory, where he had plenty of time to ponder in private how he felt.

In his room, among the statuettes of St. Anthony and the closet of clericals, Panin was only moderately pleased with his performance. He still possessed deep hungers caused by Shulamith's warm slender body and the deliberate motions of even her most innocent though provocative gestures. He felt more like a man than either a priest or a spy should have dared.

But he also felt something else.

The puzzling desire to be a teacher to this genuinely questioning woman. Panin sat in a quandary.

How, he wondered, had he gotten himself into a position so opposed to everything that he felt as a man, everything he needed to do as a spy, and everything he was called upon to do to pretend to be a Roman Catholic priest?

After Monsignor Righi's departure, Shulamith wandered about her apartment as if she had just moved in. She rearranged small ornaments from one piece of furniture to another; she adjusted chairs and toyed with empty glasses. Before leaving to find a phone booth and report to Tamir, she quickly downed a glass of straight scotch. She suspected Tamir would also be in need of a drink, once he heard this story.

There's much to be considered, she thought to herself, afraid almost to speak aloud in her own apartment.

She had not counted on this priest being a man who could reach her soul.

[XVII]

PANIN REALIZED THAT HE HAD NOT BEEN KEEPING UP WITH
Monsignor Righi's paper work. The entanglements of this
last week were beginning to exact a toll: Cardinal Devreux's visit, the parties, Shulamith . . .

The desk in the Permanent Observer's office was piled with reports and unanswered letters. Belli had a flurry of notes scattered
throughout the material. If Panin did not set aside an entire weekend of work, Righi's essential duty of reporting would fall behind
to the point that superiors in Rome would have to become concerned about their Permanent Observer.

That was precisely what Panin did not need.

For this reason, he had intended to sequester himself in the
Permanent Observer's office throughout the long Thanksgiving holiday weekend. During any spare moments not committed to parish
duties, he could dictate answers for the backlog of correspondence,
then he could scan as many reports as time permitted. It was a perfect solution. Father Belli was spending the holiday in the Bronx although he had said he would stop over for a few minutes on Saturday morning on his way to Staten Island to meet a fellow priest. He
had to deliver some Italian food Vaccaro had asked him to buy for
his mother at the stores of Arthur Avenue. So the office would be
empty, quiet, private.

As Righi, Panin settled in behind his desk and long before Mrs.
O'Rourke arrived to fix breakfast, the Monsignor had finished dic-
tating responses to nearly a dozen letters.

After a break for coffee and toast, then a rapid scanning of
two reports, Righi was surprised by the ringing of his office phone.
For a moment he was nearly of a mind to ignore it; the weekend of
work was too important. But it continued to ring.

Panin thought a curse in Russian that, to his memory, did not
translate into any other language, then he answered the phone in
English. There was unmistakable impatience in his voice.

"Monsignor Righi, I knew I could count on you being there,
you gracious rascal." The caller spoke rapid Italian peppered in an

awkward manner with Latin phrases. After a long list of somewhat embarrassing self-aggrandizements and compliments, the Italian returned to what seemed to be his original intention for the call: "I just wanted you to know that I'm settled in at the hotel you recommended to Cardinal Devreux. Everything is superb. How right the Cardinal was: you are a fine host for us visitors to New York."

The Italian continued his chatting.

And the Permanent Observer was too preoccupied to care—for Panin was rapidly scanning his memory, struggling to determine who this man was. Then the caller alluded to "the Academy" and in the very next phrase used the words "the will of the superiors" in such a manner that Panin immediately remembered who the fellow must be.

A prelate had written Righi—Panin had just read the unanswered letter this morning; the caller must be the man en route to the post of counselor at a nunciature in some Latin American country. It was in the letter. Panin also remembered that Righi and this prelate had studied at the same academy for the training of church diplomats—but to Panin's relief the two terms had not overlapped. However, Panin remembered that Righi and this prelate did have some mutual friends.

The Italian jarred his way back into Panin's attentions. "Cardinal Devreux spoke well of you at the Vatican. You're very lucky to have a *cardinal* for a friend. *Tesaurum invenisti.*" He seemed unstoppable, but Righi encouraged the chattering with "hmm" and "I see"; the prelate seemed not to notice these minimal responses, however, and continued: "The Cardinal also said that you were the most knowledgeable and that you briefed him on a number of important matters—"

Panin struggled to locate the letter in the box marked "Belli" and at the same time prodded his memory: he had to remember precisely which friends Righi and this prelate had known. Plus, he had to decide what he was going to do with this guest.

"Of greatest interest to the Secretariat of State were your indications to Cardinal Devreux that the UN is overrun by spies and Communists. The Cardinal was most impressed, not only that you seemed to know a good deal about the matter, but—more importantly—that you seemed capable of holding your own. *Omnibus non obstantibus.*"

It took all of the energies and imagination that Panin could muster just to pull together an adequate recall of Latin and a precise recounting of the Monsignor's history vis-à-vis this presumptuous priest—not to mention devising an impromptu holiday schedule.

He held the prelate's letter, just located, and read it with the probing concentration of a trapped man: Righi was being called upon for another tour of Manhattan. Perfect.

The Permanent Observer swallowed deeply and plunged into an interruption designed to regain control of both the conversation and this potentially dangerous situation. "Well, my friend, I'm truly glad to hear that you're settled and that the Cardinal enjoyed his visit here. But you know me well enough—or at least you know enough about me—so that I'm certain that you'll appreciate the fact that I did nothing to curry favor with him. I was only doing my duty, nothing more. However, I am flattered that he should go away thinking of me as a friend. But whether or not such a friendship proves to be a 'gold mine' "—the translation of "*tesaurum invenisti*" just came to him.

The prelate chuckled, then attempted to launch into another breathy sentence, but Panin's Righi persisted. "However, I must say that one aspect of His Eminence's report was somehow inexact." He had to take particular caution in wording the remainder of his correction. He intended to dissuade the prelate from believing that Righi possessed a disproportionate amount of information concerning spies at the United Nations—but he also intended to make certain that the priest could not report back that the Permanent Observer accused Cardinal Devreux of misrepresenting a conversation in some official reports. Panin was walking a tight and unfamiliar wire; each step had to be firm, well-placed.

When Panin finished stating all this in Italian, he fell silent. The letter in his hand alluded to the fact that this prelate spoke no English. The Monsignor decided to wait and let the unwanted guest reveal how much of a tour he expected from Righi during this first morning of the holiday weekend.

The prelate jumped back into the conversation as if he had gotten exactly the second wind he had needed. He quickly cataloged several museums that he would love to visit, then added a few of New York's standard tourist attractions. "But, Monsignor, this is your city," he concluded, switching the decision back to his host.

"Mmmm, let me see. . . ." Panin stalled; he knew that someone so cultivated—no matter how presuming—must be handled with subtlety. That's when a most unusual idea came to him. It was a plan that he had reserved for his own amusement. He had been doing research, bit by bit, ever since he had arrived in New York. Originally he had intended this to be a solo adventure of his own: a means of escaping the Righi role, the rectory family, all the UN personnel. A day off for Volodya Panin.

But since there did not appear to be time for that—not now, not in the foreseeable future—why not use the idea to satisfy this prelate? Panin gave in: "I have it: let's take a tour of the bridges surrounding Manhattan." He listened as the priest stammered over the prospects of this suggestion; the man's struggles made Panin even more convinced that the idea was his best. If he were to take this fellow to the Metropolitan Museum—say, to the Catello family's collection of crèche figurines—the prelate would probably criticize it to pieces or string out innumerable comparisons. The bridges, however, were certain to shut him up.

"There are about forty," Righi explained, "but we won't see them all. These bridges are an integral part of Manhattan; they radiate from the island like sunbeams. No single bridge is an example of good architecture, but all are stupendous works of engineering." He could hear the prelate's murmurings, but could not make them out. "Of course, you shouldn't imagine that you're about to see Venice's Rialto, Florence's Santa Trinita, or Rome's Ponte Sisto—"

"Before they ruined it during the last century," the prelate qualified, then he hastened to remind Righi that he had, while a student of canon law in Rome, resided just across from this bridge, living in the Ospizio dei Centopreti. Surely Righi remembered?

Panin risked the mention of a common friend from his memory of Righi's Academy days and explained to the prelate that this friend "used to speak of walks along the Ponte Sisto. . . ."

The phone conversation ended without apparent mishap, Righi and the visitor agreeing to meet tomorrow after mass. Then the tour would begin.

At least, Panin consoled himself, I'll have the rest of today for some of this work.

He took the phone mouthpiece off its cradle, wrapped it in a wool sweater to muffle the beeping that he knew would soon start, and placed the entire unit in an empty file drawer. Silence guaranteed.

Immediately following mass the next day, Panin in the guise of Righi called for the visitor at the hotel on East Forty-second Street, near First Avenue.

"We're beginning with the Verrazano," Righi explained, as soon as they had gotten in the rented car. "It's the longest suspension bridge—though the George Washington surpasses it in elegance and perhaps in daring as well." Then, affirming that they were also fellow Italians, Righi told the prelate the story of the Tuscan navigator who discovered the narrows . . . how Italian-Americans had struggled for three years to win, for his honor, the bridge's name . . . how the official name became a compromise: the Verrazano-Narrows Bridge . . . how all New Yorkers called it "the Verrazano."

On the bridge itself, the two men gazed upon the southern tip of Manhattan. Righi pointed out the city's crown of skyscrapers, explaining that it was the greatest conglomeration in the world, each building seeming to strive to outdo the others, whereas the midtown skyscrapers were less crowded together, with more breathing space between them.

"And to the left, that's the Atlantic; the spit of Coney Island is in the foreground."

"Certainly I've heard of that," the prelate laughed—making Righi wonder if his guest meant the ocean or Coney Island. One could not be sure, given this fellow's studied ambiguities.

As they drove once again, Righi reeled off a succession of statistics: the Verrazano contained ninety thousand tons of steel, its end towers were as high as a seventy-floor skyscraper, its cost had been $350 million . . . the Narrows formed the only entrance to the bay and harbor of New York . . . how marvelous was the sight of passing transatlantic and freight vessels . . .

At a particularly dramatic vantage point, Righi nodded his

head as if pointing. "What about that view of the tip of Manhattan? Not bad, hey?"

The prelate responded with a quotation from Horace: "*Vides ut alta stet. . . .*"

"I'm afraid that we have less snow piled high and more smog," Righi interposed. "Smog is to snow as drunkenness is to happiness." When the priest didn't laugh, Righi added, "Or, if you prefer, as sin is to the grace of God."

After maneuvering through a route that allowed them to avoid much of the holiday shopping traffic, Righi drove them to a parking area near the Brooklyn Bridge. When he proposed that they leave the car and cross it on foot, the prelate agreed, though not without some apparent reluctance.

"It's a walk I often take between sessions at the UN. It almost always stimulates meditation on the vicissitudes of the human race; the view, I promise, is magnificent."

From Righi's favorite spot on the bridge, he pointed out the upper bay, Governors Island, the Statue of Liberty, New Jersey's coastline, and—close by—the Brooklyn shipyards and the once-fashionable Brooklyn Heights.

The prelate appeared too stunned to take it all in—which delighted Righi as he elaborated, reciting all the legends he could remember about the bridge.

At one point, the prelate interrupted: "Monsignor, you seem to exemplify the phrase *omnia scire.*" Righi's visitor seemed to make certain that a look of understanding appeared in the Permanent Observer's expression, then he turned the phrase. "I only hope you haven't forgotten that 'to be all-knowing' is linked, in that passage, with '*et pro nihilo reputari?*'"

"I recognize my 'unimportance,'" Righi countered, "but I still try to understand this city. And it's a continuous discovery. Maybe not as gratifying as Florence or"—there was some irony in Righi's voice—"your native Bitonto, but definitely interesting. Particularly the people on the streets of New York." The Permanent Observer was a bit surprised at the enthusiasm that the subject evoked in him; his need to justify this new passion for the city had not, until now, been so completely expressed. He enjoyed continuing with renewed verve. "Most of the UN representatives escape from the paper work and the smog by spending the weekend with their families in the suburbs. Fine for them. As for me, I complete my reports to the Vatican, then walk all over the city: the Bowery, Greenwich Village, parts of Harlem. I see not only alcoholics, drug addicts, and homosexuals, but an almost limitless number of all types of antisocial persons; I take a passionate interest in them. They have, to my mind, the rare merit of not passing themselves off for something or someone they are not. . . ."

The irony in Righi's words did not escape Panin, but he finished the thought, then directed the prelate back to their rented car for a drive to Flatbush. "The Italian neighborhood in Brooklyn," he explained. "We'll have a snack there. Then"—his smile at the prelate hid the host's mischievous delight—"more bridges."

Manhattan, Williamsburg, Queensboro, Triborough, Whitestone.

By the time they reached the Throgs Neck, the prelate sat very quietly in the car. Righi was pleased with the progress.

"It's longer than a bridge might be," he said, "were they to build one across the Strait of Messina." But they did not stop the car to examine any particular aspect of the bridge.

"Aren't there any bridges built in stone or cement?" The question was asked in a manner indicating only the mildest of interest. The visitor seemed thoroughly drained. Nonetheless, Righi was determined to make certain.

He took the prelate to see High Bridge.

"As you can see," he pointed out, once they got a good view of the structure, "it's not beautiful. High Bridge used to be an aqueduct; then it must have been fine to behold. But they destroyed the rhythm of the arches when they made room for larger ships to pass under it."

But neither High Bridge nor the Harlem River nor even the prospects of Harlem itself seemed to interest the prelate. "The Romans did better," he grumbled. Then he shook his head, as if passing final judgment upon most everything he had seen; the Latin phrase which he uttered, *"Te saxa loquuntur,"* said most unsparingly, "The stones speak of you."

For once Righi conceded that his guest was right: the Romans had been better at building aqueducts. He did not argue the case;

instead he called attention to the fact that Edgar Allan Poe used the bridge to reach the markets in Harlem.

"Who's Poe?"

Righi took some pleasure in telling the prelate about the works of Poe—giving lively précis of several Poe short stories and quoting from some of the more dramatic passages in Poe's dark poetry. "He's considered, among other things, the father of the mystery story. Just the kind of writer who should interest Father Potocki at the rectory."

The prelate asked about this category of fiction and showed only passing interest in Potocki.

Righi answered with a certain generosity toward the latter and no small enthusiasm for the best among the former. "As I was saying," he said, backtracking, "Poe used to cross this bridge, coming from a nearby cottage and going into Harlem to buy food. Even poets have to eat."

"Ah," the prelate laughed, "but '*Carmina non dant panem.*' "

"Not in America," Righi countered. "Here, some writing does 'feed its author.' If an American writer knows how to use his pen, people will read and pay for their reading matter. Nice, huh? I still don't know why things aren't the same in Italy."

Close to sunset, they decided to seek out a restaurant in which to have dinner. From High Bridge, they had driven toward the Henry Hudson Parkway; they intended to head toward the center of the city.

A wall of impenetrable black clouds rose up out of the Hudson River just ahead. Around the edges of the clouds, tongues of flames darted upward—an effect from the setting sun.

From the Parkway, all they could see was about a mile of darkened water alongside the line of the Palisades, on the Jersey side of the river, and then, on the far horizon, a brick-red sky.

"It's like a volcano," Righi said. "And it gives me an idea of where we may eat. I know a restaurant called Vesuvio. We can have a volcano at our table."

Much later, as Righi drove the prelate to the front of the Hotel Tudor and stopped so that his guest could drag himself rather wearily from the car, the visitor admitted, "Monsignor, this is a unique city and you have led me on what I suspect is one of the more imaginative ways of seeing it. I thank you." However, before Righi could pull away, the prelate tapped on the passenger window. Righi leaned across the front seat and rolled the window down.

The prelate delivered his tag comment as though it was his chance to get the last laugh. "I never knew that New York could have so much water around it."

While Righi sat, cold air blowing in from the open window, the prelate waved and walked away.

On Saturday morning when Belli showed up on his way to Staten Island Righi told his assistant about the prelate's unexpected visit. When Belli asked him how the day had gone, he answered, "I found out that it doesn't take much to satisfy even so sophisticated a fellow: bridges, water, and an Italian restaurant. Too bad there isn't an Italian-type lottery in this country. I'd place a dollar on a three-number combination. Or do you think that it is criminal to gamble?"

"It's not forbidden," answered his assistant, "but have you a book which will tell you what numbers stand for bridge, water, and restaurant?"

He had no such book. "A dollar saved, Charlie."

[XVIII]

IF THERE WAS ONE THING FOR WHICH FATHER POTOCKI GAVE Monsignor Righi credit it was his professional ability. His assiduous attendance at the UN, his lucid exposition of the arguments to which he had listened, his faultless logic and his way of de-fusing headlined drama, in which events usually proved him right—all these were in his favor. And above all, his unflappability. He had the serenity of a sage, even though he was still only in his forties.

He had real know-how and was cut out to be a diplomat, no doubt of it. In spite of Potocki's feeling that Righi was an impostor he couldn't help admiring him. If only instead of betraying Mother Church, he was an honest layman, who knows what services he might render his country.

The face of a poker player, that's what he's got, Potocki, now an inveterate reader of detective stories, said to himself. That's why he cheats so well. For sheer professional competence he can't be touched. I never saw such a tightrope walker!

Every time he had supper at the rectory Righi gave new demonstrations of his competence, clearheadedness, and balancing ability.

On this rainy evening Righi was especially brilliant. Maguire had asked the usual question:

"Well, Giuseppe, what was the weather today at the UN? Rain, hail, or sunshine?"

"Hail. They were talking money. Debts. Debts that make yours pale by comparison, Frank. You're not the only one to have worries."

"Well, someone will pay them, I suppose."

"Perhaps. But France and Russia, the two that owe the most, have already said they won't pay because the UN military operations in the Congo and Suez weren't legally authorized, they claim. Not to worry, however! There's good old Uncle Sam. . . ."

"And besides contracting debts, what are they doing?"

"They're disarming. They have been talking about it for twenty-five years. But while repeating the necessity of disarmament they find that they've lost all sense of urgency. *Assueta vilescunt*."

"What's that?" asked Nevins, who had little Latin.

You see, Righi thought, filling his glass, what I got out of showing the bridges to a certain individual. He gave me the bug. Before this it never occurred to me to subject these good fellows to Latin. After taking a sip he said aloud, "It means, Tom, 'custom stales.' By talking about disarmament they began to talk in a vacuum, a familiar vacuum which occasional peaceful explosions were not enough to fill. Now, all of a sudden, they want to regain lost time. The only way to do that is to talk about disarmament seriously."

"I suppose so," said Maguire, breathing on his eyeglasses in order to clean them, as he did when he wanted to see more deeply into a problem.

"They were pushed into action for several reasons," Righi went on, "one more urgent than the next. Reasons and facts, gleaned from statistics. Take note, Tom, so that your young men can push their slogan 'Make love, not war' more aggressively. Here are the statistics. A tenth of the world's resources go into planning destruction, that is, into arms. A third of the world population is starving, almost two thirds close to hunger. Only one person out of every seven gets along fairly well, one out of twelve well. Meanwhile, even if there's not much actual shooting, we continue to traffic in arms and our dictionaries are enlarged by such horrible neologisms as 'overkill capacity.'"

"Those figures make you think," put in Potocki.

"That's exactly why the members of the Disarmament Commission, which sits permanently in Geneva, have come here for meetings. The Holy See, of course, is aware of the gravity and urgency of the problem. The arms race doesn't only devour the resources which should be used for man's well-being; it also increases the insecurity which it claims to eliminate. With more arms there is greater fear. Men have devised arms capable of wiping out the human race without setting up institutions to prevent such a thing from happening. So Rome has urged me to impress upon the delegates the importance of producing some practical results."

"And will they?" asked Vaccaro.

"I have good news for you, Sal, and for the Cardinal Secretary of State to whom I'll send a report tomorrow. They said today, 'Let's arm, since in twenty-five years we haven't been able to reach an agreement not to. But from now on let's have controls on our arming.'"

"What does that mean?"

"No need to resort to metaphysics for an answer, Sal. It means simply that an international agency should be able to see how many hydrogen warheads you have. How many guided missiles are you capable of launching? With what biological and bacteriological reprisals can you threaten us? How far along are you with the manufacture of a neutron bomb? As you see, my dear *Siciliano*, they're big problems. And to leave them unsolved means that there remain all the premises for planetary self-destruction."

"They'll never allow it, *paesano*," said Vaccaro gloomily.

"True. No one believes they will. But it's something that all the foreign ministers who have come this year said, 'Enough! Things can't go on this way. We can't invest two hundred and thirty billion dollars in weaponry.' To these two hundred and thirty billions, incidentally, the underdeveloped countries contributed thirty billion."

"So what will happen?"

"What will happen is that once men are convinced of the truth of 'the more arms, the greater fear,' and of the falsity of 'war is the fertilizer of history,' then they'll begin to disarm."

"And finish the job in the Valley of Jehoshaphat," put in Potocki.

"Never despair, Stan. The disarmament problem is complex. No one's disarming as long as he sees only a vacuum ahead. In other words, there must be a positive alternative, so that nations need not fear for their security. And the only valid alternative is a United Nations. Not the one we have today. Let's not forget either that not only is disarmament a political and military problem, it's a human necessity, to be resolved by men rather than by computers, by creativity, not inertia. The man of the future will find the answer, the man . . ."

"The 'sun of the future,' as the Italian socialists used to describe the realities yet to come," Vaccaro interpolated ironically. His interruption was unmannerly, but Righi chose to overlook it.

". . . the man who is not resigned, for whom the disarmament of the war machine is not just a pious hope but an obsession."

"You mean a revolutionary?" The Sicilian thought he had a sure shot.

"The word 'rebel' might be more appropriate, or 'dissident,' if you think 'rebel' has been discredited. Rebel against the present order of things, which is bound up, supposedly for the sake of peace, with a balance of power, that is, of arms. And if you are scared off by the words 'revolutionary,' 'rebel,' and 'dissident,' remember that St. Francis of Assisi was one of them, a gentle rebel, but a rebel all the same. And Jesus Christ before him. Do you know any more revolutionary, more radical text than the Sermon on the Mount?"

After Vaccaro, Nevins had to put in a word.

"Let's start by forbidding the use of certain weapons in the dirty war in Vietnam. Democracy can't be exported in the form of napalm."

"What sticks with me," said Potocki, "is the phrase 'war is the fertilizer of history.' Never mind the fertilizer—if Israel hadn't waged war in 1948, 1956, and 1967, it would be afloat in the Mediterranean."

"There may well be a fourth war to follow. But this time the attack will come from the Arabs."

"Monsignor, have you direct lines to Cairo and Damascus?"

"There's no need. There are signs of an explosion in the air. Months may go by—two or three years at the most—but they will go back to fighting. In those parts they live in symbiosis with war."

"Do you think Israel has an atomic bomb?" asked Vaccaro. "If the Israelis see trouble ahead, they'll bomb the Aswan Dam, and then it's Egypt that will be drifting in the Mediterranean. Do they have the bomb or don't they?"

"I say they don't," said Nevins.

"I say they do," said Potocki. "With the Israelis you never can tell. They're strong and smart."

"My question was addressed to Monsignor."

"Monsignor says that if they don't have the bomb now they'll have it in a very few years. I can tell you more tomorrow. Let me talk meanwhile to Ahmed Badr."

"Who is he?"

"I'll tell you that too tomorrow. Just remember that when he speaks he never says anything stupid, and sometimes he hits the bull's-eye."

"We should have more evenings like this in the rectory," said Francis Maguire contentedly as he rose from the table.

PART THREE

MONDAY FOLLOWING THE HOLIDAY WEEKEND, FATHER BELLI felt it necessary to remind Monsignor Righi that Christmas was coming.

The Permanent Observer had gotten a lot of work done during the weekend, and he allowed himself to joke with his assistant: "Glad you reminded me. Now it all makes sense. I was beginning to wonder why there were lighted trees on the median down Park Avenue; why all those mature, zealous Salvation Army women had begun playing trumpets and standing beside red cauldrons on street corners. On Houston Street Saturday, I noticed that the Brothers of St. Anthony were busily setting up a colossal nativity scene. Thanks for explaining it all, Belli." Righi paused, allowing the ironies to simmer. "But you must take into account: I'm not from a northern country. All this folklore, picturesque as the best of it is, is not the manner in which we celebrate Christmas."

"The point is"—Belli, humorless as usual, couldn't be sidetracked—"it's time to prepare the Christmas cards which this office sends every year. Radio and TV reminders have already begun urging us to mail them early."

"Maybe we shouldn't send any this year." Righi tapped a note which lay on the top of the Observer's in-box: it was a request from Maguire asking each member of the rectory household to help save money . . . the parish budget was in a severe strain until after Christmas. "Of course," he added, "strictly speaking this doesn't apply to us, but we are supposed to set a good example."

Belli's face flushed as if he had been slapped. "But there's no way of getting out of it. There are over one hundred and thirty permanent missions—one thirty-six, to be exact. We have been sending each of them a card for years. They'll be *expecting* it. Except Albania." The office assistant hesitated. "It happened a few years ago." There was a blend of embarrassment and outrage in his voice. "They sent our card back. But the others? We *have* to remember, um, the more important members of the Secretariat, and those media people, plus a lot of people somehow connected with the United Nations."

Father Belli went to one of the files, his quick movements implying that action might be more persuasive than words. "I'll show you last year's list; that'll give you a better idea." He spoke into the drawer of ragged file folders while he searched. "Usually we buy five hundred—but according to your wishes, we could buy more."

Righi pointed to Maguire's note once again.

"Oh, I know. But you'll probably receive many more than five hundred. And there's always the need at the last minute to cover for all the names you've, I mean *we've* forgotten."

"Would you show me some samples from previous years?"

Belli pulled a handful at random from several bulging folders and gave them to Righi. Some were very elaborate. A few were as big as a sheet of typewriter paper and decorated with ribbons—the nation's colors, Righi presumed.

"Those, as you can see," Belli added, "are from the, uh, poorer countries." The assistant opened one to indicate the inscription. "The printer does most of the work—just a message and the official's name—though some ambassadors choose to scribble their own name at the bottom."

"Sounds like an assembly line to me."

Belli continued, seemingly determined to make a particular point of his own. "Missions which have a *secretary*"—the pause meant *unlike ours*—"don't waste as much time; they don't have to drop more important matters to see that envelopes are addressed."

"Then let's not send *any*."

Belli's glasses had slipped down on the bridge of his nose and he looked over them at Righi; the Observer laughed and relented.

"Okay, okay. It's Christmas." Righi held one of the samples for the assistant to see. "So what should our message be on the cards? Most of these say simply 'Season's Greetings.' What kind of a statement is that coming from a representative of the Holy See?"

"Well," Belli pressed on, "it means 'greetings appropriate to the occasion' and the occasion is Christmas."

"Sounds like an insult to the birthday of the Lord, if you ask me."

Belli pushed his glasses further up the bridge of his nose.

"Remember, these cards go to Jews, Moslems, pagans, nature-worshippers, Shintoists, what-have-you. The Lord have mercy—even to atheists. We use such a phrase to avoid embarrassment."

Suddenly Righi got an idea and interrupted Belli. "Why not send the amount we would normally spend—the money we would have used to buy, print, and post these cards—why not send it to some charitable institution, preferably one in a Third World country?"

Belli shook his head, causing the glasses to creep downward once more. "Other missions wouldn't play the game, Monsignor."

"The game?"

"I mean," Belli reasoned slowly, "other missions would not go along. Even if one were to take it up, there would still be the need to do something so as not to appear tight with one's money: they would have to write the rest of us and say 'I'm giving my Christmas card money to the poor'—which would cost as much to send as if they had just gone ahead and mailed cards."

Righi shrugged, "Seven hundred, then."

Belli smiled, apparently satisfied and not hesitant to show it. "And what shall we have imprinted?"

"Say 'Christ is with us' and I'll pen my own signature."

"Send that to Israel? To Bar-Hillel?"

Righi leaned back in his chair and stretched as he answered, "Why not? Christ's coming is a historical truth and a divine reality. Bar-Hillel will subscribe to the first . . . we'll hold to the second."

For a number of days, Potocki had felt restless.

Throughout the Thanksgiving holidays he had taken long walks, so immersed in his fantasies about investigating that several times he came close to being run over by cars turning the corner.

When he was on duty and the secretary had gone home, Potocki plunged into the reading of a stack of adventure, spy, and political-intrigue novels. It did not occur to him that these might be the worst possible medicine for his nerves.

And lately he was becoming increasingly irritated that neither he nor Maguire could catch Righi at fault. Consistently the Observer said mass well, read his breviary, helped with confessions.

Righi even appeared to be doing his work at the UN in an exemplary manner. In fact a few of the priests at the rectory admitted that during his last few months with them, they had learned more about the UN than in the years that his predecessor, Faddini, had lived among them. Potocki was becoming frustrated.

Then Maguire infuriated him by asking Righi to give a lecture on the UN in the parish hall. When Potocki had confronted the pastor, Maguire had angered Potocki even more by responding, "The Observer's lecture will, for now, only contribute to the prestige of Nativity. And he may draw a few extra people to bolster the offering—provided the people whom he attracts also come back on a Sunday."

Meanwhile, McNeil had made no further contact with the priest.

Potocki was growing more anxious and depressed. Then on Wednesday, the parish secretary called to him as he was prying off galoshes that had only moderately protected his feet from the slush along his walk route.

"Phone message, Father. A Joe O'Brien."

Immediately Potocki's heart began pounding. "Did he leave any message—beyond his name, I mean?"

The secretary read the note aloud with no more expression than if she'd been reading a laundry list: "He said to tell you that Mildred had her baby and that he—the father, not the baby—would call again later."

Potocki felt as though he had been waiting for years just to be able to perform with aplomb in such a moment. "So the baby was a boy then?"

"He said 'baby,' that's all." She hunched back over her typewriter and peered at the place on the paper where the imprinting hammers had last struck. She gave all appearances of having fallen into a state not unlike temporary deafness, blindness, and muteness. Obviously she had work to do.

Just then Monsignor Maguire walked in. "Was the walk that good? You seem all excited, Stan."

Potocki seemed to bounce, his left foot still half wrapped in a galosh. "Oh, it's wonderful: Mildred has had a baby."

"Mildred?"

"Joe O'Brien's Mildred."

Maguire tried to match Stan's enthusiasm. "Alleluia." He

added, "Then I guess this means you'll be going to the baptism, right?"

"You bet. Joe has promised to call me back later."

When McNeil called and spoke with Potocki, it was apparent to the FBI agent that the priest was bordering on becoming too involved for him to be useful. But James McNeil made no hasty decisions. He needed this fellow. To his surprise, enough evidence had surfaced for the Bureau to require surveillance by an insider.

After McNeil established when and where he and Potocki would meet, the agent reviewed what he had learned from preliminary investigations since he had launched the first low-keyed inquiries just before the holiday weekend.

The SID (Servizio Informazioni Difesa), as he had expected, sent an immediate and unqualified response: this Monsignor Righi was without blemish. For good measure, they sent along biographical notes that told the FBI everything about the Monsignor that they already knew.

From the doorman at the Israeli women's apartment and also from sources at the Israeli mission, McNeil had mildly interesting information about the priest's activities with Shulamith Arieh. Apparently Righi had been making a number of visits—but nothing indicated that the relationship was anything more than catechism lessons. The Israeli information people had nothing else—at least, McNeil realized, nothing else that they would share. He had his doubts about the Israelis—just like the doubts he had about a Vatican diplomat giving lessons to women whose names appeared on the FBI suspicion lists.

As yet, however, no indications were leading to evidence of sexual involvement. Not yet, McNeil thought.

But then there had been earlier investigations involving Ahmed Badr and his various disguises, but none of these had produced any evidence either. This time McNeil had been informed that Badr was away making a routine visit to the Ministry of Foreign Affairs within his own country.

Information about the East Seventieth Street (potential) "love nest," he admitted to himself, had temporarily come to a standstill.

As a result, McNeil would not have phoned Potocki. But a report from the Royal Canadian Mounted Police had arrived this morning. It was vague, but intriguing to McNeil nonetheless.

There might be some link to Potocki's suspicions about having seen Righi before . . . elsewhere. Potocki had mentioned the period of 1969–70 and Manitoba.

According to the Mounties' report, something unusual had taken place at Winnipeg in 1970. Several Soviet agents had infiltrated the Ukrainain community—information confirmed that —but the extent of it or the reasons behind this activity had not as yet been determined. The Canadians assured McNeil that the investigation was not over.

As for the photograph of Monsignor Righi that McNeil had sent them, the Mounties had no immediate information. They had circulated it among their sources, but no one seemed to recognize the man. However, a key source for them, one Lev Khokhlov, had just died. An autopsy indicated that he had not succumbed to a heart attack, as the man's family believed, but that Khokhlov had fallen victim to prussic acid.

The Mounties indicated that their next steps would be in the direction of ascertaining whether or not this death had been part of what the Russians called a *mokryye,* or a "wet affair"; in other words the elimination of a dangerous enemy.

The Canadians promised an update as soon as more information was available.

Late that afternoon, James McNeil arranged to sleep in his office.

He tied up both phone lines, dialing one number from the other. According to the phone circuits, the Bureau office was talking to itself. Then McNeil stretched out across the padded throw rug that his wife had given him for his office.

McNeil had been asleep about thirty-five minutes when a loud knock at his door caused him to kick violently, driving one of his shins into the metal leg of his desk.

He groaned, swore, and then crawled to his feet from the sleeping position that had made him look very much like a corpse moments before to the young agent who had just started work, shuttling top-secret reports.

"What's th' matter?" McNeil yelled. "Haven't you even seen an agent sleep on the job?"

"Sorry, sir. Uh, no sir. Uh, just thought you might want to see this info from the Gárda Síochána." He handed McNeil two sealed reports from the Irish agency, then spun around in a military turn and rushed out the doorway.

The first report, McNeil saw at once, was mostly a duplication of information that his office had already obtained. He had run a background search on everyone at the rectory once Potocki's queries led him to believe that at least a low-keyed inquiry was in order. This Mrs. O'Rourke had been born in Brooklyn in 1913 . . . maiden name: Corrigan . . . was baptized at St. Anne's . . . had moved back to Ireland with her parents when she was five . . . had married Patrick O'Rourke in 1935 . . . was left a childless widow in 1960 . . . thereupon had returned to the States . . . had worked in two convents . . . in 1969 had been taken on by Monsignor Maguire who had been furnished with excellent references . . .

The second paper was in fact a confidential bulletin: *Please send recent photo of Veronica O'Rourke.*

McNeil was surprised.

He read the accompanying memorandum with greater interest:

The subject did obtain her passport from the American Consulate in June 1960 and her indicated destination was the United States. However, in the month of July, 1960, records confirm that Veronica O'Rourke had a heart attack and died without undertaking the projected voyage.

Further, a cousin of Mrs. O'Rourke—a Miss Dorothy Corrigan of Tralee—took one of our men to a Dublin cemetery, the Mount Jerome Cemetery, where they located a tombstone with the following inscription: "Veronica O'Rourke, born Corrigan, 1913–1960. *Requiescat in Pace.*"

This Miss Corrigan says that she does remember something about her cousin's plans to return to the States, but that she also attended Mrs. O'Rourke's funeral, remaining afterward in Dublin for a few days to help dispose of her cousin's possessions.

Miss Corrigan did not remember whether or not a passport was among Mrs. O'Rourke's effects—but the cousin does remember thinking, at the time, that it was odd that no personal papers were among the belongings. . . .

McNeil fixed himself a cup of hot coffee from the last ounces in the office pot. It tasted bitter, but he resisted the temptation to soften it with some stale coffee lightener he kept on the window ledge.

He cleared his phone lines and directed several new agents to join the investigation. He also obtained the services of an excellent and speedy photographer, who promised he would get a clear picture of Mrs. O'Rourke.

Then McNeil tied up the phone lines again.

He could not help but feel amused that Stan Potocki had led them into all of this by an incredibly flimsy intuition based upon how a priest's hands should look. Amazing.

Probably, McNeil considered, nothing would come of all this except that another illegal alien might be sent home or this eccentric priest might be reprimanded. Still. McNeil knew that small hunches were the stuff of which major discoveries were born.

He stretched out across his padded throw rug and closed his eyes.

All this work had made him sleepy.

[XX]

STAN POTOCKI WAS RELIEVED TO LEARN THAT HE COULD WEAR his clericals for the appointment with McNeil at Jacobi Hospital in the Bronx. He felt more confident when people could see him dressed as a priest and treat him accordingly. Also, he had decided that being dressed like this served him well in his new activities—it was a good cover while he worked for the FBI. He enjoyed that feeling.

Who would suspect a priest? he mused, oblivious to the irony in that question with regard to his own stalking of Monsignor Righi.

In the foyer of the rectory, the secretary handed him an envelope. "It's probably a Christmas card from the thoughtful Monsignor at the UN." There was a certain dreaminess in her expression. "He sent all of us one."

Potocki opened it as he rushed toward the subway. It was from Righi and the card was handsome. It appeared to be a personal one, rather than one of those that Potocki had overheard some of the other priests joking about—the cards that Father Belli used to select, mail, and talk about, and that Faddini, apparently, never even took time to look at, even though they bore his name.

Righi had penned a personal note to Potocki: "On this blessed day, I'm praying that your nostalgia won't be too heavy."

The Polish priest groaned.

McNeil was waiting at the entrance to Jacobi Hospital.

Together they walked to the second floor where they chatted for a quarter of an hour with a cousin of the agent; the woman had given birth to a boy just a few days before.

Afterward they went downstairs and out to the parking lot. In the agent's car, they rode north. Potocki noticed that he occasionally glanced back to see if they were being followed.

After a minute or two, McNeil spoke up: "Good for you, Father. You did a good job." Potocki felt uncertain about whether the agent meant the priest's actions back at the hospital or—more important in Potocki's mind—his instigation of an inquiry into the mysteries surrounding Monsignor Righi. He decided to presume the latter.

"So the fellow is a spy then, right?"

"No jumping to conclusions, Father. Investigating is a slow and thorough business." There was no humor in the agent's manner, Potocki noticed. "If you move too fast, you're almost sure to go wrong. Especially if the suspect knows what he's doing." McNeil turned off on a side street and drove slowly, never taking his eyes off the road. "So far, all we know is: A, your man is a glib talker . . . and B, he may be an impostor, though we don't know why. And why is important, Father." At the corner, McNeil turned and drove just as slowly as before, this time hugging the curb, as if the two were looking for building numbers. "So. We're following him and we're checking things out—but we also need help from you and your good Monsignor Maguire. What do you say?"

Potocki responded with the kind of earnestness that only priests and insurance representatives seem capable of using: "Joe, believe me, both of us are ready to go all out for you. At a moment's notice. Why just last night Monsignor Maguire and I were talking about a spy story I read, in which—"

"Whoa there, Father. We're dealing with facts. They can be stranger and more absurd than fiction—and also more dangerous. Remember that. Spy stories may amuse you, arouse your curiosity, help you kill time. You may enjoy the author's imagination as he takes you from Oslo to Sydney overnight, as you go on a safari today and an expedition to the summit of Mount Everest tomorrow. You may be intrigued by an Asian, an African, a Swede, or an Eskimo, sexy women and shrewd men, but real counterespionage is work. It's work done in silence and solitude; often it's frustrating and always it calls for infinite patience. . . ."

Potocki listened. He could sense that the agent was not only instructing, but also unburdening. The priest couldn't determine if McNeil was telling him all this in a precautionary way . . . or if the agent was actually attempting to strengthen some sort of bond between them. Potocki quickly chose to believe the latter—particularly since the agent turned the subject toward more private matters.

"My wife could tell you. . . . During the day, she has no idea what I'm up to; but at night, she sees the effects. Sometimes, it just doesn't pay. I've seen good men wrecked. But the main thing, Father, is collecting the maximum amount of information—even if the length of the process may make it all seem as if we're stalled somewhere along the line. Understand?" But McNeil did not wait for the priest's answer. "Every detail—no matter how petty—every detail may be important; conclusive clues often come from the most irrelevant trifles. And, Father: it's work which doesn't call for a 'hero' . . . no fiction. Instead, we need long-distance walkers, persistent searchers. Cars racing in hot pursuit are not our style—do you follow me?"

Potocki said "I do" as if the priest were marrying the Bureau.

"Great." McNeil snapped, "Here's how things stand. First of all, I'm afraid that you can't be told everything. The less you know the safer you are. But you understand?"

Potocki experienced an immense and immediate sense of disappointment. No, he did not understand. But he nodded in compliance.

"Good—because there's already been one murder . . . in Canada."

"A murder? Good God, whose?"

"Remember, Father: the FBI asks the questions, not you."

"Sorry." Potocki felt like a reprimanded teenager.

The agent's smile toward him was indulgent, making him feel even worse. "A man was killed because he may have known something and that something just might, somehow, connect with our Righi. But I caution you. This is all still in the investigation stage; the Canadians are doing their part and we're doing ours. That's where you come in."

Although Potocki felt distrusted, he tried to appear submissive. He tried to show McNeil that he appreciated the assignment that the agent was explaining: how Potocki was to watch Righi while the Observer was in the rectory . . . how Potocki was not to follow the Observer once Righi left the rectory. . . . To the Polish priest, all this inside work sounded dismal and not at all what he had been expecting.

Apparently McNeil realized that the priest was becoming disheartened, because the agent added: "However, the case is not without its elements of real interest. There are at least three women involved. . . ."

"Christ! Murder and sex?"

McNeil burst into loud belly laughs. He had to pull the car to the curb until he could recover.

"Murder: a possibility. But sex: no."

Potocki shook his head and felt a blush come across his face. "In the world of spies, Joe, are morals always so free and easy?"

"Too many novels again, Father." McNeil was dabbing at tears in his eyes, using a crumpled handkerchief folded more like a tossed sheet of paper than a cloth for a man's pocket.

"Uh, excuse me, Joe, but I really don't understand—"

"Sorry, Father. I forgot." McNeil appeared to sober somewhat as he very obviously struggled to explain. "A spy's life is basically austere. Appearances to the contrary, a successful spy's life is usually based upon chastity, poverty, and obedience . . . with all due respect to you and your brethren. And spies live this way not because they are so very moral, but because they know that one false step can be their last."

Potocki only half listened as James McNeil continued, explaining how spies in general do not learn state secrets from pillow talk. The priest felt as though McNeil was too deliberately destroying Potocki's myths about espionage. So Stan Potocki resisted: it was too soon in this priest's new role for the glamour to be wiped away.

"Oh, these female spies may be sexy and they may use their natural gifts to influence, to manipulate male spies—but usually that's as far as they go. Even if the women wear the latest clothes to make it easier for them to feed someone poison or steal secrets— these women sleep alone. So do most of the men. Their work demands that they drain their minds and that they avoid sentimental attachments. Sexual contact, even if only halfway pursued, is risky; it threatens embarrassing complications and the real possibility of blackmail."

"But Mata Hari—" Potocki interrupted.

"Nope. 'Fatally beautiful' women such as Mata Hari have long since left the business of spying. Today you can only find them in novels. . . . Shocking, Father, isn't it?"

More like dreary, the priest thought—but his response to the agent was, "Instructive, most instructive."

Thereupon McNeil proceeded to discuss Monsignor Righi and the few facts that he seemed willing, at present, to share with the priest. "He meets at least one, and maybe two, very sexy girls. Indications are, all they do is talk—probably trying to win over one another's minds. In any case, Father, we've got that situation covered —meaning that it's out of bounds for your surveillance. But as I said, there is a third woman and she's the one we want you to watch."

Potocki felt the sudden rush of excitement. He was getting an assignment and a woman was involved. This was real espionage.

"I'm speaking of Mrs. O'Rourke, your housekeeper."

The priest stared at the agent as if McNeil had belched.

"Believe me, Father, even if Mrs. O'Rourke isn't sexy, there are reasons to suspect that she has assumed the identity of a dead Irishwoman and that possibly she may be dangerous. What we need from you are details which may help us to determine why she came to the rectory and what, other than keeping house, she may be doing."

"If she's done something illegal—assuming an identity is illegal, isn't it?—then why don't you simply arrest her? Why have me spend my time watching her?" Potocki's questions begged more for an exit than for answers.

"Why put her behind bars, Father, when we can let her go her own way and put us onto the trail of others—higher-ups? And after all, our business is to investigate. You must not forget that."

Potocki, however, had seized on one aspect of McNeil's response. "I see: we want to land an entire network." The concept pleased him, gave him a renewed sense of worth and challenge. His chest rose as he sighed.

"That's it, Father, stay what you are—a good priest and a good American, even a good reader of detective stories." Apparently McNeil was misinterpreting Potocki's revived sense of interest. "You and Monsignor Maguire have two subjects to keep an eye on. Be alert—but don't arouse any suspicions. Overlook any instances with Righi or O'Rourke in which they rub you the wrong way." Then, driving with his left hand, McNeil used his right to finger a vest pocket and retrieve a piece of paper that contained nothing more than a phone number. "Anytime you have something to tell me, use this number." Potocki took the paper and put it into his trouser pocket, rather than in his jacket. He decided it would be safer.

"And don't ever call me from the rectory," the agent added. "Always use a booth—but not that one near the rectory, not the one at Second and Forty-seventh. Just find a booth and ask for me by my real name; identify yourself as PETE. If I'm not there, never leave a message—just say that you'll call again later. And never mention Righi or O'Rourke or even Maguire by name. From now on, just call Righi MACARONI and O'Rourke LETTUCE."

"MACARONI and LETTUCE," the priest repeated with obvious excitement.

"Now, is there anything that you need, like money for taxis or for telephone calls?"

"Oh, no," Potocki answered quickly and with dignity. "Monsignor Maguire and I are proud to take care of it."

"Fine. Then if I want to see you, I'll let you know. Otherwise, work only within the rectory and no heroics. Agreed? And be patient. Even if these people are who we suspect them to be, it will take time to prove their true identities and their reasons for being there."

Then McNeil made a sharp turn and raced his car across three lanes to reach the far corner. Potocki grabbed at the arm rest. "Just remembered a subway station," McNeil explained. "The express will take you back to Grand Central, no problem."

As the priest got out of the car, McNeil called after him, "And thanks for all you're doing. We really appreciate it."

Once again Potocki's words were jam-packed with earnestness. "I am an American and espionage is a crime. God bless us all."

[XXI]

MARFYONA ALEXANDROVNA POPOVA WAS IN HER LATE FIF-ties. Her files in Moscow Operations Center indicated that she was born in 1912 in Leningrad; hers had been a railway laborer's family that had known the city as St. Petersburg.

According to one interview, she had no memory of the time under czarist rule because when the Revolution broke out, she had been only a child.

Her record confirmed that Marfyona had joined the Party at what must have been the earliest possible age; she was reported to have been given work with the NKVD, but in a minor capacity. A couple of vague evaluations from her superiors indicated that her gifts might recommend her for intelligence activities, since she had displayed special abilities with languages and mimickry.

Educational records noted that Marfyona had studied at a spe-cial school for foreign agents, where she specialized in English and German. Her final examination reports concurred that she showed promise and, above all, the guarantee of absolute loyalty.

Her mission summaries began with the year 1938.

Using the name Margaret Doherty, Marfyona had been sent to England. There she obtained a cleaning woman's job, the kind usu-ally available to the Irish—but this position was in a historic build-ing, the Admiralty.

A few years later, she received excellent recommendations from the Admiralty, enabling her to obtain the same position, cleaning woman, back in the German Embassy in her "native" Dublin, Ireland.

Marfyona remained in the German Embassy during World War II and was instrumental in obtaining much useful information. Her list of key transmissions included references to data that could have been most beneficial to the Allies—had the Kremlin passed it along. They did not.

After the war she continued working in Ireland. Her positions were in more than one embassy and in several convents as well. From each institution, she received good evaluations and excellent references—and the KGB always managed to get copies.

Her travel record showed that between these positions she made frequent visits to England, where, she explained, she spent time with a cousin.

An unusually large number of memoranda appeared in her files prior to Marfyona being transferred, in 1960, from Ireland to the United States.

A faithful Catholic could be useful in America—provided the Soviets could get her there under the cover of the proper papers. Soviet agents in Dublin found the emigration application of one Veronica O'Rourke to be most fortuitous. They were able to steal her approved passport and also to make certain that Mrs. O'Rourke died of a heart attack at just the right time. Thus Dublin's Veronica O'Rourke took off for the next world and Marfyona was allowed to leave Ireland for the New World. No questions asked.

By the time Mrs. O'Rourke's cousin Dorothy Corrigan had arrived for the funeral and had had a chance to sort through the deceased woman's belongings, Marfyona was already adapting to her new name and role. The KGB file recorded almost all these details.

However, Soviet agents failed to note that several years later, Dorothy Corrigan decided to raise a stone over the grave of her departed cousin: it was an afterthought that occurred without fanfare after Soviet agents in Ireland had satisfied themselves that Marfyona Alexandrovna Popova had successfully assumed the safe identity of an Irishwoman whom no one, supposedly, cared to remember.

Nine years after Veronica O'Rourke's arrival in the United

States, Monsignor Maguire hired her to work as housekeeper at the Church of the Nativity. Later, after she had informed Moscow that Monsignor Faddini had been promoted and would be leaving his post as Permanent Observer, this housekeeper was given a new code name for a new project.

She became, for purposes of the HOLY SYNOD mission, an active KARENINA for this most delicate of KGB operations.

KARENINA quietly kept house at the Nativity.

Upstairs, escaping the cold night air, Volodya Panin crouched over a shaky portable typewriter that he kept in his private quarters at the rectory.

He was typing a letter to Monsignor Righi's sister.

It would go with the Christmas card that Father Belli had already addressed to Anna Maffei—a card inscribed and signed as if it were no more personal than any of the others being sent from the Observer's office.

"Here, I have a lot to do," Panin typed, then alternated a few details from the UN with personal observations about the weather and New York City. He apologized for not having written more often and promised to do better in the future, though he added as a mild warning in advance, "Politics take up a great deal of my time. Too much so, leaving too little time for my pastoral duties and for personal matters, such as correspondence. Nonetheless, thank God, my health has not suffered. Remember me in your prayers."

Panin did not sign this sheet, but merely slipped it inside the Christmas card and sealed the envelope.

Just then he heard a rapid, nervous knock.

"One moment, please," he called out, not really enthusiastic about seeing any of the priests tonight.

But when he opened his door, no one was there.

He looked in both directions down the hallway. No one.

Quickly he slipped back into his quarters and eased the door shut. Not having to be gracious was certainly fine by him; he had had enough of the priestly life for one day.

Downstairs, alone and bowed over the kitchen table, the housekeeper appeared to be saying her rosary; she clutched a beaded necklace and her manner seemed very devout: an Irishwoman at her vespers.

But Marfyona was using these beads to recount moments in her own life. She was remembering not only those things that might be found in the KGB files, but also much, much more.

She was a woman alone with her memories, a woman in the kitchen at the end of another day.

I'm a good woman, she reflected. Though to others I may appear the kind whom the English call "cabbage and potatoes." Habit has shaped me. Her mind traveled further back: There was a day when these rolls didn't cling to my waist . . . when a cleaning woman's uniform didn't present me to the world as dull, dull. . . .

However, reflection was unusual for Marfyona.

During the course of her nearly sixty years, she had not put much time into thinking about what she had done, or into scanning her own soul. Instead she had worked: a good housekeeper and a good low-level spy who found satisfaction in being useful. She took pride in both roles because she believed that her actions were helping to forward principles to which she was committed.

It was a paradox of the double life that though her years had been spent in lies, intrigue, and dissimulation, she was usually more on the level than many who were reputed to be so. "Some people fool others and themselves," one interview in her files quoted her as having said. "They do the right things for the wrong cause."

Apparently Marfyona had no qualms about doing wrong for what she considered to be right. Had she been a person capable of quoting Lenin, she might have memorized his dictum: There is no morality outside the context of man.

In fact, had Marfyona been the real Mrs. O'Rourke and these evening meditations a true rosary, then she would probably have been the kind of Catholic who if asked would have been willing to spy for the Pope.

It was almost as though the object of her total dedication depended merely upon the accident of her birth. Her life, as a result, appeared to be beyond good and evil. But not beyond jeopardy. Or discovery.

The current investigations were the first such inquiries ever to have been made into Marfyona's activities. Had she known, she would have been deeply worried, not about the danger to herself, but that such circumstances would surely cause trouble for her superiors.

Long ago, Marfyona had learned the rules. She knew that within the context of spy wars, she was a foot soldier. She understood that by definition she was expendable. These matters almost never bothered her; she knew she had been born to serve and she served well.

She also understood that people who create no problems for themselves are the soldiers who are rarely caught. She had endured, hadn't she?

Nonetheless, over the years Marfyona had come to realize that the rules were made to benefit the top agents—the intellectuals and the brilliant fellows—the ones most guilty of endangering the careers and lives of the soldiers under them. The silent and the faithful.

Marfyona had had to concede that the brilliant spies were necessary, that their successes justified their excesses. But she had also witnessed how short those top spies' careers could be. In contrast to her own.

Indeed, she had quietly witnessed many of their defections.

As a result, her only real fear was that one day, one of these brilliant spies positioned above her might turn mercenary, might begin playing the double game and sell himself to the highest bidder.

Such events, Marfyona understood, would topple an entire network, and since she was neither an intellectual nor a mercenary, she knew all too well what her fate, in such a circumstance, would be: like a soldier who dies in battle because a commanding officer errs, she would fall victim. . . .

The moment she heard footsteps approaching the kitchen, the housekeeper spoke in a quiet, meditative voice: ". . . and at the hour of our death. Amen."

"Amen," echoed the priest who had apparently attempted to tiptoe into the kitchen, but in vain.

When she saw that it was Father Potocki, she stuffed the rosary into her apron pocket and grumbled, "What is it, Father?"

"I seem to have interrupted. I'm sorry. This just doesn't seem to be my night. . . ."

The housekeeper's voice bore a keenly Irish accent. "You didn't interrupt, my boy. I was on the last bead."

"Good."

Potocki's manner was like that of a boy running into the kitchen after school, the housekeeper observed, a boy caught in the pursuit of a snack or a drink.

"Then may I have a cup of tea—if it's no inconvenience?"

The Irishwoman in her manner was pronounced as she got to her feet and started toward the stove. "Ah, but it's been a freezing cold day. Just what you'll be needing, this cup o' tea."

Minutes later, as Potocki sipped his freshly brewed tea, he stared at the woman as if to track her every move in the kitchen; once she noticed him looking intently at her hands. Soon his presence made her uneasy.

"My boy, shouldn't you be telling Mrs. O'Rourke when something is troubling you?" Her question seemed to startle Potocki.

In response, he shook his head violently, as if to object—but his eyes and manner betrayed him.

"Then something's wrong upstairs?" Her question in all honesty was innocent, earnest. Nonetheless, it sent Potocki into a stammer. Hot tea splattered from his cup.

"Uh, I just knocked on the wrong door. That's all. You know, it could happen to anyone."

But she didn't know.

All she could see was that this Polish priest had problems. He was continually awkward and disruptive. And just now, his eyes had been those she had seen in many a lean overcurious fellow—the kind searching for something. What, she didn't know.

And tonight she didn't care.

She only wished that whatever it was, he would simmer upon it somewhere else.

PART FOUR

MONSIGNOR MAGUIRE LISTENED CAREFULLY TO THE LECTURE that he had invited the Holy See's Observer to give. The pastor had been certain that such an event would either dispel suspicions about Righi or expose some more tangible means of dealing with the matter. The truth was Maguire had grown increasingly impatient with the prospect of relying exclusively upon what his assistant might discover. He wanted the matter resolved and he wanted the Nativity rectory peaceful again.

At least, Maquire thought as he looked about the auditorium, the event has attracted a large crowd. Even Mrs. O'Rourke had asked to attend. There she sat, wearing her best drab suit and an old winter hat. The sight saddened him: this faithful and irreplaceable housekeeper whom Potocki said the FBI suspected of being an illegal alien . . . or possibly something worse.

If he could have his way, Maguire would stop all this snooping today.

But the pastor did not have his way in this matter. As evidence of that fact, he glanced toward his "niece" once again. She smiled over her shoulder, then faced forward, allowing her dark hair to fall back in a rush of curls that framed her attractive face in the fashion popular with students this season.

She was Evangeline Maguire—the "niece" whom the FBI had sent to audit Monsignor Righi's speech. The pastor silently detested his having had to lie when he introduced her, telling about her studies in political science at Columbia, conjuring up vague facts about old family ties and trips years ago, when he and her parents had enjoyed Evangeline as a small child. . . .

Therefore once Righi's speech began, Maguire felt a deep sense of relief. Listening, he could be himself once again.

And thus far, the lecture was proving Righi to be virtually beyond reproach. Maguire was pleased to find the Permanent Observer abandoning his otherwise ironical attitude toward the United

Nations. In fact as Righi spoke about the Holy See and the Pope, as he detailed the benefits that the world could expect from those who glory in their faith, Maguire found the speaker positively moving.

At one point the pastor could not resist catching Potocki's glance, whereupon Maguire raised his eyebrows as if to say, See, Stan, you may be barking up the wrong tree. Potocki peevishly looked away. Maguire didn't care. This speech revealed to him something hidden and quite good within Righi. He only hoped that this benevolence was lasting and real.

"Poor countries," Righi continued, adjusting his script on the lectern so that he could look directly at more of his listeners, "are defined by their inabilities to build roads, schools, hospitals, housing. We define such poverty by how many of these essentials a particular country may lack.

"So, you may ask, why can't they build these things? The reason: they are too poor to afford even that which we consider as minimum. By definition, many of these countries would have to advance merely to reach 'poor country' status. Thus, they are caught in a vicious circle.

"And how may such a circle be broken? I suggest that the only workable way today is to put the principle of human solidarity into action. For Christians, this also means putting religious duty into action.

"But how much duty and how much action? The answer, friends, is that need becomes the only priority; need will determine the extent of our action and duty.

"And need—in times such as these—is best satisfied by the means which human solidarity can provide. Solidarity does not distinguish between friends and enemies, between whites and blacks. It allows no demarcation between Communists and proponents of Western democracy. Of course, since it does not, solidarity is difficult for governments to swallow.

"Nonetheless, fellow Christians, solidarity is the only approach which, I contend, the Church can embrace, because it's the only one stemming from the Gospel itself."

Maguire caught himself nodding in agreement with Righi's stress upon solidarity—at least in principle. But something occurred to him on a more practical level: Why should we buy Cuban sugar to prevent Cubans from starving, after those same Cubans allowed Russian missiles to be installed in direct threat to us? Maguire also noticed that his "niece" seemed to have mixed feelings about the Permanent Observer's ideas: she was rapidly taking notes. Moments later, when Righi asked for questions, Evangeline Maguire was the first to stand and call out.

"You have a question, young lady?" Monsignor Righi was polite and seemed pleasantly attracted to the woman's good looks, to her apparent sense of self-confidence. Immediate attention focused upon her from the audience as well.

"Yes, Monsignor." Maguire's "niece" paused, appearing to organize her thoughts in a more effective manner, then she continued: "We must assume that you know of Lenin's theories and that he once stated that wars are either reactionary or revolutionary. May we assume these things?"

The speaker's gestures were noncommittal.

She persisted. "But one might argue: Communists define wars according to who wages them. For example, war—to them—is part of the proletariat's struggle. If the proletariat is in power, then war is a legitimate means for achieving worldwide revolution." She paused again, this time directing her statement toward another segment of the audience. "On the other hand, if war is an attempt to overthrow a particular government which the proletariat does not control, then every means including war is justified by the Russians. It's as though the Russians still go by the rule even though they seem, at least for now, to have given up on the idea of exporting revolution." Using both hands in a gesture implying intense conviction, Evangeline Maguire returned her full attentions to the speaker. "To the point. It seems as though the Russians have no trouble criticizing everyone else: anything which opposes their ideology, they consider to be a 'war of aggression'; anything which fits, however, they call a 'war of liberation.' More specifically"—her voice sounded a challenge—"Russians consider spies as heroes . . . at least spies caught operating on the territory of the United States and its friends. However, American spies caught in Russian or Warsaw Pact territories are said to have 'sold their souls to imperialism.' What is your opinion, Monsignor, on the larger issues I've touched upon . . . as well as upon this last example?"

Maguire did not understand everything that his "niece" had

said, but he understood a great deal about her manner. While her harangue seemed to discomfort many members of the audience, the pastor was pleased that not a trace of vulgarity could be observed; to the contrary, she appeared intelligent and, he would like to believe, well-intentioned.

She had also put Righi on the spot.

Maguire noted that Mrs. O'Rourke seemed particularly offended by Evangeline's questions, as if the housekeeper believed the young woman to be unfairly intent upon provoking Monsignor Righi.

The speaker, however, appeared unperturbed. His answer sounded direct and tough-minded to Maguire. "Here, young lady, we concern ourselves with the world according to the United Nations. We have no intentions of branching out into definitions of armed interventions—whether they be by Monroe, Lenin, Mao Tse-tung, Kennedy, or Fidel Castro. Please remember: the United Nations' charter forbids not only the use of arms to settle international disputes, but also the threat to such recourse." Righi's expression became even more uncompromising, a face bordering on impatience.

"Admittedly," he continued, "the UN lacks a clear definition of aggression." As Righi proceeded—explaining how the UN coped with the ongoing accusations of both the United States and the Soviet Union against one another—Maguire seemed a deeper caution in Righi than heretofore the parish priest could recall. "Both nations speak of spy rings, intelligence services, and covert operations. But, in my opinion, what is needed is a definition of aggression—one which covers legal, technical, and political concerns. Today no such measure exists. However, if one were established and universally accepted, then such actions could be judged by a measuring stick, so to speak; it could enable the United Nations to deal effectively with such aggression, rather than *post factum* judging such acts on the basis of their consequences."

When it became apparent that Righi had said all he intended to —avoiding a direct answer to Evangeline Maguire's question about spies—an elderly man stood and from his place on the pew beside her, raised an additional question for the speaker. "I'm not satisfied with the answer you have given this young lady. Is the United Nations a den of spies who operate, of course, to the detriment of the United States?"

All attention focused awkwardly upon Monsignor Righi; Maguire sensed a definite tension spreading through the audience.

The Observer took several moments before answering. It seemed to Maguire that Righi was not hesitant, however; it was as though the speaker was bolstering up a stronger sense of resolve. "You, my dear sir, are taking up cudgels against something which doesn't exist. All that really exists are the countries which comprise the United Nations—the UN itself is no more than the sum of its member states' political aims, which seldom add up to a total. . . ."

Maguire became more deeply disturbed as Righi continued; he felt angered by the interrogators' tones and also by the Observer's burdensomely political responses. Wasn't this diplomat also a priest? Thus, Maguire concentrated upon formulating a question that, he hoped, might allow this lecture to end on an edifying note befitting Nativity.

". . . So it may be that third-class spies roam the UN corridors or waste everyone's time as they eavesdrop upon telephone conversations. But I assure you: spies are more an obsession than a reality. If there are spies, I suggest that you look for them in Washington or in Moscow—instead of two hundred yards from the serenity of the Church of the Nativity."

Then the Permanent Observer said something that made Potocki, Evangeline Maguire, even the housekeeper perk up; Monsignor Maguire could not help but notice.

"It's like this: if we in the Vatican had secrets, we'd have a counterespionage service. But as everyone knows, our only secrets are the appointments of bishops. . . ."

At this, most members of the audience laughed.

But, Maguire observed, not Potocki or Ms. Maguire or Mrs. O'Rourke. The situation was sensitive and the pastor decided to take action. He stood to ask his question.

"Monsignor Righi, I speak for all of us at the Church of the Nativity when I say how grateful we are to have you speak to us, as well as reside among us. But one more question, if you will: Why is the Holy See represented at the United Nations?"

Righi used his reply as a concluding statement for the session:

"Thank you, Monsignor, your question is really at the heart of everything I have tried to say this evening. That is, the Holy See's presence at the UN is in keeping with its spiritual mission of the defense of peace. We remain neutral so that we may defend peace most effectively. As Clemenceau once said, 'War is much too serious a matter to be entrusted to the military.' Well, ladies and gentlemen, peace is—for the Church—too precious a concern to be entrusted only to politicians."

Afterward a number of people gathered around Monsignor Righi to congratulate him.

Maguire stood to one side and enjoyed watching their reactions.

He also noticed his "niece" quickly leave through a rear door. In addition, the pastor found Mrs. O'Rourke's reactions surprising: she approached him, appearing mildly upset and nervous. When Maguire asked her didn't their Monsignor Righi do a good job, she mumbled a reply and then she too left without speaking to the Observer.

Maguire didn't care. To him, this Italian had vindicated himself and he intended to tell Potocki as much.

Just then, the Polish priest came into view. He was last among the people who waited to approach the speaker. Potocki's eyes darted from side to side. He seemed too eager to stand still.

Maguire decided that he should intervene.

But before the pastor could reach them, Potocki had guided Monsignor Righi away from the few remaining listeners and had apparently asked if the Observer was certain that no spies operated out of the United Nations.

As Maguire walked up to them, Righi was responding to Potocki's probing: ". . . dead sure, Stan; it's just as I have explained. Those that may be there can be no more than underlings—no matter how much talk about spies you may hear. Just imagine: the other day the Ambassador of Israel told me that he was a spy. Now if you were in counterespionage, would you waste time exposing him?"

Both Maguire and (he could tell) Potocki were taken aback. Was this man actually addressing, however obliquely, the issue of their recent suspicions?

Whatever his intentions, Righi left both of them in a further quandary when he left with one final remark: "So, Stan, if you know anyone who has contacts with the FBI, please urge them not to waste time . . . at least not with the Israeli ambassador."

[XXIII]

 APPARENTLY, POTOCKI DID NOT HAVE TIME TO GIVE THE FBI Monsignor Righi's advice—at least not before they visited Shulamith Arieh.

She was in the East Side apartment alone and the night was so bitter that the bus riders at the stop nearest her building were huddled together. From her window she could watch them. The sight made her feel lonelier than ever.

Gila was in Tel Aviv.

And Jehudah Tamir had met Shulamith just two days earlier, conveying the news obtained by the Israeli mission: the FBI was investigating Monsignor Righi and had identified him as being one of her visitors. She was sure to be called upon, and soon.

Tamir's instructions to her had been simple: if the American agents appeared, she was to cooperate with them, but reveal as little as possible of her activities. Tamir's advice had been even simpler: don't fail.

Shulamith sat alone and prepared for the worst. She skimmed over passages in The Jerusalem Bible, but couldn't concentrate, then glanced nervously through several new magazines that had come in last week's mail.

When the doorbell finally rang, she could not prevent herself from jumping to her feet. This encounter would not be easy. She only hoped the FBI knew nothing of her work for its Israeli equivalent: Shin-Beth. And she hoped the agents had senses of humor.

When she opened the apartment door, two men stood there; one of them held out a card identifying them as federal agents. She remembered the name, McNeil. He looked younger than the other.

After she had invited them in and offered them drinks—which, as she expected, they declined—she took the initiative and asked what she might do for them.

James McNeil spoke up. "Miss Arieh, you've been employed at the New York office of El Al since 1969, haven't you?"

She could observe no hint of his personality; his voice and manner and question were strictly business. But his eyes were softer.

"Yes, sir."

"This apartment. It's nice, isn't it, Mike? And roomy. Would you tell us how you can afford it on your salary?"

Okay, so far. She could answer straight—for the most part. "I share it with a friend who works with El Al. Just now she's in Tel Aviv." McNeil looked skeptical and she quickly added, "And I receive some money from my father."

The other agent made notes and McNeil pursued the point. "Then your father is well off?"

"Fairly." She had to go easy. She had no idea how much they knew.

The older agent—Mike—interjected, "Your father—is he a practicing Jew?" He did not look up from his pad.

"I wouldn't say so. More like Jews who go to synagogue only on Yom Kippur."

"And your mother?" From the younger agent. Shulamith recognized the alternating questions as a technique. Her nervousness increased.

"Momma died ten years ago."

McNeil, with the softer eyes, responded, "Sorry."

Then the three of them sat amid a silence that Shulamith hoped wasn't to be the calm before the . . .

"Back to your father," Mike resumed, but McNeil interrupted.

"What do you think your father would say should somebody casually mention to him that his Shula and her roommate were being taught the catechism by a Catholic priest?"

Shulamith was more curt with McNeil than she had intended: "That is my business—not my father's."

"Quite right," the older agent chuckled, then proceeded as if reading his information from a page in his note pad. "Your father passed on to a better life eleven months ago . . . and according to the settlement papers for his estate, he hadn't a red cent to his name."

Their hostess honed her voice so that it was as cool as the frost on her apartment's front windows. "You're well informed."

McNeil didn't lose a beat either. "That's what we're paid for—just the way you are, Miss Arieh."

She said nothing. His soft eyes hardened in their fix upon her.

"Miss Arieh, we know more about you than—I'm sure you'll agree—either of us would like to discuss."

Shulamith yielded nothing, stiffening her neck as if in readiness for anything these agents had to offer. "Very kind, I'm sure. Now, what is it that you want?"

"Tell us about the nature of your relationship with Monsignor Righi." The older agent again sounded as if he were reading.

"That's simple. There is no relationship."

McNeil leaned forward. "Young lady, we're no fools."

"Just as the Nazarene and I are not lovers. Are you satisfied?"

Mike started, "Well, we have reason to believe that that may be true—"

Anger flashed across Shulamith's emerald-green eyes. She could feel it. "You men certainly seem to know a lot—much more than a lady should be subjected to."

McNeil slumped back in the chrome-legged chair and fumbled in his pockets for cigarettes. His voice sounded calculatedly bland. "I remind you that you're a foreigner, that your activities outside the office are known to us, and that—unlike the man you report to, Tamir—you do not have diplomatic immunity." He tapped out a Camel with one hand and slowly lit the bent cigarette before continuing, smoke circling between him and her. "Would you really want to exchange this East Side luxury apartment for a crowded cell in an American prison? Or would you prefer the embarrassment of deportation? No, Miss Arieh, you're an attractive woman, used to the good things of life." He curled his fingers so that the red ember of his cigarette pointed inward, a fraction of an inch from his right palm. "Let me give you some advice: cooperate . . . and you will remain free, uh, to live life as you have been."

While Shulamith had been listening, she had also determined that much of this was standard bluff. However, they seemed to have their facts about Righi; Tamir had confirmed that much. By the time McNeil had tossed the challenge to cooperate toward her, Shulamith had decided upon her limits.

"Okay. I see Monsignor Righi twice a week."

"What does he want—so regularly?"

She resented the older agent's insinuations, but she answered readily nonetheless. "To tell you the truth, I don't know. I am going under the assumption that he's trying to convert me to Catholicism. At least that's all that he has indicated so far."

Mike persisted. "Has he, uh, ever tried to—"

"He doesn't seem to want to touch me—if that's what you mean. He keeps careful distance." And she resented the smirk that widened across the man's face as she added, "All he does is read the Bible aloud and discuss the New Covenant with us—sometimes Gila also takes instruction when she's in town."

"That's all?" McNeil seemed to be trying to interject a less tense approach. Shulamith had to resist a sudden liking for the man. "Just a lot of priest talk?"

She smiled at McNeil, even as she made a point of avoiding the other agent altogether. "Oh, we do talk about other things."

"Such as?"

"Anything, everything. I don't know." She hedged, hoping he would be tolerant.

But the other agent tapped his note pad with the stubby pencil in his left hand, "Specifics, please, Miss Arieh."

"Okay: the Middle East situation . . . uh, what Israelis think about peace with the Arabs . . . the Palestinian movement . . . the refugee problems . . ."

"How nice," McNeil congratulated her in a mildly mocking tone. "But how about other subjects? Has he ever asked you about military matters, about the training of pilots, the location of military airports, minefields in the frontier area, repair facilities for planes and tanks? Maybe about pipelines now under construction? Maybe about the off-limits area of the Negev?"

Shulamith matched McNeil's tone with a mocking laugh that interrupted the agent's seemingly endless catalog. "You men flatter Shula. How could I know answers to such matters, even if I or the Nazarene were foolish enough to discuss them?"

Both agents conceded to her barb with half smiles.

McNeil bent over an ashtray to twist out his cigarette and his partner flipped through his note pad until he came to a question that seemed to satisfy him. "Now for matters more personal than the Negev. What do you want from the Monsignor?"

It was a question that Shulamith had been asking herself for some time now. Her answer was more guarded than any she had thus far given. "I don't know myself . . ."

McNeil appeared unaffected. "Don't waste our time. You've got your reasons . . . and I don't believe that one of them is preparing for conversion." He used his right hand to enumerate, holding his thumb in the air for one. "First, there are hundreds of priests in Manhattan and some of them are conversion specialists. Second, it isn't among the duties of a Vatican representative at the UN to give religious instruction to a pretty kid like you. And third, lady, if you're supposed to be so interested in the catechism, any good Catholic would become suspicious upon learning how often you continue to make love to a lieutenant in our Air Corps—"

She had expected this from the older agent, but McNeil's bluntness shocked and—she realized—even hurt her. "Congratulations, Mr. FBI. You men are thorough and thoroughly disgusting." The thought that Lieutenant John Calvert might be swept into all this had honestly never occurred to her. She felt weak. And sick to her stomach.

Mike forged ahead. "We have evidence that you collect lovers in military aviation—preferably engineers and radar operators."

With all the dignity and bile she could muster, Shulamith spit an answer toward him. "Lovers—how many or how few—are my personal concern."

For the first time in this interrogation, the older agent abandoned his reading-the-note-pad manner and hurled a string of questions and insults at Shulamith: "Come off it, baby. Nobody's interested in your virtue. Fun? You're entitled to that and any privacy about it which a smart girl can manage. But the stuff we're talking about is business—serious business. And you're sharp enough to separate the two. Right? So let's start by labeling Righi as business. Got it? Well one of these days we're going to get this thing straightened out and anything you haven't told us about Righi— well, you can believe that we'll hold every tidbit against you. Have I made myself clear?"

"Crystal clear."

For the next two hours, both James McNeil and Mike Russo bombarded her with questions. Even McNeil pulled a note pad from his coat pocket.

But nothing in Shulamith's answers gave any indication that she knew anything more about Monsignor Righi's identity than what their and Tamir's sources had been able to unearth. In answer to the question, did she believe that Righi was spying on behalf of the Vatican, the young woman repeatedly assured them, "I know nothing more than you seem to know."

Finally the two men relented—but not until Shulamith had given them assurances that she would say nothing of the interrogation to either Tamir or to Righi and also, that she would report to them immediately following any future conversations with the man whom she persisted in calling the Nazarene.

However, Shulamith would make no promises when Russo asked her to break off her relationship with Lieutenant Calvert. The very sound of his name in this context appeared to evoke intense anger from within her.

McNeil motioned Russo to hold off and the two left the apartment abruptly.

By all appearances, neither the Israeli agent nor the FBI agents knew anything more about Monsignor Righi than his Vatican files had produced. The Observer remained a well-documented mystery.

And that fact seemed to be no consolation for Shulamith or McNeil or Mike Russo.

[XXIV]

 VOLODYA PANIN WAS SO SURPRISED BY SHULAMITH'S PHONE call that he left the Permanent Observer's office to be alone.

He walked for blocks along Forty-seventh Street without noticing where he was going or past which buildings he was walking. Then, at the corner of Forty-seventh and Fifth, he turned north. Instinctively he seemed to choose the Scribner's display window as the place to stop and stare and decide how best to react.

"I thought you should know," she had begun, then she proceeded to explain, quite calmly, "that the FBI came to my apartment last night and questioned me about you for over two hours." When Shulamith could not evoke a response, she surprised him further by promising to give Monsignor Righi additional details, provided he would agree to meet her.

He now realized that his blunt reply, "Not yet, Shula," had not only been too hasty, but must also have aroused even greater suspicions in the Israeli woman's mind. The implications sickened Panin. He knew that he had not dissuaded her by his rebounding suggestion, "Why don't you phone me again once you know Gila's holiday schedule? Okay?"

It was simple: he had tripped up.

As a result, there was only one thing for Panin to do: TOLSTOY would have to be told and subsequent instructions would have to be requested.

If Panin did not do this, the entire Righi mission could topple over a brink that until just moments ago had not been a real threat in his mind.

That's when the rush of feelings came.

Panin could almost taste the blend of challenge and danger— that blend which had always urged Nitchevo toward performing his best. He could feel a surge of renewal crystallizing his professional instincts into weapons as real as any soldier's gun and ammunition.

He was caught up in these emotions when he saw the reflection of that face in Scribner's window: the reflection passed by with the speed of a Fifth Avenue holiday pedestrian, but its effect had been both penetrating and haunting.

The face of an old man, crying.

Panin spun around, but could only discern the back view of a man—possibly an Orthodox Jew dressed in an austere black hat and black overcoat—as he disappeared into the floodlike flow of shoppers suddenly released into the crosswalk by the street-light change.

The man left standing in front of Scribner's could only watch the people pour into the midtown diamond district and wonder: why was that face so familiar, so powerful in its effect upon me?

By midnight that evening, Harry Goldstein was still at work in his Long Island garage. Neighbors knew Harry as a radio buff, so it seemed natural to them whenever he spent more time amid his radio gear than he spent in his office.

In the garage, plaques and award certificates lined the only wall not covered with shelves of radio equipment, spare parts, or tools. For the most part, these citations were in appreciation for Harry's radio assistance during international disasters or regional rescue missions. To this Long Island community, Harry Goldstein was known as the man to see for radio info.

But tonight, Harry Goldstein was FALCON. Earlier in the day, TOLSTOY had alerted him concerning the new developments surrounding the HOLY SYNOD mission.

Both of them had agreed that circumstances warranted a radio report to KGB headquarters at Moscow. Such a direct method would surprise headquarters and—the two men hoped—the surprise should cause their superiors to act quickly concerning what might be the imminent collapse of the New York mission.

By midafternoon FALCON had rushed home and had informed Moscow that:

—HOLY SYNOD and KARENINA were reportedly under strict surveillance.

—TOLSTOY and FALCON expected similar treatment at any time.

—The woman in HOLY SYNOD's life had just been taken to the cleaners by the TALL MEN.

—As a result, the woman's JERUSALEM FAMILY was expected to be considering cooperation in the investigation with the TALL MEN.

—Finally, as of the moment, HOLY SYNOD's credentials remained intact.

—Please advise.

FALCON began receiving transmission from Moscow at 12:27 A.M.

He did not recognize the voice, but the operator had identified himself in the prescribed code before repeating headquarters' responses in rapid, clear Russian.

FALCON taped the entire communiqué until he heard the code word for ending. The Russian operator spoke it three times.

FALCON had remained silent throughout; he knew better than to use this same air time for any additional messages to headquarters from TOLSTOY. And the Russian operator had certainly asked for none.

The Long Island radio buff therefore systematically shut down for the night.

Moments later, Harry Goldstein emerged from his garage. He wore a dark blue ski suit—his habitual after-hours attire.

He got into his Volvo and started it, letting the engine warm up; a thick haze of exhaust fumes enshrouded the vehicle. Goldstein timed the wait by his Swiss watch: five minutes exactly. Then he backed the snow-ladened car out of his driveway and drove directly into Manhattan.

Alexander Lewinson was waiting by the door in the Empire Diner.

After Goldstein's passenger joined him, the two appeared to drive aimlessly along the icy streets of midtown. It was nearly three in the morning. They used the time to decode Goldstein's tape of headquarters' response.

Lewinson seemed pleased to learn that Moscow approved his recommendation: the HOLY SYNOD operation was to be frozen.

However, both men were surprised by the additional news that an informer in the Canadian Mounties had confirmed for Moscow that the FBI was investigating possible connections between Righi and the 1969–70 Winnipeg mission that had involved Panin. Moscow Center promised to use every means to hastily double-check the security surrounding Lev Khokhlov's death, but they were eager to gain any information from the United States that might assist them in determining how the FBI got a lead on such a connection.

Lewinson shut off the recorder and stared out into the icy night. "*Oy vey*, but the goose fat has this time spilled out of the pot."

Early the following morning, December 22, a letter and a small present arrived, via diplomatic pouch, at the Soviet mission to the United Nations.

They were addressed to Leo V. Kuznetsov, the man described on the mission's list of personnel as its chauffeur. The return address indicated that Mrs. Kuznetsov had sent them under the auspices of the Minister of Foreign Affairs in Moscow. Merry Christmas.

The letter contained affectionate words from the chauffeur's wife—but the small present had been expected for other purposes.

Kuznetsov immediately conveyed it unopened to the drop-

point for the name encoded into the parcel's wrapping paper design
—a name that Kuznetsov knew only as FALCON.

An hour later, a sleepy FALCON strolled about the great hall of
Grand Central Station as though he was just one more Christmas
shopper waiting for a train home to Connecticut or the Hudson
Valley.

However, FALCON had been guarding trash can number 33 and
at the right moment he headed for it. When he had extracted the
newspaper wrapped around a small gift box, he went up the stair-
way leading to the taxi stand and entered the first available cab. It
exited onto Vanderbilt and drove him to Bloomingdale's.

He found the department store a mob scene peopled by
women in the latest fashions and bewildered businessmen—all vying
for the attention of indifferently efficient clerks. The FALCON was
more than amused.

For the next full hour, he simply rode the escalators, appearing
to be trapped in the throes of thinking up gift purchases. Then he
left the store through its Lexington Avenue doors and took an IRT
train to Wall Street. He had a broker to see and more time to kill
before FALCON could meet TOLSTOY at their usual *shul* appointment.

There FALCON would transfer this gift box to TOLSTOY via the
leather cases in which both Orthodox Jews carried their prayer
shawls.

On the morning of the twenty-third, Mrs. O'Rourke had no idea
that this routine trip to Alexander Lewinson's shop would in fact
be her last visit there.

It was just another necessary stop on her list for the day.

Mr. Lewinson seemed as argumentative as ever and Pat Maloney was once again absorbed in what looked to her to be the
same novel he had been reading during her last visit.

She had at least five more stops to make before getting back to
the rectory and the fruit and vegetable stew she had left Father Potocki to watch.

To her delight, Lewinson had everything ready: several handsomely wrapped rosary gift boxes she had ordered for a few old
ladies who had been particularly kind to the rectory this past year

. . . and the statuette of St. Anthony that she had had to return for repairs.

"Is it noticeable?" she asked, pointing to the package that appeared to contain the statuette.

"Since when does a man need glasses to notice a statuette?" Lewinson snapped.

"You old grouch, I meant the repairs."

Then she saw that the shopkeeper's face drew uncustomarily sober and his answer sounded earnest: "Do you listen to the words of an old man? If you take care, Mrs. O'Rourke, nobody'll ever know that the thing has suffered a single crack."

His words puzzled her, but she grabbed up her parcels and went her way—not fully appreciating the import of Lewinson's warning until that evening, when, alone, she deciphered her instructions.

Instructions for Panin, of course, had been sealed in the St. Anthony statuette that Lewinson supposedly had had repaired.

When Monsignor Righi retired to his quarters for the evening and found the statuette returned to his bookcase, the anxious KGB Colonel hastened to secure his door and the window curtains, then deciphered and read how his future was to be handled.

KARENINA was to abstain from all spying activity, including visits to TOLSTOY's shop. As a result, a new method of communication would be established, its details forthcoming to HOLY SYNOD from TOLSTOY at the latter's instigation only.

Further, both KARENINA and the HOLY SYNOD were hereby reprimanded for any unauthorized contacts they may have made within the rectory; hereafter, neither was to communicate with the other for the duration of the mission. In fact, KARENINA had been instructed to break all lines of communication between herself and anyone related to the HOLY SYNOD mission.

The thought saddened Panin. He had found Marfyona unusually supportive. In a way, she had been like a well-intentioned, doting aunt. He would miss that—but he also appreciated the value of insulation, and the entire HOLY SYNOD mission needed that kind of protection; these instructions underscored that fact.

Panin continued the deciphering.

It was suggested that HOLY SYNOD use the Christmas Eve midnight mass at Church of the Nativity as a means of introducing the Israeli women as possible converts to Monsignor Maguire. This act would most likely bolster his priestly identity with both the pastor and the FBI.

Panin noted that once again his instructions implicated Maguire and possibly one other rectory priest as informers to American federal agents.

As Panin sprawled across his twin bed and slowly kicked off one slipper at a time, he could not help but look out the window and into the snowy black night.

Once again the spy's dilemma seemed to have closed in upon him. Nitchevo stood virtually alone on stage awaiting a dramatic climax.

PART FIVE

PANIN BECAME EVEN MORE CAUTIOUS—NOT ONLY BECAUSE he had just been instructed to do so, but also because his instincts had for several days been warning him.

But the professional in him seemed to have forgotten a basic lesson that had been particularly emphasized during his Moscow training years: caution possesses its own dangers . . . and an excess of caution often leads men into traps.

It was as though Panin were subject to the same mishaps that overly careful automobile drivers fall victim to, as though his intense concern against making a wrong move might be the very cause of some damaging mistake in the days ahead.

He felt vulnerable and tense. Who in the rectory family suspected him? And why? His usual composure was shaken and he decided to escape. Like the millions of New Yorkers lost in the scramble for last-minute Christmas gifts, he needed a diversion.

Panin took a downtown express train to the shopping section around lower Broadway. Going there, near Manhattan's tip, he had hoped to satisfy his urge to get as far from the rectory as possible. The subway was yet another means of guaranteeing that anyone following him would encounter the most difficulties.

Once he began walking down the cold, narrow side streets in the area, Panin realized that this distance from the rectory had in fact brought him no relief. Worse, he felt that instinctive warning once again. Someone was following him.

Just then, he spotted a small card shop. He slipped in through the narrow doorway and watched the street from behind a rack of seasonal cards near the front window. Casually he looked for a card to send Cardinal Devreux (whom, Father Belli had reminded him, they had forgotten on this year's list) and another with a blank inscription page (he intended to respond appropriately to the *Christi Nativitas tibi fausta sit* that he had received today from the prelate whom he had shown the bridges of New York). Meanwhile, he scanned the street.

After several minutes, he paid the tired-looking clerk for the two cards he had selected; Panin had seen no one on the street to suspect. He walked outside and smiled, amused with the idea that he might inscribe the prelate's card with the curt reply *tibi quoque* —"the same to you"—rather than rack his brain for something lengthy in Latin.

Still no one appeared whom he might perceive as a threat.

He looked for a small shop where he hoped to find gifts for his colleagues at the rectory and also some trifle for Shula.

At the corner, once more he felt that inner warning. This time, however, his training countered, urging him to do the wise thing and continue on his way as if nothing was wrong. After all, he was going nowhere that might expose his cover or threaten his mission.

Then Panin's increased cautiousness intervened, bringing him closer to danger once again. He felt torn.

Though he knew that one does not lose a tail unless it's a necessity, Panin made an inexplicable decision, for such an old fox: he would set out to lose his pursuer.

For half a block, he quickened his pace, then sharply turned a corner; then he slowed to an almost leisurely walk. A few hectic shoppers bumped into him and grumbled their annoyance with nonholiday uses for the name of the Lord.

In the next block, Panin zigzagged the street twice—the last time allowing himself to go down one subway entrance and quickly up the other. This backtracking brought him to the basement steps beneath a small, run-down building that he had spotted earlier.

He had hardly withdrawn into the dark doorway when he heard the kind of sound that B-grade horror movies use: a door hinge creaking behind him. Turning, Panin was confronted with the face of a very old man who looked uncomfortably familiar. He could not remember where he had seen this face; he only knew that it held him, invited him.

"Father?"

The sound of the old man's voice seemed, in Panin's mind, to match the long, untrimmed beard; the sidelocks hanging over the old man's ears; the skullcap, and the black caftan buttoned to his chin.

"Are you waiting for someone, Father?" The old man's smile was like a child's. By the man's dress and manner, Panin decided that he was in the presence of an Orthodox Jew—perhaps a Hasid.

"Father?"

The old man's repetition caused Panin to respond, "Uh, no. It's so cold. I just stepped in for a moment to get out of the wind. You don't mind—" Panin had nearly been overcome by the resemblance between this man and—he had just realized—the faces among the ghettos of the Ukraine and Belorussia. The sudden memory of those people, their costumes, made images crowd into his mind from days he had purposely tried to forget. . . .

The old man was shaking his head no, causing his sidelocks to jangle silently. "Then come in," he urged, "a glass of wine will warm you."

Panin was so eager to be off the street that he went in hastily.

He found a room stacked high with books. Its shelves were overflowing with volumes; many of the longer boards were rickety and drooping. Books even burdened the room's only windowsill, its two tables, and several chairs. At least a half-dozen thick volumes leaned in the corner by the unmade day bed.

"People call me Rabbi Grynspan," said the old man.

Panin did not know why he responded, "And I'm Father Colella."

The old man shifted an armload of books from two chairs and indicated with a nod which chair Panin should sit in. "I'll get the wine."

Minutes later, the two men sat around a table, their bottle and glasses perched on top of books. In silence, they sipped wine and Panin felt an odd sense of companionship with this stranger.

"It seems that we are both men of God?" The old man was the first to speak. His gray eyes, set deep in his gaunt face, looked mild and warm. "A grave responsibility. One that might make us tremble. But we both know—do we not?—the Almighty never abandons those who do their best to serve Him . . . to serve with a pure heart and from righteous intentions." Then the Rabbi leaned sideways, allowing his eyes to make better use of the room's awkward lighting. "I see by your name—maybe even your face—you're Italian?"

Panin felt pensive and strangely malleable. "I'm from Rome, Rabbi—and you?"

As the Rabbi explained with a certain pride that he was from Kiev, Panin felt his muscles tighten. He made no response and hoped that the old man did not notice his discomfort.

Moments into the silence, the Rabbi asked solicitously, "Don't you feel well?"

"I just thought of some horrible things," Panin answered, immediately using a cover, but also realizing that the emotions behind his words were genuine. For some reason, this old man was evoking profound feelings in Panin. "Things I've been reading about lately: the persecutions and slaughter which caused so much bloodshed in the Ukraine—particularly in Kiev."

"All too true," Grynspan sighed. Then he quoted scripture aloud, as if his words were meant for a third, unseen participant in the conversation between the two men. "The Lord giveth and the Lord taketh away; blessed be the name of the Lord." The old man began a recounting in a manner that suggested that he believed his listener also knew something of the people whose fate the Rabbi described: "My whole family was wiped out . . . the Nazis and the war . . . and with them, there were other fellow Ukrainians. I can distinctly remember the day before it all happened: what a day that was. Everyone shared the light of that day and it was light bountifully bestowed by the Lord. People walked the same streets; everything seemed to be as it had always been. A few even buried their dead in the cemeteries, where the next day . . . Then came the hour of darkness, of hatred. Who among us can forget how it felt when man hunted down man? Who can silence the terror in those children's screams?" Again the old man's voice quoted scripture: "The Lord giveth, the Lord—"

In spite of himself, Panin cried out, "That horror fills me with such shame . . . shame and remorse." His feelings were spontaneous and too true to be suffocated. For the first time in his career as a spy, the KGB Colonel felt a soulful responsibility: in the face of such ignominy, he could not let himself continue the lies and the pretenses—not to the dishonor of this beleaguered old Jew.

"But you're a man of God," Rabbi Grynspan countered. "You have no reason to be ashamed. Those who took part in that cruelty, those tortures and murders, none of them were Christians. Impossible. They had to have been—as Communism had taught them—men who didn't honestly believe in God, or men who were false Christians."

Panin winced. He realized that he was, just now, a false Christian, a false priest. He could not repress the thought. In defense he shifted his attention back to the old man's words. "Then you don't hate Christians?" Panin was puzzled that he felt apologetic.

"We serve the same God; we are all His children—why should I hate them? One day, God will judge who is Cain and who, Abel." As Panin listened, the Rabbi continued, "Don't you see lies and imposture everywhere? This is an age of little faith." The old man began to tremble as he spoke of men and women who were trampling what he called the "sacred spark of conscience."

Then Rabbi Grynspan's gray eyes seemed to ignite.

"Though this is another time of darkness, Father Colella, be sure that a catharsis is in sight. Remember how Elijah prayed for and obtained a sign of fire? How heaven destroyed the prophets of Baal? Well, in this time of darkness we can believe: among us are those with sufficient fire within them. . . . They will fight this spread of evil. Some of them will have the courage to cry out, like the Archangel Michael, 'The Lord rebuke you, who but Jehovah?'"

Panin was astounded by this man. "But I've always thought that the Jewish people—understandably—held deep resentment toward the Church?"

"Absurd, foolish," the old man protested, sending his sidelocks into hectic motion. "How can such be when Judaism and Christianity are the only two religions revealed by the true God? Can the only true religions despise one another?"

All of Panin's cultivated anti-Semitism now seemed to choke him as he listened to this old man, as he came to believe that this persecuted Jew was, in fact, genuine in what he professed. "It's strange to hear these things on your lips. I have always thought that Jews didn't—"

"Have some more wine, Father," the Rabbi interrupted, filling Panin's glass. "You've touched upon a delicate subject, I admit—but a subject on which I have long meditated. In my humble belief, there are errors on both sides. Your good Pope John, I have read, also saw it this same way." He moved books about on the table as if each volume represented some aspect of what he proceeded to describe. "We Jews did not accept Christ; we preferred loyalty to our Covenant—our 'election' or security—over the words of this prophet who had come to save all nations. Remember: we had lived apart for centuries, our separateness was God-given. Can you see how difficult it was to throw off the belief that only we were the depositaries of His revelation?" The Rabbi patted one tattered volume gently. "It was too tempting just to go on believing, 'The remnant of Jacob shall be in the midst of many people, as a dew from the Lord.'" With his right hand, he seized the wine bottle and shook it. "But you—children under the New Covenant—you were quick to forget that Jesus was born and lived as a Jew and forgave those who pressed men in authority to condemn Him."

Panin then noticed that tears were clinging to the heavy, wrinkled eyelids of Rabbi Grynspan, who continued, "We have—both of us—paid a high price. We have been driven by pride or by foolishness. We have disobeyed our common Father . . . and we shall pay."

Panin felt dumbfounded—and also enlightened. He sensed that his voice sounded almost like a young man's again, as he asked: "Still—you do refuse to recognize Christ as your messiah, do you not?"

"All true. Tonight, as you celebrate the coming of your messiah, we still await our Anointed One." For the first time since Panin arrived, the old man's voice weakened.

"But we also wait . . . upon the parousia—the second coming of the Messiah."

"So it should be," the old man enjoined. "Faith and hope give life some sense. Along with love, are they not the only realities which contain meaning?" Then, to Panin, this old man seemed to grow in wisdom, even as the younger man watched. "When this end of time comes, we may discover that your messiah and ours are one and the same. God is in no hurry. And we Jews? We stiff-necked people are used to waiting."

Then Rabbi Grynspan stared at Panin as if the old man could see straight into the KGB Colonel's heart.

"Who can know the designs of the Most High?" Panin replied,

though surprised to use an expression that—until then—he could not remember ever having heard.

"Only God knows," said the old man, lifting up his eyes and his almost fleshless hands. "Now, Father, you must go to your church." Grynspan pointed to a small pendulum clock on one of the shelves. "It's time to get ready for midnight mass."

Back out on the street, the experience with Rabbi Grynspan continued to replay in Panin's mind and soul. The old man's words penetrated deeper as the man in priest's clothing walked toward the subway. "Only if we know how to listen to ourselves, only if we understand our frailty, only then can we discover the eternal which we bear within us."

It was as if Panin had heard these words in a fresh new language.

"Lord, open our eyes," Grynspan had prayed, just before Panin had left. And Panin had truly felt like a blind man being given the sight of light for the first time.

A hint of tears seemed to freeze in the corners of his eyes as Panin glanced about for the street that led to the subway station.

He remembered having asked the old man, "Shall we see each other again, Rabbi?"

And the old man had smiled broadly. "We shall surely be together at the end of time—right, Father?"

Then Panin had promised to pray for the man.

He had genuinely promised. The idea now evoked a profound sense of amazement into Panin's mind. He felt, momentarily, more vulnerable than earlier, when he had been certain that someone had been following him.

"*Shalom*" echoed in Panin's ears. Rabbi Grynspan had said it with such conviction as Panin had left the basement room. And also the old man's promise: "I feel that I shall pray for you in a very special way. . . ."

It was as though the someone whom Panin had felt to be following him were, in fact, no one other than God. And to Panin's surprise, that feeling was a comforting one.

At the subway station, Vladimir Efimovich Panin, colonel in the KGB, found himself alone in the entrance—no other person in sight. For a number of seconds, he stood still and tall. Even though, in his heart, he felt lost and perturbed, at the same time, he knew that he felt strangely happy.

He walked down the steps lightly, as if he had just learned how to walk.

[XXVI]

IT WAS A CHRISTMAS EVE LIKE THIS THAT MADE JAMES McNeil sorry that he was an agent, sorry that he was a Catholic, and particularly sorry that he had married her.

"Jimmy," she had argued. She always said "Jimmy" in that nasal tone whenever she wanted her anger armed with a barb. "This is the fifth midnight mass in a row that your son and your wife will sit like an orphan and a widow. Where is your shame? Heaven knows, I've long ago given up on your pride."

McNeil had said nothing.

Later, when he turned off the TV and pulled his overcoat from the closet, she had huddled over their son like those Irish women McNeil remembered from the immigrant photographs. Like a hovering, knot-bulged potato and a lean, gangling sprout. She was sobbing.

What could he say? Both his wife and his son knew that McNeil had a duty. He would not have picked this or any of the other Christmas Eves as a time for performing that duty.

He crammed his damp hat onto his head and plucked at his son's shoulder. "Say a prayer for your ol' man. I'd appreciate it." Then he left for the Church of the Nativity and another night's work.

Monsignor Maguire didn't appear very happy that his church was tonight a meeting place for possible spies, known operatives, and undercover agents. At least that was how McNeil read the consternation spread in a plastic smile across the pastor's face.

Even when McNeil assured the priest that "there won't be any trouble," the tired Maguire remained noticeably upset.

Otherwise, McNeil found the gathering festive.

The sanctuary was overflowing and the federal agent recognized many diplomats and UN employees among the parishioners. However, he didn't concentrate upon scanning the crowd for details. He wanted to concentrate upon the primary suspects.

He easily recognized Mrs. O'Rourke, dressed in a navy-blue wool suit and wearing a hat conspicuously garlanded with plastic flowers, her cheeks puffy and her eyes red. She looks like the model for the devout housekeeper, McNeil mused.

Then a familiar voice alerted the agent.

"Let's sit in the last pew."

He turned in time to see Shulamith Arieh walk in arm in arm with another woman whom he recognized as Gila Ben-Ami. Although he was certain that Miss Arieh had seen him, neither woman looked in his direction. He could almost feel their indignation being silently hurled at him. But he really didn't care. Certainly not tonight.

Thank God, he murmured to himself once the organist and choir began the music heralding the beginning of the service. McNeil knew that Christmas music had powers to cover a multitude of sins.

And the music was good; tonight's mass was being aired on NBC radio (according to a note printed in that evening's worship schedule) and the organist—to McNeil's ear—seemed more energetic and hearty than most.

At one point during the processional, McNeil glanced back at the Israeli women and found them seemingly fascinated by the hymn-singing of O come, O come, Emmanuel, and ransom captive Israel. . . . If they were acting, he thought, these two were as good as their files promised that they were.

Then he saw Monsignor Righi.

The Permanent Observer, wearing white vestments embroidered in gold, walked with a hieratic gait amid the other priests in the processional. Whoever he may be, McNeil observed, he certainly looks the part tonight.

This impression was further emphasized during the concelebration of the mass itself. McNeil could not help but feel—he hated to admit—a certain seraphic fervor in Righi's manner as the priest consecrated the bread, then lifted it up as the body of the Lord.

By the liturgy's Amen, McNeil felt extremely ambivalent

about this priest under scrutiny because the midnight mass had somehow touched the agent in a way that none had in years. He kept thinking, But it's impossible, as he followed the other parishioners into the auditorium for coffee and cakes as a postlude to the mass.

The Monsignor Righi who minutes later appeared in the auditorium seemed to McNeil to be almost jubilant. The priest, now dressed in his usual clericals, moved smoothly through the crowd.

"Merry Christmas, Sal." McNeil watched as Righi greeted Father Vaccaro, then patiently met each of the *paesano*'s family members. Two uncles told, in broken English, how they had just arrived from Calascibetta and how different this mass had been from those back home. "How," the stockier uncle asked, "can there be mass and no singing of *'Tu scendi dalle stelle'?*" The other added, "And the men and women here—they sit all together? What kind of Christmas this is?"

The federal agent could see that Righi was purposely avoiding a woman who appeared to be a news reporter, since she clung to a tape recorder and had earlier extended its mike among the parishioners, apparently asking for their reactions.

When Monsignor Righi left the Vaccaros and approached the Israeli women, McNeil saw the woman with the tape recorder break away from the parishioners with whom she had been talking and quite deliberately make her way toward the priest and the younger women.

"Shula and Gila, Merry Christmas."

"Oh, Monsignor," the two replied in virtual unison. "All of the music and the, uh, the words of the mass—they were very beautiful." Shulamith seemed to be describing Gila's reactions as well.

After what appeared to be some small talk among the three about the weather and Gila's latest trip to Tel Aviv, to McNeil's surprise, Righi led the women across the room to Monsignor Maguire. The Permanent Observer appeared to be introducing his Israeli "women of experience" to the pastor. McNeil reacted with amusement, imagining what the easily shocked priest might be thinking about his Monsignor and these unmistakably attractive women. . . .

Then the reporter intervened. McNeil watched her slice between Righi and the Israeli women like a basketball player driving through a tight zone defending the goal. Microphone in position, she seemed to be asking the Observer a question when Righi stopped her midsentence.

"Excuse me, Miss Winthrop. Tonight is not an appropriate time for interviewing." His coolness caused her head to bob like a jarred Christmas tree ornament. "But if you must, try those two priests over there." McNeil observed that Righi pointed toward two sad-faced priests apparently embroiled in some argument. "I can assure you that they're experts—not on the Palestinians, but one of them on the depths of the unconscious and the other on the dangers of metaphysical commitment. Won't those be two good subjects for your lunchtime broadcast on St. Stephen's Day?"

An annoyed Miss Winthrop walked toward the two priests.

McNeil then eavesdropped as Righi continued his conversation with the Israeli women and Monsignor Maguire.

"So this is the first time you've been to a midnight mass?" The pastor seemed to have difficulty hiding his mix of embarrassment and attraction; he looked to either side of the women's faces, rather than look at them directly.

There was soft laughter in Shulamith's voice as she answered, "Oh, this is the first time we've been to a mass of any kind." She reached for the priest's arm, then pulled away; the young woman seemed intent upon making a good impression, but uncertain of just how best to go about it.

Monsignor Righi hastened to add: "My friends, Frank, are interested in the Catholic Church."

McNeil noted a genuine incredulity in Maguire's voice as he responded, "Well, uh, that's good news—now, I'm sorry, but I must be moving on. I hope you'll understand. Tonight I must greet every single parishioner: it's a beloved custom which we Irish brought to America. Ladies, see you again soon, Merry Christmas and God bless you all."

Many parishioners had left and most of the cakes had been eaten. The auditorium contained maybe one fifth of the people who just minutes before had filled it with conversation and festive greetings.

Those remaining seemed to be gathered into three or four loosely arranged groups. Some women were making talkative trips from the serving tables into the kitchen; others seemed to be washing cups and saucers and dessert plates.

Of course there was a group of priests, several of whom had a rather loud discussion under way. Vaccaro and his sleepy-eyed uncles formed an edge for this group.

Then there were those who persisted in lingering around the still-lively Monsignor Righi. McNeil sat with Evangeline Maguire and Father Potocki, the three posing as new friends only recently brought together by a holiday project organized by Miss Maguire's "uncle."

But McNeil had grown uncomfortable.

He had the distinct feeling that Shulamith Arieh had, in fact, broken her promise and told Righi about McNeil's earlier visit to her apartment. He had grown more positive about this intuition as the reception progressed. His reason: neither the Israeli women nor the Permanent Observer had as much as glanced in his direction. McNeil felt as though the three had quarantined him.

The agent had just decided that he should leave when Righi raised his voice and began telling the small, informal group about his encounter with Rabbi Grynspan. "Wasn't Our Lord Jesus Christ born in Bethlehem, didn't he live at Nazareth, travel through Galilee and Samaria and Judea?" The Monsignor's questions seemed to be both rhetorical and also for the benefit of the Israeli women. "Then we must not forget that Jesus was a Jew from start to finish —right up until his death near Jerusalem."

A few others edged into this group now listening as the Monsignor described his encounter with the Rabbi; McNeil noted that Mrs. O'Rourke, her wide-brimmed hat now clutched under her bosom, was among them.

"I now see," Righi continued, "that God was somehow behind my meeting this wise old man. I must admit that I don't yet know what to make of my feelings, but I do know that just talking with this man of God, this Jew among Jews, has affected me deeply." Still others moved closer to the priest as he spoke; it seemed, at least to McNeil, that there was a peculiar earnestness in what Righi was saying. Like the priest's fervor during the mass, it puzzled McNeil.

"That's why I prayed for Rabbi Grynspan during the mass tonight. I prayed for this man on Fulton Street because, quite simply, he promised to pray for me. And he said it in such a way that I can't help but believe that such praying will reach God this night."

REQUIEM FOR A SPY

Mrs. O'Rourke coughed, nearly choking on a piece of cake. Others gathered around the priest seemed immediately touched, almost embarrassingly so.

McNeil had had enough. It was time he went home to his wife and son.

The next day, Christmas, agents from both the FBI and the Israelis made visits to Fulton Street.

The two pairs of men, recognizing one another, took turns inspecting mailbox tags without interference. After all, it was Christmas. Later, the Bureau men inquired at the few restaurants and bars that were open, but no one seemed to know anything about a rabbi named Grynspan.

The Israelis had already checked New York City's rabbinical federation listings and, over beers, joked with the Bureau men about this futile search on a Christian holy day for a Jew who probably existed only in the mind of an Italian priest.

"Some Christmas," complained one of the federal agents. "Why couldn't this have come up on Hanukkah?" He elbowed the closer of the two Israeli agents. "Then you guys could have holiday pay instead of us—hey, hey?"

The shorter of the two Israelis gestured with two hands, as if pushing away some invisible barrier. "Better you than me. You guys started nosing into this UN stuff, remember, not us. It's a joke. Who cares what these diplomats say? Particularly one who's a priest. If you want to know my opinion, both your boss and mine have gone batty over nothing. We're not gonna find a rabbi and we're not gonna nail a priest. All this rabbit-chasing is just so Israel and America can look good next time they sit down to compare complaints. Am I right, or am I right? Then buy this joe another—"

[XXVII]

DURING THE NEXT DAY, PANIN WAS QUIETLY PLEASED TO find that the rectory was virtually deserted. By midday everyone had left for other holiday settings; only Potocki and Righi, with relatives in Detroit and Rome, and Evangeline

Maguire remained behind—each isolated in his or her separate and lonely room. Evangeline had promised her "uncle" that she would stay at the rectory and cook dinner for the two stay-at-home priests while Mrs. O'Rourke had the day off.

Nonetheless, Panin felt glad. He expected the isolation to give him time to prepare a major report to the Vatican concerning the General Assembly session just ended December 21. He also knew that he could not comfortably work any place other than in the rectory office. No one from the UN dared to be seen between sessions. "It is not chic, Monsignor, to look as though you have not done enough work during the General Assembly's twelve week fall/winter session. . . ." Or so he was informed by Martha Winthrop when she had asked the Permanent Observer where he intended to spend the holidays. He had answered, "The rectory office," and she had protested, cataloging all the other places where his colleagues had told her they were going: "Florida, Montego Bay, Acapulco, several to the ski resorts in Vermont and the Laurentians."

Well, chic or not, the Permanent Observer had no intention of moving. His office was more than sufficient for him this holiday. He had work to do, for Righi and—he hesitated—for Panin as well.

After about two hours of concentrated effort, Panin's mind became overburdened by the range of subjects he knew that he had to include in his "comprehensive" report for the Vatican.

"Comprehensive" was a Vatican adjective; it meant that their Permanent Observer at the UN had to address issues such as the Third World countries, what one key African leader had described as "a bold, clear-sighted, global concept of economics," what a Western minister of foreign affairs had termed "the call to self-criticism on the part of nations both rich and poor," what the Communist countries were labeling the "sins of the multinationals," plus corrupt finances and raw materials and the problem of freighters flying a flag of convenience and . . .

By two o'clock Panin had to find diversion. He had to get away, to break the concentration. In fact, this last need had lately become an additional worry for him: he could no longer concentrate the way he had always been able to.

Since his encounter with Rabbi Grynspan, he could not seem to shake the thought of the Last Days. They conjured terrifyingly lucid memories within his mind and soul, a tragic sense of time, an uncompromising sense of morality that was new to him.

These thoughts about the Last Days seemed to support his certainty that a man (even he, Panin) is saved provided he believes that faith is for the sake of salvation. He asked himself: what good is all the rest?

Panin walked to his dingy window. There, looking out upon a virtually empty East Forty-seventh Street, he felt pangs of solitude, which on second thought he identified as self-disgust. He pondered: had Christmas caused these feelings? If so, then he thought it strange—Christmas had never meant anything to him, at least nothing more than isolation. His new sense of salvation compelled him to question: isolated from whom? And why this self-disgust? Hadn't he always lived apart and always known isolation? Why then these sad feelings?

Outside, snowflakes swirled around trees that he could see in the small park around the UN. He remembered that it had been snowing since dawn.

Until today, these trees were nothing more than nude skeletons. Now he could see that they precariously held curving lines of inch-deep snow. It was like a greeting card picture. At any other time Panin would have delighted in the sight.

But today he could only think of the Ukraine: its endless stretches of bluish-white snow clinging to his native steppes, while bitter winds galloped over them, as if to mock the birches and poplars caught in their wild gyrations. The trees! Panin took pleasure in the sudden memory that often the movement of those trees had been the only clue he could find as to the direction in which some broad, slow-moving, ice-coated river might be flowing.

And so many other memories! The gurgling call of the samovar in the damp heat of the *isba*, the aroma of the tea made by *matushka* . . . his grandmother, who now lay buried beneath just such a sheet of snow as this. His grandmother. Such stories she used to tell. He could almost *see* her just now: pouring tea, talking of *muzhiks*, all the while lugubriously wrapped in her worn black caftans. He remembered how she described earlier times: waiting for days until the frozen roads cleared for travel. "How many times," she repeatedly told him, "have I seen the *troika* bring a loaf of bread when I could not see—even along the horizon—the kopeck with which to buy it?"

Had Rabbi Grynspan also remembered such poverty? Panin wondered. And was the old man also reminded of the wintry desolation of those Ukrainian steppes—even now, when the beggars and *startsy* are gone? Did Grynspan know the proverb, "Under the snow there is bread"?

It was certainly a proverb that Panin had never heard quoted at the United Nations. Today it was a proverb that represented the voice of hope.

Panin decided to go upstairs.

He knocked on Stanislaus Potocki's door and waited, holding a bottle under his arm. From inside the Polish priest's quarters, Panin could hear the playing of a record that sounded to him like Rubinstein playing Chopin.

When Potocki opened the door and asked, "What can I do for you, Monsignor?" Panin could see surprise written across the Pole's open, peasantlike face.

Panin tried to make his proposal sound genuine. It was; he did not want to be rebuffed. Not today. "What do you say, Stan, to our keeping one another company? After all, it is Christmas and I've got this bottle of first-rate scotch to share—" He could see no immediate acceptance in Potocki's expression. "It's a Christmas gift and I thought it would be uncharitable if I drank it all alone. What do you say?"

Potocki immediately changed, now showing no hesitancy. "Come in, Monsignor. We'll have a party all to ourselves." This sudden change put Panin on alert. "Who knows what kind of a good time Monsignor Maguire and Vaccaro and Nevins may be having, right?" he continued, then added a remark that sealed Panin's suspicions. "By the way, should we invite Miss Maguire to join the party?"

The suggestion for the company of women was, for Potocki, quite out of character; it confirmed Panin's intuition that this "niece" of Maguire might somehow be connected with the investigations of which he'd been warned. Rapidly he reasoned, if she is, is Potocki also aware of her clandestine efforts? And what would that imply about him?

"I'd say no, Stan." Panin spun off an excuse. "At least not right away. Just what kind of a party do you think two priests and a student of political science can have? She's bright, I grant you, but we'd risk hearing how I should work to make UN procedures more reasonable . . . or how you should persuade Poland to act as a bridge between East and West toward the 'global strategy for peace.'"

Potocki seemed perplexed. "Well, uh, since it is Christmas, I just thought that—but you're right. And I do welcome your company. This Polish music was getting to me. You know: nostalgia will hear no reason."

Panin noted that the priest seemed purposeful as he marked his place in a novel, then crossed the room to turn off his record player. "Stan, I see you go in for spy stories." The Russian saw Ian Fleming's name on the book's spine.

Potocki blushed, as if at odds with himself. "Well, yes. I admit that I like them. How about you, Monsignor?"

Panin could feel his half bitter, half ironical smile spreading across his face. "Not much. I find them—how shall I put it?—too fantastic." Panin could see puzzlement in Potocki's eyes. "But if you care for the real thing, try reading the court stenographer's records from the trials of spies—the ones who've been caught. They may be less entertaining then these novels, but they'll be much more enlightening. For example. Has it ever been ascertained what the Soviet spy Colonel Rudolf Abel got out of the Americans? No. And yet a Fleming would claim to tell you." He could see that he had Potocki's hungry attention. "Or read the *White Book* of the Royal Canadian Commission—it details Soviet spying efforts to discover atomic secrets during the war. Or you can buy the stenographic account of the Klaus Fuchs trial; he was responsible, some years later, for transmitting those secrets to Russia. In any case, don't bother with imaginary tales."

Potocki gulped down a particularly hearty portion of the scotch in his glass. "Oh, I know such books are likely to exaggerate."

"Yes, but I also mean that such writers don't seem to know about what Americans call a 'thick' spy: one who is complex, difficult to understand." Panin had decided to see just how far into this subject Potocki would plunge.

The priest showed no caution. "What do these 'thick' spies do? Do you know?"

Panin proceeded to give the naïve fellow the kind of generalized answer that he thought Righi might be capable of: examples from diplomatic service, noting how unheroic the lives of such real spies had seemed to him. All the while, Panin made certain that his manner was unmistakably casual. He studied Potocki's quarters, silently noting that the priest's study and bedroom and bath were smaller than Maguire's, much smaller than those reserved for the Permanent Observer's use.

"But," Potocki interrupted boyishly, "don't most spy-story writers get their material from personal experience?"

Panin shrugged. "Who knows? No one but the writer can know for certain. Believe what you like."

The priest leaned against the upholstered arm of his chair. His face lined up, in Panin's perspective, with the photograph of a man. The portrait on Potocki's desk appeared to be that of his father. "But earlier didn't you say you also objected to the way these novelists describe their heroes? Didn't you mean to say 'villains'?"

"Heroes, villains—what does it matter? He's a villain who spies for their side, a hero if he spies for yours. Isn't that a crazy distinction? It reminds me of our Secretary General when he talks about offensive and defensive weaponry. He doesn't know—or pretends that he doesn't—that it all depends upon which big gun you're standing behind."

Potocki's expression became as righteous-looking as that of Our Lady of Częstochowa—the only picture adorning his bleak walls. "But spying's a crime!"

"A crime, Stan, only because it violates a law. Are crimes bad because they're forbidden, or forbidden because they're bad?"

Potocki shook his head wearily. "But isn't a country's safety at stake and doesn't that limit how we view such distinctions?"

"Only inasmuch as all countries have spies and all countries make severe laws to neutralize the situation. Both are necessary evils. Anyway, I'm not condemning governments for jailing or even shooting spies. I'm only criticizing romantic writers who invent fantastic stories. Why, they make up soliloquies which no self-respecting spy would ever address to himself—"

Panin could see that Potocki appeared locked into this subject, .

as if he was attempting to memorize every word the Permanent Observer was saying. "But there must be something more that you object to?" The priest did not hide his eagerness for his guest to continue talking.

Panin continued, once again firing a double-edged smile at his listener. "Our famous moneymaking mystery-story writers forget that spies are human, that there is a soul involved. Oh, here and there spies are presented as human; a human touch does no harm and it may even make a story more plausible. But I ask you, with what devices do such writers clothe their characters? If you haven't yet found out, then I'll tell you, Stan: sex, drunkenness, and nightmares. They give their characters only the most bestial qualities."

Panin relented. He realized his vehemence had caused him to stare at Stan as if he was attempting to hypnotize the Polish priest. He got up and went to Potocki's single dreary window. From there he could see that snow was still falling, that East Forty-seventh Street remained deserted. It was still a melancholy Christmas.

Then he faced his colleague once again, as if to say by his expression, Now are you convinced?

Potocki spoke up. Apparently he had reduced the discussion to a level he understood. "Then these spies are sinners."

"Sinners?" Panin echoed as he returned to his chair. He could feel himself using immense self-control with this unknowing fellow. "Let me recall for you, Stan, that the Church finds something in even the most hardened of sinners, something which neither the late Ian Fleming nor his fellow writers ever attribute to their characters."

"And what is that?"

"Father, need I remind you of the immortal soul? Surely you'll agree that a spy has a soul—won't you?" Panin was surprised at himself for taking this discussion so close to his personal concerns . . . as surprised as Potocki was embarrassed.

"Uh, I must admit, Monsignor, I haven't given the matter much thought."

"Well, Stan, I have. Spies can be as responsible and sensitive as anyone else. But the ones I've encountered also appear to be among the loneliest and most isolated beings on the face of this earth. Even the writers who grind out this trash seem to misunderstand, to despise, to belittle them." Panin glanced around the room again, realizing that it contained very few personal belongings. "Now, Stan, I don't mean any personal offense. I just think you'd be better off, for instance, rereading Mark Twain."

Potocki laughed awkwardly. "That's exactly what Monsignor Maguire said to me." Then the priest immediately appeared regretful.

Panin let it pass. "I guess, Stan, I'm only suggesting that you extend the same compassion to spies that you do for thieves and murderers, prostitutes and—"

"You mean pray for them? Is that what you do, pray for spies, Monsignor?"

"I pray for anyone who feels the sting of solitude, for anyone who doesn't pray, for people who don't believe. I ask God to give them the grace of light. Remember how the blind man asked the passing Nazarene, 'Master, let me see,' and He gave sight to the man? Do you know any appeal more marvelous? And finally, I pray for all those who are forgotten by people who ought to cherish them—"

"I'm surprised," Potocki interjected, appearing quite sincere. "And I hope you'll forgive me, Monsignor, but I didn't imagine you to be so introspective a priest. I guess that I imagined you as only interested in the United Nations."

"Introspective?" Panin joked with his host. "Let's just say that my introspection has led me to the conclusion that a spy may do the wrong things for many right reasons."

"And what is 'right'?" Potocki hazarded.

But Panin could tolerate no more. Not tonight.

"Please, Stan. Enough of all this. It's Christmas! Why don't we down another glass of scotch, then go to see what Miss Maguire has prepared for our supper? Surely she's a better cook than Mrs. O'Rourke. But even if she's not, we can always fall back on the cannoli which Sal Vaccaro's mother sent us for a present."

"Cannoli?"

"Oh, yes. Prepare to have your mouth water. Cannoli is a cylinder of pastry. It's made with eggs; browned in olive oil; then stuffed with ricotta cheese, candied limes, and spices. You'll see what Italians can do!"

[XXVIII]

MCNEIL LOOKED AT THE PHOTO PRINTS THAT EVANGELINE Maguire had given him at nine in the morning on December 26. What interested him most was the picture of the camera. No proper ecclesiastic would own a camera that complex and costly—the kind used only by a few professional photographers . . . and spies.

He phoned Father Potocki to request another meeting. Since Evangeline's search of Monsignor Righi's quarters proved so fruitful, McNeil intended to ascertain exactly what Righi and Potocki had discussed—while the pastor's "niece" had stolen the opportunity to search the Permanent Observer's study and bedroom and bath.

"But you didn't find any papers?" McNeil had asked when Evangeline Maguire delivered the photo prints.

"The usual UN stuff—notes on outer space and the environment, on population increase and urbanization." The woman had looked to McNeil as though she had not slept well, as if she had done some holiday partying not related to the Righi investigation. He refrained from asking.

"But there was one scribbled phrase which intrigued me: 'One human race, with a single conscience.' What do you make of that?" She had seemed almost hesitant to ask.

McNeil had laughed, then dismissed it as the "usual gibberish out of the UN."

To which Evangeline had added, "Well, I just thought it might be a quotation from Teilhard de Chardin?"

McNeil had enjoyed the last word. "Isn't it all the same?"

Just before noon, he picked up Potocki and the two drove through the roadways in Central Park that had not been closed off for pedestrian use.

"This one's top secret, Father—just thought I'd remind you."

"Of course. You have my promise from before and you have my solid assurances now. I'm here to serve—not to hinder." The

Polish priest, naïve as he remained, still appeared trustworthy. McNeil decided to tell Potocki as much of what he had learned as was feasible.

"Maguire's 'niece' did search Righi's quarters while you and he chatted yesterday. Was the scotch good?" He could see that Potocki was embarrassed at the revelation that somebody outside the rectory knew of the priests' holiday drinking.

"Okay. It was just okay. But back to the search: did she find anything important?"

"She photographed a camera. A small, highly sensitive device."

Potocki blurted out his presumption. "The kind spies use?"

"Maybe." McNeil didn't want the easily excited priest to run any further with his conclusions than the federal agent knew Potocki was capable of doing. "The point is this: evidence of his having such a camera in his possession may be useful—should any of this get to court—but we also need to put any such evidence into context. What I mean is that the things he said to you are equally important. Now, Father, what did the two of you talk about?"

Carefully Potocki reviewed everything he could recall from his conversation with Righi.

"Interesting," McNeil interrupted. "If this Righi is a spy—and I use the word 'if'—then such an outburst would fit. Spies are given to occasional indulgences. Believe me. As a counter-spy, I'm virtually the twin brother to such people. And I know that even the best of them will spill out their feelings to somebody."

"In my opinion," the priest countered, but with some timidity, "a spy would either have avoided the subject altogether or affected ignorance, indifference. Anything other than what he did."

McNeil kept his eyes on the roadway. "You're wrong there, Father. Spies are lonelier than those saints who spent their lives atop a column in the desert. What were they called?"

"Stylites."

"Right. Well, a man can live in a world unto himself, even when he's walking down Broadway. A spy may spend an entire day on crowded Times Square and still feel damnably alone. He has no one to talk to and no ivory tower in which to take refuge; yet inwardly he feels an urge to communicate. That's why he is ready, every now and then, to risk talking—particularly when he thinks that his listener is innocent." McNeil glanced at Potocki and saw that the priest took no pleasure in what the federal agent was saying. "Well, Father, if that's the impression you made on Righi, congratulations. You may have gotten a spy to talk about spying."

"But isn't that a gamble on his part?"

McNeil had his own doubts as to why Righi had discussed spying with Potocki, but he held them to himself like a rare coin. "Maybe he was making fun of himself, Stan. Maybe he was just falling victim to fatigue and self-pity. Christmas is a prime time for that. I don't know. But I do know that spies lead a hard life. I can't condemn them."

The Pole's bovine eyes appeared wide open as he stared across the car at the man from the FBI. "You don't mean that you have sympathy for them?"

"Why not?" McNeil realized that this was a subject that the priest might not fathom, but he knew he had to try to make his point. "We don't hate them, Father. We fight them. It's our job. And we don't shoot them down just because they're spies; on the contrary, we respect them. Some of those men are brilliant and courageous. They are dedicated to their work even though they are always in danger of capture and prison—even death. What does the Bible say, Father, about 'ashes on the dinner table'?"

Potocki's response was prompt. "Psalm 102: 'I have eaten ashes for bread. . . .'"

"Exactly. And believe me, ashes are no picnic."

The Central Park roadway had led McNeil's car to exit onto Fifth Avenue. McNeil knew a good coffee shop on Lexington Avenue and decided it might be the best place for this conversation to continue.

"What would you say, Father, to a good cup of coffee?"

"Fine." But there was little enthusiasm in the priest's voice. "As long as I can also get some tea."

McNeil parked illegally near a police station where he had some pals, then the two of them walked to the coffee shop, no more than a hundred yards away. Along the street and within the shop, McNeil made quick, thorough studies of everyone in sight. He wanted no surprises today.

After the waiter had taken their orders, McNeil reminded Potocki that the two of them should be careful of what they discussed when anyone was within earshot.

"So, Father, why do you think Righi spoke so passionately about the life of a spy? Have any new thoughts?"

Potocki answered in a more clear-sighted manner than McNeil expected. "He seemed uneasy. That's it. As if something inside him had given way. As if he was profoundly dissatisfied." The priest halted and appeared to be thinking. When he resumed talking, he sounded a bit guilty. "It was like Righi was calling for help. You, uh, you don't think—provided he is a spy and all—that Righi is on the point of defecting?"

It was an idea that had honestly not crossed McNeil's mind. "I can't say, Stan. If it's difficult to say why a man goes in for spying, it's even more difficult to explain why some men chuck it." The agent fumbled with a greasy sugar container; he pulled a paper napkin from the holder and automatically began cleaning the sugar container. "We're speaking now of real spies—not merely informers. The motive of informers is usually either money or hate. When the motive disappears and if they haven't been gunned down, informers just fade. But spies have higher motives: from love of adventure to love of country. Usually spies don't get out until they're caught." Maybe, just maybe, McNeil pondered, this Righi is becoming dissatisfied. "Who can say, Stan, how sincere Righi was about the sermon he dished out to you? It could have been a skillfully phrased attempt to bolster his own priestly identity, or"— McNeil hesitated—"it could have been a genuine expression of how the man feels. If he is a spy and if he—God forbid—has been impersonating a priest, maybe he's beginning to believe in what he has been saying?"

"So you think a change might actually be taking place within him?"

McNeil didn't know what he believed—but some of this felt right to him. An intuition. "I can't say right now. That's why I need more information from you. Details. What the man says and how he acts. Facts about the exterior man so we can make at least educated guesses about what's going on inside him."

The priest smiled knowingly. "Like the Gospel: 'From their fruits you shall know them.'"

"Exactly." McNeil spotted the waiter heading back toward their booth. "For the time being, let's confine ourselves to certainties. And it's a certainty that spies are good liars and good actors. The more sincere they seem, the more they lie." Then he nodded to indicate someone's approach behind the priest's back.

Potocki sat quietly while the waiter served them. When they were alone again, he whispered. "What are my instructions?"

McNeil sipped at the hot coffee and answered, "This thing still may take a long time. Watch him carefully. That's your ongoing and primary instruction. He may continue talking now and it will be stupid on his part. Or he may shut up. That may last for months. Who can say why he does or doesn't act the way you've described him?" He used his fork to stab at the cake he had ordered, but then failed to taste it. "I could swear that today he's feeling better—like a woman after childbirth—and that he won't talk again for a while. The main thing for you to remember is don't change the way you behave toward him. If he thinks of you as *innocent*, then go on being that with him. And don't remind him of yesterday's conversation. If he wants to talk again, just listen. No questions and no pressure. Got it?"

Potocki stared into his cup of hot water. He had not even bothered to drop in the tea bag. "You know, I'm beginning to feel sorry for him—"

McNeil agreed, but he could not let this priest know his feelings. And he had to make certain that Potocki's sympathies did not jeopardize the already delicate position in which this investigation rested. "Watch out, Father. Have pity on his soul, but leave your personal grief out. Don't get your emotions tangled up in this. Remember: you're an American and this Righi is suspected of being dangerous to your country's security. Whatever we ultimately find as evidence against him, he's not going to overturn the Roman Catholic Church. Am I right?"

The priest nodded, but did not look up.

"But don't you forget: he may do other damage which could affect all of us."

[XXIX]

 HOLIDAYS FOR THE UNITED NATIONS WERE CUT SHORT. ANother terrorist attack in Israel and the subsequent reprisals had created yet one more crisis.

As usual, the crisis quickly spread throughout the Middle East, then bounced from there into the lap of the United Nations. Delegates were called back from Acapulco or Florida or wherever to an emergency meeting of the UN Security Council. Grumbling diplomats with half-baked suntans were filing into the glass and concrete tower and each person seemed to resent, more than usual, the gusty winter wind that flapped the flags of a hundred and thirty-six nations—making their entranceway noisy, chilling, almost like a worldwide joke at their individual expense.

As Monsignor Righi, Panin was one of the first to enter the North Lounge once the Security Council had ended its meetings with the release of one more watered-down resolution condemning everybody in general and nobody in particular. At least that's how he read the resolve.

Still, he knew that it didn't matter. News reports indicated that tension had already subsided spontaneously, as it often did, even before the distinguished Council members could get back to the city, meet, and agree upon their tranquilizing commonplaces. Panin suspected that the only realities in all of this would turn out to be the graves—dug one by one on either side of the frontier separating Israel and Lebanon.

Deaths once again in the Holy Land, Panin thought, but not a single drop of blood to spot the thick carpets of this glass house.

"Don't tell me, don't tell me: espresso without lemon." Chico Ramirez interrupted Panin's melancholy.

But when the young man seemed to recognize how dark was the Monsignor's mood today, he became more solicitous. "I'm sorry, Monsignor Righi—is there anything wrong?"

"Only the coffee, Chico. Please bring me tea with lemon for today." Panin had been out of sorts for days.

His opinion of the United Nations had fallen rapidly as he faced the cold realities of describing the organization's strengths and weaknesses in the comprehensive report he had just completed and sent off to the Holy See. Oh, his report had been positive—Panin dared not make it otherwise. But it had not been the truth as he sincerely knew it.

That's what truly bothered him. He could not help but wonder what Rabbi Grynspan would think, should the old man know that Panin had been dishonest once again . . . that he had lost confidence in the United Nations, but still had continued to extoll its virtues?

Am I doing nothing more, Panin asked himself, than compounding a life that has already been entrapped in its own tissue of lies? What's the use of my being here?

He sipped his tea and stared out the wide window past the terrace that overhung the East River. He asked himself the question that had been simmering within him for days, but most particularly following his encounter with Rabbi Grynspan: Why should I go on with this living lie? I no longer know where Panin ends and Righi begins.

Had he not argued with Potocki? "A spy has a soul."

Had not the saving of his soul and the awareness of the end of time become two ideas that now ceaselessly hammered at his mind?

And who was speaking—Panin probed into his own heart—when he had asked, face to face with Grynspan: "Who can know the designs of the Most High?"

Some minutes later a deep voice interrupted Panin's meditations.

"May I keep you company, Giuseppe . . . or would you prefer to linger over your tea alone?" The speaker was, Panin looked up to see, Shimon Bar-Hillel; the Israeli Ambassador held an espresso in his broad Teutonic hand.

"Glad to see you, Shimon. Do sit down." Panin tried to recapture his Righi perspective. "How goes it?"

Bar-Hillel pulled out a chair. "Look out the window: there's nothing new under the sun."

"Solomon." Panin answered, playing the game that Righi and Bar-Hillel usually enjoyed.

The Israeli continued. "Solomon, right. So. We've been censured and so have the others. The accounts have been balanced. Such tightrope walkers they are in this place. But surely you've noticed that: no differentiation."

"That's correct." Panin replied but he also needed to say more. "You have lost lives . . . and so have the Arabs."

Bar-Hillel looked momentarily puzzled, as if he were unaccustomed to the mood that hung over Righi. "We shall continue to shed blood and so will they. You know that. But then death isn't a popular subject in this building, now is it? Death is too black a notion for distinguished diplomats called back from the Caribbean beaches. UN members prefer to garner statistics, to discuss articles of the Charter, or to hold solemn commemorations of the Universal Declaration of Human Rights." The Israeli gestured with his espresso cup, as if making a proud toast.

"You're becoming cynical, my friend." Panin had to respond with these words—yet inwardly, he yearned to admit to Bar-Hillel that the Israeli's thoughts were almost precisely his as well.

"And who wouldn't?" Bar-Hillel rejoined. "This is the best school of cynicism in the world. And the joke is, governments actually pay great sums of money to keep this leaking boat afloat. Do you know: they've censured or condemned my country a hundred or a hundred and fifty times over—relying upon a mechanical vote. Ha. If this is democracy, you can have it!"

"When I said you were a cynic I wasn't attempting an act of revenge. I was thinking that you are as wise as Solomon, which may mean as bitter as Ecclesiastes. You know I agree with many of your points, or almost agree. But tell me this: what would we do without the United Nations? It's a place where, despite the drafts, everyone seeks shelter. If a nation acquires independence at midnight, at eight o'clock the next morning it knocks at the door of the UN. Where would we be without this refuge of . . . sinners?"

"We'd do what nations have always done and will continue to do after this building has collapsed. We'll spy and cheat and make war and then write history books to justify it."

"Don't you prefer the UN's slogan 'Better speak than shoot'?"

"A false comfort, as you well know. And hypocritical, to boot. Said by someone who, even involuntarily, was 'puritanizing.' We talk, while others are killed."

"Well, some say that imperfect as it may be, the UN is better than the vacuum left after the end of the League of Nations."

"Do you see a difference between the vacuum of yesterday and the so-called reality of today? Everything goes the same way—that is, badly."

"So you'd throw this fine building into the East River, would you?"

"The river's polluted enough already. It would be an ecological crime to make it any worse. Better remodel it into the headquarters of some big company. . . . Now you'll tell me that I've all the cleverness of a Jew!"

"I'm not telling you, even if the thought did occur. . . . But I'm not sure your bitterness stems only from this last meeting of the Security Council. There must be something else behind it."

"Yes, there is," said Bar-Hillel. He looked at Righi as if to question how he knew. "There's a new wave of anti-Semitism in the Soviet Union. Cleverly contrived and widely trumpeted accusations of a 'Zionist threat.' It looks like an upcoming trial, in which the lucky ones will be submitted to treatment in a politico-psychiatric institution and the unluckier to a work camp in Siberia. Does this make any impression on you?"

Righi nodded emphatically.

"It does indeed. A considerable impression. To the point that I might find your question offensive if I didn't know your feelings about me. But we mustn't stop with these hateful and shameful events if we want to get at the root of our uneasiness."

"No?"

"We're in crisis because faith is dead. And when the supernatural is relegated to the world of the absurd, we have total bewilderment as a rule of life. Now that technical advances have freed man from many of his material preoccupations, he is supposed to have more time for the things of the spirit. Instead, the ground seems to have been cleared for a process of desanctification and self-worship. What a paradox. We live in a world which denies God and boasts of being able to get along without Him. It's a life without divine grace, love, or any prospect of eternity to follow. God have mercy on us, all of us. Sometimes I wonder how long the Almighty will be so patient about us. . . ."

Bar-Hillel looked at him in surprise. Had he understood him right? There was a new tone in his voice. "What do you mean by 'us'?"

"Just what I said: Mercy on us, patience with us. All of us. I didn't mean Communists only, but this whole generation of vipers, as the Scriptures call it."

The ambassador smiled knowingly.

"Including spies who pretend to be religious?"

"Of course. And they're the worst, because their hypocrisy borders on sacrilege. But there may be redemption for them, too.

Someday they'll discover that there is a last day, a day of reckoning."

"This isn't the way I've heard you talk before, Monsignor," said Bar-Hillel, using the title for the first time and with a tone of respect. He stood up. "Please excuse me, but I must make an urgent telephone call."

While those whose job it was to listen in on other people's conversations tried to interpret the one between the envoys of Israel and the Vatican, Panin fell back into what Potocki would have called introspection.

I wonder what Rabbi Grynspan would say about this place? Probably: "Who knows? We'll find out at the end of time." The end of time isn't on the United Nations agenda. If it were, the discussants would arrive at different finishing posts. This institution isn't on the edge of imposture; it's not a world of prefabricated truths, as Bar-Hillel claims. But without a doubt, nobody here knows, when the chips are down, to what extent he has pulled the wool over the eyes of his neighbor.

And here I am, wisely embittered, or bitterly wise. I'm drawing my inspiration from Solomon, and his wisdom is too pessimistic. Pessimism has never made any man better. I prefer his father, good King David. Ironic, Panin thought. I know the Psalms by heart, without their ever having touched my heart. You, wise old Grynspan, might quote me number 23: "The Lord is my shepherd; I shall not want." But does it fit a lost sheep that wants, that is, lacks everything?

He left the North Lounge frowning—without saying goodbye to Chico. As he went back to the rectory the hundred and thirty-six flags were still moving in the wind that had cleared the sky. But Volodya Panin had no eyes for anything around him.

[XXX]

THAT EVENING PANIN WENT TO BED EARLY, BUT HE COULD not go straight to sleep. Insomnia.

Over the years of his work as a spy, insomnia had been a regularly recurring affliction—often in times when the possibility of discovery was greatest. Like now. And each time that insomnia had befallen him, Panin had fought back—but never with the weapon he used tonight.

Panin read the Psalms. They were—he had come to understand —a tonic for his soul. Uncannily, they had a way of meeting him at the point of hurt. "When in trouble I sought the Lord," he had read earlier this evening in Psalm 77, "my soul refusing to be consoled." It was as though when David had written the words to this particular Psalm, the Biblical poet had been thinking of him.

"I am forty-nine years old," Panin confessed to the walls, "and twenty-six of those years have been spent in disguises, in danger."

No answer, no response returned from the rectory's plaster and woodwork. The impostor priest was left with nothing but his deep discomfort; this was his hour of greatest need. He understood that.

Tonight Panin felt anxious in a way he had never before known. He felt that he was losing control. What was left within him wasn't fear. He knew fear. Fear had concrete objects—death, the displeasure of one's superiors, loss of confidence, loss of a job— Panin had encountered all of these in the past and, without too much difficulty, had overcome them. Fear, then, he could handle.

He knew too that what he was feeling within was not remorse.

He had never killed, except during the war (and even then he had no way of being sure); during his missions for the KGB, somebody else had done the killing. Panin's recourse had always been his mind, not a gun. In fact this trait was a matter of record.

The most he had done was to steal secrets—but to accomplish that he had also lied, deceived, plotted. So had many other spies on both sides of what the West called the Iron Curtain. In this guilt then, Panin knew he had company. If to Americans he might someday be known as a "dirty spy," to his fellow countrymen he might be known as one of the "heroes of the Soviet Union." This balance relieved him of most of the remorse he might otherwise feel.

So what was he feeling?

From the street he could hear an assortment of car horns, an airplane, and somewhere an unusually loud radio. It was just another Manhattan night—except for his insomnia.

Two hours later, he saw by his clock, and Panin was still awake.

As far as he could tell, he was no sleepier than when he had first crawled between the now damp, twisted sheets. His skin felt hot, his temperature must be up, but his mind was unaffected. It hummed like the motor in an electric typewriter.

That was it.

The comparison inspired him to get out of bed and write out his thoughts. Panin slipped into his robe and slippers, and turned up the heat in his study. He even placed a glass of fresh water by the portable typewriter on his desk.

Then he poured out his feelings on paper:

> Do I really want to desert the cause? Not for a minute. Deserters have always been despicable to me: they only seek to save their skins or to make money.
>
> And how would I feel if my fate became the same as my colleague Abel's? Could that happen to me?
>
> Of course. TOLSTOY, FALCON, KARENINA—any of them could turn me in, as some underling had done to Abel. Or I could also be caught without any disloyalty on the part of my comrades. The mission could fail. Such endings are always possible and such failure could lead to arrest and trial—just as it did for Abel.

Panin stopped typing. Like his mind, the typewriter motor continued to hum. When he did start typing again, it was with an even more somber expression, which he could feel tightening the skin of his face:

> Then there is always execution. Richard Sorge was executed by the Japanese. Who among us can forget that? Of course, Sorge's circumstances did involve the war; executions in time of peace are a rarity.
>
> Still, execution is one of the possible ends to all of this. And to be honest, the idea of being caught is not altogether displeasing. Execution or no execution. With or without an exchange of captives such as that effected between Rudolf Abel and Francis Gary Powers. . . .

Panin shut the typewriter off. Its hum sank in pitch until it ground into silence. Nothing but the car horns and, somewhere, that radio remained in Panin's sleepless ears.

Slowly he removed the paper from the carriage and with a pair of scissors began shredding what he had just written. It had been stupid of him, he knew, to write such thoughts in the first place. As evidence, they were the equivalent of loaded, cocked guns aimed at his temple.

When he finished the shredding, he burned each piece, then dropped the remnants unceremoniously into the toilet. One consummative flush sent them down into this island.

Another hour passed. Vainly he rolled his head on the pillow in search of one corner not wet with perspiration.

There was none.

Panin got up, checked the clock, found the time to be 4:11. He went into the bathroom and faced himself in the bluish mirror under the bare fifty-watt bulb. "Nitchevo, be honest with yourself. Is it really America that tempts you?" He stared into his own eyes and examined his own face as he had learned to examine the faces of others.

No. He knew his answer was honest. Others might be bitten by this America bug, but not he. He didn't particularly care for Americans and he would never, never help them undermine a Soviet spy ring. From morning to evening, a man does not turn into a traitor. He could not think of a defector whom he believed to have sincerely opted for the States because of the American way of life. "Tell me another one," Panin challenged himself in the mirror.

That's when Vladimir Efimovich Panin admitted that he was locked in combat with something else. Hadn't Rabbi Grynspan called him a man of God? Could Grynspan, as a Ukrainian, have addressed Panin this way in order to bring him around? Was this night like Jacob's wrestling with an angel?

To Panin, the circumstances surrounding his soul were very much like those of a saint about whom he had recently read. The saint had said, "If I didn't know that there was only one God, I'd have seen one in this soul." Tonight, Panin realized, that one God was dealing with his soul. On the battlefield and crippled by a shattered leg, "Nitchevo" was something that Panin had been able to say.

But in the face of God, Panin knew that he would be lying to both himself and his Redeemer were he now to say, "It's nothing." But how could he—defenseless, deprived, tormented—how could he address God?

And had Panin not promised Rabbi Grynspan that he would pray for the old man as the old man had promised to pray "in a very special way" for him?

To Panin's heart, it felt as though his choices had been limited to just one.

"Lord," he murmured, going back to bed, "teach me to pray." The words had virtually floated into his mind. It was as if something he had read during his months of preparation at spy school had, ironically, stuck within his heart—only to appear in this hour of his need. He could only remember the phrase in French: *Le désir de la prière est déjà une prière*. And who has said that a man is great only when he is kneeling?

His mouth had become painfully dry.

In the darkness he reached out until he found the switch and could turn on the light. He got up for his drink of water. It was then that his eyes fell—as in a vivid dream—upon the crucifix that hung on the wall over his desk.

Christ was looking at him. Was it possible?

Panin felt an unspeakable trepidation, then fell, as if conquered, onto his knees. Like a child, he hid his face under the bedspread.

Seconds later, Panin cried out—his voice muffled from his own hearing by the bedspread. "Lord, make me less unworthy of Your mercy—please, Lord." Then he was silent. Waiting. Listening. Hoping for the voice of God.

"Lord," Panin beseeched. "I feel unworthy even of Your listening to me. . . ." Then the Russian hid his face once more, deep into the bed covers. He felt an exhaustion that moved over him like a body fever. He felt almost too weak to speak. "You can see, Lord, I can't even find the words with which to pray. I beg You—help me." It was all that the longing of his soul could say.

Still kneeling lightly, Panin fell asleep. Later he would remember this sleep as white and soothing and dreamless. He would remember it as having also been long and timeless. A sleep of sleeps.

Yet here in his quarters, he suddenly woke up.

He felt drawn. He knew he was being urged to look, once again, at the crucifix. Slowly he raised his head until the silver crucifix gleamed against the blue wallpaper. The face that met his was suffering—the suffering of Christ—but it was also serene. And crying.

"Is it you?" Panin whispered—for he realized that what he was seeing looked just like the face of Rabbi Grynspan. Yet the face was unmistakably the visage of Christ.

Then it was over. In a half daze, Panin felt free to climb back into bed. As he did, his body felt relaxed and refreshed—as after a hot shower. Immediately he dozed off and slept, without dreams or nightmares, until his alarm rang at six o'clock.

As he awoke, the first thing to become recognizable in his mind was the Psalm:

> *I spent all night meditating in my heart,*
> *I pondered and my spirit asked this question:*
> *If the Lord has rejected you, is this final?*
> *God, your ways are holy!*

[XXXI]

STAN POTOCKI HAD NOT SLEPT WELL, BUT HIS PROBLEM HAD not been insomnia. He had used the night to search the Permanent Observer's rectory office. No one had instructed him to do so. And he had found nothing that to him looked even remotely like important evidence. By breakfast Potocki was both exhausted and disappointed.

"Bacon or ham with your eggs, Tom?" Sal Vaccaro was asking as Potocki entered the rectory kitchen. Vaccaro wore an apron over his cassock.

"Neither, thanks, I'll scramble my own," replied Nevins.

Since Mrs. O'Rourke was nowhere to be seen, Potocki realized this must be her morning to come late and Sal's morning to cook. To Stan, the Italian priest looked like a character straight out of the Fellini movie that he had seen by mistake a couple of weeks before at the Little Carnegie Theater.

Somebody had told Potocki that the film was inspirational.

"And how about you, Monsignor Righi? Do you want toast or pancakes with your tea?"

Righi mumbled, thanks, but he couldn't eat anything.

Then Potocki noticed for the first time that morning how weary and tired the Observer appeared. Maguire also noticed Righi's condition.

"Giuseppe," he asked, "you're very pale and you look more worn than last night. Are you okay?"

"Frank, to tell the truth I don't feel very well."

There was a peculiar vulnerability in Righi's voice—a kind of humanness that Potocki had not noticed before. The Monsignor looked like a boy who had just lost his first friend, Stan decided, or maybe had just learned a crucial, unforgettable lesson. At any rate, there was a boyishness to the man's weary manner.

The pastor suggested, "Should we call Dr. O'Grady? He lives nearby, is here at the eleven o'clock mass every Sunday—"

"When he isn't out playing golf."

Potocki had meant his quip without malice—as a fast, helpful joke. But no one laughed. So he felt foolish and immediately fell silent once again.

"Oh, it'll go away," Righi responded. "Last night I thought it must be the flu, but I don't have a fever today. Probably just a cold that will go away."

That's when McNeil's phrase came to Potocki's mind. Poor fellow, he thought, Righi must have eaten ashes in his bread. And the thought made him feel a mixture of pity and triumph as he looked at the weakened Monsignor Righi. Ashes are no picnic . . . that was obvious to see.

"Did you sleep?" Maguire pursued. "You don't look as though you did—or you, Stan, for that matter!"

"You're right," Righi answered. "I had too much on my mind."

But Potocki was so caught off guard that he blurted out an alibi that at once made him sorry he had used it. "Uh, I was praying, Monsignor."

In turn, each of the priests seated around the table stared at Potocki as if no one believed that he spent last night in prayer. No one.

"Stan, that's admirable." Maguire's tone sounded a fine balance between priestly blessing and paternal skepticism. "As for you,

Giuseppe, you can have the UN on your mind too much. Remember that."

Vaccaro added, yelling from the other side of the kitchen, "Better a live donkey than a dead diplomat. There are still some of Momma's cannoli. I'll bring them to you. Maybe they'll turn out to be a miraculous cure for the UN germs that have got you down."

"The UN can go its own way," Righi snapped, then immediately seemed sorry about his comment. "At least the waters are calm after this latest crisis has blown over. I'd love to get away. But soon enough I'll be making a trip to Rome."

Potocki caught the look of surprise and concern in Maguire's eyes as the pastor asked the question that both of them wanted answered: "And when would that be? Uh, I only ask because of the mass schedule."

"February tenth. That's when I'm supposed to be in Rome—but I'll also get some time at home, far from everyday problems here." Righi looked up, glancing around the rectory kitchen. "I'm not speaking of you—you have put up with me and have extended such good graces. It's just that I'm a bit stale where the UN is concerned."

Potocki couldn't help but be surprised and perplexed by what the Permanent Observer had just confessed to them. When taken in context with his weary manner this morning, Potocki thought he saw a distinct change in Righi. He decided to phone JOE O'BRIEN about the date of February 10 as soon as breakfast was over. Righi could be on the verge of making some move.

"Good," Monsignor Maguire responded. "February tenth and your cold will be gone."

Sal Vaccaro began serving the priests. The men crowded around the table, then rushed through the blessing and proceeded eating in a hungry, aggressive manner—one, Potocki noted, that they did not employ when Mrs. O'Rourke was around. Men relaxing in the exclusive company of other men.

"Oh, Giuseppe, I forgot to tell you that one of those Israeli women telephoned for you yesterday while you were out. I'm sorry that I didn't give you the message sooner." Monsignor Maguire was talking with a mouth full of breakfast. Quickly he washed it down with Vaccaro's hearty black coffee.

"Which one?"

"Miss Arieh," Maguire answered and Potocki noted that Righi appeared pleased to hear her name. Then the pastor explained, "We had quite a chat on the phone and I tell you, she seems to me to be a pleasant and bright young woman. Imagine this: she wanted to know why my first name is Francis—in fact, why this name is so widespread among the 'Nazarenes,' as she calls us." A couple of the priests chuckled, but no one interrupted their eating to comment.

Finally Righi asked, "And what did you answer, Frank?"

"Giuseppe, what do you think? I told her about St. Francis of Assisi and St. Clare."

"Good, Frank. She's quite sincere—despite her calling us 'Nazarenes.' She's even collecting prayers, though I admit she doesn't make much distinction between Jewish and Christian—"

Maguire interrupted, talking even as he wiped his mouth with a napkin. "Now I see why she asked if I knew of any prayer written or said by St. Francis. I quoted the prayer to her and—can you believe—she took it down using shorthand. By the way, Giuseppe, she said that she'd call again today. Do you honestly think she may be a serious candidate for conversion?"

Potocki listened carefully to Righi's answer that Miss Arieh was "intelligent and open-minded, open to the truth." The Polish priest was not convinced. Then Righi concluded with words that Potocki thought O'BRIEN would be most interested in: "And if she concludes that we have the truth, I believe she'll be ready to accept the consequences." Potocki felt an immediate sense of disgust. It was one thing, he decided, to have sympathy for whatever this fellow Righi might be tormented by, but another thing altogether to sit and nod in agreement when he spoke of converting women like Miss Arieh.

Vaccaro, carrying another plate of hot toast, asked Maguire: "Monsignor, which prayer did you recite to her?"

"Sal, surely you know the one: 'Lord, make me an instrument of Your peace. . . .' Isn't St. Francis a favorite *paesano* of yours—even if Assisi isn't Calascibetta?"

"Of course!" Vaccaro joked. "And who among you would believe that I agree with an Irishman for once? I say that prayer often."

Potocki was reaching across Tom Nevins' plate to get the jelly when he saw puzzlement on Righi's face, as if—impossible as it seemed—the Permanent Observer did not know what Vaccaro and Maguire were talking about. Then Righi asked a question that made everyone stop eating.

"Frank, what's the English text for that prayer? Does the translation render the beauty and Franciscan simplicity of its original?"

"The English version? Well, here it is."

Lord, make me an instrument of your peace. Where there is hatred, let me sow love. Where there is injury, pardon. Where there is discord, union. Where there is doubt, faith. Where there is despair, hope. Where there is darkness, light. Where there is sadness, joy. Grant that we may not so much seek to be consoled as to console; to be understood as to understand; to be loved as to love. For it is in giving that we receive; it is in pardoning that we are pardoned; and it is in dying that we are born to eternal life.

Potocki noted that Maguire seemed to take Righi's question at face value. But the Polish priest remained incredulous. How could any priest not know the Prayer of St. Francis? That is—provided the man was a priest. . . .

Guardedly Potocki watched Righi's reactions while Maguire quoted the prayer and he had difficulty hiding his own astonishment as he saw the Permanent Observer's eyes—usually so cold and cutting—slowly fill with tears.

When Maguire had finished, Righi spoke up in a choked voice. "Please excuse me. You know I'm not feeling well and I think it best that I go back to bed."

Maguire and Vaccaro asked if there were things they could do for him and Nevins asked if he might help Righi up the stairs—but the weakened Monsignor declined. "Don't worry," he called to them as he walked through the dining-room doorway, "I'll call if I need help."

For a few moments, the priests sat in silence, almost stunned.

Finally Vaccaro asked Maguire, "Maybe there's something serious with the *paesano?* Has he mentioned anything to you?"

To Potocki, the pastor's answer seemed risky, almost too revealing. "Sal, the Prayer of St. Francis could make even stones repent." Then Maguire seemed to realize how his answer might be interpreted, so he added, "I guess the diplomat has just proved he's human too."

Potocki lost no time.

He asked to be excused as well, then grabbed his coat in the hallway and left the rectory for a nearby stationery store, where he used a telephone booth to call JOE O'BRIEN. Slowly and accurately, Potocki recounted every detail of the morning's breakfast. However, to his disappointment, the only item that seemed to interest the agent was Righi's date of departure for Rome: February 10, 1972.

For the rest of the morning, Panin meditated or slept.

His prayer had been answered by a prayer. God had, he now believed, sent him the Prayer of St. Francis as an answer to Panin's beseechment: "Lord, teach me to pray."

And the answer made Panin sob as he had not remembered doing since the days of his childhood.

He now understood: it was all so simple.

"Where there is despair, hope. . . ." An answer to his sleepless night: "Where there is darkness, light. . . ."

It all depended upon him, Panin realized.

He now had a prayer of his own. And so did Shula. What a feeling of forgiveness, of divine caring—Panin had finally found a comfort and warmth that had been missing throughout the long, torturous night.

God, he now knew, answered back when called upon. Prayer was not just playacting for the pious. For men who seek, there is a way.

[XXXII]

WHEN SHULAMITH ARIEH COULD NOT REACH MONSIGNOR Righi by phone and after her travel arrangements arrived by messenger, she realized that she would probably never see the man again.

Jehudah Tamir had made that clear.

He had explained her instructions most carefully: Jerusalem wanted her to understand that no further link between "associates" of their mission at the UN and the Permanent Observer of the Holy See were to be tolerated.

"I know the meaning of 'tolerated,'" she had assured Tamir.

He had continued, seemingly unaffected: The most recent crisis in the Middle East had underscored the fact that Israel's relationship with the Vatican was hindered by certain "soft areas"—a fact that key officials in Jerusalem chose to interpret as a signal. Therefore all Vatican officials were to be treated with the utmost cordiality and caution. In particular, this meant the Holy See's Permanent Observer at the UN. Did she understand?

"Fine," Shulamith had consented. It's just fine, for everyone except me. These last words she had muttered only in her thoughts.

She knew that Jehudah would go on as if nothing had happened. He always did. And she knew that those men from the FBI, McNeil and what's-his-name, would follow this particular "game" to its resolution, then file her story along with thousands of others.

She even suspected that Monsignor Righi would go his own way—wherever that was—and merely remember these last days as but an interlude. Then, of course, there was Gila. Poor, unquestioning, impervious Gila Ben-Ami. She was already back in Tel Aviv and probably involved with a new "assignment." Shula's airline tickets and exit visa indicated that Tel Aviv would be her destination as well.

But not before one last note to the Monsignor, Shulamith suddenly decided.

She made a hasty trip to a stationery store around the corner. There she purchased handsome parchmentlike notepaper and envelopes.

Back in her apartment, as she packed her bags, she thought carefully of what this note to him should say.

She put The Jerusalem Bible in the bag.

The message had to be genuine.

Finally, her packing completed, Shulamith sat cross-legged on the thick carpet and penned her thoughts and feelings into a quotation. It was all she could honestly say, yet she knew that these were words that would make him understand how she truly felt:

It is in giving that we receive.
It is in pardoning that we are pardoned.
With gratitude and affection, Shula.

Monsignor Righi never received the letter. In fact, for the next five days he saw no one outside the rectory—because he was found unconscious on his bed.

Earlier Monsignor Maguire had become alarmed when nothing could rouse Righi into answering his door. The pastor had authorized the younger priests to use the rectory passkey and to enter the Permanent Observer's quarters.

Potocki and Vaccaro found him, his Bible clutched to his chest. The book was opened to the Psalms.

Maguire made the phone calls: first to Dr. O'Grady and secretly to James McNeil at the FBI.

When Dr. O'Grady arrived, he was dressed in wool slacks of a vivid plaid, his winter golf outfit. He helped them bring Righi back to consciousness and diagnosed exhaustion—not acute enough to warrant hospitalization (*yet*, he added), but certainly serious enough to necessitate complete bed rest, a special diet, protein tablets, nursing care. . . .

Maguire seemed to employ an intuition as he suggested that maybe his niece, Evangeline, might be suitable as a nurse to see the weakened Monsignor through this confinement—

But Mrs. O'Rourke bristled as if the parish priest had told a bawdy joke in her presence. "What will people say? A young woman coming in and out of this house. I can hear it now: 'Poor ol' Mrs. O'Rourke, she just can't keep up the way she used to.'" The housekeeper hammered at Maguire's chest with her sturdy forefinger. "Now, I ask you: Do I deserve to be treated this way—and publicly?" Then she made the only threat to the parish priest that anyone could remember her ever making. "If so, Monsignor, then this lady'll be packing her bags. Am I clear?"

Reluctantly, or so his expression conveyed, Maguire retreated. He and Potocki exchanged quick glances, the pastor said the housekeeper could care for the Monsignor as she saw fit, Dr. O'Grady asked to be excused so that he might phone the drugstore nearby, and Mrs. O'Rourke immediately went to put on her coat. "I accept your apology," she said, nodding toward Maguire, although he had not said anything close to an apology. "And I'll be back after I've picked up the items I know will do the poor Monsignor Righi some good. Don't anybody feed that man a bite until I get back."

Even Dr. O'Grady seemed to understand that the Irishwoman's edict also included him.

To Panin, the loss of consciousness was like a dream.

And later the attentions of Dr. O'Grady and Mrs. O'Rourke seemed no more than hazy intrusions into his thoughts, into the sorting out of what he should do, now that his soul had begun its return to God.

He could feel himself slipping in and out of attentiveness.

All the while, Mrs. O'Rourke kept a wordless vigil with him. As she brought in broths, tender veal steaks, fish fillets, carefully stuffed chicken breasts, Panin could hardly resist the aromas that filled his room like a family's kitchen. He found himself eating more heartily at each successive meal.

And between meals, Mrs. O'Rourke brought small portions of various liquids to him. Included among these were what she seemed to remember as his favorite teas to accompany pastries and an assortment of delicacies.

Near the end of the second day, Panin secretly decided that KARENINA must be acting out of a sudden devotion that stemmed from some almost perverse pleasure at having the Colonel at her mercy.

By the third day, Panin had decided what he must do, though he had no idea as yet how he could accomplish it.

He took a chance. When Potocki came to visit in the afternoon, Panin asked, in Mrs. O'Rourke's presence, if he would do a favor for the Permanent Observer. Immediately Panin could see hasty, unguarded suspicion flare up in the housekeeper's eyes.

"Sure, Monsignor, you name it."

"Stan, it's for my already scheduled trip to Rome. Would you reserve a place for me on an Alitalia flight for the evening of February ninth? I'd like a round-trip ticket."

"But—" Both Potocki and Mrs. O'Rourke spoke the same word at the same time.

The priest deferred to the housekeeper.

"But, Monsignor, Dr. O'Grady hasn't given any indication—now has he?—of just when you'll be well enough to leave the rectory. And you'll be making arrangements to fly?"

Panin purposely ignored her and continued with Potocki. "I'm asking you, Stan, because Maguire is busy and the others would probably pass the request on to the secretary. There can be no mistake in this—it's for the Vatican, you know. Now I can trust you, can't I? It's for the ninth, you understand? And the return is to be left open." Then Panin returned his attention to the now-irritated Mrs. O'Rourke. "I hope, dear lady, you know that I dare not move without instructions—"

The housekeeper appeared incredulous. Panin realized that she was interpreting this as the first time since both of them had received instructions for absolute silence within the rectory that either of them had hinted at double meanings or oblique communication. Her taut expression seemed to chide: not in front of this guy—are you really sick?

Panin added most casually, "Stan, I'm a perfect patient. I take Dr. O'Grady's instructions second only to the Gospels."

Later that evening of January 15, Panin felt as though one more door had been closed to him, but that it indicated his next passageway. The maze was unfolding for him.

Monsignor Maguire had visited. Earlier Mrs. O'Rourke had left some special pastries for their tea, then she had left peevishly. Subsequently, when Panin had gone for his scotch, he had found that she had taken it from its shelf and put a note in its place: "Sorry, Monsignor. Doctor's orders."

When the pastor arrived, he seemed edgy as he repeatedly crossed his legs, rubbed at his weathered face, and stammered.

Panin decided he could not ask Maguire to hear his confession. It was not that Frank Maguire couldn't be trusted. He could. However, during the conversation Panin had realized that the pastor did not have his best interests in mind. Maguire virtually refused direct eye contact during their chat. It was as though he knew that his direct manner—which had endeared him and made him so trusted among the rectory priests, even among the parish at large—this direct manner could not be offered to this man. Panin reasoned that somehow Maguire knew. Confessing to Frank Maguire would have put the pastor in a position that he could not handle. How could he cope with the confessions of a spy?

Even as Maguire sat in the ill man's quarters and talked about rectory finances and quarrels among the priests and scheduling problems for masses, Panin had understood that his confessions as a spy and also as a new believer must be said to no one outside of the Vatican itself.

Another midnight. The one between the fifteenth and sixteenth of January. Again Panin knelt beside his bed.

"Lord," he prayed in a whisper unnatural for a rectory. "I have no one to talk to—but You." Outside, the street noises created almost unearthly, muffled sounds that echoed in his quarters. Grayish light danced about his ceiling. "Lord, You know that I would do nothing of value were I to give myself up to the Americans. What would it mean to my soul if I ended up a defector whose picture and story appeared on the front pages of newspapers? And what good would my life be living as an ex-spy, guarded by the Americans and left to write memoirs which the average American would demean? Please, God, help me see the way out. Guide my journey. Lead me."

[XXXIII]

FRIDAY OF THAT THIRD WEEK IN JANUARY, FALCON RE-ceived what would turn out to be the last encoded message from his contact at Moscow Operations Center.

From his garage on Long Island, Harry Goldstein taped the message, then telephoned TOLSTOY at another Manhattan deli to establish one more late night meeting. FALCON agreed to pick TOLSTOY up at the Empire Diner. The two would decipher another message while they rode around town in Harry's Volvo.

"Don't forget, sonny," TOLSTOY added in closing, "there are still dangers in driving late at night. Some drunks haven't heard that the holidays are over."

Harry Goldstein knew what TOLSTOY meant: surveillance and

tailing remained a real threat. "Me?" he quipped. "I'll drive like every car on the road was out to run me down." Then FALCON hung up and headed for his zigzag route through the Island and Queens before reaching Manhattan and Alexander Lewinson.

What they learned from deciphering the tape was that Russian informants in Canada had discovered additional new results from the Mounties' ongoing investigation, pertinent to the HOLY SYNOD mission.

An as-yet unidentified Russian agent had defected. Protective custody around the defector was, for the moment, preventing any "silencing" actions. But one fact had been confirmed: from this defector, the Mounties knew enough to identify Colonel Panin's role in the Ukrainian-colony subversion of 1969–70.

Once that information reached the Bureau in America, the HOLY SYNOD cover was within days, possibly hours, of being exposed. KARENINA and TOLSTOY, possibly even FALCON were all in immediate danger.

As soon as possible, exit documents would be coming to each of them, according to final instructions they had been given before the mission began.

Lewinson whistled through his widely spaced lower teeth. "Kiss it all good-bye."

Goldstein said nothing. Instead he continued to drive with his left hand and rewound the recorder with his right. Slowly the FALCON replayed the entire tape, as if straining to make certain that what they had deciphered was no mistake.

Later, when Goldstein returned to the Empire Diner, where he intended to drop off TOLSTOY, the old man slapped at the younger man's knee in a friendly gesture. "Next year in Jerusalem—maybe —what do ya say?" Still, the FALCON remained silent. As the short-legged Lewinson got out of the Volvo, he called back, "Then somewhere, at least. And be well . . . be well."

Into the darkness engulfing the streets near the shiny, twenty-four-hour diner, the shopkeeper named Lewinson disappeared. FALCON's Volvo drove off—its motion was the jerk one normally associates with a taxi.

Midway back to Long Island, Harry Goldstein realized that their original directives with regard to final instructions had all exit documents coming first to KARENINA. But now she was insulated from the rest of them.

It could snag.

Even the hint of that possibility made the FALCON feel more uncomfortable than he had felt since those first illegal days in America.

By noon the following day, Panin received what at first he thought to be a delayed Christmas gift from Monsignor Righi's sister in Italy. That's what the package size and return address indicated.

However, when Panin opened the package, he immediately recognized the ploy for getting his final instructions to him. "They'll come like a thief in the night," General Rostov had forewarned him months ago. "To spring a priest, one needs to think as the pious think."

Now here it was: a hand-crafted, ivory crucifix that bore the imprint of a craftsman in Righi's native province. But this was only a fine copy. A Rostov copy.

Quickly Panin locked himself in his bathroom and proceeded to decipher the message encoded in the prayer imprinted on the back of the crucifix:

Moscow had received the HOLY SYNOD's request for permission to return home, via Rome, departing February ninth. KARENINA and TOLSTOY—possibly other operatives—were also being called back, but their exit plans were more difficult to arrange.

HOLY SYNOD was instructed to use his time in Italy to everyone's best advantage. Moscow approved earlier contacts with an American naval officer now stationed in Italy; HOLY SYNOD should, upon arrival, renew contacts with this officer, then proceed to obtain all information that the officer, currently attached to the south command of NATO in Naples, might offer. He was expected to extract a promise of long-term cooperation in furnishing information on the codes used by the Seventh Fleet in the Mediterranean.

HOLY SYNOD was strictly instructed not to return to New York. He was to pass any information about the Seventh Fleet to the Soviet military attaché in Rome, then make his own arrangements for an incognito return to the Soviet Union.

Panin stared without actually seeing the basin or towel bar in front of him. He was overcome by an immense sense of relief. It was, he realized, as if God had intervened. The bewilderment of these last days of illness suddenly gave way to undeniable hope.

He felt like the prodigal son before his return, his forty-nine years of wandering now coming to an end. Admittedly he had no real scheme for how he might make his plans happen, but Panin now believed. No one could cheat him of the joy. He was returning to his Father's house.

By January 27, when James McNeil and Mike Russo were going over their checklist, the Bureau was virtually certain that they held all the strings to pull in the whole network.

At least that's what their evidence showed: the housekeeper, the shopkeeper, the chauffeur, and possibly one other, all to support the man who (McNeil was now privately convinced) was a masterful impostor. The Mounties' report had been the light switch. It was now time to expose one *Colonel Vladimir Panin*. But first the Bureau needed witnesses in custody.

McNeil double-checked. "The rectory, Lewinson's shop, and the current location of all other suspects?"

Russo read from yet another note pad. "No slips, no changes. Surveillance reports from them all within the last half-hour."

"Great. How about medical info on the Observer from Doc O'Grady's office?"

"Patient still confined to bed. All vital signs positive during the noon exam. Slight chest congestion. Nothing else."

McNeil fought off the fleeting feeling that something somewhere was not being covered. "What about the airports, the docks, the Canadian border, train stations? Any look-alikes stopped for questioning? Any instances of visas or passports having been doctored?"

"Nothing out of the ordinary. This thing is tight. I promise you."

The agent rubbed at his tired, tense face with both hands and leaned across the desk as if to emphasize the point. "Russo, any worries in your own mind, man? Spill 'em. Otherwise, I don't want any moans, once we start pulling in the net. Do you read me?"

Russo frowned. "Look. Nothing short of an act of God could save these fish. Believe me."

James McNeil, as both a good Catholic and a tired Bureau man, took no comfort in Russo's weak attempt at a joke. He decided to phone Maguire and ask him, if he was willing, to pray a special prayer. Something important was coming up; the Bureau needed God on their side. At least until February ninth . . .

That evening a small parcel was delivered to Mrs. O'Rourke's West Sixty-ninth Street apartment. She had never seen the deliveryman before, but she decided to risk a question. Any information could be crucial.

"Any trouble with this? Any interference getting this here?"

The man's eyes contained hours of conversation focused into a few direct gazes. "Lady, I got through because some guys like the smell of my cash." His pause spoke louder to her than his words. "If I were you, I wouldn't expect any other friendly visitors."

She knew exactly what the stranger meant. She watched him walk away and locked the door carefully before opening the parcel. The sight of her exit documents felt like a reprieve, but the documents for FALCON and TOLSTOY—what was she to do with them, now that she had been insulated from all the others?

The next morning, January 28, she had her plan in mind.

She sent a message from an East Side walk-up where the Singing Telegram Service of Manhattan had its offices. She could only hope that TOLSTOY would recognize the final-instructions code in which the telegram had been prepared. Even if he did, she did not know if he could act upon the information. Still, she had to signal where the documents were being sent.

Afterward, she returned to her apartment and sealed their documents in an envelope marked "Special Delivery" and addressed it, per the telegram code, to Richard P. Johnson, 201 West Seventy-second Street, New York, New York. Then she left the apartment without taking a single item.

Marfyona was a woman who long ago had learned how to say good-bye.

Panin got the idea for his escape as he stood barefoot on the cold rectory floor. He was flipping through the bulky Manhattan Yellow Pages when he saw the heading: "Ambulance Services." The words made him rush back between the covers of his bed and study most carefully which company he should choose for conveying him out of the rectory.

A hospital and its emergency room, he knew from previous experience, were far better exits than this Church of the Nativity rectory.

Marfyona used that evening to convince herself that she had shaken any possible "shadows," then to abandon her Mrs. O'Rourke identity.

She checked into the Dixie Hotel on West Forty-second Street, where she spent most of the night making her appearance match her passport photo, the image that some unknown superior had supplied for her. She sheared her hair, then dyed it. She tried various makeup combinations until she could see in the hotel mirror a face she had never known before. By dawn she could see a face that gave her comfort.

There was just one more errand to run, a stop in Brooklyn, then she intended to return to Times Square and go to the Cunard Line docks, where she could double-check her booking for the ship scheduled to sail on January 30.

Two hours later James McNeil gave the order to arrest her.

"You say she's just dropped an envelope off at the Tillary Street post office and the address matches the one we intercepted in the singing telegram sent to Lewinson? Check. And you've searched her apartment on Sixty-ninth. Nothing?" McNeil cupped his hand over the phone and ordered Russo to handle the court procedures for warrants. "Then yank her in," he yelled back at the agent reporting in. "And tell your buddy to guard that envelope at the post office until we can get papers in his fist."

Five minutes later, amid phone exchanges between the Bureau and other agencies, the same agent called in again. McNeil was so eager to grab the phone that he jammed his knee, with a deep thud, into the desk drawer encasement. "Aaaah," he groaned into the phone. "McNeil here. Make it fast, this line is handling emergencies—"

"It's me, boss, at Tillary Street. I got a problem."

The pain in McNeil's knee was the hot, crazy-bone kind. "Shoot."

"It's this housekeeper. She's not resisting or anything. She just wants to do something funny."

" 'Weird' funny or 'ha' funny?"

The agent sounded perplexed. "More like 'nice' funny, boss. She says she wants to call the Church of the Nativity and tell them that she's just been to a doctor and that he says she won't be able to work for a while. Can she do that, Jim?"

McNeil felt as though something more than his knee pain had gone crazy. Then the reporting agent spoke away from the phone, though McNeil could faintly hear, "Lady, you tell him—"

"Hello there, Mr. McNeil, sir. This is Mrs. O'Rourke." As the woman continued, all McNeil could be concerned about was the hope that this woman was in handcuffs. "I certainly don't mean to make trouble for the FBI, but I do know that the good Monsignor and my priests at Nativity don't deserve to be left without sufficient help and sufficient notice. In all my years of household work, I've never done that. Can an old woman have your permission to call in and say I won't be available for a while?"

It was a situation that McNeil had never encountered—that was for sure. "You're right, ma'am. You probably won't be available for a long while. But Blessed Mary, something tells me you're sincere. It's amazing. I guess your thoughtfulness does you credit." He paused to weigh the options. "Well, I'll call Monsignor Maguire for you. You understand?"

The woman sounded oddly appeased to McNeil. "Thank you, young man. It means a lot."

In spite of himself, he responded. "I guess there aren't many people like you left in domestic service now, are there?"

"Believe me," she answered, "there are no more."

Within the hour, Harry Goldstein and Alexander Lewinson were also arrested. McNeil got a report that the old man was arrested after agents awakened him from a nap behind a counter of rosaries. As for Goldstein, agents had found him waiting on the brownstone steps of 201 West Seventy-second Street. His alibi had been that he was a new tenant, waiting for the mailman from whom he intended to get a change-of-address card and instructions for putting his name on the mailbox. The men from the FBI got Goldstein to answer to the name Richard P. Johnson.

"Tell the fellow," McNeil concluded, "that we're holding a 'Special Delivery' package just for him."

Questioning of the housekeeper and the shopkeeper and the Long Island radio buff proceeded into the afternoon of February 2nd.

But the Bureau got nowhere, other than giving Mrs. O'Rourke the nickname "the Rock." When Russo came in to take his turn with the housekeeper, he saw McNeil's concern. The agent rigidly held to the approach that the Mounties' information was not enough for them to risk bringing the Permanent Observer of the Holy See into custody. Surveillance, yes. But an arrest?

Monsignor Righi enjoyed diplomatic immunity, moreover the position he held was an important one that demanded that the Bureau have cold proof behind any challenge.

"Listen, Jim," Russo encouraged him. "We've got at least until the ninth."

But Volodya Panin left New York the afternoon of the second.

He did not have to resort to the escape route of the ambulance service or to the confusion of an emergency ward in order to evade those agents he knew to be hounding his every move beyond the rectory.

It was as if God, in fact, had intervened.

About four o'clock, Panin told the parish secretary that he would be calling upon the provincial of the Scalabrinian Fathers on Carmine Street. She agreed to take his phone messages and also asked if the Monsignor was certain that he was up to a trip around the city.

"Just getting out will do me good," he answered, then left the rectory. He was carrying nothing but a briefcase.

On First Avenue, he caught a taxi and rode directly to Kennedy Airport. I have only one hope, he kept telling himself. If they intend to prevent me from leaving the country, I cannot escape them. And if they are following me, I cannot lose them.

Not this late in the game.

My only hope is to do what none of them will expect me to do.

At Kennedy Airport, Panin spotted two FBI agents before they seemed to see him. He knew there must be others.

He proceeded nonetheless to the TWA ticket counter, where he purchased a round-trip ticket, New York to Rome, and paid the ticket agent in cash. While she was counting his change, he prayed. Only God could get him out.

Then ticket in hand, he walked to the passport area. Immediately, the two agents moved toward the section that Panin was heading for. He was certain there would be others as well. His heart pounded within him as he walked forward, still praying.

"Father?" The shorter of the two apparent agents called to him. "Use this line, please."

Panin followed the instructions, knowing that he dared not resist at this point. Nitchevo he might be, but he was also no daredevil.

When he reached the agent, the other man turned and walked away, leaving Panin and the shorter man by themselves.

"I need the truth from you, Father. Please."

Panin had no idea what to say and merely shook his head in puzzlement.

"Are you the priest who was a friend of Shulamith Arieh?"

Was this a trap? Panin knew that at this moment, he had no way of knowing. He decided to answer with the truth—even if it cost him his freedom. He took a long, deep breath, then responded.

"Shula is very special to me . . . and to my Lord."

The agent then took Panin's ticket from him and firmly seized the Russian's right arm. "Then come with me and ask no questions. I have orders to stop you. My orders could keep this plane on the ground until next Christmas. But I also have a debt. Even if it costs me my job, my career, I must pay it."

To Panin's astonishment, the agent led him onto the plane, then waited just outside the passenger's compartment entrance until the stewardess sealed the door. Later, from Panin's window, he could see the watching man's figure at the terminal window.

Whoever the man was, Panin reflected, Shulamith had been the key. And whatever his motivation, some power beyond them all had done the persuading and the arranging. Like the parting of the Red Sea . . . but without drama, without theatrics.

Just the mystery of men protected by their God.

PART SIX

THE TWA PLANE ARRIVED ON TIME AT ROME'S LEONARDO DA Vinci International Airport.

Panin had no luggage to pick up, so he went straight to the terminal entrance, got into a taxi, and said to the driver, "To the Vatican." It was half-past nine.

"I suppose," the driver joked in a Roman dialect, "you have an audience with the Pope?"

"Yes, I hope to see him." Panin's head leaned forward, as if to use the remainder of the ride for a nap.

He had not slept during the night flight. He had not even accepted the hostess' offer of earphones for the film. Instead, he had taken a New Testament out of his briefcase and had immersed himself in it.

A man rose from the seat in front of him. Apparently a Jew, he put a prayer shawl around his shoulders and turned his back to the screen before launching into his evening prayers. He seemed determined to avoid the movie's distraction.

For many passengers, the scene became a show within a show.

But not to Panin, who knew that this fellow had faith and was not ashamed to practice it openly. A changed Panin could no longer laugh at such zeal—first, because it reminded him of Rabbi Grynspan, and secondly, because Panin now realized that God would judge according to faith put into such action.

If Christians had such faith, Panin silently pondered, as Christ said, they'd move mountains . . . they could turn this world around.

Panin was meditating on St. Paul's Epistle to Timothy as the sun rose and the plane flew over England's southern coast.

When breakfast was served, he left the toast and drank only the coffee. He hoped to receive communion in Rome. And for this communion, Panin wanted to observe the rules: no solid food, and liquids only up to three hours before.

To the hostess' question, "Aren't you eating anything, Father?" he had responded, "No, dear. I have to do penance for the greed of which I was guilty in New York: too many good restaurants." She laughed understandingly, so he asked, "Are you from the city?"

"From nearby—across the George Washington Bridge. I live in Fort Lee. Ever heard of it?"

Panin smiled back at her. He remembered the bridge tour for the prelate. "I know Palisades Amusement Park better."

"Lucky man. I never have time to go."

Neither had he, Panin realized. "I know it only by reputation."

The taxi moved rapidly down the highway toward Rome.

The anticipation reminded him that he had never been to Rome. In fact, the only Italian cities Panin had visited were Venice and Florence—to which he had gone on his own—and Trieste.

Panin remembered posing at Trieste as a member of the Allied Control Commission. In those days, Trieste was considered by the Kremlin to be a barometer for Western relations with Yugoslavia. Panin's mission had been to determine what instructions these Commission representatives had been given with regard to relations with Tito.

When his colleagues organized a bus trip to Rome, Panin's KGB superior had directed him to play sick, enabling the impostor on the Commission to go through papers from the British, French, and American governments. He had succeeded by bribing a petty French official, who showed him secret papers indicating that the three Western Allies doubted the sincerity of Tito's detachment from the Soviet orbit and that the Allies were ready to oppose, with force, any expansionist aims on the part of Yugoslavia. . . .

But there had been time for a private excursion.

An intelligent guide had taken Panin to the Piazzale Michelangelo overlooking Florence and had recited, "Florence, city of the mind; Rome, city of the soul."

The quotation had reminded Panin that the Russian patriarchate of the Orthodox Church once considered Moscow to be the third Rome. What then had become of this glorious Christian name? He remembered that historically, Constantinople had become the second Rome when the Roman Emperor Constantine transferred the empire seat there. Later the czars took over this title after the Turks captured Constantinople in 1453.

The thought saddened Panin: Moscow, the third Rome, now ruled by political power.

Street noises from the city roused Panin within the taxi and his spirit rebounded. He was not in Moscow, but in the city of the soul . . . of his soul so miraculously rediscovered.

Urbs aeterna: the Eternal City.

"What's that dome to the right?"

The taxi driver responded, his hands waving even as he snaked the car through heavy traffic, "The Church of Saints Peter and Paul in the new EUR section. Mussolini planned this Esposizione Universale Roma." His eyes quickly checked his passenger's expression through the rearview mirror. "I don't know what you think, Reverend—but for me, Mussolini was a great man."

A sudden whiff of gas fumes caused Panin's reply to be peppered with coughs: "A dictator—even if he improved some things. But we're better off without dictators whatever their successes." Before he could utter his last remark, a spasm erupted, making Panin's question sound more like a bark. "How far to the Vatican?"

"If there isn't too much traffic on the Via Aurelia, we'll make it in twenty minutes."

Half an hour later, Panin subtly checked his watch so as not to offend the driver, and the taxi turned onto the Via della Conciliazione. The facade and cupola of St. Peter's appeared in their majesty.

The driver interrupted a low whistle to ask, "Which entrance, Father?"

"The middle of the Square, thank you."

Left alone and holding his small briefcase, Panin was overpowered by wonder as he stood beside the obelisk. The semicircular colonnade seemed to embrace him with its massive granite columns. Suddenly, Cardinal Devreux's descriptions of the Square came to Panin's mind. Bernini had meant this colonnade and these columns to symbolize the Church's encompassment of peoples of every race and tongue. He had intended the multitude of saints atop the colonnade to stand for the "fecundity of faith in Christ." Mother of saints: the Church.

It all seemed so profound to him. How arduous, but not impossible is this road to sainthood: where had Panin read that, he wondered? Or the other phrase that also came to him: A Christian's only sorrow is in not becoming a saint.

Then Panin's eyes rose to the cross that topped the obelisk and he understood what the inscription at its base must mean, celebrating Christianity's triumph over paganism. His glance shifted to Michelangelo's dome, which amazed him with its power and harmony, its equilibrium and elegance, all as in a divine balance.

And there, to his right: the Apostolic Palace, where soon he intended to confess his imposture. He felt compelled to pray: "God, strengthen my resolve and assist me with Your grace."

Joining a band of pilgrims, Panin moved toward the basilica. As he was about to enter, a guard stopped him. For a quick moment, Panin panicked.

"Reverend, you can't go in with either a camera or a briefcase. Please check your items here." The handsomely uniformed guard spoke Italian clearly and Panin felt relieved as he realized the man was only carrying out routine security. But he foresaw another problem. His briefcase contained the lock combination for the safe containing the Permanent Observer's code secrets. Panin had carefully kept this paper for delivery to the Cardinal Secretary of State. It would be, he hoped, proof of his sincerity.

"Very well." He relinquished the case, realizing that the Cardinal could easily send for it once Panin had told his story. "But let me take out my breviary."

"By all means."

Panin removed the breviary and made certain that the lock combination was positioned on top of the other papers in his briefcase; then he volunteered the case and entered the church.

He had decided to say a brief prayer before this most important encounter of his life. Ahead, under the great bronze canopy, lay the Altar of Confession. At the railing, he knelt. More than a hundred lighted lamps, each symbolizing a prayer, surrounded him.

"Beneath me, O Lord, is the tomb of Peter, prince of the

apostles. He too denied Christ. But Peter was saved by a loving look from You, the Divine Master, on Your way to shed Your blood for all mankind." Soundlessly, Panin concluded his prayer with that of Peter and the other apostles, allowing their words to echo in his mind: Lord, increase our faith.

On his way out, Panin paused to say an Ave Maria before Michelangelo's "Pietà," then the new Christian felt ready to face those whose confidence he had betrayed. He approached the bronze doors with a feeling of serenity.

The Swiss Guard sprang to attention, presenting his halberd as he did each time a priest passed by. Fifteen feet further, the pontifical gendarmerie waited in civilian dress. Panin held out Righi's card.

"Monsignor, you've come from New York?" The gendarme continued to scrutinize the card, then copied Righi's name.

"Yes, and I wish to see the most eminent Secretary of State." The two men looked at one another as if the gendarme was probing for some recognition. Is this the Righi he remembered?

"I'll call His Eminence's secretary for a pass. One moment." He dialed the number, then asked Panin, "Monsignor Righi, how's the weather in New York? It's too bad that you've run into a cold wave here in Rome. A lucky man you are, working there these days. In Italy things are very bad. *L'America è sempre l'America!*"

Panin began a reply, but the gendarme's attention returned to the phone.

After several seconds, the gendarme cupped his hand over the receiver and whispered, "You can go up now. Of course you know the way." Along with the return of Righi's card, the gendarme gave Panin a pass.

But Panin did not know the way, though that had rarely hindered Nitchevo before. He simply followed a priest who seemed to be at home, reading a thick report as he walked. The two climbed several flights of broad, solemn marble stairs, then entered the vast courtyard that Panin recognized, remembering photographs: San Damaso.

There another Swiss Guard stopped him, examined the pass, then directed Panin to the elevator.

From there, everything was easier. The elevator operator left

Panin on the first floor of Raphael's Logge, where a third Swiss Guard indicated the office of the Secretary of State.

Panin felt, walking through half of the Loggia, the vernal effect of the frescoed vaults, their pastoral themes appearing as a succession of airy pergolas populated by birds of nearly every color, each peeping from among the painted leaves and branches.

He entered the wide, open door. Its shiny leather screen attracted Panin's attention until a young priest greeted him: "Our representative at the United Nations?"

"I am called Monsignor Righi, yes."

The other obviously did not understand and smiled cordially. "I know that you want to see His Eminence, but I'm afraid you've chosen a bad day. Audiences today are for the diplomatic corps." The smile broadened.

"I regret not having given notice. I only ask that His Eminence spare a few minutes." Panin could get no hint of the secretary's mood from the man's dull eyes. "I just arrived—hardly two hours ago. Straight from New York. I consider the conference so important that I came directly—"

The secretary's eyes brightened. "Have you been to the Secretariat of State?"

As Panin stuttered, "No," the secretary continued: "That's the procedure."

Panin's expression responded, I know, and he softened his voice in a steady tone, "I should like to report directly to His Eminence. Please."

The secretary appeared to enjoy getting to make the last comment: "His Eminence will decide."

Back in New York, Father Potocki went to four different phone booths along Third Avenue before he mustered up enough courage to complete the phone call.

When McNeil had listened to a catalog of apologies, he asked that the confused priest repeat the facts. "He didn't sleep at the rectory last night and his briefcase is missing from his room. He didn't appear in the sacristy for the six-thirty mass assigned to him."

"Okay, Pete. Just keep waiting. We'll talk about it later." The agent rubbed his temples with his thumb and middle finger. Headaches and his sinuses and now this. "Oh, Pete—what time you got? Nine? Why not call me at noon? And take care—sure."

During the three-hour interval, the FBI ascertained that the Permanent Observer of the Holy See had, indeed, left the city undetected.

Indications now placed this Monsignor Righi in Rome—thanks to a slip at TWA and to Father Potocki. If James McNeil had not felt so ill he would have asked why it had taken Pete so long to report all of this from the rectory.

[XXXV]

CARDINAL GIULIO RESPIGHI HAD BEEN READING A LENGTHY report prepared for him on *"Humanae vitae."* Yet another controversy was emerging on the subject and the Secretary of State intended to keep current on what had been written about this encyclical, both the bitter attacks and the feeble defenses.

Using an ivory letter opener, the Cardinal scratched his bony chin. "Responsible procreation," he thought aloud, "a problem which didn't exist in my grandfather's day."

His black robe brushed at the edges of his polished desk as the Cardinal moved to the tall window that overlooked St. Peter's Square. Today was the feast of St. Blaise. Yesterday's crowd from Candlemas was gone. Cardinal Respighi took hope. Yesterday had been a mild, sunny day, affirming the proverbial belief that winter's backbone had been broken. His arthritis sorely needed relief.

Hadn't his secretary understood him this morning, following mass in the Cardinal's private chapel? He had given the Cardinal the blessing of his throat with lighted candles. "By intercession of the blessed Blaise, Bishop and Martyr, may the Lord free you from ills of the throat and all other ills."

A knock on the door interrupted his reflections. His secretary entered, but Cardinal Respighi continued staring out the window. So his secretary began explaining about the Permanent Observer of the Holy See at the United Nations. . . .

His Eminence's mind quickly connected Monsignor Righi's

name with a note that the substitute of the Secretariat of State had left yesterday: ". . . a comprehensive report on the most recent session of the General Assembly. . . ."

"If you agree, Your Eminence, an appointment might be arranged for, say, late this afternoon?"

"If Monsignor Righi says it's urgent, let me see him right away." The Cardinal's mumble sent his secretary back out of the room, but not without a sigh, once out of His Eminence's earshot.

What the Cardinal was looking upon were the magnificent pines, the ones towering on the slopes of Janiculum around the American College. Those boys, he reflected, they come to Rome "from every state in the Union." Here they find all that Rome means and should mean to a Catholic priest. But do they take it away with them? Now, with the opponents to *Humanae vitae* rising up even from among distinguished seminary professors who once studied here?

The statue of the Redeemer shown through the pines and cypresses from the ridge where the Society of Jesus . . . "Your Eminence, Monsignor Giuseppe Righi, Permanent Observer of the Holy See at the United Nations."

Respighi turned to see a man who looked vaguely as he remembered the Monsignor, but not exactly. Something about the face was different. An expression of suffering.

Panin heard the Cardinal speaking: "Monsignor, we received a very well-documented report from you. The substitute was very complimentary." Panin watched as the Vatican official gestured toward the stack of folders and booklets across his desk. "As soon as I can, I intend to read it most carefully." But Panin felt compelled to stand in silence.

How was he going to tell all to this man?

"Monsignor, you look very tired. We weren't expecting you before next week. I hope nothing has happened?"

Panin heard nervousness in his voice as he responded. "Your Eminence, I deeply regret disturbing you without asking for an audience. But the matter at stake is serious. Very serious."

Respighi motioned toward a pair of chairs. "Please do sit down. And tell me, what is it?" Panin could see that the Cardinal recognized his visitor's deep concern.

Even as Panin sat, he began speaking—though he could not bear to look directly into His Eminence's probing eyes. Rather, Panin stared beyond the Cardinal and examined the luminous room as he explained, "I fear what I have to say will disturb you and I beg your forgiveness in advance." What he saw was a sixteenth-century vaulted ceiling and richly covered walls hung with Flemish tapestries. In them, Panin found much-needed relief from the pain of confronting the kindly face across from him.

"Don't speak *per speculum et enigmata*, Monsignor. Please lay politeness aside and say frankly what you have come to say." Cardinal Respighi's long fingers, suddenly shifting across the letter opener, were the only evidence that the churchman was feeling impatient as well as curious. "Is there something which interferes with your work in New York? Then let me tell you at once that we highly esteem you." Panin slowly bowed his head. "I know how difficult it can be, living in a local rectory, no home of your own. Cardinal Devreux said as much. I found some of the same difficulties when I was a young secretary in Latin America: I know what local conditions can impose by restricting one's movements, prohibiting entertaining when or where one wishes. . . ."

Panin listened only vaguely to these reminiscences.

Instead he focused upon the red trimmings on the black robe that the Cardinal wore. Somewhere—in Canada or back in Moscow?—Panin remembered learning that the cardinal's red had a symbolic meaning: the wearer's readiness to shed his blood, if necessary, for his God.

Finally, Panin forced himself to interrupt the Cardinal in midsentence.

"Your Eminence, you are not talking to Monsignor Righi."

Earlier Panin had taken particular notice of the Cardinal's cross, studded with rubies and hanging around his neck on a handsome gold chain; now, apparently in reaction to the Cardinal's genuine surprise, the cross jolted as the older man leaned forward.

Panin continued: "The man you see before you has only pretended to be Monsignor Righi." He saw a glaze settle on the Cardinal's eyes. "No, Your Eminence, I haven't lost my mind, nor have you. There's no need to become alarmed, either. I am telling you the plain truth. And I'm only sorry that it's painful to hear. But believe me, it's equally painful to tell."

Sorrow slowly replaced disturbance in the Cardinal's expression. When he finally responded, he emphasized his gestures with the use of his ivory letter opener.

"Tell me, Monsignor Righi, that this story is a Carnival joke. The Carnival season is well on its way." Respighi's throat grew raspy. "Or say that you're tired and that your condition has affected your imagination." Again, the Cardinal leaned forward, his black robe creating a wall-like effect. "But tell me—not out of respect for me, since I am of little value, but for my position—if you are not our Righi, who are you?"

Panin spoke more clearly than he had done in years: "Colonel Vladimir Efimovich Panin, an officer of the *Komitet Gosudarstvennoi Bezopasnosti*. The KGB, Your Eminence."

The Vatican official rose. As he walked toward the tall window, he continued to watch his visitor, fearfully now.

In spite of himself, Panin proceeded to spout a passionate and lengthy statement of deep conviction. Unconsciously, he switched from Italian to his native language.

"Monsignor, since when do you speak Russian?"

"The Monsignor does not," Panin responded, back in Italian, "but Russian is my native tongue."

Against the window light, Respighi's face grew even more pale. Still, he seemed determined to restore some control over the situation. "There was an inquiry, just a while ago. The Italian SID. We learned about it only yesterday and were about to send you a cable in code. . . . I beg you, once again: who are you?"

"Who I have been from the beginning: Volodya Panin."

The Cardinal shook his head, evidently incredulous. "But you have Monsignor Righi's looks and voice and gait . . . ?"

"Physically, I may be his double. But morally, Your Eminence, I'm a bad copy, an impostor." Then Panin attempted to calm the Vatican official: "You have no need to fear. I'm not carrying any weapon."

With a wave of his hand, Cardinal Giulio Respighi interrupted Panin. "Afraid? I am not afraid. But I am bewildered." The churchman went to his desk and raised the receiver on his telephone. "This is urgent. Please send Father Zalenski."

When he had concluded the phone call, he explained to Panin:

"Zalenski's our Russian translator. We shan't speak to each other again, not until he arrives."

"One request, Your Eminence." Panin halted the pacing that the Cardinal had resumed. "Please ask that my briefcase be brought from the entrance. It's important."

Without saying anything further to Panin, Respighi returned to his phone, made the call to fulfill the request, then turned his back upon his visitor.

During the long minutes of waiting that followed, Panin watched the Cardinal appear to lose his thoughts in the hunting scenes on the tapestries lining his office walls. Panin wondered what the churchman was thinking as both of them stared into the imploring eyes of the stricken boars or, there, into the bloodthirsty eyes of a pack of dogs.

"He speaks perfect Russian, Your Eminence. Very refined. He seems to be well educated. But I don't understand. Isn't he Monsignor Righi?"

Cardinal Respighi appreciated the great disadvantage under which Father Zalenski had been placed, having listened to the visitor's lengthy statement in Russian without knowing anything of the earlier conversation between Respighi and the man who until now had posed as Righi. However, the Secretary of State needed this control. "Please, Father Zalenski, just interpret what he told you."

What Zalenski reported in Italian seemed to Respighi to be direct confirmation of his visitor's earlier admissions. He had been a Soviet spy, he was sorry for his imposture, and he now came to ask forgiveness and to make a sacramental confession. "He says, finally, that he'll resume talking to Your Eminence in Italian as soon as I have left the room."

Respighi could not help it: the ivory letter opener broke neatly into two pieces, snapping between his long fingers. He threw the pieces into the waste basket, felt ashamed, and asked Father Zalenski to excuse him. The Cardinal enjoined the priest, "Speak to no one of what you have seen and heard, under the bond of the Holy Office." Then he phoned his secretary and repeated this injunction.

The full weight of this crisis seemed to press down on his shoulders like a corpse that had fallen to his lot to carry.

The Cardinal again sat across from his visitor—this man who said he's Panin. The Secretary of State felt older than his sixty-five years, he could feel his red skullcap slip and he didn't bother to straighten it. He felt more vulnerable than he had allowed himself to feel in many, many years. "Where is our Monsignor Righi?"

The visitor's reply was like a stab. "In Russia. Which is why I'm here."

"Unheard of! Incredible! A Russian spy the double of—"

"I'm here to help bring him back to Rome."

The Russian's words made Respighi feel foolish. The Cardinal could hear himself stutter as he continued: "—our Observer at the United Nations? And how long has this shameless, unbelievable game been going on?" The Secretary of State knew his shock was quickly giving way to anger.

"From the eighth of September, 1971. On his flight to New York, the Monsignor was kidnapped at the London airport. I was the switch."

Respighi calculated the consequences as if he were playing a chess game with life-and-death rules. "But the code book and files —if these have been revealed—"

"Neither, I assure you, were revealed to anyone." The Russian gestured toward the briefcase, which Father Zalenski had brought in earlier. "I have here the combination to the safe containing the code. It had been sealed in Monsignor Righi's luggage. I found it and did not even show it to the assistant, Father Belli." The visitor extended both of his hands, palms upward. "At the moment, nothing is endangered. Belli is conducting day-to-day affairs. And Monsignor Righi—or rather, the KGB on his behalf—retains his diplomatic passport. You have no need to fear. I am, Your Eminence, merely a man who has come to make an act of submission."

Respighi felt compelled to believe this man, but the Cardinal also yearned to prove to himself that no more deception was being harbored. He took Panin's hand in both of his. "In the name of God to whose minister you wish to confess, tell me the truth. Please relieve me of this nightmare." And during the man's answer, the Cardinal probed the Russian's eyes for any hint.

"Every statement I have made so far is true. But there is more to tell." As the Russian spoke, Respighi could see nothing in the man's eyes other than the reflection of red—apparently the red from the trimmings on the Cardinal's black robe, the red from his buttons and embroidered buttonholes, the red from his broad red-fringed sash.

Respighi felt powerless. "One thing I must know: why did you come here to make what you call an act of submission? Why didn't you hand yourself over to the Americans? And—what has made you speak of a confession?"

The visitor's hand trembled as he wiped perspiration from his brow. "May I have a glass of water?" he asked.

The Cardinal poured it from a carafe on his desk. This fellow is suffering, he thought. Whether or not he's telling the truth, I have no way of knowing—but his suffering is plain to see.

"Speak, my son, whoever you may be."

Panin drank the water, and with great relief, began his story.

He told Respighi of his baptism into the Catholic Church by Byzantine rite in the Ukraine, stories from his boyhood, and of how he joined the Party. To the Cardinal, his visitor's words and experiences sounded like unimaginable make-believe.

"Then last September, after I began masquerading as a priest, something happened which had not been in either my plans or those of the KGB." As the visitor paused and took another drink of water, the Cardinal caught a glimpse of Panin looking at Respighi's ring, resting atop papers on his desk.

"I found—or rather, I was found. In all these years, Your Eminence, I've never been caught by the French or the British, the Canadians or the Americans, but I was caught by the mercy of our God." These words were accompanied by a warmth that touched the Cardinal.

"On the plane which brought me here, I meditated on the words of St. Paul, how he described himself, and in them I saw both my present and my past selves." Respighi recognized the *First Letter to Timothy* as Panin began reciting verses, apparently from memory:

> *I thank Christ Jesus our Lord, who has given me strength, and who judged me faithful enough to call me into his service . . .*

The Cardinal realized that he was silently mouthing these words along with his visitor. . . .

*even though I used to be a blasphemer and did all I could to injure
and discredit the faith. Mercy, however, was shown me, because I
had been acting in ignorance. Christ Jesus came into the world to
save sinners. I myself am the greatest of them; and if clemency . . .*

Respighi interrupted with a whisper: "St. Paul repeats 'mercy.'"

*mercy has been shown to me, it is because Jesus Christ meant to
make me the greatest evidence of his inexhaustible patience. . . .*

The Cardinal's heart compelled him to believe the man before
him. His weary eyes of pale blue appeared to hide nothing. It was a
moment such as the Secretary of State had not, he realized, experienced in years. The Holy Spirit did seem to accompany this man.
But how? Respighi hastened to ask: "And how did it go—your encounter with God?"

As Panin briefly described how powerless he had felt; then
how much stronger than his will God's had been, the older man
found himself listening intently. But he was surprised when Panin
concluded, "Will you hear my confession, Father?"

"Of course. But first, you must rest." Respighi needed time to
think. He returned to the telephone. "I'll have them prepare a room
for you here. Take a bath, if you wish, have something to eat and a
long nap. This evening, I'll hear your confession."

The Russian looked uncomfortable and explained why. "And
one more thing: a suit of clothes. I haven't a right to wear these."

The Secretary of State agreed, but also felt a certain sense of
empathy. "You can trust me to take care of all the details."

[XXXVI]

CARDINAL GIULIO RESPIGHI FOUND MORE SERENITY IN EX-
amining proposals for sainthood than in dealing in diplomacy. He knew that.

In this respect, he was true to his lineage. The Respighi family
numbered few priests and many policemen, the well-educated kind
who sit behind desks. Therefore, this case of the false monsignor

not only disturbed his spirit, it also stimulated his mind. The story of a converted Russian spy had been astounding—but Respighi did not intend to accept it at face value. An investigation had to precede the Cardinal's attending to this man's spiritual misery. The policeman in him would not allow it to be otherwise.

Cardinal Respighi phoned for an urgent meeting with the Holy Father.

"When he says that he has made a career of lying, we must have proof now that this man is telling the truth." The Holy Father's manner was cautious and businesslike during his time with Cardinal Respighi and the substitute of the Secretariat of State. Both men were impressed and, in a sense, relieved. "We must have some facts which confirm or deny that the Monsignor is an impostor."

Minutes later, the two men hurried to write down their assignments and, after showing appropriate politenesses, rushed back out. They were so preoccupied that neither of them noticed the ceremony or decorum in the movements of the Swiss Guards—the gestures and salutes that surround any visit to or from the presence of the Pope.

The woman interrogating Cardinal Respighi was a smaller, younger, near-replica of Monsignor Righi. Her voice was hysterical in tone.

"Has something happened to my brother?"

Instead of the Monsignor's cold, somewhat forbidding air, her expression seemed the kind that was usually warmhearted; her eyes, usually laughing. Usually, though not now; not after having been brought to the Vatican by special car, then rushed to the office of the Secretary of State.

"Please, Your Eminence, don't tell me anything but the truth."

While the Cardinal explained a few necessary details to this widowed sister of Giuseppe Righi, a portly man sat beside her and attempted to comfort her by occasional pats on the arm. Signora Anna Maffei seemed interested not in these attentions by her brother's personal physician, but only in Respighi's ongoing explanation.

"That's all we know as yet, Signora. I asked you and Dr. Prignano to come in order to ascertain more facts. But I must tell you

from the start that our meeting must remain strictly confidential—
in the interest of all of us, especially your brother."

His two visitors nodded.

"Well," Respighi continued uneasily, "our Observer at the
United Nations arrived today from New York—"

"But Peppino wrote me that he'd be coming on the tenth—"

"He told us the same thing. But—and I beg you, Signora, to
remain as calm as you can—the man who arrived today and who is,
even now, here in the Vatican . . . this man says he is not Giuseppe
Righi."

The Monsignor's sister was restrained, but firm. "I must see my
brother."

"I pray that you shall," the Cardinal reassured her, "but there is
much to do if that is to happen." The three discussed as much of
Panin's story as the Secretary of State thought advisable.

"But where is Peppino?" The woman leaped to her feet as if
she could bear no more.

Like a brother the Cardinal rose and took her in an embrace.
"Nothing, so far, has happened that you should consider as beyond
remedy. I have been promised this. The visiting gentleman told me
that Giuseppe is in Russia, and that he wants to do everything he
can to bring your brother home. You must trust me." From within
his robes, Respighi produced a linen handkerchief, then helped Signora Maffei back to her seat. "Now I'm asking you, for your
brother's sake, help me. When did you last see him?"

She explained how her brother had visited them the day before
he left, last September. "But only for a quarter of an hour." Then
she remembered an earlier visit, in July, when Righi had spent three
weeks in the country with her family.

"Did you notice anything unusual about him then?"

She shook her head. "He was the same old Peppino. Very reserved, even with us, his family. As if he were living in a world all
his own. We always said he wasn't typical of our native province,
Romagna. My children teased him about 'living with his head in the
clouds.'"

Nothing. Cardinal Respighi felt completely frustrated that he
could pry nothing from this woman that seemed to help. "Maybe
his letters," he asked in near desperate tones, "did you notice anything out of the way? The handwriting, maybe?"

"No, Your Eminence. He typed all his personal letters. Always."

Dr. Prignano had been listening and was just then cleaning his fragile-looking glasses when the Cardinal thought of a question that might produce answers from the portly physician. "And you, Doctor, was there any unusual symptom when you last examined Monsignor Righi?"

The physician launched into a detailed explanation of the Monsignor's general health and medical history, aided now and then by the Signora's memory. "Giuseppe was, as you can see, a model of good health. I examined him just before he left for America. Let me see . . . yes, he explained that he'd undergo another exam here at the Vatican. He described it as 'a checkup on checkups,' as I recall. Otherwise, no problems—isn't it so, Anna?"

Respighi had nearly reached his limits with these two; he would have to try other sources. He was about to interrupt Signora Maffei's answer when she said something that intrigued him.

"Please. Would you repeat what you just said?"

"Well. I said, 'Yes, God be praised,' then I said, 'I remember only two times in his life when Peppino had to take to his bed.' But—"

This could be productive, Respighi hoped. "When was it that he took to his bed. And why?"

"They took out his appendix—I think he was about fifteen at the time. Then he broke his leg. He had been skiing on Mount Abetone. It must have been 1942 because we were living in Ravenna and that's where they brought him. Oh—and it was his left leg."

Even though Respighi's inherited policeman's instincts had caused him to ask for this information, the Cardinal had been nodding to her answers as if to say, we know. "But listen to this," he said. "The man who arrived here today claiming to be an impostor, he also had a slight limp and I think it was his left leg, too."

Dr. Prignano interrupted excitedly, as if surprised by his own insight. "But does he have an appendectomy scar? I know that Giuseppe has one."

"Now that's an interesting bit of news," the Cardinal responded. This could produce the kind of fact that the Holy Father had ordered them to search out. Respighi calculated the options. In seconds, he knew what he must do. He turned to the telephone and placed call after call, making various arrangements, including the sedation of Volodya Panin so that Righi's physician could check for this telltale scar.

The entire procedure took about two hours.

When Dr. Prignano returned, he explained how impressed he had been by the manner in which the *Stato Città del Vaticano* was handling their fatigued and mysterious guest. Then the physician assured His Eminence that the patient was not only in good health and resting, "but he also has no operation scars."

Cardinal Respighi felt a strange sense of relief mixed with fear, but Anna Maffei's composure immediately gave way to tears.

When the two men had helped calm her, Respighi repeated his admonition that all of this was top secret and that they had promised to keep it that way.

The pair had barely left his office when the desk phone rang. Respighi listened as the papal nuncio in Italy delivered a most urgent message to the Secretary of State: The SID had just received a cablegram from the FBI; in code, it requested a search for Monsignor Righi. Further, it indicated that he was "suspected of espionage" just prior to what they described as a "mysterious disappearance."

"Good," the Cardinal exclaimed, causing the nuncio to sound astounded over the phone. He explained that he had just gone through the awkwardness of expressing embarrassment to the SID; did the Secretary of State realize that—

"You'll understand tomorrow," Respighi hastened to assure him. "Can you be here at three o'clock?" The Cardinal double-checked his calendar. "In the meantime, don't call the SID back. And if they call you, tell them that you know nothing."

"Believe me," the nuncio responded, "I'll be telling them the truth."

When Cardinal Respighi hung up the phone, he leaned back, allowing his black robe and his tired arms to fall across him. Much of the tension that had wrapped around him like a movie cowboy's lasso now slipped away.

He still had no answers. But the policeman in him also knew

that now he had some facts. Facts, he understood, were the best beginnings.

Quickly he made one last phone call. An attendant in the
building near Volodya Panin's quarters assured the Cardinal that
Panin continued to sleep soundly. The exhausted churchman decided that the Russian's confession could most propitiously wait
until tomorrow.

[XXXVII]

THE ROOM IN WHICH PANIN AWOKE WAS BY NO MEANS A
bedroom. Its vaulted ceiling and walls were frescoed with
scenes depicting the events of the reign of a Pope. Its floor
was polychrome inlaid marble surrounding a papal coat of arms at
the center.

Judging from the clock on the small table beside his bed, he
had slept for eighteen uninterrupted hours. Apparently the doctor
had done his job well; Panin appreciated that. The jet lag, the exhaustion produced by the revelation of his imposture—for these,
sleep and vitamin B_{12}, which the doctor had given him, were the
best remedies.

He knew that sleep probably gave them time to check his
story. It only surprised him that he no longer cared how they went
about it. He was a changed man.

Panin smiled, seeing that they had even left breakfast for him;
the juice was still cold.

Later, after he had finished eating, Panin learned that finding
the bath was not as easy as waking up. A sign had been hung on
one of the four doors in the room: Beyond this door and two
others, you will find a bathroom. In fact, it took considerable mean-
dering to find the place where he could bathe and shave.

The marble hallways were chilly, so he ran back to his room,
where he found civilian clothes laid out across a great onyx-topped
walnut table. In moments he was enjoying the comforts of wearing
a double-breasted blue jacket and trim gray slacks, instead of the
clericals and collar that had been his "costume" these long months.

At exactly eight o'clock, the Cardinal knocked at the door. As Panin opened it, Respighi began speaking immediately.

"Good morning, Mr. Panin. Am I pronouncing your name correctly? I hope you slept well and weren't cold. It's almost impossible to heat these large rooms." To Panin, the Cardinal appeared more refreshed and more confident than the Russian had remembered him from yesterday. "You'll have to excuse us. We're not equipped to receive overnight guests. These rooms, known as the Bologna Apartment, are handsome, don't you agree?"

Panin started to describe his favorable reactions.

"They were decorated by Gregory XIII"—the Cardinal was chattering again—"he came from Bologna, you know. And did you notice that scene on the right? It recalls his reform of the calendar. On his account, it was called Gregorian—"

Panin caught Respighi taking a breath. "To be sure, but we Russians use the Julian, making us always thirteen days behind everyone else." Both men laughed, dispelling much of the tension they both felt.

Finally, the Cardinal sounded a bit apologetic as he continued: "There are guest quarters at the tower of San Giovanni; it was Pope John's idea to have the tower refitted. But that's on the crest of the Vatican Hill and—well, I wanted to have you close by, you understand?"

Of course, Panin thought. But he also could not show ingratitude. "Please, Your Eminence, I slept very well indeed: as we say in Russian, like a stone. And I appreciate all your attentions."

Cardinal Respighi nodded, and the two men moved toward two chairs that seemed so out of place to Panin he was certain they had been brought to the Bologna Apartment specifically for his use. Both men sat down, though neither was exactly at ease as yet.

Respighi seemed to seize upon the furnishings as a safe topic. "We had to move quickly—but the *Floreria* was most helpful in providing what we requested. It's our office for the maintenance of the Apostolic Palace, an enormous warehouse of furnishings not currently in use."

Then the Cardinal's thoughts seemed to stumble into the subject of their having drugged Panin. "The physician . . . well, you needed a checkup and—" He looked at Panin as if to ascertain whether or not the Russian understood. "And Monsignor Righi's personal physician was available. . . ."

Panin showed his host that he was totally unguarded. "Did the doctor find whatever evidence you needed?"

The Secretary of State seemed to know no other way of coping with Panin's directness; he simply matched it. "Yes. When Righi was fifteen years old, he had an operation: his appendix was removed."

Panin's laughter made the vaulted ceiling ring.

"Whereas the KGB unwittingly allowed me to keep mine! Ah —clever as my chiefs are, they can't foresee everything, now can they?"

Both men laughed, enjoying each other's honesty as a welcome relief.

"Then you don't hold my investigation against me?"

"On the contrary, Your Eminence. I admire your flair. The KGB foiled by a cardinal. They would choke."

Respighi seemed to relax as he leaned toward Panin as one conveying a confidence. "But you see, my son, I was born into a family of police; both my father and my grandfather worked at the police headquarters near Sant'Eustachio. Do you know that Renaissance jewel of a church?"

Panin reminded the Cardinal that this was his first visit to Rome, whereupon Respighi proceeded to explain how the beautiful church had inspired him, as a boy, to abandon his father's dream of his becoming a chief of police . . . how Respighi had turned to the Church . . . and how when he had been named a cardinal—anybody can be cardinal, he joked, the proof of this is that I have become one—the Pope had made him the titular of Sant'Eustachio. "By an ancient tradition," he elaborated, "six of the cardinals resident in Rome are bishops of small dioceses surrounding the city. To the others as well as to those cardinals who reside abroad, a city church is assigned. It furnishes them with their title; hence, titular. And the churches in this category, like Sant'Eustachio, are most noteworthy for their great age or their artistic merits. The Holy Father graciously gave to me the church which had originally inspired . . ."

Several minutes later, Panin finally broke the conversation away from the exchange of background stories to remind the Cardinal of the Russian's most urgent intentions. "Now that you know I am the impostor, that I have been telling the truth about all of my past lies, may we discuss just how we are to proceed?"

"—the sacrament of penance?"

"Yes, Father, and also effecting the exchange which will bring Monsignor Righi back home."

The Cardinal looked steadily at Panin as he asked, "Is that what you really want, Mr. Panin?"

"Your Eminence, consider me at the service of the Holy See until such arrangements are complete. And remember: I serve very well."

"But are you certain that Righi is still alive?"

Panin couldn't determine the Cardinal's motives for these questions. Was Respighi truly concerned for him as well as Monsignor Righi? "I have no reason to doubt it—unless, God forbid, he has died a natural death." Both men grew quiet.

It was the Cardinal who finally broke the silence. "Was an exchange ever discussed—maybe as a precaution, as a fallback?"

"That's why I believe Righi is safe. The plan was to have him placed under house arrest. Then, if the Americans caught me—the Kremlin has exaggerated ideas about the Vatican's influence on the United States government—my superiors were to be ready to effect an exchange."

Respighi appeared sincere when he responded, "But—and I'm sorry to speak of such, Mr. Panin—but what if your mission had been accomplished? What would have happened to the Monsignor then?"

Panin felt safe in confiding in this man: "He would have been returned quietly, arriving in Rome a bit unsteady over the whole thing. We were fairly certain that the Vatican would not reveal the fact that one of its diplomats had been kidnapped and that its listening post at the United Nations had been manned by a Communist."

Dismayed, the Secretary of State nodded in agreement.

Then an idea occurred to him: "Did Moscow ever propose, as one of your options, that you should come of your own free will to the Vatican and recommend an exchange?" Panin could see new suspicion in the churchman's expression.

"They did not imagine a conversion, if that's what you mean. And neither did I until . . . until God opened my eyes."

The Cardinal immediately apologized, but another complication seemed to cloud his feelings. "I think you are telling the truth. But won't such a drastic move as this place you under their suspicion? And won't that harm the prospects for an exchange?"

"Not at the start." Panin smiled, thinking abut the possibilities probably being tossed around among his former colleagues, even now, at the Moscow Operations Center. "My chiefs knew that I was under FBI surveillance. My last instructions said that I shouldn't return to New York once I had gotten out during the trip set for the tenth. When they hear from you and when they are asked to arrange an exchange, I suspect that my reputation will convince them that Nitchevo—my nickname—has once again been quite clever."

Panin knew there would be more, though he had not yet allowed himself to imagine all the possibilities. "Of course, when I arrive in Russia—"

"Then you will confess, you'll tell them about your conversion?" Panin could see that until this moment, the Cardinal had never considered that the Russian would do such a thing.

Panin responded emphatically that, yes, he would not deny his new-found faith. He could tell that his answer was meant as much to convince himself as to assure the Cardinal. "After all," Panin continued, "I am equally certain that Soviet retribution will be firm and immediate."

"You are serious then." Respighi seemed to be slowly accepting Panin's sincerity. "And the retribution you mentioned would be?"

"A bullet in the head or a mental institution."

"Is this really awaiting you?"

"Just as night follows day."

Panin could see an immense sense of fear and admiration flood across the Cardinal's face. It was as though Respighi had suddenly seen the heart and soul of his visitor. "Then it was the wish to free Righi which prevented you from defecting while in America?"

"Plus the realities: what sense would it have made for me to have been exchanged for an American spy who had been caught in Russia? Or for me to have lived as an ex-spy in America?"

"So you are ready, my son, ready to lose your life?" The Cardinal's question sounded more like a statement of faith to Panin.

But it was a faith he had already accepted. "To gain it, Your Eminence. Will you hear my confession?"

The confession took two hours. Afterward, the Cardinal went to pray in his private chapel. He later told Panin that he had commended the Lord's new servant unto Him for the heavy cross Panin had borne and the heavier one that would soon be his.

When the two men met for lunch, Respighi immediately commented upon Panin's manner. "You seem happier, if I may say so, than the real Monsignor Righi, as I remember him."

Panin felt what he was confessing as he explained, "Spiritual joy is a totally new feeling for me."

"But your future is very dark, my friend."

Panin resisted the concern in the Cardinal's voice. "Now that my soul is relieved of its burdens, it feels light enough. If God grants me his help I can bear whatever I must face."

Respighi seemed to believe him, seemed to observe something rare in him. Panin could see this as men see other men's purest feelings.

The Cardinal made a promise. "I'll send you a book for meditation this afternoon. *The Little Flowers* by St. Francis. You are ready, I think, to appreciate the passage on perfect joy. Then, tomorrow morning, you can receive communion."

Panin knew it would be the long-awaited nourishment for his soul.

[XXXVIII]

"IT WILL BE A SIMPLE MEAL," RESPIGHI HAD SAID WHEN he gave Panin an invitation for supper in the Cardinal's apartment. "I have to stick to a strict diet." He had rubbed at the dents his knees made in his black robe. "Arthritis."

However, what Panin found arranged on the Cardinal's table that evening was anything but simple: Franciscan sisters had prepared fettuccine.

"They're very dear," a much more relaxed-looking Respighi explained. "The sisters keep house for me and I explained that tonight's meal would be something of a celebration. They know nothing about the nature of this occasion, but from the tone of my voice they must have realized how glad I am to have your company."

After the sisters had departed, leaving the two men to their food and conversation, the Secretary of State resumed his questioning. Panin could tell that the churchman had spent the hours since their last meeting pondering the implications of all that had transpired.

"Tell me, if you can and will, my friend, what Soviet intelligence was trying to accomplish by having you assume the identity of the Holy See's Observer? You'll pardon me, but it all seems like a joke, as if Moscow merely wanted to show what they could do."

The fettuccine was perfect and Panin was particularly hungry. He struggled to finish his mouthful so that he might respond. "My answer may reveal objectives which may seem too small to justify such a colossal hoax, but we had our reasons, I assure you. Most immediately, though, I was to gain new experience in an unusual role. That's important. I expect that I was being prepared for later, more important missions, ones in which success would depend upon my playing an undetectable role as priest."

Panin could see the worry that understandably came upon the Secretary of State's face.

"But, Your Eminence, I assure you that I have no idea what such larger roles may have been. Secondly, I was instructed to use the authority of the Holy See in efforts to bolster the policy of peaceful coexistence. This is very important to the Kremlin."

The Cardinal said nothing, giving Panin every opportunity to continue. The Russian, however, knew that he had already been as truthful as was necessary. "There were other aims, but they in no way involved the Holy See. I hope you understand my not speaking of them?"

"This is no confession, either sacramental or secular. Feel free to use the restraints you wish."

For the next course, the sisters served poached cod to Respighi, but Panin was given roast pheasant.

"I am told that your pheasant came just today from the farm attached to the papal villa at Castel Gandolfo. Enjoy—since I cannot."

Thereafter the man ate quietly. To Panin, the food was the best he had eaten in years. He felt wonderful.

After a while, the Cardinal pursued the subject that Panin had expected to come up much, much earlier. Did the Russians' efforts achieve any results via the office of the Permanent Observer's office?

"Very unimportant failures," he answered, not with much confidence in his voice. After all, Nitchevo had been accustomed to success. "The fault lay in the field of operations. The United Nations is not the place for any investigations, other than what might be termed 'low-level spying.' Washington would have been a more productive setting, but—"

"But such concerns are no longer of interest to you—is that it?"

"I have different ideals, now, it's true." Panin was relieved when the sisters returned, interrupting, asking if anything else was needed. Converted he was, but not completely reconciled to all the changes that such conversion made necessary. All of this would take time—time which, apparently, Panin would not have.

"Have some more pheasant," the Cardinal urged.

"With pleasure." At least the food was excellent.

"Like the food in your New York rectory?" Respighi quipped, as if he had been reading Panin's thoughts.

"That was as good as American-style can be." The Italian and the Russian smiled knowingly. "Plenty of food—but monotonous. Lots of roast beef and occasionally steak. Also overcooked spaghetti —when we had it—though nobody seemed to mind, except Father Vaccaro and me." Panin had to resist thinking of KARENINA as he spoke of her food. He hoped she was unharmed. "Ah, but then there is breakfast, at which Americans excel. There's a bit of everything."

The last sister, having served the pheasant, was about to leave the room, and the Cardinal called after her, "If we need you again, Sister, I'll ring the bell."

It was then that Panin decided he should ask the Cardinal a question: "Your Eminence, though there may still be concerns in your mind about my life as a spy, I would love to talk about conversion. May we?"

"But of course." Respighi seemed pleased. "Why not start with the first, even the most remote of the causes for your conversion? I remember that you told me the immediate cause was your encounter with Rabbi Grynspan, no?"

"It was one of them, that's right. But another was my disillusionment with the United Nations. The fact is the UN is a waste of time. I know the phrase is a strong one and I don't mean for a second to criticize the Holy See for maintaining a Permanent Observer there. You have made contributions: the Holy Father's visit shattered all precedents and his encyclical '*Populorum progressio*' is another milestone."

While Panin continued explaining, the Cardinal moved politely from the table. He brought a box of cigars from a nearby cabinet and when Panin had finished, the Cardinal offered his guest one. "The nuncio to Cuba brought these as a gift—please." As Respighi lit his, he returned to Panin's remarks. "Are you one of those who believed that the UN would be the demiurge of a new world order? Were you a Marxist who kept his options open?"

"Not at all. But once I began preparing for my role at the UN, I found myself taking to heart the words of its Charter: a mandate 'to save succeeding generations from the scourge of war.'"

"And you think it has failed?"

The Russian was moved as he responded from his heart after his experiences during the last months. "Failed? How else can you describe some fifty-five armed conflicts, large and small, since the Second World War? Even when the UN has brought the firing to an end, the results have been disappointing. Meanwhile, the great tragedies of these years have been resolved—for better or worse—without the United Nations. The *coup d'état* in Czechoslovakia in 1948, the blockade of Berlin that same year, invasions of Hungary and Czechoslovakia, the Cuban Missile Crisis, Vietnam, and above all the Palestinian problem . . . Even after the Security Council was unanimous in pointing to a solution following the Six-day War of 1967, it was powerless to either impose a solution or even to find a way of proposing it to the conflicting parties."

"Your historical summary contains none of the animosity so often voiced by most diplomats I've known—the kind who have moved from one post to another. But my friend, this is so contradictory to the enthusiastic and encouraging reports you sent us."

Panin could see that his most recent deceptions troubled the

Cardinal. "That's true. In the beginning I meant them. Mostly. Then sheer conformism took its toll. Conformism, you see, is a spy's stock in trade. Under no condition can he afford to be original. But, of course, professional conformism may extend to his way of thinking and living outside the realm of spying."

All this deception and the memories associated with it—the impact of it settled into Panin's heart. He pointed toward a decanter on the Cardinal's buffet. "Is that vodka, Your Eminence?"

"Especially for you." Respighi smiled shyly, then poured glasses for his guest and himself.

The Italian continued sipping at his, even after the Russian downed his glass in one gulp. Its burn felt like a warm bath to Panin. It seemed to free him, make him nostalgic and confident. As he spoke, his voice deepened and he could hear his own remorse. "I have played many roles, so many, Father: traveling salesman, porter, bank clerk, fruit vendor, sailor, businessman. In Winnipeg, I was even an impoverished Russian grand duke."

"No wonder you moved so imperceptibly into the life of a priest in New York City." Panin could hear the hint of vodka in the Cardinal's voice.

"But not without a price. Perhaps God wanted to show me that one can't touch the sacred with impunity—is that possible, Father?"

The Cardinal answered as if from some very personal recess in his soul. "It is our awesome condition, *dispensatores mysteriorum Dei:* we are dispensers of the mysteries of God. We lose faith or we gain it. Some become saints. It is peculiar—did you not feel this when you were at the Church of the Nativity?"

For a moment the memory of the priest whom Panin had been became vivid in his mind. "Each time I had to hear confessions. I was the only one who knew Italian; Father Vaccaro understands only English and the Sicilian dialect. So the confessions affected me —it was unavoidable." He rubbed at his left palm with the thumb of his other hand. "Until forty years ago, the neighborhood had been inhabited by people from Parma and Piacenza. Now only a few old women remain; they confided in me. Their sufferings, what they had endured as immigrant brides, the loneliness of their widowhood, how bitter they had become since their Americanized children had moved far away. They asked advice, what to do with their meager savings. When they asked for absolution of their past sins or that I pray for God to grant them a good death, I felt like a worm, having abused the good faith of these ingenuous souls."

The Cardinal poured a second vodka for himself, then responded to Panin, speaking just over the rim of the glass. "When the Lord brings us back to Him, His ways are mysterious."

Panin held his empty glass gripped in his fist and unconsciously he squeezed it as he continued. "We didn't take into account what a risk God is. That there is no way out if we put God to work for us. Is that not true? My chiefs and I thought that Marxism had vaccinated me against any infection or deviation. I was an actor who could sustain any role. But I had no way of knowing that I could not repeat those powerful words and at the same time continue to deceive myself. They have a mystique: This is my blood of the New and Eternal Covenant, given for you and for all men for the remission of sins."

These words also seemed to affect the Cardinal, for the robed churchman coughed away a hint of tears, then he pushed himself higher in his chair. It was as though Respighi was undergoing a spiritual experience with the Russian of an intensity he had not known or approached in years of official duty.

"Was it then that the Rabbi met you?"

"Actually, Your Eminence, I was led to the truth by a woman . . . a woman who, like myself, was a spy. In the end I fell in love with her."

The Cardinal's next question surprised Panin. "Was she pretty?" Somehow it revealed a more human side of Respighi, one that the Russian had not expected him to have.

"It shouldn't astonish you that I ask," the Cardinal hastened to explain. "Another cardinal once asked it—and it didn't prevent him from becoming pope. Pope Benedict XIV, who was Cardinal Lambertini, archbishop of Bologna. He first asked, if the girl was pretty. It was during the course of a confession. If she is pretty, he is reported to have reasoned, then the sin is one of weakness. If ugly, then the sin is vice. . . . But then there are so many stories about Lambertini!"

"She is beautiful." Panin spoke slowly, the memory of Shulamith making him suddenly nostalgic. "But she was also so eager to learn and so open to the truth that I felt compelled to take soundings in my own soul. What I found was a terrible abyss between what I was asking her to declare and to practice, and the life I was actually leading." Panin could almost envision her sitting on her couch, her legs pulled under her as she listened to him. "When I realized that out of sin there can arise a longing for certainties, then I began to see the same possibilities for myself. For this I am grateful to her."

The Cardinal seemed to state his next reaction cautiously: "But, my son, you did not go into this matter even briefly during your confession."

"She had a charm I've rarely encountered, Father. But my relationship with her involved no sin. At least none that I'm aware of."

"That depends." Respighi was probing, not comforting.

"Mine was visual, not carnal enjoyment, Your Eminence. And she was sincere in her journey of faith as well. I don't doubt that even now she is on her way to a new life."

Thus, with the promise that both men would pray for her as well as for one another, Panin rose from his chair to depart. He realized that it would not be easy to dismiss the thought of Shulamith Arieh. The memory of her clung to him too keenly.

PART SEVEN

THEY GAVE HIM TWO MORE BOOKS TODAY. THE VOLUMES were stacked beside his Bible, where he found them when he awakened.

The jacket copy indicated that one of them, *Le roi des aulnes*, had won the *Prix Goncourt* for Michel Tournier last year in France. Was that a fact that he remembered? Righi had to keep check on such things; he had to keep his mind satisfied that it was working properly.

The other appeared to be an American novel about the South. There was a time, he remembered, when he had intended to travel there. Now, he wondered. . . .

This second book had, he realized, an ironic title. As he did so often these days, Righi thought this without speaking aloud. He almost never spoke these days.

The book's jacket was green and its title was *Deliverance*.

Over the months they had given him books in various languages.

After he had become friendly with his guards, he learned that he should be pleased. The volumes he received were books usually not made available to Soviet citizens. He was pleased enough that he had any books.

Righi had come to enjoy entire afternoons, lost in devotions and reading. The *dacha* was comfortable, well-heated. Every week it was cleaned, though Righi was never allowed to remain in the same room while they worked.

Yesterday had been good. He had cleared rocks from among the shabby flower beds. Apparently the garden had been neglected for a number of years. He had made the beginnings of a fine mulch bin, mounding debris into a sturdy box, using the frame they had built for him.

For that he had shown his appreciation—hadn't he?

Yesterday afternoon he had worked until the cold bitterly

drove him back inside. Then he had concentrated for an hour upon the carefully regimented exercises that he had designed for himself earlier. Righi's body was becoming taut and limber.

One never knew. . . .

He had had to devise an array of other methods to keep himself from losing his mind. How else could a priest endure a place where the saying of mass and the receiving of the sacraments were impossibilities?

The situation was absurd. He had even come to resent that they no longer came to interrogate him.

During those first weeks, he had been visited by government officials—the KGB he had presumed—nearly every day. They had asked him hundreds of questions. And asked them again. Questions about the Vatican. Who really financed it? Who would be the next Pope? Had it liked Togliatti better than Longo and Berlinguer? And what did the Holy See think of the policy of peaceful coexistence?

These relentless probes for "secrets" had continued: Did he possess any information about Cardinal Mindszenty, who left Hungary, or about Tito and his relationship with officials at the Vatican? Finally they had satisfied themselves that Monsignor Giuseppe Righi knew no "secrets."

Next they had flooded him with Marxist literature—until they saw that he read it dispassionately, like a scholar filing summaries for unknown colleagues to list in bibliographies.

Then they had left him alone.

The guards became unfailingly polite, but distant. Loneliness began seizing him with the grip of lingering flu and fever.

He had surprised them by asking to study the Russian language. They seemed flattered and gave him a Russian dictionary and grammar book. Soon the guards changed, became patient again, even cooperated when he sought opportunities to practice conversation. In this way, Righi came to learn of their childhoods, their native villages. He memorized jokes and learned when to allude to them, making his companions laugh heartily.

Eventually he realized that, based upon the temperatures and various hints in his Russian conversations, he was being confined somewhere in the Crimea. He saw peasants work from morning to night, almost never leaving the fields. Of course he had seen Italian laborers on the property of his sister's in-laws, but he had been a different man then. There he had been a visitor, smoking a cigarette and seated in a deck chair under a shady garden tree.

Here it seemed that Righi was becoming less cold and insensitive; he was deeply affected by the vulnerability of these Russian peasants. Perhaps there was more happiness here than in the gilded drawing rooms of diplomatic residences?

Of one thing, however, the Monsignor was certain. This hard test had removed him from an ivory tower and had flung him into everyday life. That had to be through God's will, a will that seemed somehow to be making him a more capable man.

At Moscow Operations Center, the various reports on Panin had been evaluated, analyzed, argued over, double-checked. There remained a few among his KGB superiors who quietly harbored their suspicions. Nitchevo had not been in touch with any contacts for days—what else were they to think?

But General Leonid Rostov laughed away their arguments.

As soon as he had looked over the latest material, his eyes had flooded with tears that spilled down his round cheeks as he repeatedly broke into fits of laughter. Earlier he had termed this turn of events "Panin's Roman holiday."

To his assistant, the General explained: "Nitchevo's no sorcerer's apprentice: he's right on target." Rostov counted off on his fingers, as if to mark each of Panin's moves. "He slips out of the Americans' hands, goes to Italy—don't be surprised if he digs out secrets about the American fleet—then he lands in the Vatican. He is so adroit. I can just see him playing his part, kissing the cross . . . all improvisations while the jack asses continue to fall for it. What do the Americans call a trick of this kind, Pyotr?" The assistant, who had spent some years in New York, appeared puzzled until the General added, "Something about a cake, huh?"

"To have your cake and eat it, too."

"And what a cake. Homemade using holy water." The General was drying tears from his eyes with a handkerchief. "As a nuncio detailed the story to our ambassador in Rome, Panin went straight to the Cardinal Secretary of State. He told him his real name and begged to have his confession heard. What a coup!"

Pyotr appeared deeply confused. "But Comrade General, a confession?"

"No, *durak*, you idiot." Rostov mocked at a sign of the cross with a toss of his hand in the air. "He made a religious confession, whose hearer is bound never to quote from it."

Pyotr shook his head, unconvinced. "I know enough, sir, to be leery of popes and *startsy*. I have seen enough, the worst, from the one in my village . . . that jailbird in Kuban who associated with kulaks and was always talking about Babushka-Czar. . . ."

Rostov let the assistant ramble, then the General cut his words short with a dismissal as sharp as a knife. "Listen, you with a head as big as a Cossack's. You are still too simple to understand this Catholic nonsense. A priest is bound by what they call the 'seal of the confessional.' Not even the Pope could force a priest to repeat what he has heard. Capitalist courts won't accept a confession in evidence."

Pyotr seemed unimpressed; his doubts seemed to shoot flares. "Then you are not concerned about what Vladimir Efimovich may be telling such priests?"

Rostov had no hint of a laugh in his voice as he answered. "Whatever they are told, they'll have nothing."

Pyotr shrugged and began stacking Panin's folders in order. "It must be as you say—but I still don't like these people rooted in superstitions."

Rostov whispered his response, his manner intense. "Their superstitions play into our hands. It is at home that we must not tolerate them. Meanwhile, we must get Nitchevo back as soon as possible. To keep up the morale of all our men, to make certain they do not lose their taste for risky missions—Panin must return safely."

[XL]

RESPIGHI COULD NOT HELP BUT OBSERVE THAT PANIN seemed to be living these days as if they were his last days of peace. The Russian seemed determined to get the most out of them.

Each morning, Panin heard the Cardinal's mass, then used his free time to tour the beauty of Vatican City. Various officials and priests were eager to share their time and knowledge, showing him around the buildings where they worked and worshipped.

The Cardinal knew that this quiet man would impress them, but Respighi also gave Panin a VIP pass, just in case.

The Secretary of State also made certain that none learned Panin was a converted spy, or that the priest accompanying him was an SID guard, authorized in his disguise by the Cardinal himself.

Meanwhile, Cardinal Respighi had enormous difficulties trying to give the appearance that nothing had happened while his office continued at a frantic pace, using every contact and source he could trust to effect negotiations that might bring about the exchange.

The SID made the situation clear. The KGB considered an exchange to be the final resort. They would spend time considering how to free their valuable agent. And exchanges often took years to work out.

Respighi thanked God that during Panin's work, the security of the Republic of Italy had not been seriously threatened, nor had Monsignor Righi been seized on Italian soil. Either of these would have made the Cardinal's current efforts impossible.

But the SID did not tell the Cardinal everything.

Another factor was motivating the Italian Communist Party and the Russians to satisfy the Vatican as soon as possible. All of them were afraid of what exposure might bring.

Of course none of them knew about Panin's conversion; the SID and the KGB operatives in Italy only knew him as an active colonel who appeared to have been helped in his deception through covert efforts of the Italian Communist Party. How else could the Vatican have been so successfully duped? It mattered little that both the Italian Communists and the KGB knew that the facts of Panin's operation suggested the contrary. Panin's residence at the Vatican was a situation that out-argued all facts.

To the outside world, should the story be leaked, the situation looked as though Moscow and the Italian Communists had mixed Soviet intelligence with Italian Party work. In the eyes of the

Kremlin, the complications of such an appearance could be cata-
strophic.

Therefore Moscow, its embassy in Rome, its contacts with the
SID, everyone scurried to see that Panin was removed from the
corridors of the Vatican, where he was within a prayer of the
Pope. Certainly before the Americans could devise a scheme to turn
everyone's discomfort to their advantage.

The documents that finally arrived in Cardinal Respighi's office
were papers worded so that all of this was considered as nothing
more than a mild entanglement. Respighi was almost amused as he
read the query: How, then, can we best oblige the Holy See by
aiding in the return of one of its diplomats from temporary, invol-
untary exile?

Once the Cardinal knew that a resolution would soon be within his
reach, he took an afternoon off to accompany Panin on his walks.
"Volodya, you may be interested in knowing that Signora Maffei
was deeply touched by what you said to her yesterday. She told me
so when we met this morning."

Panin's cheeks still looked hollow, but his eyes, Respighi was
pleased to observe, had brightened since his arrival. "It's thoughtful
of you to mention it, Your Eminence. And I'm equally grateful that
you arranged for that meeting between the Monsignor's sister and
myself."

"She said she was touched that you should ask her to forgive
you for having caused the kidnapping and detention of her
brother—"

"And she answered that she thought it was an act of divine
providence. She says she is praying that her brother will have, upon
his return, the same truly Christian outlook that she sees in me. She
is greatly overestimating my merits in comparison with her
brother's," responded Panin humbly.

"She may be quite right." Respighi contemplated aloud. "Giuseppe Righi is a good priest and a devoted servant of the Church.
But I wonder if somehow, like the rest of us here in the Curia, he
has not forgotten his mission to the people? And who knows what
bitter experiences might do to him over there?"

Grim concerns hovered in Panin's mind, just as they did in
Respighi's. Nonetheless, both persisted with individual, determined

efforts to share the pleasures of the time together, the inspiration of the places in which they walked.

Inside the Pauline Chapel, the Cardinal phrased his comments carefully: "You see those two frescoes—the 'Conversion of St. Paul' and the 'Martyrdom of St. Peter'? They're the last works of Michelangelo, done when he was past eighty. See with what power he painted?"

Panin absorbed what he saw like a thirsty man who has been given fine wine.

Later the two men spent a long and quiet time looking down at St. Peter's interior from the height of the Hall of Blessings. Panin realized that the Secretary of State had to sacrifice valuable time for this escort. "I am delighted, as always, with your company, Your Eminence, but I don't want to trespass on your time. It's too precious to the Church."

The Cardinal silenced his friend with a calm, sure gesture. "Don't think of that. A single soul is as important as the whole world." Yet Respighi knew there was more. How could he tell this man how much he had come to mean to the Cardinal? "The problem is, I don't have the energy to accompany you up to the cupola. Go admire the panorama of Rome. And if you have time, you may go to the *Terza Loggia,* where you'll find sixteenth century maps. One of them labels North America as the 'Unknown Land' and your native Russia by the Latin name 'Sarmatia.'"

As the Cardinal left Panin, he seemed to ignore the gendarmes as they leaped to attention. All doors opened. He walked uninterrupted.

This daily drama was his life.

Yet it was the drama in the other man's life that, now and for some time to come, would dominate the Cardinal's thoughts.

Panin walked slowly in the darkness.

He was alone and felt vulnerable in his cold bedroom. He stretched his arms out like a blind man and felt his way toward the great walnut table where he remembered the lamp was placed.

When he reached it, his fingers shivered from the touch of the great onyx top. He heard the lamp switch click and saw a small orb of amber light surround him; it seemed to create a one-man island in the immense darkness of this chamber of a room.

Almost immediately he felt comforted. He began rubbing his warm hands across the onyx until gradually the surface coldness and his body temperature came closer together. He remembered seeing an old woman do this very thing, before beginning her prayers at the marble rail of the altar in a small chapel in Kiev. Her prayer had been long.

Tonight Panin intended to use this table for writing and he suspected that he would be here for a long, long time:

> I could have defected to the Americans.
>
> But death is a duty, not an escape. It is possibly my last debt payable to truth. In effect, it is my profession of faith. Is this not so? For if I had died at Kharkov, people would have said: It was his duty to Mother Russia.
>
> Does this not make going back a duty?
>
> And what an irony: though it was part of my job to feel at home the world over, I now understand that I'd rather die at home than abroad. . . .

This writing became like a dream. Panin knew where he was and what he was doing. Only his emotions became caught up in what felt almost like deep dreaming.

Thinking of Russia, Panin realized that his country was extraordinary and mystical, beautiful and cruel, a land of contrasts, virtually inexplicable. And its people? At this great distance, Panin felt that he knew them better than when he had lived among them. "As God wills," the old Russian expression he had heard so often; it still said so much, even in its disuse, about the people of Russia— their goodness, their compassion, how resigned they had come to be.

Still, Panin could not help thinking of the other characteristics made clear by distance and time:

> We are like artificially fed capons—we are regimented and conditioned, treated like instruments and products from our birth until . . .

Panin's pen smeared ink across the page.

The toss of Shulamith's hair suddenly crossed his mind. She had been the person who made him realize that he, too, had become anti-Semitic, that he too acted without any idea of the reasons behind his actions:

. . . like artificially fed capons . . .

But that was before the compassion of Rabbi Grynspan.

Now, away from both of them, Panin could more clearly see how he and other Slavs had been led into practicing anti-Semitism. Panin understood all too well. The old man's face appearing, as a surprise, on that cold night, the absence of fear in his eyes—such had not always been the case for Ukrainian Jews.

His pen made quick scratching sounds as he resumed the capture of his thoughts upon paper:

It's small consolation that the Nazi concentration camps—rather than the Russian and Central European pogroms—will go down in history as the worst examples of persecution against the Jews.

How can I forget my father's account of Pobedonostsev's plan? "Russia's Jewish problem will be resolved when a third of the Jews has emigrated, a third has been converted to the Orthodox religion, and a third has disappeared." My father used this statement from the czarist government minister for church affairs as explanation for—I can almost see my father now—the savage story of why a Jewish dynamiter assassinated Prime Minister Stolypin in our native Kiev . . . why, under the very eyes of the czar, Mordka Bogrov killed Stolypin. A pogrom of huge proportions was avoided at the last moment by sending a whole division of Cossacks into the Kiev streets.

I can remember my father's exact words as he explained: "When Cossacks make a cavalry charge, no human force or artificial barricade can hold up against them. . . ."

The chill of Panin's room became gnawing. He rose from his chair and began pacing in the shadows beyond the lamp's immediate light. The room was virtually empty. His leather soles made faint rubbing sounds against the polychrome floor.

"How could God have reached out to bring peace into the heart of an anti-Semite like me?" His words, whispered aloud, were probes into the darkness. There seemed to be no answer.

He remembered what a colleague at the UN had said. The two of them had been arguing in private over the Palestinian problem; earlier they had engaged in heated, public debate. Panin's adversary/friend had then quoted Maritain: "It seems as if the Jews exist in order to irritate, exasperate, stir up and push ahead the rest of human society. They form an extraneous body—a leaven."

Now, standing in the darkness within the Vatican, Panin understood this concept of "leaven." It was as though his becoming a Christian was a call to bring leaven into Mother Russia's battle against God. It was possible. The present leaders were slowly following Stalin's example. They moved against the Church as he had, first liquidating the Ruthenian Church, then muzzling the Catholic Church of Latin rite in Lithuania and Latvia, even in the former Polish territories; only then had Stalin turned to persecuting the Jews. Through it all, most leaders of the Orthodox Church had become puppetlike. Today the Kremlin was simply continuing the destruction.

But could Panin make a difference?

That was the question. Was not everyone else in his country being instructed that the destruction of religious faith brings about the liberation of man?

Yet Panin knew that his new-found liberation had come from God. It was inseparably a part of him, as Jewishness was to a Jew.

And the thought of that made Panin realize: any evidence of this liberation within me will be like a leaven. And, as for a Jew or any other believer for that matter there will be danger ahead, because in Russia, there is a plan for resolving such problems. . . .

"Your faith is strong, Volodya; it's the faith of a convert."

Cardinal Respighi grew more animated as he spoke. This man's influence inspired him and the churchman no longer hesitated to show his feelings. "You're like Daniel, unafraid to go into the lions' den."

The two men had renewed their discussions about faith and the decisions of life. Several days had past and again they were enjoying a meal in the Cardinal's apartment. This time the Franciscan sisters had prepared velvet tender veal in Panin's honor.

Soon, however, the Cardinal fell silent. When he resumed conversation with his guest, Respighi's voice conveyed a poignant tone.

"My friend, this is the last time we'll sit together at such a meal. I say it with genuine regret."

Panin's hand trembled as he placed his glass of wine back on the table. "Am I to leave so soon?"

"It was agreed upon just today, between the papal nuncio to Italy and the Soviet ambassador to Rome. You're to leave tomorrow afternoon. In Prague, you'll be exchanged for Monsignor Righi—"

"Then he's safe?" It was as if for the moment his own peril was forgotten.

"Signora Maffei and some SID agents will go with you as far as they are allowed." Respighi watched as Panin slowly bowed his head. "And my blessing. You can be sure of that."

The Secretary of State could not understand Panin's immediate response, which was the Russian for "as God wills," until Panin resumed speaking Italian: "At least I'll see my beloved Russia."

The Cardinal's black robe made its whispering sound as he rose from his chair. "You'll also go with the blessing of the Holy Father. He'll give you a private audience tomorrow." Respighi enjoyed watching Panin's expression change gradually toward a faint smile of gratitude; still the Russian remained virtually speechless. Something within him had suddenly been hushed.

The Cardinal decided to prepare Panin for the papal audience. "I suspect that he'll receive you on the terrace above his apartments. From there one gets a magnificent view of Rome. It's his favorite place." He continued, explaining about the Pope's hobby, in so far as any pope can have one, of growing flowers. "He once said to me, 'Every budding flower is a luminous proof of God's existence.'"

Nonetheless, Panin remained distant and preoccupied until Respighi interjected, "Your letter touched the Holy Father deeply, my friend."

"Then he read it? I'm so grateful to His Holiness. I've been writing a great deal these days and that letter somehow seemed to say best what I've been thinking. Will there be time for me to attend his mass?"

"Just before the audience—you'll receive communion."

A great sense of relief settled upon Panin as he answered, "I'll need that for the trip. From Rome to Prague is only two hours of travel—but the journey from the KGB to eternity may be long indeed."

The two men used their last minutes together as a time of remembering. The Cardinal shared boyhood stories and even a few moments of spiritual triumph. Respighi was doing everything he could to lengthen their time together. Finally, however, he glanced at the bronze clock on his mantel.

"What do you want to take with you tomorrow?"

"Nothing, Your Eminence, but the clothes on my back. I have my dignity for the moment when I arrive face to face with them."

The Secretary of State extracted a small box from his robe pocket and held it out to Panin. "Will you accept this small gift?"

"Oh, but you shouldn't—"

"Look inside, please—"

Panin opened it nervously to find a small Byzantine cross on a gold chain.

"To remind you of your baptism and the faith of your grandmother. I'm certain that in Heaven she has been—is even now—praying for your return to the house of the Father."

"I'll wear this as long as I—as long as they allow me to." Panin appeared strengthened as the cross lay on his palm. "Your Eminence, I don't know how to thank you."

"Let me thank you. For you have given me a great deal." The hint of tears rose in the Cardinal's eyes; he could feel them. "In the beginning, you gave me the greatest shock of my old age . . . and in the end, my greatest consolation."

"But why should you thank me?"

"For hope—even tinged as it now is with sadness. My friend, you have affirmed God's presence in a time when, to many, He seems to be absent. And you have restored confidence for the future of your Mother Russia. . . ."

To the Cardinal, Panin's protest sounded humble and sincere: "Don't tell me that God picked up a spy on the streets of New York—"

"Oh yes—and sent him to this jaded bureaucrat, to remind me, I suspect, that He will sustain His Church till the end of time . . . with or without the devices of so brilliant an investigator as yours truly."

Panin leaned over to kiss the Cardinal's ring, but Respighi drew back. He could never allow such a thing—not from this man. "God be with you, my son," he said, and the two men embraced, "and give you strength."

How he would miss this Panin.

At the *dacha* that February 25, Monsignor Righi was awakened at three o'clock in the morning.

The guard who had taught him so many good jokes in Russian now appeared somber. He spoke in terse Russian as he instructed Righi to dress quickly and pack everything in one travel bag.

Just as he had been transported without explanation on that September 10, so, Monsignor Righi now realized, he was being rushed toward Moscow.

This time, he thought to himself, at least I have not been given an injection, then shuttled from vehicle to merchant ship, traveling half-conscious, like a corpse in the care of men who have only their orders in mind.

[XLI]

"THE AGE-OLD PROTOCOL OF KNEELING THREE TIMES HAS been discontinued since the time of John XXIII." The Holy Father's private secretary had a cold; he dabbed at his nose with a well-starched handkerchief of pale blue linen; after each use, he meticulously folded it. "Just kiss the Holy Father's ring." The secretary repeated the answer that apparently he was most often called upon to give. "And don't be afraid; His Holiness will put you at ease. Why, he told me this morning, as he looked over today's schedule, he is eager to meet you."

Panin could hardly suppress his amusement: the priest's handkerchief stood upright within the clasp of his hand like a restaurant napkin.

Minutes later, as Panin followed the secretary into the Pope's working quarters, he was struck by two unexpected impressions. First, the Pope looked exactly as he had expected the man to look: slender, handsome, groomed in crisp robes of pure white; the presence of this great man did not disappoint. In Panin's experience, great men had rarely been equal in person to the images of them portrayed by the media.

This man, Panin thought, appears to be all that I thought a pope could be.

Secondly, he was fascinated to find the Pope's quarters so simply furnished.

Just then, as if the Supreme Pontiff had heard his visitor's footsteps and turned to meet him, the Pope's figure showed at a new angle against the light from the tall windows. Beyond them, the midday panorama of the city of Rome. The sight was a feast for Panin's soul.

The Pope held out both hands in greeting.

Vladimir Efimovich knelt, then kissed His Holiness' ring. He felt shivers down his spine and, as he got up and his eyes met the Pope's, Panin saw in them what he genuinely believed to be compassion and serenity.

"I'm afraid, my son, this greeting must, at the same time, be a farewell." The wistfulness in his voice sealed Panin's trust; he believed in His Holiness' empathy as surely as he believed all that he must soon face in Russia.

"Your Holiness understands: I'm going home."

The Pope nodded slowly, then took Panin's shoulder in a half embrace; the Pontiff's hand and white sleeve bolstered his visitor, guiding Panin out and along the hanging garden situated over the Pope's private apartment.

The cold air on this late February morning was crystal clear. Panin followed His Holiness' indications as the Pope pointed beyond the city itself, toward the farther-reaching landscape. "That's Agro Romano." Panin could see that it was already green, leading from Mount Soracte to the chain of the Lower Apennines. "And there, the Alban Hills." He described them as the site of his summer residence at Castel Gandolfo.

"While I was waiting for you," the Pope continued, "I stood out here and said the rosary. It's a fine place for that—don't you agree?"

Panin's voice was almost lost in the open air. "Yes—"

"And I thought of St. Luke's parable about the Pharisee and the publican. Do you know it?"

In fact, Panin had read it during those painful days of decision when he was ill and confined to his quarters at the Church of the Nativity rectory. "I remember it, though vaguely—"

"Well, it is written that the publican 'went down to his house justified.'"

"But"—Panin smiled as he responded—"is a spy worse than a publican?"

The Pontiff curled his lower lip and shook his head. "I don't know—but I also don't believe that the Lord judges men by their professions. Yours, my son, was merely more unusual and risky than most."

"Believe me, Your Holiness, spying is a world unto itself. It is adventurous and there is some romance attached to that. But it's almost always a lonely life, cut off from love or grace." Panin paused; he could see that the Pope continued to listen intently, exhibiting the patience one might expect from a shepherd of men. "Yet at the beginning, one doesn't suffer. To the contrary: if a man is operating under a false identity, there are many comic moments. I must admit that for many years, I enjoyed it. I was laughing inside. Like most spies, I was sustained by a sense of humor."

"But then, one might say, your soul became arid for a long time?" The Pope's understanding struck Panin's heart. The Russian felt free to tell this man anything, everything.

"In a parched land, yes, and a man unaware that he was thirsty. It all continued, this life-long deception, until I realized that I had become a tired actor no longer amused. The show became petty in my eyes. For you see, a spy's most bitter disappointment is to act, not only without a public, but also without the satisfaction of applause from within."

The Holy Father considered Panin's words carefully. After a few minutes, he motioned toward the study and asked if his visitor would enjoy tea or an espresso.

"After New York, espresso is a nightmare to me! But a Russian never refuses tea. On that score, I assure you, we are even more fanatical than the British."

Back in his study, the Pope indicated that they should sit in armchairs that were positoned before an alabaster-topped table. "Volodya—I feel I should call you by this name—we are all glad that God has rescued you from your solitude, but we are also concerned. Your homecoming may be tinged with bitterness: are you not afraid of what may await you there?"

The chairs had been turned so that the Pontiff's visitor faced a great ivory crucifix, several contemporary landscape paintings, and a "Christ in Agony," which Panin quickly determined was painted by Georges Rouault. He felt a strange comfort as he looked into the face of pain.

"I have lived many years outside the law and I have had many moments of fear. However unnatural it may sound, I am no longer afraid of any man. Perhaps it's because I feel absolutely free—"

The Pope interrupted: "*Veritas liberabit vos:* the truth will set you free."

Again Panin smiled. "It happened to me."

The Pontiff alluded to Pascal as he leaned toward his guest and quoted, "You wouldn't seek me, were I not already seeking you." Seeing understanding in Panin's expression, the Pope continued: "So, my son, did you feel fear then, when you heard God's call?"

"I was terrified." The question caused Panin to momentarily relive those agonizing days of his illness at the rectory. "The first moments were the hardest. I didn't know how to defend myself. I wanted"—the Russian felt himself stumbling to say all of this in Italian—"to dig into myself, even though it felt like my will had become paralyzed. I felt mortified and dulled." Suddenly Panin felt so inadequate: how dare he speak about the soul's journey in the presence of the Vicar of Christ? "It may sound trite, but truth can hit like a flash of lightning, so close that it blinds. After a while, however, everything begins to clear."

"You are very eloquent in describing your *itinerarium mentis in Deum:* the journey of your mind toward God. Sincere and eloquent. St. Paul says that during such liberation, the spirit groans. Conversion is a movement within the soul which is difficult for the mind to follow—is it not?"

"For me, Your Holiness, conversion has not been as difficult as the realization of what its consequences are. I suspect that many men come close to truth, but draw back once they see what its acceptance implies for their future."

The two men exchanged knowing looks, and the Pope said, "May God grant you the grace of perseverance, for it is hard to burn bridges with the past." And again Panin felt astonishment at how understanding of human frailty this Pontiff was.

As if the private secretary had been watching for the right moment to interrupt, he entered and was followed by another, who proceeded to serve tea. Panin and His Holiness sat quietly. The aroma of hot tea grew strong and invigorating.

After seeing that both the Pope and his guest had what they needed, the man knelt and kissed His Holiness' ring before departing. Panin noted that the private secretary followed like a well-starched shadow.

Then Panin used the opportunity of the Pope tasting his tea to confess, "I have done a great wrong to the Holy See."

The Pope made a gesture of denial. "Cardinal Respighi heard your confessions, did he not? Then you have no further need to carry any of that on your conscience, Volodya. The good Secretary of State and his assistants will take care of everything else. As for spying, it will continue as long as this world remains torn apart by selfishness and faction."

These words, like the warm tea, washed within Panin; he felt like a boy again, running, yet also very old. He felt forgiven.

Seconds later and quite casually, the man clad in white stood up. He held one finger in the air, as if to say *un momento;* then His Holiness moved toward a pair of portraits on the same wall as the Rouault.

"May I share something with you?"

Panin nodded, not knowing whether to follow the Supreme Pontiff across the room or to stay seated, sipping his tea.

"These are my parents." He gestured toward the paintings. Even from the distance at which Panin examined the likenesses, the woman's hands appeared to have been marvelously captured. "After God, Volodya, they are responsible for my vocation. On the anniversary of my mother's birthday I chose to wear the chasuble made from her wedding dress. It was her gift to me upon my ordination to the priesthood. I pray for my parents at mass every morning. I think there is no better way to show my gratitude. May they rest in peace." Then the Pope turned back, facing his visitor. "I feel very close to them, even now . . . and I assure you: they join me in beseeching God's protection on you and upon people like you in your native Russia."

The telephone's ringing startled both men.

His Holiness moved to a small table and answered the phone. During the conversation, Panin noted that the Pope's responses were whispered and concise. The Russian's eyes shifted from the trim and tailored back of the Pontiff's robes to the warm colors of his parents' portraits. Such a son, Panin thought, to have become such a man.

When the Pope hung up the phone, he apologized for the interruption and explained: "A message from the chamberlain. It seems that at this afternoon's general audience, there'll be a group of legislators from Colombia. I gather that their ambassador to the Holy See is hoping that I'll utter some reference to the presence of his countrymen. Of course, I shall."

Panin smiled. "While I was at the UN, my actor's status notwithstanding, I heard great praise for Your Holiness' gift of words. The delegates were most appreciative." He enjoyed gleaning some good from reports which those days had brought to him.

"God's gift, my son—" The Pope actually seemed embarrassed. "But what, if anything, may I do for you?"

Panin did not hesitate. "It would be a great joy for me if you would send your Apostolic blessing to the priests of the Church of the Nativity."

"It shall be done." The Pontiff uttered the promise even as he moved toward a drawer in the alabaster-topped table. "And also know: what you have endured will not be forgotten. I have a memento to give you. It's an emblem of our blessing, which goes with you to all your countrymen. And, Volodya, it's for you to remember our meeting by. . . ."

Panin received a leather-bound volume with gold-leaf frontispiece. He translated the Latin title, *Imitation of Christ*.

"For a man who cares, as I'm told you do, about the special details in life: the typeface is Bodoni."

Both men laughed the laugh of men who have unexpectedly gotten glimpses of each other's heart.

"Thank you, Holy Father. It will go with me as far as Moscow. After that, I don't know. In any case, the edition will be judged too fine to be thrown into the fire. Who knows? There are always people ready to read what will be considered 'the aberrations of the bourgeois world.' "

As the Pope led Panin away, they came back to the hanging garden's edge. Groups of pilgrims could be seen streaming in lines across St. Peter's.

The Supreme Pontiff stopped. "Is it true, Volodya, that Stalin once asked ironically how many divisions the Pope could put at the Allies' disposal?" Panin realized that the question was rhetorical when the Pope pointed outward. "Do you see how the faithful throng from every part of the world to the home of their common Father? That is our army, my son. They are moved by faith—not just to see a man who, after all, is visible on television in their homes. They are moved by a faith which can never die."

Within sight of that army, Panin knelt and received the Pope's blessing. And as he knelt, Panin enjoyed the wonder of this army whose sounds were not marching or the noise of artillery wheels, but the distant sounds of laughter and the chatter of tourists.

These memories would sustain him when his plane landed in Prague.

In Moscow later that day, a guard shoved a man through a doorway. General Leonid Rostov noticed that the man put up no resistance; these days, he observed, they almost never did.

Maybe that was why interrogation had lost some of its appeal for him? He honestly didn't know—though it certainly had.

The General used his thumb to snuff out his cigarette; he used the thumb as most men would use the sole of their shoes.

From the marble mantel, the new electric clock chimed. Rostov looked at his watch—right to the minute. There's time for a few more folders, he decided.

Outside his enormous window, one could see the rooftops of Moscow and, since it was a February dusk, the gradual flicker of street lights as they came on, section by section. Rostov did not notice; he almost never looked out this or any window.

And particularly not this evening.

The folder through which he was leafing belonged to the man whom he had believed in all these years: Nitchevo. It contained memo after memo, recommendation after recommendation. The man was something of a marvel—all these missions, all these varied roles.

Yet the most recent entries were Rostov's problem.

Queries had come from agents in New York. There were damaging questions about Panin's last days there. Also about the silence. Several of Rostov's colleagues had inserted negative memoranda: a man, even one such as Colonel Panin, had to give an account for such a protracted silence.

Out of habit, the tired interrogator lit another cigarette.

In seconds he coughed as the smoke lodged in his wheezing lungs. The room echoed. Its ceilings, seventeen feet high, echoed with even the smallest of sounds.

He was reminded of a writer who had once remarked that the offices in Lubyanka were never meant for interrogation; they are too spacious and airy. Rostov remembered laughing. "So, what are they better suited for?" he had asked. The man replied, "A metal chair through the window . . . and a leap to the flight called death."

"Such a fool," the General whispered aloud, just as he had that day.

Now, alone, Rostov's eyes scanned the top report in Colonel Panin's file. Every colleague in Moscow Center had come to the conclusion that either Panin had been brainwashed in some new, uncanny manner . . . or Nitchevo had this time gone too far. Only Leonid Rostov's scrawled note spoke in Vladimir's favor.

The General thumbed out this second, half-smoked cigarette, then shoved the stub into his jacket pocket. He hoped this star agent of his was not making a fool out of himself. And he pitied the man if, somehow, Panin ended up making a fool out of General Leonid Rostov.

For that, everyone knew, there was no forgiveness.

PART EIGHT

PART THIRTY

THE NEXT AFTERNOON, VOLODYA PANIN SAT ON A BENCH IN Prague's Ruzyně Airport. The room was so cold that the metal of the bench felt like ice.

Outside the room's two doors, pairs of Czech guards stood, chatting to themselves. Inside, one Italian guard sat beside Panin while the other, a nervous fellow with one leg shorter than the other, pressed his face against the frost-covered window. He seemed to be making an awkward attempt to thaw a space with his breath so he could see out. Whenever he spied any movement beyond the gray window, he described it in detail to his partner. His Italian was choppy and he spoke as if only he and the other SID agent were in the room. But Panin did not think his tone unfriendly.

Today was apparently just another day on the job to him.

At Panin's right, Signora Maffei sat quietly. She rubbed her cuticles as if they were rough edges on pottery that she was not quite ready to relinquish to the kiln.

At least, Volodya thought, I feel calm.

He wore a well-tailored gray suit, a loden coat, and a Homburg. Earlier a clothier in Rome had come to his room at the Vatican, had fitted him for the clothes, then departed. The man politely refused any explanation. The clothes had arrived pressed and ready to wear. A card in the suit pocket had read in handsomely written Italian: compliments of Sant'Eustachio.

Twenty-seven, twenty-eight, twenty-nine—by the clock on the wall, they had waited a half-hour before the side door opened and a wave of cold air rushed in ahead of four stocky men in uniforms.

"Peppino!" Signora Maffei called, and the man surrounded by those uniformed escorts pushed his way forward. Panin and Signora Maffei sprang to their feet and the SID guards scurried into place.

Monsignor Righi appeared uncomfortable in his clericals and his face was drawn; Panin could see that for this man it had been a long time since September.

His sister embraced him. "Oh, Peppino, I thought I'd never see you again."

"Everything's all right now, Anna." Panin noted that the sound of Righi's Italian appeared to sound peculiar to the man. "It's all over," Righi added.

Surrounding the brother and sister and Panin, the agents stared silently, their eyes moving from Righi to Panin. It was too obvious. Panin smiled: except for their clothes, he and Giuseppe Righi looked almost identical.

The shorter Italian agent's whisper could be overheard: "Like two peas—no?"

General Leonid Rostov and Signora Maffei would confess later that they had been startled; neither could, at the time, identify the change. It was just that the colonel and the priest had seemed possibly more gentle or more indulgent—judging from the expressions in their blue eyes. The detached and almost haughty air was gone from each man's manner. Both the General and the sister had thought, "He's changed," but had kept the thought to himself or herself.

Only later would they individually realize that these two men had become more alike than either the General or the sister would have previously thought possible.

After the Russians had disappeared into the dulled light of the Czechoslovakian dusk, Righi sat on the bench that Panin had just abandoned.

Anna embraced her brother as he succumbed to his emotions. "I can't believe it," he kept repeating until his sister finally interrupted.

"All that you must have been through," she murmured. "Talk to me, Peppino."

The priest leaned his head so that his face became half-buried in her hair. "Are you well, Anna?" He could feel her nodding. "The children?" He added the nicknames he used for other family members.

"We are all well. Believe me. Now tell me about you."

The SID agents turned their backs, affording the couple all the privacy possible.

Slowly Monsignor Righi began a frenzied summary: how, in

fact, he had been well-treated . . . how he had missed communications with his loved ones . . . how difficult the isolation had been . . . how much he had missed his priestly functions . . . the sacraments. "I kept asking myself, Why are they doing this? and then, Am I not, in some way, responsible?"

Signora Maffei patted her brother's arm. "Cardinal Respighi will answer all your questions. He is waiting for you with open arms, and without your having to tell him, he'll understand your torment. He's been so good to me—why, before I left, he made me promise to bring you the Holy Father's blessing."

As the Monsignor grew calmer, he smiled and pulled away from his sister. He took her hand and squeezed it gently as he continued, "But there were blessings in all of this. The grace of God. Through it all I found that new horizons opened for me. . . ."

Anna Maffei's eyes brightened. "That's what Volodya said to me—"

"You don't mean that spy, that impostor?" Her brother bristled. "Didn't you notice how he made fun of me when we met just a few minutes ago?"

"My dear brother, you have no way of knowing. That man's sincere." Her eyes moved toward the side door where Panin and the Russian agents had exited. "He gave himself up at the Vatican." She appeared unable to see anything more than the Czech guards, their backs to the door. "It's very possible that he may be sacrificing his life—"

"Anna, he's a KGB agent—a Communist—"

"Was." Signora Maffei covered her face with her hands so that the SID could not see her tears. "He's a real Christian now."

The priest seemed both puzzled and alarmed. "How do you know?"

His sister tearfully told him portions of Panin's conversion story, whereupon Monsignor Righi's face turned pale. He jumped from the bench. "We must do something." The priest moved toward the door. "Perhaps there's still time."

"It's finished, Monsignor." The taller SID agent restrained him. "Please, sit down. There's nothing we can do. Rome did all they could. Please sit. Our special plane leaves in half an hour—not much time. Just relax and think how happy you must be to go home."

Mechanically Righi obeyed; he sank back onto the bench as months of imprisonment had trained him to do.

"Yes, Anna, I'm going home. But if what you tell me is true, then there is certain trouble ahead for him."

"Peppino." Signora Maffei pulled her brother toward her again, but she also looked toward the door. It was as if she now had two brothers and was torn between comforting the one and worrying over the other. "He wanted it this way."

In the Russian military jet, Leonid Rostov and Vladimir Panin sat side by side. The General had arranged it this way. Panin gathered that Rostov wanted to get some feeling for what Nitchevo had gone through before allowing the other agents access to him.

Panin made no effort to speak to anyone until after the plane had gained altitude. He did this even though he was aware that to Rostov this silence implied further complications.

Finally the General was unable to tolerate the distance between himself and this subordinate; he quipped, "So, Comrade Panin, did you not learn enough curses from your mother language? I heard you. What was that oath you exchanged with the priest when you two met in the airport?" The General's eyes searched deep into Panin's as he awaited a response.

"It was no oath, General. I said, '*Orare pro me ad Dominum Deum nostrum,*' and he replied, as I had hoped, '*Misereatur tui omnipotens Deus.*'" Panin could feel the danger he had just entered into.

"So translate this gibberish."

Panin responded with confidence, slowly. "General, I asked that the priest 'pray for me to the Lord our God,' and his response was an assurance: 'May God have mercy upon you.'"

General Rostov's large hands fell on Panin's arm; the grasp felt shuddering but relentless. "Stop it."

But the Colonel had to continue; his voice remained unshaken. "I said those words with conviction—"

The General's grip, like an electric charge, shot pain through Panin's body. "I said that's enough." The grip penetrated with ceaseless fury. The pain was almost unbearable. "At the airport, I saw that you had changed, but, *Gospodin polkovnik,* your Roman holiday has done you in." Just as suddenly, Rostov's hands released their hold. His voice laughed out, apparently for the benefit of the other agents, but his aside was just loud enough for Panin to hear: "In this bourgeois incarnation, we'll call you 'Mister Colonel.' Remember the czarist style? You should like that. Meanwhile, shut up and consider yourself under arrest."

The other agents looked from one to the other, trying to guess what was transpiring between the General and the Colonel. Therefore Rostov spoke up, again with a laugh: "The rascal. See why our military attaché in Rome never got any news? Hah—the information on the code of the Seventh Fleet. This fellow must have been pulling our leg again."

Vladimir Efimovich bowed his head.

No longer *Nitchevo*, but *Gospodin polkovnik*. This sarcastic remark would have, in earlier times, aroused him to defend his honor; now these words were a source of joy—perfect joy.

Like the words he remembered from *The Little Flowers* of St. Francis, the book that the Cardinal had given him. As the Beatitude promised in the Sermon on the Mount:

> *Blessed are ye*
> *when men shall revile you*
> *and persecute you.* . . .

As the plane flew over his native Ukraine, Panin prayed for strength . . . and blessings upon his people down below.

Later that night, the Alitalia plane touched ground at the airport in Rome. Monsignor Giuseppe Righi felt the jar and awakened. The long sleep had felt good.

"Home, Peppino," his sister whispered.

The interior lights of the plane blinked, then all but a few went black again. In the darkness, the priest spoke and felt as if he was apologizing—not only to Anna, but also to someone not there. "I didn't deserve his choice, Anna. It's such a sacrifice."

"He said as much—but about himself. The Colonel said he wasn't worthy of the grace which God had given him."

In the gray-blackness, the brother clasped his sister's hand in his. Outside the passenger compartment, he could hear the engines whine and see lights flicker along the runway.

"Who does deserve the gifts of God?" He knew that his words

carried the weight of all he had learned during his imprisonment in Russia.

His thoughts were silently conveyed to Anna, as sometimes happens between close siblings, so that she responded as if she had understood things that he had not yet told her.

"You've changed, Peppino. Not only have you lost weight, something else has—"

"Anna, it was God's will: I was so arrogant, so self-sufficient. I needed the lesson."

Minutes later, the passengers were allowed to leave the plane. Monsignor Righi and Signora Maffei walked arm in arm down the stairs. At the base, two ecclesiastics were waiting. Cardinal Respighi was the first to embrace Righi.

After exchanging greetings, the three men and the woman walked toward the terminal; SID agents followed at some distance. Finally Righi spoke in a low voice to Respighi. "I have been told a great deal, Your Eminence."

"Then you understand about our brother Volodya? You saw him?"

"Yes . . ."

"And?"

"I have much to learn from him."

The voice of the Secretary of State sounded to Righi like the sound of memories flooding upon memories. "We all do. . . ."

[XLIII]

 THE INTERROGATION BEGAN AS SOON AS GENERAL ROSTOV could get Colonel Panin off the military plane and, via a waiting car, to Moscow Center.

This was the General's last effort, this trip to the KGB offices.

If Nitchevo had been acting a grand role all these months, then taking him to the headquarters and recording his explanation would be treatment befitting such an imaginative and amazing agent.

But if Panin should have other answers, then Moscow was also the best place for putting the Colonel in the hands of specialists who would soon learn the cause of Vladimir's change.

It only took about an hour of listening for Rostov to decide that Panin's answers were most definitely incredible.

"Nobody brainwashed me in New York or in Rome," Panin repeated. "It was my school teachers and the Party and the KGB who did that. Now I'm free." Finally General Rostov shut off the recorder and called in the specialists. One was beckoned from his mistress' bed and the other was pulled away from an all-night interrogation of a dissident who persisted in learning new languages to use for his pro-imperialist writings.

These two alternated their efforts to determine just how the Colonel had been used, then how he might be debriefed, unlocked. General Rostov demanded that they not stop until they discovered Nitchevo's key; Panin had been too valuable.

The process took two uninterrupted days and nights.

Sometime during the third day, new sounds awakened Panin: boots upon hard floors . . . and a pouring sound . . . then spills.

Panin tried to get up, but a sharp pain in his shoulder made him fall back against the cot. He tried to open his eyes, but the right one resisted; with his hands he gingerly felt the swelling around his cheeks. Another pain shot through him.

With his one good eye, Panin examined the cell.

Immediately he recognized Lubyanka. The high ceilings, nearly as high as those rooms in the Apostolic Palace. And there, at the top of one wall, a window, like a gun portal in the bricks, unreachable, dingy, covered by bars as thick as poles.

In addition to his cot, he saw that this cell contained four others. No. Five. The others were empty, their mattresses rolled up. And there a table, positioned in the most visible spot in the room. Atop it was a teapot and what looked to be a chess set.

Panin reflected: As if I'll have any leisure time here.

From the outside he heard other sounds. Marching. No. The erratic walking of many men. And a frightening echo, as if these men were walking in some narrow well around which high walls towered.

"Hands at those backs. Line up in pairs."

Russian orders growled in a lazy bass voice. "Don't stop, don't talk."

Prisoners were exercising by walking between the Lubyanka

building and the enormous wall. He had seen it so many times as he had ridden along Dzerzhinsky Street and onto the square. In his mind, he saw the pillared turret hovering over the square itself; the Lubyanka water nymphs, half-reclining against that turret. . . .

This time his view of all that—should he be allowed outside—would be from the side of the wall where no one wanted to stand.

Minutes later Panin crawled from his cot and knelt on the cold parquet floor, its sections worn to the size of old bricks. He remained in this position for some time until the clank of metal against metal alerted him that someone was outside his cell.

From the peephole in the door, Panin saw eyes peering in.

Leonid Rostov's voice was loud and grating. "Pyotr, did you ever know a man to lose his wits to such a degree? What those priests can do."

A guard opened the cell door and the two KGB officers entered. Behind them, Panin could see the shiny finish of the corridor floor, striking in its contrast with his dark, greenish cell.

"You there, get up. What's this nonsense on the floor?" The days of interrogation had taken their toll. Panin got stiffly to his feet and stood at feeble attention.

For what must have been several minutes, the two officers waited in silence, tormenting the tottering Panin. Soon the only sounds he could recognize were the guard's footsteps, pacing along the corridor.

Then Rostov barked into the silence, "Sit, dog, on the floor."

Panin felt himself crumble backward; his body settled only when he felt the wall smack against his back. Then he raised his head. Bruises burned as his facial muscles strained to smile.

The General muttered an oath and hunched over the prisoner so that his wide, animal-like face thrust within inches of Panin's. The Colonel could smell meat on the man's breath. "You're mad, *Gospodin polkovnik*, quite mad."

All the while Panin could see Pyotr, the General's shadow, as he stood disinterestedly cleaning his fingernails. He used a penknife as if he was acting the familiar role of villain's assistant. But to Panin the performance was so lame that it gave him strength.

"For yourself, Vladimir Efimovich, have you nothing to say?"

"I was saying the Apostles' Creed when you came in—"

"Which makes your crime," Rostov sneered, "all the more damning, for yours is a rational paranoia."

Panin felt his mind struggling to keep pace with the General's manipulations. "But I'm quite sane. Believe me. Or are you leading up to the announcement that Nitchevo is ripe for a mental institution?"

"Ha—do you think we would allow you to preach your idiocies to others?"

As Panin smiled again, he felt the swelling around his eye begin twitching violently. "General, don't tell me you're afraid I might be listened to?"

"Afraid?" The General turned his back to Panin. "I am disgusted." He spoke as if more reasonable men stood in invisible attendance, standing along the wall, layered as it was with various coats of paint and paper and scratches long-since forgotten. "Disgusted that such an experienced and able agent, a man who once had his feet more firmly planted on the ground than anyone I had ever known—"

Panin interrupted, trying to sound as encouraging as an old friend can. "The most realistic man I know, Rostov, is the Roman centurion whose story is told in the Acts of the Apos—"

"Leave the gospel to those with cerebral hemorrhoids, like yourself, Vladimir Efimovich." Rostov twisted toward Pyotr, apparently so that the General's assistant would not mistake his words. "I am a Communist and happy to be one." Then he turned once more, facing Panin in a challenging posture. "As you used to be—"

"Rostov, why won't you admit that we have been brought up on slogans?" Panin struggled to lift himself so that he might lean on one arm. "Slogans are the opposite of what I'm talking about. Let me tell you about the courage of that centurion's convictions—"

For a moment, Panin thought that the General was going to thrust one of his heavy, highly polished boots directly into his chest. The prisoner flinched. Instead the General moved almost sadly toward the table in the cell. When he nodded to Pyotr, the assistant laid a folder before Rostov.

"Volodya, use your head. Be yourself, be what you used to be. The Party needs you. Locked away in a prison like this, you are no good to anyone." Panin believed the sincerity that he heard in Rostov's voice and he saw that the General's tone surprised Pyotr.

Panin decided to be equally sincere. "Leonid Konstantinovich, you're the one living in a prison." But he could see that his intentions made no impression upon the General.

Rostov's response was to open the folder and slowly begin a handwritten statement on the topmost piece of paper.

Panin continued, not quite certain of his motivations. He only knew that he had to say these things to a man he had known so long. "Yes, you and most of our Russian people are living in a prison which Communism has built. You're no more free than those you have sent to the *gulags*, or writers in the mental institutions, or Jews waiting to be tried on the basis of prefabricated accusations—"

"Thank you." The General stopped writing. "I was waiting for that. Give me the right words to explain how that tearjerker of a rabbi infected you in New York."

Panin had told them the story dozens of times. He knew exactly which sentence to repeat. "You can write that Rabbi Grynspan is the man I owe for my first impulses to return to God." But before Panin could continue, Rostov spat at him, barely missing the prisoner's face.

"Do you think the Party spent money to educate you so you could read the Bible, quote the Gospels, kneel down, and string out prayers? Were you raised to be an icon-kisser? What if Lenin had been swallowed up like you during the years he spent in bourgeois Switzerland, indeed in affluent Zurich? We'd still be back in the times of the Babushka-Czar or, worse still, of Kerensky." General Rostov could no longer hold back the force of his rage.

Panin, therefore, no longer held back himself. "The Party's purpose was headed for failure as soon as our leaders tried to make a mockery of God." He labored to pull himself onto a chair opposite Rostov. "God won't be mocked. Strange, isn't it, General? If there's madness, it's what Christians call the 'foolishness of the Cross.'"

The interrogator did not look up; his hands moved steadily as he wrote. When he finished the last paragraph, he scratched a slanting line across the bottom half of the page. "Colonel, you can wallow in that rubbish if you like. I have heard enough." He spun the folder around so that the statement would be in position for Panin to read it. "Sign it, then tell me what good all this brings you, what you feel as you lay your life on the line."

Without reading it, Panin took up the pen and wrote in Russian, "May the Lord have mercy on you, Leonid Konstantinovich," then the prisoner added his signature.

The General ignored Panin's note and watched for the signature. "You are no longer Nitchevo—if indeed you ever said that word. But, Panin, you are still a good actor. Are you playing Christ?" To Panin, the General's eyes were an army closing in on its conquered.

"God forgave me that life. My playacting is over."

Rostov smacked his hand over the folder. "Enough." He shoved it, causing it to sail across the cell. Pyotr caught it at his waist. Rostov's voice became dispassionate, official. "You understand, we can't submit you to a regular court trial."

Panin became unusually alert. He could taste copper in his dry mouth. "I realize that, General. How could you explain that a colonel of the KGB has defected to God?"

It sounded like a joke—surprising all of them.

Both Rostov and Pyotr appeared unable to stop shaking with laughter. The noise brought a corridor guard to the cell door. Again Panin saw eyes peering in.

"Ah, what a fine Ukrainian humor, worthy of your countryman Gogol," the General chortled in his deep voice. "Stand up. I'm certain you know the rules." He motioned to Pyotr.

The assistant nodded to the guard.

Panin sensed everything after that as slow, muffled, somehow buffered. He could hear the metal scrape against metal, the moan of the door hinges. He could see the man in uniform step in. Only two steps. He could see their silhouettes against the light reflecting off the corridor floor. Like the sheen from the floor of a fine Moscow hotel.

Then Panin heard the crack and felt a tinge in his neck—something cold and hot. Bitelike. He felt himself falling, as in a dream. And words came to him; he remembered Cardinal Respighi quoting them to him. Volodya had virtually no control of his own tongue as he murmured, "*In manus tuas, Domi*—"

Rostov flinched at the sound of the guard's second shot—the one that struck directly into the nape of Panin's neck.

And the General suddenly felt afraid, without knowing why.

Methodically, Pyotr placed Colonel Panin's folder on the table and wrote across the top of the signed statement: FEBRUARY 28, 1972 AT EIGHT-THIRTY IN THE MORNING, THE TIME IN MOSCOW.

Rostov sat very still. Had his assistant seen him flinch?

Other guards stepped in and picked up the body. One of them asked the General, "Excuse me, Comrade General, but the man has a gold cross and chain around his neck. Shall we bury it with him?" There was unmasked self-interest in the man's voice.

Rostov motioned them away with his hand. "I had hoped the fool would use it to do himself in."

They moved quickly. Pyotr and the General were left to themselves as the guards actually stumbled as they hurried away with Panin's body. From the stairs at each end of the corridor, footsteps indistinctly rumbled. The other prisoners were returning from their daily walk in the courtyard or along the eagle's perch above Lubyanka.

Leonid Konstantinovich mumbled in a voice that sounded lonesome even to himself. "But then, I guess he did. . . ."

[XLIV]

JAMES MCNEIL HAD ALMOST NO DESIRE TO GO BACK TO THE Church of the Nativity. The place was, in his mind, too wrapped up with the Panin case, and that was one episode he had tried hard to forget. As a good Catholic, he felt he could hardly do otherwise.

Then Monsignor Maguire phoned to tell him that new information about Volodya Panin had just arrived from Rome. Would McNeil come by so that he could give the letter to the Bureau directly?

En route in a clattering taxi, McNeil rolled down his window as far as the cab door mechanism would allow and let the nippy spring air smack against his face. It felt brisk, fresh.

By the time he reached the rectory, he felt invigorated.

"Joe, I mean, Jim. Welcome." Stan Potocki met McNeil at the

rectory door. "Won't you join Monsignor Maguire and me in the living room?"

When McNeil and Potocki entered the rather drab room, the federal agent noticed a new and large framed picture of the Pope. As he drew closer to it, McNeil saw that the oversized photograph had been autographed.

"It just arrived," Maguire explained as he greeted McNeil. "The Cardinal Secretary of State sent it to us along with the letter I thought you should see." Then the parish priest pointed toward the inscription included with the Pope's signature. "Look, isn't it marvelous? No other parish in New York has anything like it. I know His Holiness' words by heart: 'To Monsignor Maguire and his zealous assistants at the Church of the Nativity—We are deeply happy to impart our Apostolic blessing, in the hope that it brings down blessings from Heaven'!"

McNeil complimented the Monsignor and his parish upon such an honor, then tried to get down to business. He wanted to spend no more time here than necessary. But Maguire would not be speeded along.

"And how's my 'niece'?"

"Evangeline? She was sent to a post on the Arizona-Mexico border where there's heavy traffic in drugs."

Maguire seemed jolted a bit when McNeil said nothing more.

"I should also thank you for having our new housekeeper cleared. At least now we can be certain she won't turn out to be another Mar . . . uh, what the devil was her name?"

"Marfyona Alexandrovna Popova," McNeil answered in a stumbling pronunciation of the Russian syllables.

"Oh, glory! Pronouncing a name like that could spoil a man's digestion!"

While the pastor laughed alone at his own joke, Potocki interrupted. "What happened to the . . . the people we helped apprehend?"

"Behind bars. The two men got harder sentences because they're American citizens."

"And Mrs. O'Rourke?"

"She was deported for fraudulent and illegal entry."

Potocki's overactive imagination was in high gear as he asked, "Did they confess?"

"Sorry, Stan. None of them would admit to what they had been doing. But we did find a code book among Goldstein's children's toys, or so he called them, stored in a trunk in his Long Island garage."

"So you lost the 'game'?" The Pole looked too disappointed for comfort.

"Stan, we didn't lose an inch. We uncovered a spy network and used the Mounties' information to discover an impostor's identity. Panin had to abandon the Vatican Observer's office. Does that seem insignificant to you?" McNeil stared directly at the priest, as though to drive his point into the mind so permeated by spy stories. "If you're judging by mystery story standards and think an 'admission of guilt' is necessary in order to score a success, just give me the address of one of those writers and we'll send Popova to him. We'll see if he can break the 'Rock.' "

Maguire intervened. "Then there's the letter we received—"

"Which is why I'm here. Great. May I see it?" The agent was glad to get back to business.

Almost ceremonially the pastor put on his wire-rimmed glasses and straightened his collar. Then he leaned back in the overstuffed armchair. Slowly he scanned the letter's many pages and James McNeil was just about ready to curse under his breath when Maguire began. "Let's see now, here it is: 'To prove what a fine man Mr. Panin is—apart from the life he led before—I want to give you this information in confidence. With all that apparently lay in store for him, Mr. Panin found time and compassion to ask that I do something, if possible, about your parish's indebtedness. He suggested that I write, in the Pope's name, to tell the New York chancery that Nativity should receive some aid. Monsignor, I was deeply affected. Can you imagine anyone else doing that if they were in Mr. Panin's place?' "

McNeil tried to keep impatience from his voice. "Monsignor Maguire, I am also impressed by all this—but what does it have to do with the Bureau?"

"Oh, sorry." The pastor fumbled with the pages. "Here, Jim, read the letter aloud . . . beginning here, with 'Before leaving Rome for Prague . . .' "

The federal agent took the letter and read in a clipped near-monotone. "Before leaving Rome for Prague, Mr. Panin asked me to transmit to you, to Father Belli, Father Potocki, as well as all the other priests at Nativity, his greetings and the assurance that you are in his prayers. He wanted your forgiveness for all the deceptions he practiced upon you.

"As for Colonel Vladimir Efimovich Panin, trustworthy sources have informed us that he died of complications possibly related to his medical problems evidenced during his last days in New York—" McNeil interrupted his reading and added a comment of his own. "The word 'complications' usually covers a multitude of Russian sins. I'm sure you know that." Then the federal agent continued reading aloud: "He had been detained in the Lubyanka prison. We at the Vatican believe that he died in a state of grace, as a martyr to the faith, but we ask all of you who knew him to join your prayers for his soul to ours. . . ."

McNeil handed the letter back to Maguire. "I suspect, Monsignor, that you think all of this is something of a miracle?"

"At the least, Jim, a mystery."

"Like Rabbi Grynspan?" the agent asked, actually interested in the priest's perspective on this point.

"We'll never know." Maguire smiled, then took off his glasses. "He's not a case for your files, Jim. Investigation must stop where mystery begins. A good Catholic like you should know that."

The three men looked at one another as if the months had somehow drawn them closer, even as they remained worlds apart. Potocki coughed. He seemed sad—perhaps anxious that he not be left to fall back into his priestly concerns.

"Jim? Have you checked on the credentials of the new Permanent Observer? Shouldn't—"

"Stan, please. I already have half of New York to cover today. What's more, with Lent coming up, I'm going to have to cut my cigarettes down to five a day. A promise to good Father Kelly, years ago. As for nagging, I've got a fine wife for that. Please, leave the suspicions to us. Okay?" McNeil was up and already headed for the door.

"But," the Polish priest ran after him. "What if you, if all of us are deceived once again? It's possible!"

Maguire held Potocki back and concluded the conversation for them all. "My boys, God reads men's hearts like a book. The Lord can't be deceived—even if clever men try to put Him off track."

McNeil agreed. "You're right there, Monsignor." He hesitated and then added, "How about an offering to celebrate a mass for the repose of the soul of Volodya?"

The pastor looked at the FBI man, who continued. "Under another name, of course, and with another donor. I'm sure you understand."

"Of course, Jim. We'll find other names for you and Panin when we list the requiem masses in our parish bulletin."

And leaning back again in his armchair he added in a soft voice, "This experience, once you strain out the incredible and the unthinkable, can lift up the heart and soul of an old man like me. Think about it, Jim."

And McNeil did. Not just during the minutes it took to walk toward Second Avenue and then north along the row of shops and restaurants, but often in the months that followed. Still, he would never tell anyone that this case—or any other, for that matter— had reached him. He would keep it to himself.

Just the way he would have answered had a passerby recognized him on Second Avenue and asked why he had tears in his eyes. "It's the wind," he would have said.